FIREGLASS MACHINE

Dushma hurried across the landing, the floorboards rattling. Then halfway across she froze. What if they were waiting for her on the stairs?

As she hesitated, a tiny noise nearby made her turn her head. She was standing opposite the entrance to the derelict flat next door to her own. At first it seemed untouched, but as she looked more closely she noticed fresh scratches in the wood of the jamb next to the lock. Then she heard the noise again: a faint squeak like a rusty bicycle, or. . .

Almost imperceptibly, the handle was turning.

Also by Patrick Wood

Electric Dragon

Point

FIREGLASS MACHINE

PATRICK WOOD

SCHOLASTIC

Scholastic Children's Books,
Commonwealth House, 1-19 New Oxford Street,
London, WC1A 1NU, UK
a division of Scholastic Ltd
London ~ New York ~ Toronto ~ Sydney ~ Auckland
Mexico City ~ New Delhi ~ Hong Kong

First published by Scholastic Ltd, 2005

ISBN 0 439 96337 0

Printed by Nørhaven Paperback A/S, Denmark

10 9 8 7 6 5 4 3 2 1

PROLOGUE

There was a thick glass window in the floor by Dushma's feet and through it the sea looked very close. The swell was immense. Hill-sized waves reared up towards her, then slumped back into valleys of water vast and grey as lunar craters.

In the pilot's seat beside her Arbilow struggled to hold the helicopter steady. His face, pinched with the effort, glowed a sickly green in the faint light from the instrument panel.

The wind came in sudden gusts, unfurling ribbons of spray from the crests of the waves. Sometimes the air seemed almost too thick for the helicopter's shuddering rotors to slice through. Then the next moment the whine of the engine would rise an octave in pitch like a drill bursting through the far side of a wall. For a few breathtaking seconds the helicopter would plunge seawards as if through a vacuum, before the rotors bit into the air again and pulled it upwards.

Arbilow had the joystick clenched in both fists to stop it

being wrenched from his grasp by the lurching motion of their flight. He was hunched forward in his seat, harness tight across his chest, his trembling forearms braced against his knees.

"A helicopter is basically very simple to fly," he had said. "There's one control to make it go up, and another to make it go forward. That's all there is to it."

"So how come there are so many dials and switches?" Dushma had wanted to know.

"Oh, that's just for doing complicated things," he had replied with confidence. "Like winching people up and flying in the dark."

They had taken off a little after dawn in good weather. The storm didn't break until after they had left the coast well behind and were out over open sea. They should have been almost able to see their destination by the time the banks of black cloud came rolling in around them, reducing visibility to a few hundred metres. Arbilow had to try and navigate using the compass on the dashboard, forcing the joystick left or right when the swinging needle told him that their course had veered.

Water blistered the windscreen, making it even harder for them to see where they were going. A single stubby wiper lay folded along the lower edge of the glass, but Dushma had no idea which control would activate it.

Without taking his eyes off the compass needle, Arbilow shouted, "See if you can find some flares or lifejackets. In case we have to ditch!"

Dushma loosened her harness and slid carefully out of her seat, holding on to a handle above her head to keep herself steady as the helicopter rolled. The most obvious place to try was the hatch at the back of the cockpit. The space was cramped, and she only had to take a single step to be able to reach it and pull it open.

A gust of hot, oily fumes spilled out. Right behind the bulkhead was the helicopter's engine. Its greased axles and pistons gleamed in the dim light, twisting and pumping like the limbs of some writhing, captive creature.

Dushma slammed the hatch quickly shut again, coughing from the acrid vapour.

There was nowhere else to look but under the seats. Bracing herself, she crouched and reached beneath the nearest. Her groping fingers touched a cold metal cylinder wedged against the footrest. She pulled it free, but it was only a fire extinguisher.

As she sat down again, Arbilow shot her a quick sideways glance and saw her shaking her head. He grimaced. "I'm sorry!" he yelled.

I could've jumped out when you took off, thought Dushma. *After all, you did tell me to*. But it didn't seem worth the effort of shouting it aloud above the noise of the wind and the engine.

It was now almost completely dark. Arbilow was leaning as far forward as he could, alternating his gaze between the faint glow of the compass binnacle and the blurred view through the windscreen.

Out of the corner of her eye Dushma glimpsed a flicker of light away to starboard.

"Look, there!" she cried, pointing. "Is that it?"

Before Arbilow could reply the deep, grinding sound of thunder reached their ears. The next instant a glaring wire of bluey-white light wriggled across the sky in front of them. A side window blew in with a bang and fragments of glass showered the cockpit.

Dushma had not yet strapped herself back into her harness. She tumbled sideways, hitting her head against a metal stanchion as she fell. The fire extinguisher spilled from her lap and rolled away.

The helicopter plunged, spinning and see-sawing in a wallowing motion that made it feel as if the craft might flip over at any moment. Arbilow gripped the joystick, his only idea of how to regain control being to hold on as tightly as he could.

Clinging to the back of her seat, Dushma pulled herself upright from where she had been thrown to the deck. The wind howled in through the broken window, whipping strands of hair across her cheeks. She screwed up her face to squeeze the tears from her swimming eyes, then stared in breathless disbelief at the impossible view in front of her.

The sea reared up almost vertically before them, close enough for every ridge and furrow in the water to be visible. Specks of foam flashed on its rippling surface like reflected light in a wall of frosted glass.

Rolling loose across the floor, the fire extinguisher clanged against the rear wall of the cabin. Slowly the helicopter tipped back on to its tail, as if cringing away from the surging wave. Still swaying, it began to climb again, passing metres above the frothing crest, tendrils of spray clutching at its undercarriage.

Their course had stabilized but there was panic on Arbilow's face as he leaned over the compass binnacle. "Look at it. . . The thing's gone wild!" He was shaking his head. "I don't know where we are!"

Blinking rapidly to try and clear the lightning bolt's after-image from her vision, Dushma peered down at the helicopter's dashboard. The compass needle was whirling randomly.

"*Now* we've got to turn back," she said without thinking.

"But I don't know where 'back' *is*!" His voice was cracking. "I've no idea whether we're heading back to the coast, out towards France, up into the North Sea. . .!" He twisted frantically in his seat, scanning the furious sky for any variation that might indicate the direction of the sun.

Dushma too looked around her but there was nothing helpful to be seen. Whichever way she turned, the smoky grey of the horizon was interrupted only by broken stilts of lightning. No longer even sure which way was down, she swayed on unsteady legs and clutched at the back of her seat, her mind blank except for the useless instructions of primitive instinct: run; curl up and hide; shriek for help.

It took her several terrified seconds to remember what to do. "Wait, it's all right, I can tell. . ." She realized she was talking aloud, though far too quietly to be heard. Trying to relax the tensed-up muscles of her face and neck, she began moving her head slowly from side to side.

She felt nothing. Perhaps it was the lightning, or the shuddering of the engine, or. . .

Her locket. She was still wearing her locket. Tipping her head forward, she pulled at the collar of her blouse. One arm still hooked round the back of her seat, she reached behind her for the clasp of the gold chain she wore at her neck. It was too stiff for her to undo with one hand. After a moment's fumbling she lost patience and wrenched at it. The chain snapped, grazing her skin. A lozenge-shaped locket slipped from the broken links, bounced off the dashboard and dropped to the floor.

"Which way, which *way?*" Arbilow was shouting.

Dushma closed her eyes and tried to ignore him, tried not to let his panic infect her. She had used to be able to do this, if she concentrated. She had used to walk for miles, losing herself in warrens of narrow, winding streets and then finding her way unerringly home again. It was like a breeze on her cheeks, an almost imperceptible stroking sensation that would brush across her skin if she could hold herself steady enough, if she could turn her face just so. . .

"*That* way." She pointed. "North. It's that way."

PART
I

I

Dr Marlstroy Lights the Firetrees

Dr Marlstroy was having a party, or a soirée as he liked to call it. It was autumn, but the high brick walls of his Italianate garden had soaked up the day's sun, and now made the evening warm enough for the guests to stroll among the urns and statues and enjoy the sunset.

Dushma stood on the patio with a tray of orange juice. She had been there for fifteen minutes and was already beginning to feel bored.

Most of the people at the party were quite old. She recognized two or three of them from television. Those that Marlstroy introduced her to all seemed to treat her as if she was about five. One of them had asked her what she wanted to be when she grew up. All she had been able to think of were far-fetched professions such as lion-tamer and steeplejack. She was sure the serious-looking man with grey hair and steel-rimmed glasses would think she was being facetious.

"I . . . well, I don't know, I thought, maybe . . . an accountant," she floundered.

"Splendid!" said the serious-looking man, and patted her on the head.

The only other person there of Dushma's age was a boy called Alex. "Why don't you go and introduce yourself?" Marlstroy suggested, taking her tray. Nobody seemed to want orange juice anyway.

Alex had retreated to a place of relative privacy behind an ornamental hedge. He was a fleshy boy with a buttery forelock flopping down over his brow. He wore a blue blazer with silver buttons and sleeves that came down to his knuckles. In his hand he clutched something which shone like a globule of greeny-gold light in the pale rays of the evening sun.

Seeing Dushma approach he clumsily tried to hide the sherry glass under his jacket. When he realized she had already noticed it he grinned weakly.

"Hey, don't tell pa, OK? I'm not really supposed to." He glanced about and then held out the glass. "Here, try some."

Dushma took a cautious sip, then grimaced as the acidic, oily liquid scorched her palate.

"Horrible, isn't it?" said Alex. "Pa never gets anything but ten-year-old Amontillado. I'd've preferred gin and tonic myself but the chap dishing them out didn't look dozy enough for me to get away with it."

"So what will your father do if he finds out?" Dushma asked, handing back the glass.

"Aha, he won't! If anyone comes to talk to me I'll just hold my breath, see?" Alex inflated his chest with a deep lungful of air and assumed an expression of moonfaced innocence.

"You're right, you'll be quite safe," said Dushma hastily. She was worried that if he stayed like that for long she was going to be unable to stop herself laughing at him.

Alex exhaled with a snort and took a gulp of sherry. "What about your pa then, eh? He looks like a fierce old bird."

"He's not really my father. I'm his ward."

"His what?" A slow frown creased Alex's forehead. "Oh, I know. You mean like Bruce Wayne and Robin. Wow!"

"Not really," Dushma had been about to say. But seeing that Alex was starting to look impressed, instead she said casually, "Yes, something like that."

"He's a doctor, isn't he, your . . . well, not your pa, your. . ."

"Guardian. Yes, that's right. He's a neurologist. Why?"

"Well, you know. . . Brains and things, isn't it? Must be pretty interesting."

"I suppose so."

"So, er, does he talk about it then? Has he got books and things? I mean, you know, with pictures?"

"Oh yes, he's got thousands of books."

"Really? Has he got, what is it, Gray's *Anatomy*?"

"I'm not sure. He's got the *Elegy*, so he's probably got his other ones too."

"Well, in that case, I *suppose* we could go and have a look, if you like," said Alex wearily, as if Dushma had suggested it. "Come along, you can show me." He swallowed another mouthful of sherry, then poured the dregs into an ornamental urn and strolled away.

Dushma was tempted to let him go on his own, but looking around the garden she could see no one else who looked like they might be interesting to talk to. Shrugging, she turned and made her way towards the house.

Back inside, she happened to glance in through the pantry door as she passed. There were several empty bottles of sherry on the table. *Amontillado fino, 10 años de edad*, said the label on the nearest.

"Hey!" she exclaimed, hurrying on after Alex. This should prick his pomposity a bit.

"Listen," she said indignantly, catching up with him in the hall. "You know that sherry. . .?"

"Sh!" Alex glanced furtively about. "Can you smell it? Don't worry, I've got some mints." He began fumbling in the inside pocket of his blazer.

"No, I mean. . ."

"So where's this library then?" interrupted Alex. "Come on, we haven't got all evening you know. Is it upstairs?" Rattling a mint noisily against his teeth, he set off up the wide, curving staircase.

They had just reached the first landing when they heard voices from the hall.

"Great heavens, is that an original?"

It was Marlstroy and one of his guests.

"No, just a copy, I'm afraid."

"Still, a splendid painting."

"Yes, they were the perfect subject for him, weren't they? You may have noticed I've some of my own. At the end of the garden. You'll have the chance to see them working later."

"I say, isn't that illegal these days?"

"Oh, I'm sure you're all very discreet."

Alex had been holding his breath. As the voices receded he fell into an extravagant fit of panting, rolling his eyes and clinging on to the banister as if he was about to collapse.

"Oh honestly," said Dushma a little sharply. "We don't have to hide. It's perfectly all right for me to show you the library. That is, as long as you haven't got dirty hands," she added, deciding to try and assert herself a little.

Alex immediately wiped his palms vigorously up and down the front of his blazer and then held out his hands for Dushma's inspection. They were in fact perfectly clean.

"Yes, yes, that's fine," said Dushma, somewhat taken aback by such a meek response.

The library was an imposing room on the first floor, two storeys in height and lined with bookcases. Almost every shelf was full. The volumes ranged in size from pocket books no larger than a pack of cards to brass-hinged ledgers as big as paving stones. Some were so old they looked as if they would crumble apart as soon as they were opened. Others might have been bound only the day before, their gold-embossed spines gleaming in the evening sunlight.

It was Dushma's favourite room in the house and she could spend hours there at a time, sometimes reading and sometimes simply exploring the huge collection. She had never had the chance to show anyone round it before, and she was determined to try and make the most of it, even with someone as unlikely to be impressed as Alex.

"Well," she said, pausing on the threshold to inhale the familiar smell of polish, leather and musty paper. "What do you think?"

"Mm," murmured Alex, staring appraisively round the library. "So are these all medical textbooks, then?" He seemed unsure where to start.

Most of the spines were dark cloth or leather. Some bore embossed titles, while others gave no clue as to their identity until they had been pulled from the shelf and opened. But the uniformity of the bindings belied the variety of the books they contained. As Dushma had discovered, a volume selected at random was as likely to be a classic novel or a radiantly illustrated collection of poetry as a textbook or a learned journal.

"Oh no, there's all sorts of stuff," she said airily. "There are some beautiful maps, with illustrations and everything. Some of them are hundreds of years old."

"Old maps? What use are they to anyone? I mean, you

might be going along, and suddenly find the road you were following wasn't even there any more!"

He reached out towards the nearest shelf.

"Careful!" warned Dushma.

But rather to her surprise Alex seemed to know how to handle books. He slid each one gently out and held it properly, cradling the spine as he turned the pages. Soon he was engrossed in his browsing, moving systematically from shelf to shelf, examining a book or two from each.

Dushma went to one of the wide bay windows and looked down into the garden. The guests were still enjoying the last of the sun, their long shadows stretching out across the gravel paths and beds of herbs. There were muffled sounds of laughter and the clink of glasses.

At the foot of the garden was a strange assembly of what looked like twisted, wrought-iron fencing. Beyond this was a high wall tipped with sparkling triangles of broken glass. In the distance, among the sharply etched silhouettes of cranes, churches and office blocks, Dushma could clearly see the arches of the viaduct where she had once lived, and beyond them, higher than any of the surrounding buildings, the soaring spire of St Gotha's Cathedral.

"Hey, look at that!" exclaimed Alex from behind her.

He had managed to find a book on anatomy. He had laid it down on a table and was poring over the illustrations. Dushma came to peer over his shoulder.

The page he was examining contained a large and detailed picture of a man's head. There was no skin on the

15

face. Instead the illustrator had painstakingly drawn the overlapping strands of muscle and tendon that lay beneath. The man looked as if he had been covered in finely combed strips of plasticine.

"Wow, look at that!" breathed Alex again, his mouth ajar, lower lip sagging with amazement. He bent closer, his nose just a hand's breadth from the page, and began making faces. He bared his teeth and then pouted, pulling and prodding at his plump cheeks as if trying to work out just how his own body corresponded to the illustration in front of him.

"Imagine," he said. "We're all like that underneath! You said you liked maps: well this is like a map, but of a person, isn't it?"

Dushma had to admit there was something morbidly fascinating about the picture. "But at least a map might be useful," she argued. "*This* is only going to be any use if you're going to operate on someone."

"Ah, but it's artistic too. They were always putting bones in paintings. It was, a . . . a *memento mori*. There's a rich cultural tradition. The skull beneath the skin. And that chap in the play. You know, 'Alas poor whatsisname'. And have you ever played *Craving*? It's excellent. You have to shoot these zombies, and to start off with they're almost normal, except they're dead and want to eat you of course. But then as you get further in first their skin peels off, and then their flesh decays to reveal their putrefying organs! I suppose when I get to the highest level they'll just be skeletons. They might finally have got rid of their shorts by then too. . . What are you looking at me like that for? Curiosity is healthy. It's perfectly natural."

Alex turned back to the shelves. He had begun to examine another book when a thought struck him. "Hey, has he got anything in jars? You know, like specimens?"

"Oh, probably. There's usually one or two in the fridge. He says sherry's best for keeping them fresh. Shall we go and have a look?"

"What?" Alex's eyes bulged with surprise. Then a slow grin spread across his face. "Oh right, you're having me on! You had me going for a minute there. In the fridge, eh? That's good! Our biology teacher kept them in the store cupboard. He had some really disgusting ones. Rats and mice and a dissected starfish. He even had a pickled finger, he showed it to us once. He had to leave though. Anyway, what d'you think of this? I had this idea for a film about a starfish that mutates because of radioactive waste and starts growing human fingers. Wouldn't that be horrible?"

"Yes," said Dushma coolly. "All the other starfish would laugh at it."

She drifted back towards the nearest window and watched the last sliver of sun drop below the horizon. She could make out nothing of the garden more than a few metres from the house.

"Look," she said, "it's nearly dark. I think we should probably go downstairs."

Alex looked up from the book on leprosy he had found.

His face wore a greenish tinge. "Actually," he said thickly, "I think I could do with a bresh of freth air."

They turned off the lights and went down to join the guests on the patio.

"Hurry up!" someone called as they arrived. "You'll miss them!"

The bottom of the garden was now in darkness. Most people were gathered in the pool of light cast by the drawing-room windows. The breeze was freshening and several of the women had drawn shawls about their shoulders. Conversation was muted and there was an air of expectancy.

"I might have to go and lie down," Alex confided to Dushma. "I think those mints must've been past their sell-by date."

"Then it's a good job you didn't offer me any, isn't it?" she retorted unsympathetically.

Marlstroy came out of the house and moved quickly through the assembled guests. He held a burning taper in one gloved hand. The dancing light accentuated his sharp nose and chin, and the deep-set sockets of his eyes.

A hissing sound came from the bottom of the garden. Dushma thought she could smell gas.

There was a whooshing noise and gasps from several of the guests. Down by the garden wall long yellow ribbons wriggled in the darkness like the flames from Bunsen burners. The hissing grew into a low roar. More ribbons of fire appeared, while the first ones increased in intensity, turning from yellow to orange to tapering tongues of vivid blue.

In the light from the flames the apparatus that produced them could be fitfully discerned. In front of the wall at the end of the garden ran a line of black cast-iron pillars. At about head-height these branched out into an angular network of spreading pipes. Gas flames spouted like fiery leaves from vents along these pipes. As the metal heated up, the mouths of the vents themselves began to glow a deep cherry red like clumps of spring blossom.

Marlstroy returned to the group on the patio. He was close enough to Dushma for her to be able to smell the smoke on his clothes.

"Very impressive, Arthur," said a tall, bearded man admiringly. "I didn't know there were any of those left."

"I'm not aware of any others. Not in working order anyway," replied Marlstroy. "The last public ones were removed in, when was it? The fifties, I think. The V and A's got a couple, but they're disconnected."

"I've seen them in newsreels. Black and white, though. I'd no idea they were so striking."

"Yes, they were very common in London in the nineteenth century. The main source of light on most of the major streets, for a time. You know Whistler's painting, I take it? I've a contemporary copy in the hall. One of his finest, I think. *Nocturne: Piccadilly with Firetrees*."

"If old Jenkins over at Environment knew you had these he'd have a fit," said the man in steel-rimmed glasses

Dushma had met earlier. "He'd be round in a jiffy with a court order."

"This is a listed building." Marlstroy spread his hands helplessly. "I can't dismantle them. And as I understand it, they qualify as an industrial appliance. So under the applicable bylaws I have to carry out regular checks to make sure they're working properly." He looked very serious, but Dushma thought she caught the twitching of his lips that betrayed his hidden amusement.

"There's the cause of your energy crisis, Ashpool," said someone.

"And climate change," said someone else. "How much carbon dioxide do those things produce? They can't be very sound. And you know they say it's getting worse. There've been storms in the Channel this summer like no one's ever seen."

"Oh, I hardly think Dr Marlstroy's firetrees can be making a substantial contribution," said the man called Ashpool, the flames flickering in the lenses of his spectacles.

"That's right," said Marlstroy. "I've been well within my quotas ever since they were introduced. Just take a look round the house: low-wattage light bulbs everywhere."

"Call me old-fashioned," said a voice nearby, "but I think you should have some roses."

"You know I don't like roses, Fordyke," said Marlstroy, a little wearily.

Down at the bottom of the garden, more flames spluttered into life as automatic valves fed gas further up into the crooked metal branches of the firetrees. Guests drifted off again along the gravel paths, drawn towards the light and warmth.

"So you're his new project, eh? Congratulations!" A hulking, stooped man in late middle age was standing at Dushma's elbow. His fleshy face appeared sallow and sweaty in the light of the firetrees. His cheeks looked as if they could be spread across his face with a knife. He proffered his hand. It felt warm and slightly damp.

"I'm Dr Marlstroy's ward, if that's what you mean," said Dushma.

"Something like that. How nice. Do you like toffee?" He began patting the pockets of his jacket.

Dushma looked around for Marlstroy but he and Ashpool had drifted out of earshot.

The fleshy-faced man abandoned his search for toffee, took a swig from a large glass of wine and leaned closer to Dushma.

"Do you like a good naval yarn?" he asked with a wink. "That's my line. Bit grown-up for you though. Too much blood and severed limbs. Marlstroy's a fan, you know. He's got them all. So you're his ward, eh? Why don't you ask him about, what was her name? Nicola, that was it. Nicola . . . something. I forget. Anyway, shall I tell you my latest idea? It's about this girl, a bit like you actually, dark, and with this fierce frown. And she runs away to join

Nelson's fleet, disguised as a powder monkey. What do you think of that?"

"It sounds a bit grown-up for me," said Dushma impassively. "But how about they don't discover she's a girl until she mutinies and gets keel-hauled? Or would that be too tame?"

"No no! Keel-hauled, that's an idea. Blood and barnacles. Yes." He licked his lips. "Must remember that." He finished his wine and then peered about him with a puzzled look. "I say, you haven't seen my lad, have you? Where's he got to?"

Dushma assumed he must mean Alex. When she thought about it there was some resemblance.

"I'm not sure. He was here a minute ago. He said he wasn't feeling very well."

"Poor lad. He's quite delicate, you know. I suppose I'd better go and find him. . . Oh, Auquin, that was it. Nicola Auquin. Ask Marlstroy about her sometime, why don't you?"

"Yes, isn't she? I tell you I feel years younger."

Marlstroy stood in the hall talking quietly to Ashpool, the grey-haired man with steel-rimmed spectacles. Most of the other guests had already taken their leave.

"Even something like this, tonight," he went on. "You know how much I used to hate having to do these things. Waste of time, much rather be working. Present company excepted, of course. But tonight, trying to see things as she must be seeing them. . . Well, I almost found myself enjoying it."

"From your description, when you called that time, I thought she must be some kind of wildcat," said Ashpool. "And what about your work with her? It's going well, I think you said?"

"Better than ever. I can't tell you any details yet, but I believe I could soon be in a position to announce something really significant."

"Splendid! One for *The Lancet,* eh?"

"Oh at least. The Royal Society too, quite possibly. God knows, I've been successful enough, but this could be what brings me the recognition I've always wanted."

"Good, good. Excellent. But you will let me know, won't you, before you publish, if there's something that could be useful to us? I mean, if there's anything that might have implications for national security, say, we mightn't want all the details to be publicly available."

"Of course, don't worry. I won't forget that if it hadn't been for you I'd never have had the chance to do these experiments."

"Well then, I'll look forward to hearing something. Heaven knows, at the moment it would make a change to have some good news for once."

"Are things that bad?"

"It's everything coming at once, that's the trouble. We knew our own oil-fields wouldn't last for ever, but now with the problems in the Middle East and South America

23

we can't import enough to cover the shortfall. Then the unions see a chance to kick us when we're down and go on strike. So now we've got blackouts, petrol rationing, and everyone blaming the government, of course. And the whole thing's a gift for the environmentalists. They've been pressing us to cut consumption for years, and now they see these shortages as the chance to force our hand. We have a little bit of unusual weather, a stormy summer and a warm autumn, *complete* coincidence but it seems to back up their arguments about climate change and the end of the world as we know it. They want energy quotas, reduced emissions and crippling fines for polluters. The demands get more extravagant every time I hear them."

Marlstroy shrugged. "Maybe some of them make sense."

"Listen. If they had their way we'd be back in the dark ages. Reduced energy consumption and economic growth are simply incompatible. People would realize that soon enough when they started to lose their jobs. No, we can't give in to them. If we can just last out until Christmas. The strikes can't go on much longer than that, and by then the Estuary oil-fields should be on line. . ."

"And if they're not? Come on, I know you. You never put all your eggs in one basket. What's plan B?"

Ashpool pulled off his spectacles and rubbed a hand across his face. "Look, I've kept you long enough. I should go, it's late." But instead of turning away he hesitated, and then said, "Actually yes, there was an alternative. A long-term project of mine. But to tell you the truth, I've had a big setback recently. Can't really talk about it at the moment, not even to you. But it would've been extraordinary. It would've confounded them all."

"I thought the firetrees were beautiful."

Dushma stood at the foot of the stairs, ready to make her way up to bed. Marlstroy was at the door of his study, his thin form little more than a dark outline against the faint light from within.

"Yes, they are aren't they? Oh, I'm glad you liked them. I'll tell you what, you can have a party, if you like. On your birthday. Invite some friends round. We can light them again then."

"Thank you," said Dushma politely, although she could think of no one from school she would want to ask, apart from Moth.

"And what did you think of the young chap . . . Alex, wasn't it?"

"Oh, him! Well actually, I thought he was a bit weird," Dushma admitted. She grimaced at the memory of Alex saying goodbye to her on the front steps, earnestly shaking her hand over and over again while telling her in a slurred voice what a grey, grey plair it had been to meet her. "And he was rather morbid, too. He wanted to see all your medical books."

"Yes, his father was telling me he's having problems with him."

Dushma remembered the thickset man with the damp,

sagging jowls. There had been something he had thought she needed to know. The name he had mentioned had been familiar; she had heard it before, she was sure. She opened her mouth to ask Marlstroy who Nicola Auquin was, but then changed her mind. It might be something he didn't want to talk about, and she didn't want to spoil his mood. He wasn't often this expansive. Instead she said, "Apparently he's delicate."

"Is *that* what it is?" Marlstroy snorted. "I saw he'd been at the sherry, but I didn't want to make a fuss. None of my business really. And to be honest I think if someone's going to drink themselves to death they're better off doing it sooner rather than later, before they've had the chance to pass their failings on to another generation."

"Oh, I don't know if he was that bad. . ." Dushma protested.

Marlstroy tipped back his head and stared up at her, eyes glittering. "You think I'm too harsh? Yes, I suppose you're still an idealist. You think people can change, overcome their circumstances or their unfortunate heritage. I'm surprised, after what you've been through, that you still believe anyone else thinks like that. You're the exception that proves the rule, my dear. And now, bed!"

Dushma turned obediently and began to climb the stairs. The hall was in darkness, as it had been on most nights since the introduction of power rationing, and so to guide her she carried a candle inside a lantern like an old-fashioned miner's lamp. It hung from a loop round her left wrist, throwing a cone of light down on to her feet that swayed with each step she took.

But before she could reach the first landing Marlstroy had called after her.

"Oh, by the way, you don't really want to be an accountant, do you? I mean, not that I'd stand in your way or anything, but. . ."

She stopped and turned round again. "Well, no, not really. . . But, he looked very serious, so I thought he'd think I was pulling his leg if I said I wanted to be . . . oh, I don't know, an acrobat, or an astronaut."

For the first time that evening, rather than simply baring his teeth in a mirthless grin, Marlstroy smiled a genuine smile.

"Oh, that's much better," he said, his crinkling eyes gleaming in the light from her lantern.

II

In the Cathedral

Dushma had grown up in a flat in the arch of London's monumental railway viaduct. She had lived with her self-appointed guardian, Auntie Megan, a shady one-time associate of her long-dead mother. No one else had known the flat was there, apart from the lodgers Auntie Megan sometimes took in to help make ends meet.

Although sparsely furnished and chilly in winter, there could be no denying that their eyrie was splendidly located. From her bedroom window Dushma could see clear across the city. The only buildings higher than the viaduct were a few office blocks, churches and factory chimneys, and the rearing, shingled spike that was the main spire of St Gotha's Cathedral. They were far above the noise and fumes of the streets. The regular express trains that sizzled and thrummed along the electrified rails overhead were all that disturbed their isolation.

As an unregistered minor Dushma had been unable to go to school. Instead she had spent her days wandering the streets. She had explored the neighbourhood exhaustively, coming to know every cobbled lane and alleyway for as far as she could walk in every direction.

However, Auntie Megan did make occasional attempts to bring Dushma up correctly, before she began to grow resentful of her charge and devise sinister plans for her future. So it was that Dushma was at least taught enough to be able to go and learn more on her own.

As soon as she was able, she began reading whatever she could lay her hands on. Before long she much preferred to spend her time with a book than watching their old television with the picture that broke up whenever a train went across the viaduct.

By the time she had reached her early teens she rarely spent time at home other than to eat and sleep. She knew every church in the vicinity, and was happiest reading leaflets on their history, investigating their neglected chapels and half-forgotten crypts, and deciphering the worn inscriptions on their tombs of long-dead saints and gentry.

Of all these places her favourite was the vast and labyrinthine cathedral dedicated to the horrifically martyred Gotha Angstrom. She was thrilled by the austere, lofty vaulting and the macabre gargoyles, entranced by the ornate statues and the radiant stained glass, and fascinated by the tragic story of its patron saint.

On the run from the authorities, having fled her viaduct home, she came to identify with the persecuted St Gotha. It was to the cathedral that she had come when an explosion in an underground railway tunnel had destroyed her new-found refuge and almost taken her life.

Frightened and bruised, burns on her legs and cuts on her hands and arms, she had let herself quietly in through the heavy main door. Although the cathedral had only just opened for the day she was careful to keep to the shadows, in case a verger or an early visitor should catch sight of her. She was sure she must look frightful, her clothes torn, her face streaked with smoke and tears and her once thick and lustrous hair reduced to singed clumps.

Moving aimlessly from one dark corner of the nave to the next, she had no clear plan as to what she might do. Coming upon an unlocked door at the back of a side chapel, she opened it cautiously and peered into the corridor beyond. It was empty save for piles of boxes filled with hymn-books. A vague idea forming in her mind of finding a priest and throwing herself on his mercy, she shut the door quietly behind her and set off down the corridor to explore.

Taking a few turns at random, she came at last to a deserted vestry. Judging by the amount of clutter it contained it appeared not to have been used in a long time. At one end of the room was a wardrobe which turned out to be the size of her old bedroom in the flat in the viaduct. Further investigation revealed a box of old communion wafers lying in one corner. Dushma devoured them all before falling into an exhausted sleep on a pile of cushions.

She slept for the rest of that day and the whole of the

following night, although it wasn't until later that she realized this. When she awoke, the idea of seeking sanctuary from a priest no longer seemed such a good one. The fire in the underground tunnel would surely be in all the papers by now. She might be a wanted person, her description all over the national news. As soon as this possibility occurred to her she scrambled to her feet, determined to be gone before she could be caught.

On leaving the wardrobe she found that this annexe she had discovered was far more rambling and extensive than she had thought. She quickly lost her way trying to retrace her steps back to the main part of the cathedral. She took a wrong turning and was soon wandering up and down crooked staircases and through long rooms lined with cupboards full of robes and hymn-books. There was even a kitchen, although its cupboards contained nothing but teabags, instant coffee and a tin of powdered milk. After glancing back out into the corridor to make sure there was no one coming, she prised the top off the powdered milk and ate some with a teaspoon.

Eventually she found the door that led back into the cathedral. This time it was locked, but the key hung from a nail nearby. Dushma let herself out, locked the door again behind her and pocketed the key.

Her first thought was to find a newspaper. She fished several abandoned ones out of rubbish bins, discovering in the process that it was now one day later than she had thought it was, due to her long sleep in the vestry.

Surprisingly there was nothing in any of the papers about an explosion on the Underground. Some carried the story of the viaduct catching fire, but it didn't seem to have been serious so there was only minimal coverage. There was no mention of how the fire had been started by flames from the ventilation shaft under the arch containing Dushma's one-time home. Nor, to her relief, was there any suggestion that anyone fitting her description had been involved. She was still anonymous, with nothing more than her distressed appearance to draw attention to her. At first she felt only relief, but it didn't take long for this to be overtaken by a growing sense of outrage. Terrible things had happened, she knew; people had been killed. Yet there was no mention of this anywhere. There were some articles about the sudden closure of an Underground line for emergency engineering works, and the disgruntled testimony of several passengers who had been led to safety from an incapacitated train, but that was all. The public was being deceived.

That evening, having nowhere else to go, she let herself back into the cathedral annexe with her stolen key. Ravenous, she was hoping to find another supply of communion wafers, even though they tasted of nothing and felt like brittle cardboard in her mouth. In fact she found better fare than that. In a storeroom next to the kitchen she discovered what she supposed were provisions kept for feeding the congregation after Sunday morning services. There were biscuits, fruit, trifle sponges, custard powder, cubes of jelly, and currants and sugar for cakes. There was enough for her to take what she wanted without it being obvious that anything had gone.

Having eaten, she returned to her makeshift bed in the wardrobe at the back of the vestry. The next evening followed a similar pattern, and the one after that. She began to feel more relaxed in her new surroundings. She took advantage of the kitchen's plentiful supplies of soap and hot water to wash herself fairly thoroughly. She even found a comb in the vestry with which she was able to bring a little order to her ruined hair.

During these first few days she had heard only the most distant sounds of human activity in the annexe. She could almost believe that she had the place all to herself. This feeling was confirmed when, in a room that was clearly used as an office, she found a summary of the activities for which the annexe was used. There seemed to be hardly any. There was a weekly cleaning schedule, and a list of when and where the priests and altar boys changed in to and out of their vestments. And each Sunday the congregation came for refreshments after the mid-morning service. But otherwise the annexe appeared to be completely unused.

If she was careful, Dushma began to realize, and avoided certain rooms at the busiest times, there was no reason why she shouldn't stay here undetected indefinitely.

She washed her clothes at the sink in the kitchen. While

they dried she wore a cassock and a surplice taken from the altar boys' changing room. Greatly daring, she made a foray into the cathedral dressed like this, carrying a hymn-book and a candle. To her delight several visitors had seen her but none had given her a second glance.

She wondered if she could become an altar girl. Did they have them? Would she get paid? She had no idea. She resolved to attend a service one Sunday to see what it was that the altar boys did. It couldn't be that difficult, surely.

After the fear of being discovered had worn off, she found that the most difficult aspect of her new existence was the boredom. Although a solitary girl and used to her own company, she had never gone for so long with no one to talk to. She even found herself beginning to miss Auntie Megan, despite the fact that during the last few months of their life together in the viaduct they had done nothing but fight.

She began to set herself tasks to do, just to try and keep herself occupied. In one room of the annexe was a cupboard full of discarded hymn-books with missing covers and pages torn out. She set to work repairing them with some sellotape she'd found in a drawer. She assembled the loose pages into the right order, taped them together and then stuck the covers back on.

When she had finished with the hymn-books she busied herself tidying the vestry. At first it had seemed a dingy room, but once she had managed to open the leaded windows and clean the outside of the stained glass, it became much more cheerful when the sun was shining.

Among the stacked-up chairs and boxes of junk stood a brass lectern in the shape of an eagle. It hadn't looked too bad when the vestry was in semi-darkness, but it was now obvious that it was dreadfully tarnished. Dushma set to work on it with a rag and some metal-polish. She was meticulous, glad of the excuse to empty her mind of everything but the job in hand. She burnished every millimetre of metal, even wrapping the cloth round her thumb and running her nail along the grooves of the eagle's feathers. It came up beautifully, twinkling in the light from the newly cleaned window.

She was soon feeling quite at home in the vestry. Now that it was tidier it could, with a little effort, be made rather cosy in the evenings. There was no shortage of thick yellow beeswax candles to light when it grew dark, and there were heavy velvet curtains that could be drawn across the shabbier alcoves. It was only later, after she had found the story, that it started to seem not an intriguing refuge but a frightening place full of secrets and potential danger.

Eventually, she became so accustomed to her surroundings that she began to feel quite bold. After being in the annexe for several weeks without seeing a soul she had almost stopped bothering to be careful. She began to walk the corridors openly rather than flitting guiltily from one doorway to the next. Even if she did meet someone, she reasoned, they would probably think she had as much right to be there as they did. Particularly if she was engaged in some useful-looking task.

The storeroom next to the kitchen was replenished every Sunday. Her discreet pilfering seemed to be going unnoticed, and so, as her confidence grew, she began to steal with hungry abandon.

One night, unable to sleep, she had let herself into the darkened cathedral. Moonlight filtered in through the windows high above her, glinting on the gold chains of the hanging chandeliers and picking out the silver stars painted on the vaulting. It would still have been too dark for her to see her way, but she had brought a candle from the vestry. Its reflected light gleamed in the polished wood of the pews and glittered in the jewelled eyes of the statues in their niches round the walls.

Dushma walked across the wide expanse of the nave towards the cathedral's central aisle. As she went she imagined how she must look to anyone gazing down from the height of the vaulted ceiling far above her. There were hidden passageways up there, she knew, that would allow an observer to gaze down through chinks in the masonry across the whole expanse of the cathedral's interior. But now they would see nothing but a flickering speck of light gliding across a dim grey field of paving.

She stopped and peered around into the darkness until her eyes ached and swirled with colour. How many other secret passageways and observation points must there be?

There might be ones that she had no idea about, ones much closer than the roof of the nave, perhaps in the walls or in the columns close to her.

She cupped her free hand round the flame to shield it. Her fingertips shone a luminous pink like heated metal. She shouldn't be afraid of anyone who might be watching. They should be afraid of her, because they would see not a terrified girl with a candle but a set of disembodied fingers glowing red hot in the dark. They would fear her fiery hands.

A drop of wax splashed her knuckle. She flinched but did not drop the candle. *I'm impervious*, she told herself.

She set off across the nave once more. Fighting an urge to run, she walked with deliberate slowness, her eyes on the floor in front of her.

Within a few dozen paces she had found what she was looking for. She crouched, setting her candle down beside her. By its light she could just make out the inscription on the gravestone set into the floor. "Here lie the mortal remains of Selwyn Champion Esquire", it said.

She ran her fingers over the deeply incised lettering. She had seen this whole gravestone lifted up to reveal an opening into a tunnel that ran the length of the nave. She could feel the hole in the centre of the C of Champion that would allow an implement of a suitable shape to raise the stone. But without such a tool it was clear that the task would be almost impossible. So snugly into the surrounding paving did the gravestone fit that Dushma couldn't find a gap even big enough for her fingernail.

She abandoned her vain attempts to lift the stone and instead laid herself down flat, pressed her ear to it and listened. Could she hear a faint rushing noise? Perhaps, but even if she could, she told herself, it was probably only an Underground train, or the wind scouring the cathedral's exterior.

She was about to get to her feet again and go back to bed when she noticed something peculiar. The stone beneath her cheek was warm.

She sat up in surprise. Sweeping her palm across the floor around her she felt not the numbing, night-time cold of indoor masonry but a level of heat that could have come from a sun-warmed pavement in summer. Only when she moved several feet away from Selwyn Champion's gravestone did the warmth give way to the chill she would have expected.

Could it be coming from the cathedral's heating? But surely it was too late for that, it must have been switched off hours ago. And besides, she knew there could be no pipes under this section of the floor.

She lay down again to enjoy the warmth and ponder the problem further. Within half a minute she had fallen asleep and was dreaming she was toasting muffins by a bonfire in the tunnels beneath the cathedral.

When she woke, the nave was already filled with bluish early morning light. The gravestone beneath her was still warm but the side of her not touching the floor was cold and her joints ached.

She sat up stiffly. Her candle had melted into a flat cake of hard grey wax by her elbow. She picked at it with her fingernails but couldn't prise it loose, so she had to leave it there and hurry back to her hiding place before she was discovered.

Apart from the abandoned magazines and newspapers she scavenged on her excursions from the cathedral, she had nothing to read but hymn-books. After a while she never wanted to see one again. She searched the annexe for something else to read: a history book, a thriller, even a collection of poetry. She would have been delighted with anything substantial that might provide some interest. But when eventually she did find something, she would come to wish she hadn't.

The annexe was large and rambling. There were a lot of places to look, and it took her some time to search them all. What was more, she hadn't grown bored enough to be reckless. She still took care not to leave more signs of her presence than were absolutely necessary.

At first she found nothing but yellowing sheets of newspaper lining drawers of cutlery, and a page of instructions for the hot-water boiler. It was only when she returned to her hideaway in the vestry that she had more success.

The room was huge and unusually shaped. Apart from the wardrobe where she slept, she used only a small section of it, a clearing she had made for herself among the clutter out of sight of the door. Beyond her own tidy area, narrow passages ran through piled-up furniture, leading to ceiling-high cupboards and deep alcoves, some of which were themselves the size of small rooms. Behind one thick velvet hanging she had found a large, dark space filled with a forest of candlesticks, each one taller than she was.

Most of the cupboards were empty, or contained nothing but rows of hymn-books. She hadn't bothered to look carefully before, but now she took a chair and went from one cupboard and alcove to the next, reaching up to sweep the higher shelves with her hand.

Dust and the crumbling husks of dead insects cascaded down on top of her. She sneezed, loudly the first time, then more quietly, nose and mouth muffled in the crook of her elbow.

She had been about to give up and go and wash her by now filthy hands, when, at the end of the last shelf, her fingers touched something dry and crackly. Blinking away the falling shower of dust, she took down a sheaf of antique paper, yellowed and wreathed in cobwebs.

She crouched down on the floor, spread the pages out in front of her and began to sift through them. As she progressed her disappointment grew. They were accounts, containing nothing but lists of purchases, items in one column, prices in the next. She skimmed the text. Candles, vestments, furniture, perhaps the very things that surrounded her now. Hymn-books (of course). More hymn-books.

Occasionally there was a date. The documents were from the 1870s, round about the time the cathedral was being built. Were the hymn-books really that old? No wonder they were falling apart. She looked at the prices. They seemed very cheap. A bargain, perhaps. Maybe that was why they had bought so many.

This, she supposed, was how history got written. People ploughed through papers like this and discovered things, made deductions. She felt a flicker of interest. It was preferable to hot-water boiler instructions, anyway. She might find out something about the cathedral that nobody knew.

She stood up, brushing cobwebs from her hands, intending to go somewhere more comfortable. As she gathered the papers together, an envelope slid out from among them. Inside were more sheets of paper, the topmost of which was a letter, dated November 4th, 1878. She had to hold it up to the fading light to try and make out the words.

Dear Father Jardine,

As per your instructions I have made discreet enquiries regarding the destruction by fire of parish property in Cutlery Lane. The facts of the matter are elusive and consequently, as you anticipated, rumour is rife. Most worryingly, I discovered that a leading "penny dreadful" had plans to run a lurid fictionalized account of the proceedings. At considerable personal expense, I was able to obtain what I am assured is the only manuscript. This I enclose for you to do with as you see fit.

To save you the trouble of reading it, let me say that it is a scurrilous farrago which to the educated eye can quite obviously have not the slightest basis in reality. Nevertheless, even in this modern age, it is an unfortunate truth that there are all too many gullible riff-raff who would have been prepared to give it credence, to the possible detriment of the dean and chapter of our new cathedral.

As I mentioned, the acquisition was not cheap, but since the matter is so sensitive I felt sure you would not have wished me to hesitate. I hope I may make so bold as to suggest that the question of reimbursement should arise at our forthcoming meeting.

I wish to remain, sir, your most humble and devoted servant,

The main body of the letter had been difficult enough to decipher, but the signature was illegible. The rest of the contents of the envelope, however, was in a different hand: a dozen or so pages, densely written, but in a fine, careful script that was easy to read.

Conrad Vastruglin swept stiff-legged through the noisome streets. . .

No title or author's name preceded the opening sentence. A story, the letter had said, about a fire. But a story so scandalous or dangerous that the unknown letter-writer had bought or stolen it to keep it secret.

This was better than accounts. With increasing excitement Dushma flicked through the sheets of paper.

This might be, she thought, a story that no one alive had ever read. She should ration herself, a page a day.

It was nearly dark outside. She lit several candles and settled herself down on a cushion to read.

When she had finished she rose and lit all the other candles she could find. But even with a light flickering in every candlestick and on every flat surface in the vestry, there were still shadowy corners that she couldn't quite be sure were empty, however hard she stared at them.

Whichever way she turned, there was always something behind her that she'd rather not have out of her sight. Things she had thought merely interesting before – a piece of statuary, an embroidered shred of cloth like a face – now seemed as if they might move or alter their shape as soon as she looked away.

A panel of stained glass, propped against the wall, shimmered eerily in the wavering candle-light. The scene it depicted was not quite discernible, as if the glass was still liquid, the colours still running one into another. The moment they solidified, she was sure, she would see something she'd very much wish she hadn't. She laid the glass flat on the ground, trying not to look at it too closely.

She didn't get much sleep that night.

III

Firefoal

Conrad Vastruglin swept stiff-legged through the noisome streets, his heavy cloak swirling about him and shielding him from the worst of the effluent thrown up from the gutters by the wheels of passing carts and hansom cabs. It was early evening in one of the busiest parts of London, and the pavements were crowded. Hawkers jostled for space, shouting out their wares with piercing cries and sometimes darting out to snatch at a sleeve and importune a particularly likely-looking passer-by. Clerks hurried home, their thin coats pulled tight about their shoulders against the autumn chill. Top-hatted gentlemen, sticks in their hands, picked their way fastidiously through the mud and litter. A gang of workmen, already drunk, staggered across the road. And around them all weaved the urchins, some innocently engaged in childish games of chase, others, already more worldly, searching the ground for fallen coins or watching the pockets of unwary adults in the hope of snatching a purse.

Yet despite this press and clamour, Vastruglin ap̣
pass without hindrance. There was something in his
that caused the crowds to melt before him. Perhaps
his height. Or perhaps it was the deep-set eyes that
glittered beneath the wide, dark brim of his hat. Or the
venerable fullness of his long grey beard, or the cruel,
hooked appearance of his aquiline nose. Whatever the
reason, other pedestrians veered away at his approach. They
seemed almost unconsciously to step back or twist aside
rather than block his path, and thus he was able to brush his
way almost effortlessly through the multitude of people
like a boat gliding through a windswept bed of reeds.

Reaching a street corner that afforded a view of the
twilit city skyline, Vastruglin paused, staring into the
distance over the heads of passers-by, his thick, grey brows
knotted into a frown. He waited, leaning on his cane, for
the boy hurrying along behind him to catch him up.

"Look there, Ynoul." He spoke in Romanian, one
crabbed hand lifted to indicate the half-completed
cathedral that reared up on the horizon.

"Master?" Ynoul raised a hand to shade his eyes and
peered in the direction of Vastruglin's pointing finger.

Even in its unfinished state the cathedral towered above
all the neighbouring buildings. The setting sun streamed
along the length of the roofless nave, silhouetting the
skeletal masonry of unglazed windows against the evening
sky. Scaffolding clad the soaring, buttressed walls like a
prickly growth.

45

"Monstrosity," muttered Vastruglin. He leaned forward over the gutter and spat. Then he spun round and strode on through the crowd.

Before he could follow, Ynoul felt someone clutch at his arm. He flinched in surprise, then coughed as a cloud of rose-scented perfume enveloped him.

Beside him was a girl, scarcely older than he was himself, as far as he could tell. She wore a fine, lace-trimmed bonnet and her made-up face was beautiful in the manner of a porcelain doll. When he hesitated, unsure of her intentions, she tilted her chin prettily and, in an unmistakable signal of invitation, winked suggestively.

He shook his head and pulled himself free of her. As he turned to walk quickly away she leered at him and for an instant he was looking right into her mouth. She had almost no teeth. Those that remained were crooked and black, like charred wooden pegs, and he was close enough to see a whitish down furring the gums in which they were embedded.

He shuddered as he stumbled away down the busy street, pictures from his master's grimoires crowding unpleasantly into his head.

Night was almost upon them by the time they found the house they were looking for. It was a tall, many-windowed edifice which at first sight seemed if anything even more imposing than those on either side of it. But on closer inspection its ill-kept condition was clear. The light of the gas-lamps sputtering to life on the pavements up and down the street revealed a sorry facade of blistered paint, crumbling stucco, loose bricks and patches of moss and ivy. Nor had the roof escaped dilapidation. Clusters of tall chimneys stroked the clouds of drifting smog like upthrust fingers, but here and there a fallen stack left a gap like a missing digit.

A footman answered the door and ushered Vastruglin and his apprentice inside. They climbed a wide staircase to the first-floor landing, where they were shown into a large and comfortable study. Leather-bound books lined the walls, gas-fittings hissed and a coal fire glowed in the grate. A clock ticked.

"Sir Jeremy," said the footman, "Mr Vastruglin has arrived."

A tall man was sitting behind a desk in the far corner of the room. Seeing Vastruglin he immediately sprang to his feet and hurried towards him, arms outstretched. "Maestro!" he cried.

Vastruglin ignored him and walked stiffly across the room to an empty chair in front of the fire. He sat with some difficulty, taking his time in finding the right position for his long limbs. Then he hunched his shoulders, leaned forward and stared into the flames, a brooding expression on his face. He did not remove his hat.

"Delighted I'm sure, a pleasure," muttered Sir Jeremy, his smile sagging a little on his face. Recovering himself, he gestured towards a figure slumped in an armchair to one side of the fireplace. "Allow me to introduce His Grace the Bishop of Smithfield."

The bishop was a huge, florid man dressed in threadbare clerical garb. Pouches of fat hung beneath his small, dull eyes. From under his sunken chin thick, pink folds of flesh billowed down over the stained front of his cassock. He held a large glass of wine or port which he sniffed periodically but did not put to his lips. He grunted when introduced, but made no other acknowledgement of Vastruglin's presence.

"So, well . . . some refreshment, perhaps?" asked Sir Jeremy. "Tea? Wine? A little light supper?"

"I am fasting," growled Vastruglin. "It sharpens my senses."

The bishop looked up sharply and stared into the distance over the rim of his raised wineglass. "Truly," he said in a gurgling voice, "it is meet and fitting to strive to subjugate the desires of the flesh." He nodded approvingly to himself, jowls quivering.

Ynoul was not fasting and was in fact beginning to feel extremely hungry. The faint smell of gravy lingered in the study, as if from a meal recently consumed, and his stomach squelched in anticipation. But the three men seemed unaware of his presence and he did not dare to speak out.

"Of course, of course, absolutely. Whatever you wish," said Sir Jeremy. He walked back round behind his desk and resumed his seat. He was not accustomed to being treated in such an offhand manner. It cost him dear to swallow his pride, but, with an effort, swallow it he did, for in truth Sir Jeremy Elkie was a man on the verge of desperation. Sole heir to the vast fortune of his great-uncle, the mill-owner and philanthropist Sir Terence Elkie, he had squandered his inheritance on a life of dissolution and excess. Now close to bankruptcy, hounded by his creditors, he sought by any means possible to ward off ruin and restore his wealth. But he did not have his great-uncle's business acumen, and his various money-making ventures had invariably ended in disaster. Most recently, he had been involved in an ingenious aerial transportation scheme, designed to alleviate the congestion on the capital's roads. Workers would be shuttled back and forth between their homes and the city centre by a network of steam-driven overhead pulleys, supported on giant metal pylons that could be raised or lowered to control the speed and direction of travel.

Following the spectacular failure of this ambitious plan, Sir Jeremy had been left with only one chance of avoiding destitution. Playing on his family background, he had ingratiated himself with the Bishop of Smithfield. Having gained the bishop's trust, he now sought financial advantage from the construction of London's newest cathedral. This vast and magnificent edifice was to be dedicated to his great-uncle Sir Terence's protégée, the martyred St Gotha Angstrom, or "that gold-digging strumpet", as Sir Jeremy was wont to refer to her, although not in the presence of His Grace. Such a grandiose venture was bound to provide a shrewd entrepreneur with opportunities to make money through entrance fees, guided tours and merchandise. And if the attractions of the building itself were augmented by work from Europe's foremost artists, paid for by the cathedral's generous but unworldly future congregation, then the potential profits were surely even more substantial.

So, Sir Jeremy told himself, he must humour this man, this foreign sculptor, this rude and surly genius. He must ignore his insolence, flatter and cajole him, persuade him to accept a commission by whatever means at his disposal.

"Well, tell me then," he began. "I believe you're lodging on Cutlery Lane. You find your accommodation pleasant, I hope? We did our best to satisfy your requirements."

"It is adequate."

"And, er, I trust you saw our great venture taking shape as you made your way here?"

"I did."

"Splendid! And what did you think? Is it not, even in its uncompleted state, a truly magnificent torso?"

Vastruglin raised his head and for the first time looked Sir Jeremy straight in the eye. "It is not," he growled. "It is a monstrosity."

A hawking sound rose in his throat. His cheeks worked as he gathered the rheum into his mouth. Stretching out his neck, he expelled a thick gobbet of phlegm right into the heart of the fire.

"Well, really!" exclaimed Sir Jeremy. Then he recovered himself with an effort and said in a conciliatory tone, "Perhaps not to everyone's taste, I admit, but I am assured that when complete it will be a wonder of the modern age. The biggest in Europe! A worthy setting, surely, for a sculpture by Conrad Vastruglin, the greatest ecclesiastical artist of the century. I know you've been retired for years, but what better way to crown your career, what more fitting swansong than a final masterpiece for the mightiest edifice in Christendom? The crowds will flock to see it, I promise you, and at tuppence a time for a tour of the crypt and the same again for the tower . . . why, the returns will be damn handsome, sir! Damn handsome indeed!" He rubbed his hands together, barely trying to conceal his glee.

"I have promised you nothing."

"But you're here, you've travelled all this way — surely you're not going to turn me down now? Tell me what you want! Fame? You'll be in every newspaper in the land. You'll dine with royalty if that is what you wish. Money? I offer you forty per cent of all proceeds — that is, after His Grace has taken his allotted share for distribution among the needy."

Vastruglin said nothing. He glared out from beneath his thickly knotted eyebrows, a sneer of pure contempt spreading slowly across his face.

"Fifty, then!" babbled Sir Jeremy. "It's an unmissable offer. How can you refuse? You'll earn a king's ransom in weeks!"

Slowly Vastruglin turned away. For a long time he did not speak, and the only sounds in the study were the ticking of the clock and the rustle of the settling fire.

"Your blandishments are pitiful," he growled at last. "Riches and esteem are meaningless to me."

"Well, then . . . I, in that case. . ." Sir Jeremy wrung his hands, a hysterical grin frozen on his face.

"Let me tell you why I am here. Then perhaps you will see what it is you can do for me."

"Why of course, I'm sure, by all means. . ."

"This is no time for false modesty. Yes, I have earned greater wealth and fame than any living sculptor. I have been showered with gold by emperors and popes. My work has been celebrated in every major capital of Europe, and beyond. But it has never been enough." Vastruglin lowered his head and his voice dropped to a whisper. "Even in my moments of greatest glory the rich trappings of success felt like sackcloth on my shoulders. I achieved everything an artist could wish for, but none of it was enough to bring me satisfaction. I was the master of my medium but at the height of my renown I turned my back on it. I sought out new materials. I forsook marble and bronze for obsidian and quicksilver. I obtained hermetic texts and pored over them in pursuit of forgotten techniques and esoteric formulae. I craved knowledge. I vowed that I would be more than a maker of baubles. I had come to yearn for mastery of an altogether different order."

Vastruglin drew himself up in his chair and swept the

room with his fiery gaze. "I threw aside my carving tools!" he cried, gesturing extravagantly with an outstretched arm. "I gave up my sculptor's bench to toil instead at the mouth of the furnace. I worked now with anvil and bellows, vitriol and precious metals . . . yes, and other things too, yet harder to come by. For in the course of my searches I discovered secrets that would have turned the mind of a lesser man and sent him scurrying, mewling and feeble-witted, to end his days huddled and shivering beneath his counterpane. Yet I, Vastruglin, did not flinch. At last I had found a worthy use for my abilities. I had it in my power to create substances of a beauty and strength undreamed of in five hundred years. But the price was heavy. Few were prepared to pay, and for those that did the consequences were catastrophic."

"St Vitus's," breathed Sir Jeremy. "I heard the rumours. . ."

"They were fools and peasants!" snarled Vastruglin. "But I learned so much. I came so close. And now I have another chance. It will be more difficult for you than you think, as you do not yet realize what it is you have asked for. As for myself, I realize all too well. Yet despite this terrible knowledge . . . I accept your commission."

Sir Jeremy's eyes sparkled with delight. "Sir!" he cried. "You honour us too much. What can I say to express our humble gratitude? I'll have my lawyers draft a contract first thing tomorrow. In the meantime may I suggest that, without further ado, we should turn our attention to what is surely the most important matter of all: that is, the subject of your forthcoming masterpiece. I believe that on this vital question His Grace, my spiritual guide throughout this great venture, has had some thoughts that he may now care to share with us."

He turned expectantly to the bishop. The huge prelate passed his wineglass back and forth beneath his nose and inhaled deeply.

"The sufferings of the martyr," he rumbled, staring intently into the purple liquid. "The mortifications of her tender young flesh."

"Oh, yes! A splendid suggestion!" cried Sir Jeremy, clapping his hands together delightedly. "That'll bring them . . . I mean, bring their, er, bring their minds to bear on their sinful condition."

"I will sculpt whatsoever I choose," snapped Vastruglin. "Nor is that my only condition. Think for a moment. They clamour for my work in the richest cities of Europe. I could name my price in Paris, Cologne, Vienna or St Petersburg. I could insist on payment in advance, without having to sully myself with the takings of the turnstile. Yet I am here. Because it is here that I believe I will be most able to obtain the things I will require."

He reached inside his cloak, drew forth a folded piece of parchment and held it out. "Look," he said, the trace of a thin, cruel smile visible behind his beard. "The translation of an ancient chemical text. I believe it makes my requirements clear enough."

Sir Jeremy took the parchment and moved closer to the lamp on his desk in order to be able to see more clearly.

As he read his mouth sagged open and his face turned ashen grey. When he had finished he tried several times to speak but could not. At last, after swallowing several times and moistening his lips with a nervous, darting tongue, he croaked, "This . . . this is monstrous. You cannot be in earnest."

"Oh but I am. Deadly earnest. The question is, are you?"

"I've heard rumours, of course. I've heard you called mage and arch-chimic. Some said you were an adept; others, a Rosicrucian. Jealousy, I thought, or superstition. I paid them no heed. But this . . . this smacks of alchemy."

"It is no such thing! It is simply science for which the scientists themselves cannot yet find an explanation."

"We can have no truck with it!" Hands trembling, Sir Jeremy let the parchment fall. "And besides, how could such horrific ingredients be transmuted into anything that might enhance our great cathedral? What is it exactly that you're offering us?"

"Listen to me. I promise you gargoyles of unparalleled grotesquery, twisted and glistening as if plucked straight from the tar-pits of hell itself. I promise you statues made from extraordinary new materials that will astonish and delight all who behold them. I promise you yourself, Sir Jeremy Elkie, a place in history as one of the greatest patrons of art and learning the world has ever seen."

Hesitantly, Sir Jeremy picked up the parchment again,

his face contorted with indecision. "A noble goal, it's true. . . But is it one that can justify the acts your document requires?"

"It is your will. You have the power. What further justification is needed for men such as ourselves? Look around you! Your empire covers a third of the globe yet the streets of your capital city are awash with filth. The slums are seething with whores and degenerates, lowlives and criminals. Why should men like us be bound by consideration for such creatures? Without the pursuit of knowledge and beauty we are merely animals. If in achieving our ends there are obstacles to be overcome then so be it. Some rise up, others are trampled. You are anything but naive. Do not come the hypocrite with me by trying to claim that the world works in any other way."

Sir Jeremy licked his lips again, quickly, like a snake. He shot a calculating look across at the bishop, who seemed to be paying no attention to the discussion. Turning back to Vastruglin, he said delicately, "I think that further negotiations should remain strictly between ourselves."

Seeing that Sir Jeremy was weakening, Vastruglin pressed home his advantage. "I would not hold you to the terms you have previously offered me. A sum to cover my expenses would be sufficient."

Abruptly the bishop raised his glass, tipped back his head and drained his wine to the dregs. "Oh weak, weak vessel!" he shouted. Hauling himself upright, he lurched towards the door, pulled it open and staggered out into the corridor. His uneven footsteps could be heard receding into the distance, accompanied by the sound of retching.

Sir Jeremy ignored his departure. Coming close to Vastruglin he murmured, "It can be done." Then he crumpled the parchment in his fist and hurled it on to the fire. "But no one must know of this, or I am ruined."

At the height of his fame, Conrad Vastruglin had employed dozens of assistant sculptors, stonemasons, draughtsmen and apprentices. So great was his renown, and so in demand were his services, that the number of commissions he received was far greater than he could possibly have fulfilled without help.

For all but his most illustrious patrons he would often leave most of the work to others. He might only supply an initial concept and some preliminary sketches. Then, with most of the work completed, he might return to put the finishing touches to the most difficult parts of the sculpture. Such intricate details as the locks of Samson's hair, the look of lust on the face of King Herod, or the tears welling from the eyes of the Madonna – all these would merit the attention of the master.

The crowning glory of his career was a commission from the pope: a statue of Moses for St Peter's. It was a triumph, and at its unveiling Vastruglin was the toast of Rome. Afterwards, however, he had withdrawn from commercial sculpture almost entirely. As his outstanding commissions were completed, he had gradually dispensed with the services of all of those in his employ. Eventually, a year or so after his Roman triumph, his Bucharest workshop was empty.

He travelled, returning infrequently to his homeland over the next few years. After his first absence, when word spread that he had returned, a stream of visitors came to his door. There were rich patrons wanting to commission work, artisans seeking employment, and parents eager for their talented offspring to become apprenticed to the world's most famous sculptor. But he would see none of them, and soon took his leave again on another long trip abroad. On his next return, fewer people sought an audience, and the next time fewer still, until finally everyone appeared to have forgotten about him, or given up trying to see him.

At last Vastruglin's eyes began to fail him. His hands, after a lifetime of hammering, drilling and sanding, began to stiffen with arthritis. Reluctantly, he accepted that it was time for him to take an apprentice once more.

He chose carefully. Acting through an agent, he made enquiries at schools throughout the city and in all the surrounding towns. He did not want someone who would simply be attracted by his one-time fame. He wanted someone he could trust with the secret lore he had acquired in his years of hermetic study. He was beginning to feel the weight of advancing age pressing on his shoulders, and needed to be sure that his dangerous and difficult knowledge would not die with him.

Finally, at an orphanage in a nearby village, he found the very person he was looking for: sharp-eyed and still sharper-witted, nimble and dextrous, capacious of memory, linguistically gifted, circumspect and intensely curious. His new protégé did not yet know it, but Vastruglin had found the heir to whom he intended to unveil his hard-won secrets. The right bribes were paid, the adoption papers were signed, and for the first time in many years, someone other than the master himself was admitted to Vastruglin's innermost chambers.

For anyone familiar with the sculptor's workshop at the height of its productivity, the change it had undergone would have seemed considerable. Where once the walls had echoed with the sound of hammers, now furnaces breathed, bellows hissed and acid-filled retorts bubbled and fizzed. Air that had once been filled with clouds of marble dust was now hazy with tendrils of multi-coloured smoke and full of the reek of noisome chemicals.

Yet Ynoul was far from overwhelmed by his new surroundings. He seized upon the opportunity presented him, learning with eagerness and aptitude everything he was taught.

His apprenticeship was rigorous and varied. He became adept at smelting iron, casting bronze and blowing glass. He studied languages, ancient and modern. He familiarized himself with the precepts of astronomy and the fundamentals of science and mathematics. He pored over the wrinkled pages of the heavy brass-clasped tomes that lined the workshop walls. His appetite for knowledge was almost the equal of his master's.

He had been with Vastruglin for almost three years when at last the sculptor agreed to accept another commission. For Ynoul this was the chance he had been longing for: the chance to display his new skills, to apply his learning for all to marvel at.

Though it was small in scale compared with the projects he had undertaken in the past, Vastruglin seemed extremely excited, not to say nervous, about the work he was to do. The commission, from the Archbishop of Prague, was for a new stained-glass window for St Vitus's Cathedral on the subject of imaginary animals. Vastruglin's bold and colourful designs included unicorns, griffins, dragons and mermaids, and several examples of a creature so esoteric that only one ancient bestiary included it: the firefoal, mythical offspring of a salamander and a seahorse.

To Ynoul's disappointment he was not allowed to take part in the manufacture of the glass itself. The procedure, said Vastruglin, was delicate; the involvement of an apprentice was too much of a risk. Not permitted even to watch, Ynoul had to content himself with helping to make the metal frames in which the glass would sit.

Despite the small part he had played, he was still able to feel great pride at the reception given to their completed work. The colours were remarkable, everyone agreed. Experts averred that such deep and vivid reds had not been produced since the Middle Ages. The secrets were thought lost. How had Vastruglin done it?

But the sculptor would not say.

Crowds came from all over the city and beyond to admire the new window. At first the praise was unanimous. Then rumours began to circulate. It happened at sunset, people whispered. When the evening light caught the glass just so, the animals seemed to stir. Moving slowly, as if floating in liquid, the unicorns nodded their heads, the dragons stretched their wings, and the firefoals rose from their flaming pyres, arched their forelegs, shook their manes and unfurled their smoking tails.

Superstitious nonsense, the archbishop declared. He was already discussing new and grander projects with Vastruglin.

But the rumours persisted: the glass was haunted, the cathedral possessed, Vastruglin a heretic. All manner of misfortunes were linked to the installation of the window: bad weather, lame cattle, a mysterious disappearance.

The archbishop appealed to the citizens' reason but his words were ignored. A crowd assailed the cathedral. Stones were thrown and the window was broken.

Some said that the glass had not shattered at all, but had splashed on to the paving stones inside the nave and then trickled down through the cracks in crimson rivulets.

It was soon after this that Ynoul and Vastruglin had fled to London.

*

After the visit to Sir Jeremy's house, several days passed uneventfully. Vastruglin stayed in his room, poring over the books and manuscripts he had brought with him, eating little and talking less. He had no time for his apprentice.

Left to his own devices, Ynoul tried to concentrate on his studies, but without his master's attention he found it difficult to progress. His surroundings were no help. Their lodgings, in a converted cellar, were dark and claustrophobic. Vastruglin had been most insistent that they stay somewhere quiet. He slept lightly, he said, and the slightest noise disturbed him.

So Ynoul abandoned his books and instead spent his time in the open air, exploring the capital and mingling with the jostling crowds that thronged the streets. Having travelled widely with his master, he was no stranger to city life. The towering buildings held no awe for him, nor did he find the noise and dirt intimidating. Yet from the moment he began his first excursion he was conscious of a feeling of vague unease. It did not take him long to realize that, no matter in what direction he set out, sooner or later his footsteps always turned towards the street corner where he had been accosted by the girl in the bonnet.

The more he dwelt on their fleeting encounter, the harder it was for him to banish her from his thoughts. He remembered her vividly: her rose-scented perfume, her golden hair, her large, shining blue eyes, and then, when she had parted her scarlet lips, the dark, rotten cavity of her mouth. This image soon came to exert a powerful hold on his young and impressionable imagination, recurring unbidden in his mind's eye, at once loathsome and fascinating. Not understanding why, he found himself compelled to return again and again to the place where he had seen her. But although he saw many other girls of dubious repute, he did not glimpse the one he both hoped and feared to find.

In due course, Vastruglin began to receive deliveries of the items he would require to carry out Sir Jeremy's commission. Tradesmen arrived on a regular basis, their carts piled high with crates of equipment, boxes of tools and jars of chemicals.

Ynoul was kept busy answering the door, helping to unload the goods and checking lists of what had been received. He no longer had the leisure to venture abroad and loiter on street corners vainly scanning the passing crowds. Indeed, with so much to occupy his time, he suffered hardly at all from the disturbing thoughts that had previously so troubled him.

Before long the living room of their lodgings began to resemble the inside of Vastruglin's Bucharest workshop. A table of laboratory glassware stood along one wall; a portable furnace squatted in the corner, flanked by bags of charcoal; chemicals and vats of acid lined the shelves; a pair of bellows and an anvil stood by the fireplace.

When everything had arrived, Vastruglin set his apprentice to work preparing the compounds he would need. Glad to be busy, Ynoul applied himself diligently to his tasks. He used a set of fine brass scales to weigh out precise amounts of the chemicals he required; he dissolved them in acid, mixed the resulting solutions and filtered the precipitates. Coaxing the furnace to a fine heat, he melted down sand with a variety of substances he did not fully understand the purpose of, and obtained a handful of smoky glass nuggets. Then, although he had no idea why, he used a mortar and pestle to grind a bagful of porcelain shards down to a fine powder.

When he had done, he found that he had produced a set of substances more unusual than any he had ever known his master to work with. He was curious, but knew better than to ask for what they were intended.

For his part, Vastruglin kept almost entirely to his room. On the few occasions when he emerged to encourage his apprentice or issue some new instruction, he seemed to be uncharacteristically agitated. Ynoul guessed that he awaited some news from Sir Jeremy, although he could not imagine what it might be.

His preparations complete, Ynoul found himself becoming obsessed once again with the girl in the bonnet. With nothing to distract him, her delicate features and ravaged mouth once more began to dominate his thoughts. But before he could venture forth once more in search of her, Vastruglin at last received the message he had been expecting.

It was a single sheet of paper folded several times and sealed with wax. The horseman who made the delivery would not wait, almost throwing the note at Ynoul and then vanishing into the rain as if pursued.

His expression impassive, Vastruglin read the message and then immediately thrust it into the flame of a nearby candle. The paper flared up, highlighting the jutting bones of his grey, emaciated face and flickering in the inhuman glassiness of his eyes.

The document consumed, he swept the ashes to the floor without a word of explanation and turned to the chest of drawers that stood by the fireplace. Unlocking the lowest, he pulled it open and took out a bolt of dark velvet. He laid it on his workbench and lifted a hammer from its folds.

"Mjölnir, the hammer of Thor, the god of storms!" He swept the hammer high into the air, turning it so that the metal gleamed in the candle-light. Then he directed a piercing look at his apprentice. "Do you believe me, boy?"

Silently, Ynoul shook his head. Vastruglin laughed harshly.

"And you are right. I have always taught you, have I not, to winnow the ancient texts you have studied, in order to rid them of the chaff of fantasy. Thus the grains of scientific truth may be exposed for those that care to see them. A hammer is a hammer, and vitriol is vitriol. Do we care if it was distilled by a virgin on the night of the full moon? No! We are rational creatures, interested only in demonstrable cause and effect. But we do not discard what we do not understand, rejecting it simply because it does not fit with our philosophy. We may not know exactly why it is that the more outlandish substances we use give the results they do. That is a question for those who follow after us along the trail that we have blazed. Suffice it for us to know that there must indeed be an explanation, and that the reasons for it are based on the forces of nature, and not the unquantifiable influence of the supernatural."

Eyes flashing, Vastruglin tilted back his head as if addressing an imagined audience of thousands. With a wide rhetorical gesture he indicated the scales on the workbench beside him. Ynoul stepped back a pace.

"Some people talk of higher things!" cried Vastruglin. "Of fate and balance, a life for a life. But they are wrong. Do I cross myself when a black cat walks in front of me? If an old crone curses me do I in my turn mutter imprecations? I do not. Nor shall I fear this cosmic justice that the weak invoke. There is no force that cannot be measured, no substance that cannot be weighed!" He picked the scales up from the workbench and raised them high in the air. The brass pans jiggled and swung, sending circles of candle-light rippling across the ceiling.

"I have read that even colour has mass," offered Ynoul. "They say that if you make glass thick and dark enough the light will ooze out of it like treacle."

But Vastruglin's thoughts were far away and he said nothing in reply. Instead he returned the scales to their place on the bench and laid his hammer carefully on the anvil by the fire. Then he beckoned his apprentice close and warned him that later in the evening another visitor would call.

"Take what he has to give you, but on no account look inside," he instructed. Drawing forth a heavy purse, he handed it to Ynoul. "If he seems to expect it, then give him this. Use your discretion. I dearly hope that fool Elkie has not tried to gull him."

With that he retired to his room once more, leaving Ynoul to wait by the fire. It seemed to the boy that he had only been sitting for a minute or two, staring into the caverns of glowing coal, when a knocking roused him from his fitful doze and he saw from the clock that it was almost midnight.

He ran up the flight of steps that led to the entrance of their lodgings, almost losing his footing in the dark. Reaching the top, he fumbled with the bolts and chains that secured the door, fearful that the visitor had already been outside for some considerable time and might take his leave at any moment.

The night was cold and foggy. Ynoul stood in the doorway and peered up and down the street, but could at first see no one. He held his breath and listened, but heard only the distant sound of a bell tolling the hour. Then a shoe scraped on the cobbles and the tall figure of a man loomed out of the mist beside him.

"Is the maestro at home, young fellow?"

The visitor wore a wide-brimmed hat pulled low, shading his eyes from the faint light of the gas-lamp across the street. All that could be seen of his face was a curved, sensual mouth and a sharply pointed chin.

"I'm afraid not, sir," answered Ynoul politely. "I am his apprentice."

"A pity. I had hoped to meet him. Please tell him that I have seen his work and find his treatment of muscle and sinew quite outstanding. His grasp of anatomy must be almost the equal of my own." He raised a hand to his face as if to stifle a cough, but instead drew the tip of his middle finger slowly over his parted lips in a horizontal stroking motion.

"Thank you, sir," replied Ynoul. "I will tell him when he returns. I am sure he will be most gratified."

"Yes . . . please do that." Still gently stroking his lips, the man turned to look cautiously around him. Satisfied that they were unobserved, he took a step closer to Ynoul and drew a leather package from his cloak. "Still warm," he whispered, smiling.

Ynoul took the package. It was surprisingly light, and sagged in his hands as if the contents were loose and floppy.

"By the way, did your master mention my expenses? There were some I had not foreseen. . .Why thank you, he is too kind." The stranger took the clinking purse and tucked it away inside his cloak. "A very good evening to you." Touching the brim of his hat, he turned and vanished into the mist.

The package was indeed still warm, although it was

impossible to tell whether this was due to what it contained or from its recent proximity to its bearer's body. Balancing it on the palm of one hand, Ynoul pulled the door shut behind him and made his way back down the steps.

He did not know how much money had been in the purse that Vastruglin had given him, but from its weight it must have been a substantial amount. He tried to guess what might be in the package for it to have cost so much. He was sure from the feel that it could not be tools or chemicals, nor paper or a book. Food, perhaps? He bent to sniff the package.

A faint, rose-scented perfume, tantalizingly familiar, reached his nostrils. He tried to think where he might have smelled it before, but could not. He breathed more deeply, and detected something else beneath the sweetness: a hint of rottenness, the stench of decay.

Back in the makeshift laboratory, he stood hesitating by the dying fire, wondering whether to rouse his master. Before he could decide what to do, Vastruglin's door swung open and the sculptor stepped into the room.

"He has come?" He caught sight of the parcel in Ynoul's hands. "Very well. Then it is time."

Ynoul could not recall ever having seen his master look afraid before. But now his expression was troubled and his deep-set eyes seemed haunted. His breathing, quick and shallow, came in rasps from his chest and his hands trembled as he took the package and placed it on the workbench.

"Beware of certainty, Ynoul," he said. "It is the preserve of the mediocre. People have sometimes asked me if I knew what I was doing. But when the great man, the risk-taker, the discoverer, knows what he is doing, then he knows that he is wasting his time."

Ynoul's gaze was fixed on the package, but Vastruglin did not unwrap it. Instead he reached inside his frock coat and, beckoning his apprentice close, drew forth a sheaf of crumpled papers covered in spidery writing.

"Here." He held out the papers. "My journals: everything I have learned from my years of hermetic study. Secret techniques, experiments and formulae that could make the adept who understands them rich beyond the fantasies of Bedlam. I entrust them to you now for safety. If anything should befall me, they are yours to keep. Use them wisely."

Reluctantly, Ynoul took the proffered documents. "Master. . ." he began, but Vastruglin silenced him with a glance.

"There is an inn two streets away. You must spend the night there. They expect you. Take this. It will more than suffice." He pressed a handful of coins on his apprentice. "Return in the morning. No, do not argue. What I intend to do must be done alone."

"But, master. . ."

"*Go!*"

Ynoul flinched from the look of ferocity on Vastruglin's face. Not daring to try and say more, he thrust papers and money into the inside pocket of his jacket and backed away. After a few steps, no longer able to stand the intensity of his master's gaze, he turned and fled the room.

He was halfway up the steps to the street when he heard the laboratory door slam shut behind him. Then there came the muffled sound of a groan more terrible than any he had heard a human utter. Part moan of despair, part growl of determination and defiance, it was enough to draw cold sweat from the brow of any who might hear it.

Ynoul froze in mid-stride. Prompted by curiosity, and now also by concern for his master, he felt a renewed urge to stay and witness whatever might be about to happen. But another, more rational impulse told him to run, to leave the cellar behind, to escape into the night and seek out the noise and comfort of people and laughter.

He took another step, recalling the terrible expression with which Vastruglin had banished him from the laboratory. Then he thought of the stranger who had delivered the package, waiting in the mist, smiling and stroking his lips. This was enough to make him hesitate once more.

Many times in his later life he would think of how easily he could have spared himself the night of horror that was to follow. He could simply have followed his master's orders, abandoning him in his laboratory along with its mysteries and sense of impending dread. He could have hurried out into the fog-shrouded streets, found the inn as he had been instructed, and spent the night in peace and safety. He could have put all thoughts of hermetic experiments out of his mind, thrown away the documents he had been entrusted with and become a carpenter, or a stonemason, or a scholar in some subject of repute.

But he had not done so. Hands clammy, heart knocking at his ribs, he had turned round and crept silently back down into the cellar.

Holding his breath, he turned the handle and let himself back into the laboratory. He had no idea what he would say when he confronted Vastruglin again, but in fact the room was empty. Hand pressed against his pocket to stop the coins he had been given from jingling, he stepped quickly behind the open door of a wardrobe, put his eye to a convenient knothole, and waited.

At last Vastruglin emerged from his room wearing a heavy leather apron much stained by chemicals. In some places the dark brown leather had been burned by acid; in others it was streaked with silver, gold and copper where these and other molten metals had splashed and then solidified.

Beneath this well-used garment he wore a loose white shirt, sleeves rolled up almost to the shoulder to expose his wiry arms. His wild hair was pulled back from his forehead by a torn piece of cloth. His face looked greyer and more deeply lined than Ynoul had ever seen it. In his encrusted apron, and with the bronze-coloured liver spots on his hands and arms, he seemed like a thing made of stone and metal, one of his own creations.

Moving stiffly, he strode towards the laboratory door and for a moment Ynoul feared discovery. But Vastruglin merely turned the key in the lock and did not glance sideways at the wardrobe.

Having thus ensured that he would not be disturbed, the sculptor now took a crucible and began filling it with the substances which Ynoul had prepared for him. Then he built up the fire and, seizing the bellows, blew it to a fine blaze. The flames roared yet Vastruglin was not satisfied. Still he worked the bellows, the sweat streaming from him, until the heat was so great that even on the far side of the room Ynoul had to turn his face away from the hole in the wardrobe door.

When next he dared to look, the coals were glowing white-hot and the flames filled the mouth of the flue like an incandescent pillar. Peering through the slits between his fingers, he saw Vastruglin hurl more fuel into the grate and then take up his bellows again.

The flames reared up even hotter than before. A roar like the sound of a waterfall echoed round the room.

When Vastruglin could endure no more he sprang away, smoke curling from his beard. Throwing down the bellows, he plunged his hands into a bucket and doused himself with water. Steam hissed from his skin.

He leaned on his workbench, clearly exhausted, his breath grating painfully in his throat. His eyes were bloodshot, the lids red and swollen. They stood out eerily against the grey of the rest of his complexion.

After the briefest of pauses to gather his strength, he pushed himself upright again. Taking a pair of long iron tongs, he picked up the crucible and, flinching from the heat, thrust it into the heart of the fire. Sparks showered up the chimney, and within a few minutes the contents of the crucible had begun to seethe and bubble. A noxious smell filled the air.

Now Vastruglin turned to the package on his workbench. He reached out to touch it then snatched his hand away. Steeling himself, gnarled fingers trembling, he reached out again and this time pulled the bindings loose. The leather wrapping flopped open.

At first Ynoul thought it must contain some kind of cloth; a garment perhaps. He glimpsed a cloud of fine gold thread, a few patches of white splashed with scarlet, some black pegs like carved toggles. Then, as Vastruglin scooped up the package and flung its contents on to the fire, he realized that what he had seen were human remains and the bile rose in his throat.

Choking black clouds of smoke rolled across the room, overwhelming both the stench of chemicals and the faint scent of roses that had briefly been discernible. When the fumes cleared Ynoul saw Vastruglin crouching by the hearth, one hand shielding his face. With the other, now wrapped in a damp and steaming rag, he picked up the tongs and reached into the flames. Lifting the crucible, he slowly tilted it and poured out the molten contents like a libation.

A dark shining flux trickled over the coals, crackling and spitting as it dripped down through the grate. Rather than subsiding, the fire blazed up even more intensely, yet now instead of glowing white the flames were duller and more smoky, like an oil-lamp seen through a soot-covered shade. The light in the room took on an eerie quality, like that of sunshine oozing through a dense black smog.

In his hiding place behind the wardrobe door Ynoul was beginning to grow dizzy. His back ached and his feet were numb from the strain of standing so still. Yet he did not dare reveal himself. So terrible was Vastruglin's expression that he feared what his master might do. Hoping fervently that the experiment was almost over, he shifted his position slightly, trusting that the noise of the fire would drown out any sound he might make.

Now Vastruglin had taken up his hammer and positioned himself before the anvil. There was nothing on it, yet he swung the hammer high and brought it crashing down. The room rang with the impact.

He gathered himself and struck again, and then again. With every blow his whole body shuddered.

The room began to resonate. Ynoul felt the wall behind him trembling and the floor shaking beneath his deadened feet. Glassware rattled and the side of the wardrobe next to him started to thrum.

Something touched him on the back of the head and he almost screamed aloud with fear. He twisted his neck as far as he could, but saw only the wall behind him. Again he felt the touch, like a breath or a fingertip, this time on his cheek. Dust or grit, dislodged by the vibrations, was drifting down on top of him.

No sooner had he realized this than a large section of plaster slid from the wall opposite and crashed to the floor, exposing the bare brick underneath. Immediately afterwards a glass retort, shaken to the edge of the workbench, toppled and smashed.

Yet still Vastruglin beat the anvil. Ynoul had his hands over his ears now but each clang seemed to pierce his skull. How long could he stand this for? The key was still in the door; if he fled now would Vastruglin, swinging his hammer like a machine, even notice his departure?

With a crack like a pistol shot the hearth split from side to side. Splinters of stone rattled against the ceiling. A jagged hole appeared in the floor and the flaming grate toppled forward into it. A cloud of writhing smoke spouted up to fill the alcove where seconds before the fire had blazed.

By now Ynoul had reached what felt to him like the limits of terror and fatigue. He would later think that perhaps, having endured as much as it was possible to bear, he had begun to hallucinate. Perhaps he swooned and was held upright in his faint by the rigid muscles of his cramped and stiffened legs. Perhaps everything he thought he saw was nothing but a feverish dream.

He would ask himself many times whether he could really have been sure about what seemed to happen next, but at the time he had been in no doubt. Despite the smoke and tears in his eyes, despite the fumes that filled the room and the disorientation he felt from the relentless ringing in his ears, he had been certain that what he saw was real. He would have been glad of any excuse to believe that his eyes deceived him.

As Vastruglin continued to smite his anvil and the smoke thickened and billowed about him, a figure emerged from the fissure in the hearth-stone. At first just its head and shoulders were visible, silhouetted against a curtain of illuminated smoke. Then its whole body emerged and crouched for a moment, immobile, before leaping upwards and outwards into the room.

It glowed like a red-hot poker, clouds of fire streaming behind it like the tail of a comet. It leapt and spun so fast that its face and limbs could not be clearly glimpsed. One moment it seemed like a naked woman, hips swaying invitingly; the next it could have been a capering demon, horned head tossing exultantly.

It sprang on to the table and danced across it, leaving a set of smouldering marks like hoofprints on the wood. It ran and stamped and kicked its legs, showering the room with shards of broken glassware. Crouching and twisting, its hands scooped up a sheaf of papers and sent them whirling through the air, flapping and flaming then falling to the ground like the charred skeletons of bats.

Ynoul could not have said for how long the creature danced to the rhythm of Vastruglin's hammer. He lost count of the number of times it hurled itself in cartwheels from one end of the room to the other like a living firework. He forgot the pain in his legs and back; he forgot his hunger and thirst and his fear of discovery. He even forgot to be frightened by what he beheld, and felt only astonishment that anything so foully conjured could appear so beautiful. Only occasionally, averting his gaze when it seemed as if he might catch a glimpse of the creature's face, did he sense the icy finger of terror running down his spine, and wonder what price he might have to pay for having witnessed a performance by this acrobat from hell.

It may have been hours or merely minutes after the creature first appeared that its dance began to slow. The room was darkening. The upward-streaming light from the crack in the hearth had begun to grow dim; the shining column of smoke was fading and dispersing.

The rate at which Vastruglin pounded the anvil was slowing, whether from intent or exhaustion Ynoul could not tell. His master was now a hunched shape barely visible against the dying glow from the fireplace.

As the rhythm of the hammering slowed so too did the speed of the creature's dance. Its steps became jerkier, its leaps and pirouettes less frenzied. It was also now harder to see: the orange radiance was fading from its skin, leaving its body a glistening black like smoky glass or heated tar.

When at last Vastruglin ceased hammering the creature froze. Then it leapt towards the fireplace, only to find

Vastruglin barring its path, hammer raised. It veered away and lost its balance, feet scraping on the bare stone floor. Ynoul could no longer see it behind the workbench, but could only hear it scrabbling at the flagstones. Glass crunched and skittered as it twisted and flailed in its efforts to right itself.

Gradually the noises lessened as the creature's writhings grew feebler. Its movements became more spasmodic and the crunch and scrape of broken glass died down to an intermittent gritty whisper. Eventually it was still. Vastruglin too was immobile, a slumped silhouette against the fading light from the hearth, and there was silence in the room.

Ynoul pushed the wardrobe door away and tried to step forward but his legs would not support him and he fell. He lay full length for several minutes while the feeling returned to his limbs, then hauled himself painfully upright. Leaning against the back of a chair, he groped through the debris on top of the workbench in search of something he could use to strike a light.

With the flickering stub of a candle in his hand, he made his way slowly round the table towards the fireplace. With every step it felt as if a dagger had been plunged into the back of each leg. Plaster dust and chips of glass crunched beneath his feet, but he did not dare look down at the floor.

Vastruglin did not move at his approach. The sculptor's eyes were open and glassy and the skin of his face was taut and grey.

Ynoul opened his mouth to speak but no sound came.

He swallowed, then tried to gather enough moisture in his parched mouth to wet his blistered lips. "Master. . .?" he croaked.

There was no reply.

He reached out with trembling fingers and touched Vastruglin's cheek. It was already cold and hard as stone. He snatched his hand away.

Stumbling backwards, the sour burning of nausea in his mouth and throat, he forgot to keep his gaze averted from the floor in front of the workbench. For a moment the light of his candle shone on the dulled and twisted limbs of the fallen creature. In the instant before he could close his eyes, he found himself looking straight into its face.

Nothing in his experience had prepared him for what he now saw. No human visage could compare with it, even *in extremis*, nor any etching from the most graphic of his master's grimoires. No corpse could have been more hideous or pitiable, no gargoyle more grotesque.

Ynoul staggered towards the door, teeth chattering and an incontinent keening rising in his throat. The candle slipped, forgotten, from his shaking, wax-spattered fingers, plunging him into darkness.

Even then, as he fled stumbling from the cellar, he already knew that what he had glimpsed would haunt his nightmares for the rest of his life.

Dawn was breaking as he pushed open the door at the top of the steps. He half ran, half tumbled out into the street, blinking and ducking in the dim grey light. Although stale and filled with smog, the early morning air tasted to him like the purest mountain breeze and he sucked it in with deep and grateful breaths.

His head swimming, he staggered for a few dozen yards before a wave of sickness overcame him. He slumped into an alcove, his empty stomach heaving. Bracing himself against the wall, he doubled over and hawked into the gutter. His spittle was black.

The street had been deserted, but after Ynoul had been leaning against the wall for a minute or two he heard a clamour approaching from round the corner. He drew instinctively back into the alcove as a hansom cab came trundling into view, followed by a small crowd of people.

The cab clattered to a halt and two policemen emerged. Between them they held a handcuffed man, still in his nightshirt, his hair disordered and his face ashen. It took Ynoul several seconds to recognize the captive as Sir Jeremy Elkie.

The policemen stepped down from the cab, half dragging, half carrying Sir Jeremy by the arms. They seemed to be about to make for the door from which Ynoul had recently emerged, but before they could reach it the crowd had surrounded them and prevented their further progress.

". . .through, will yer now? Duty . . . the law!" Ynoul heard one of the policemen say, his words mostly drowned by the shouts of the spectators.

"She was murdered!"

"Poor thing!"

"No, serves 'er right!"

"Cut up an' 'er teeth pulled out!"

"There's Elkie, 'e'll swing for it!"

"String 'im up!"

"Aye, serves 'im right!"

A stone arced from the crowd and smashed a window of the cab. The policemen raised their truncheons nervously.

"He's in there! He made me do it!" babbled Sir Jeremy, wild-eyed, pointing at the entrance to Vastruglin's lodgings.

The taller of the two policemen shouldered his way to the door. He hauled it open and a cloud of smoke belched out into the street, driving him back. Ynoul remembered the candle he had dropped.

"Let me go! He's in there, I tell you!" shouted Sir Jeremy. "Don't let him get away with it!" Pulling himself free from his escort, he too began barging through the crowd. Reaching the door, he plunged without hesitation into the smoke. Several gasps could be heard, and someone screamed.

No one was taking any notice of Ynoul. As the press of people around him grew larger and more vociferous, he emerged cautiously from his alcove and began to make his way towards the end of the street.

At the corner he paused to look back. Flames were now leaping from the open doorway, forcing the onlookers to withdraw. Sir Jeremy was nowhere to be seen.

Drawing his jacket closer about him, Ynoul turned away. As he walked he felt Vastruglin's documents against his chest and remembered his master's last words to him. *Rich beyond the fantasies of Bedlam*, Vastruglin had said, and Ynoul shuddered at the recollection. It was, he realized with hindsight, a horribly appropriate turn of phrase.

He knew that what he had seen in the cellar that night, sprawled beneath the workbench in the faint light of his candle, would assail his sanity for as long as he lived. He knew he would never rid his memory of the creature's face, shrivelled as if consumed by fire, gleaming as if wet, lips smeared back from the teeth in a rictus of pain, eyes like pebbles crushed into a slick of black ice. And on the floor beneath it, spreading out like a halo as its head dissolved, a dark and shining pool of viscous liquid, smoking like molten glass as it trickled away through the cracks between the flagstones.

IV

Confessional

Dushma awoke cold and uncomfortable early the following morning. Wax had gathered in glaucous patches on the floor around her. The candles she had lit had melted into long, pale stalactites that hung from the tall candlesticks around her like the bars of a cage.

Shivering, she broke through the hanging threads of wax and made her way to the nearest window. She pushed it open, letting in a thin slice of fresh air.

Although weak, the light was painful for her tired and puffy eyes. Hugging herself, she turned back to face the interior of the room.

The documents she had found the previous evening still lay spread across the floor. The night before, having finished reading them, she had briefly thought of feeding the pages one by one into the flame of a candle, as if once the words were devoured the images they had planted in her mind might also somehow fade away.

Now she admonished herself for her suggestibility. In

the early morning light there seemed nothing to be afraid of. The statues and carvings that lined the vestry were obviously inanimate, their chipped features and broken limbs more pitiful than frightening.

Suddenly industrious, she swooped down on the scattered pages, gathered them up and flung them back on to the high shelf where she had discovered them. The scribblings of an opportunistic journalist letting his imagination run away with him. She brushed dust and cobwebs from her hands. She would forget about it, go and wash, find something to eat, and then. . .

She stopped. And then what? She wasn't frightened, she told herself. That wasn't it at all. But something had changed. She knew that her clandestine existence could no longer go on.

And it really wasn't that she was frightened. She had never minded the dark. She was lonely, that's what it was. With someone to talk to, to share them with, her fears of the night before would have straightaway seemed groundless. This time it had been a story, next time it could be anything, throwing her into confusion, stopping her from thinking properly. . . She looked angrily at the latticework of wax hanging from the candlesticks. What she had done really hadn't been sensible at all. It could take hours to clean up. If anyone should happen to glance into this corner of the vestry they would be sure to notice something unusual.

Now that she had come to a decision she felt a rush of optimism. Full of energy, she strode back and forth between the candlesticks, arms folded and head bowed in thought. She would have to give herself up, confess where she'd been hiding, ask for permission to stay. But instead of being worried she felt relieved. She couldn't expect to live here unnoticed for ever, could she?

As she paced a plan began to take shape in her mind. It was so simple she was amazed it hadn't occurred to her before. Here was a way in which she could approach the cathedral authorities with minimal risk to herself. The more she thought about it the better it seemed. She need not reveal who she was, how she had got there, even what she looked like, until she could be sure that they would look on her situation sympathetically.

And, she asked herself rhetorically, *why shouldn't they?* She hadn't done any damage during her stay in the annexe. No one had even noticed her. Of course they would let her stay. She could be helpful, do useful things. Hadn't she already proved it? She thought of the hymn-books she'd mended, and the tidying she'd done. They'd be glad to have her here. She would be looked after properly, get paid even. She needn't mention her adventures underground: the fire, the explosion, her narrow escape.

On her way from the vestry, full of resolve, she caught sight of herself in a sliver of mirror propped up on one of the nearby shelves. Her face was thin and desperate-looking, streaked with grime from her dirty hands. Her eyes looked hunted beneath lids swollen from lack of sleep. With a shock she realized she appeared no different from the dozens of waifs who could be seen on pavements and in shop doorways in all the main streets of the city centre.

Her feelings of hopefulness vanished as suddenly as they had come, to be replaced by a fuzzy cloud of self-pity. She blinked back tears, her self-confidence crumbling. There must be hundreds of people more deserving than her. Why should she be treated any differently? But then what would happen to her? Would she have to stay in hiding for the rest of her life? It simply wasn't fair. She hadn't done anything wrong, not deliberately, anyway. She clenched her fists, sulkily defiant. She should just curl up behind the tapestries in one of the alcoves and stay there maybe for years, not coming out at all until they found her dead and it would serve them right.

She stumbled to the kitchen to wash her face. The water was cold and the sting of it on her skin helped to calm her down. This was why she had to do something. She was panicking at the slightest excuse, swinging from one mood to its opposite within the space of a few seconds. Before long she would be incapable of doing anything.

Back in the vestry she tidied herself up as best she could, examining her reflection in the broken mirror as she did so. She certainly looked better than when she had first taken refuge in the annexe. Her burns, cuts and bruises had nearly healed and her hair had grown back to a more normal length. She had no brush, but had to pull it into order with her fingers and the comb she had found, and then secure it with the few hair-grips she hadn't lost. When she had finished she decided that, in a dim light, she might seem almost respectable.

Before she could change her mind again she unlocked the door of the annexe and let herself out into the cathedral. She walked quickly across the flagstoned floor towards the line of pillars along the far wall of the nave.

A dark wooden booth stood in the shadows. It had two tall doors, each cut with a pattern of leaves and branches. Behind the fretwork hung curtains of some heavy-looking material, completely hiding the interior.

She looked for the blackboard she had seen propped nearby on previous mornings. There it was, with "7.30–10.15: Father O'Hara" written on it in large chalk letters.

The nearer of the two doors was ajar. She swung it further open and stepped inside.

There was no seat, but rather a padded kneeler facing the partition that divided the confessional. She settled herself and drew the door towards her until it shut with a click. She was now in complete darkness.

She reached forward cautiously. Her fingertips touched the grille that separated her from the priest. She swallowed. She had never done this before. She didn't know what to say. Something about "bless me", she thought.

The silence lengthened. "Bless me!" she blurted out at

88

last. And immediately afterwards, because it hadn't sounded very friendly, she added, "And how are you, father?"

"I'm very well thank you my child," replied the priest. "And how would you be doing yourself?"

She realized, as she began to talk, how long it had been since she had spoken to anyone. As she stumbled through her explanation, she began to worry that she wasn't making herself clear. Her story was coming out incoherently, with the events in no particular order other than that in which they happened to occur to her. She was muddling things up. Helplessly, she heard herself talking about the documents she had found in the vestry, the firefoals moving in the broken panes of stained glass, her midnight excursion to the gravestone of Selwyn Champion and the heat she had felt from beneath the cathedral.

This was no good. Had she mentioned the hymn-books? Or how helpful she could be in other ways? She couldn't remember. She paused to gather her thoughts before beginning again.

The instant she stopped talking the silence screeched into her head like an out-of-control car. She strained her ears for a sound from the priest. A murmur of encouragement, even just the hiss of his breath. There was nothing.

"Hello? Father?" There was no reply. Was he still there?

She heard a dry, scraping noise beside her. She turned her head and stared into the darkness, momentarily unable to think what it could be. Then she was lurching to her feet, elbows banging the sides of the booth in her panic, nails snagging the curtain as she scrabbled for the door. She found the handle and threw her weight on top of it but it was too late. The door had been locked from the outside.

Part of her was amazed at the fury she felt rising up within her. At that moment she could have hurt someone, wilfully and with pleasure, so outraged and betrayed did she feel. Instead she drew herself back and lashed out at the door with her foot.

Her toe struck the wood with all the force she could muster. The whole confessional shuddered but the door stayed firm. She beat at it with her fists, skinning her knuckles, but still it didn't give.

It was stronger than it had looked. She couldn't break it down. She was trapped.

V

The Chimney of the Soul

They had taken her laces. She had to shuffle along with her toes curled up to stop her shoes falling off. It was so she couldn't run away, she presumed.

A uniformed woman was gripping her tightly by the upper arm, almost lifting her off her feet as she dragged her down a long concrete corridor. They were being careful, after what had happened to the priest.

She still didn't regret what she'd done to him. She had no idea whether it was going to make any difference to what was in store for her, but at least she hadn't gone quietly.

"It's for your own good," the priest had said. He had smiled at her as if he'd just given her a treat and was waiting to be thanked.

She had struck out at him, and with immense satisfaction had felt her jagged thumbnail sink into the springy flesh of his cheek.

"Well at least that's *one* of us," she spat, eyes hot and wet with angry tears. "Because it hasn't done *you* any good, has it?"

There had been blood on his face as he had spun away from her, hands rising to cover the wound. In the moment before he turned aside she saw his complacency displaced by panic. She had made him afraid of her. She had felt a wild surge of triumph even as she had been dragged captive from the cathedral.

It hadn't lasted. At some point she had banged her head, she wasn't sure how. It might have been an accident. The next thing she remembered was a feeling of relief. She was being taken somewhere and she didn't have to do anything. She didn't have to hide any more, or try and make decisions. Everything was out of her hands now.

She was pushed into a room at the end of the corridor and left there without comment. There were no windows, just a thick glass partition through which could be seen another small, bare-walled room. Fixed to the roof was a camera in a wire cage.

After a while her sense of fatalism wore off and she began to be frightened. Eventually she became convinced that something awful was going to be done to her at any moment. When at last the door opened she cringed away in terror, but it was only someone bringing her a cup of tea and a plate of sandwiches.

Slowly her fear turned to boredom. Time passed. She sat slumped in a hard chair in one corner, apparently forgotten about.

She supposed she was in prison. She listened to the noises in the distance. The rattle of keys, the bang of a door. This was the clink. The slammer.

Her mind wandered. What time was it? She had no idea. There was nothing to do here, nothing except time. It was like the punchline of a bad Christmas-cracker joke. The nick. The nick of time.

At last she fell asleep, waking some time later slumped against the wall, her neck stiff, her mouth dry and her eyes sore and gummy.

A little later a woman appeared and spoke to her from the other side of the glass partition. Her voice came flat and crackly from a metal-grilled speaker. She talked about a state-sponsored residential care and skills programme. "It'll prepare you to take a productive and fulfilling role in society, Dushma. Won't that be *exciting*?" She didn't sound like she believed it.

Staring contemptuously at the wall behind the woman's head, Dushma didn't bother to reply. She now regretted telling the priest even as much as her name. She resolved to say nothing else.

The woman shrugged and slid a piece of paper and a pen through a gap at the bottom of the glass partition. "All right, so you don't have to like it. Just put a cross on the dotted line to show you've understood."

A cross? Dushma stared at the pen uncomprehendingly. Then she realized that the woman must think she couldn't write. She opened her mouth to say something, but

93

thought better of it. Instead she picked up the pen in her fist and drew the point in a clumsy zigzag back and forth across the page from the top to the bottom. She pressed so hard that the paper tore.

After that she was dragged back along the concrete corridor, arms pinioned and feet shuffling, to another room where a man in a white coat was waiting for her.

At first she was sure that this was where her punishment would happen, for whatever it was she was supposed to have done. For everything she had ever done. She squirmed and tried to fight. When someone held her she twisted her head away and screwed up her eyes.

Only the needle hurt, and that hardly at all, just a cold point of pressure on her forearm. By the time she realized what it was it had already been withdrawn and the doctor was dabbing at her skin with a wad of cotton wool. The hypodermic in his other hand sloshed with blood. A sample, for some kind of test. She was glad she hadn't been warned in advance. She would have been certain it was going to be agony. She had often had to listen to Auntie Megan, usually the worse for drink, expressing her mortal fear of needles.

Then the doctor was listening to her chest, peering into her ears and, when she had calmed down and begun to cooperate a little more, shining a light into her eyes. Dushma began to feel curiosity threatening to overcome her sullenness. She wanted to ask the doctor what all these things were for. There was a rubber tube he wrapped round her bicep and inflated, a hammer he tapped her knee with, and a large machine that hummed and clicked. After each test he wrote something down on a piece of card.

Now that she no longer seemed in immediate danger of being harmed, a new fear crept into her mind. What if the test results showed something peculiar? A scan, someone had said, when they held her with her head next to the machine. Just the memory of the word brought on a feeling of unease. It had been a scan that had lost her the right to be registered: a photograph of herself in her mother's womb, the film illuminated with vivid patches of colour inexplicable enough for the hospital to declare that such a baby was unfit to be granted the help of the state. If Dushma was to be born at all, her every need would have to be met at her mother's expense.

Was she to be betrayed again by a picture of herself? She stole a glance at the doctor's face. He was still writing, paying her no attention. She noticed a faint stubble on his chin and hollows under his eyes. There was nothing in his expression except tiredness and boredom. Surely he would look more animated if he had noticed anything unusual about her? She allowed herself a glimmer of hope. Her situation wasn't as bad as it could have been.

The tests concluded, Dushma was taken to a small, cube-shaped room lined with unplastered breeze blocks. A single bright light in a metal cage hung from the centre of the ceiling and the floor sloped towards a drain in one corner. In another corner crouched a girl with her back to the door, scratching at the wall with a piece of stone.

The door slammed and the girl turned round and glared at Dushma. "Piss off," she said. She was broad-shouldered and bony, with dyed blonde ringlets straggling down on either side of her face and black mascara daubed thickly round her small and glittering eyes.

"Piss off, I said!" she repeated.

"It's not my fault," Dushma defended herself. "They decided where to put me." She edged away, arms raised protectively across her chest.

The girl looked at her for several more seconds, then seemed to lose interest. She shrugged and turned back to her scratching.

The wall nearest her was covered with a repeated pattern of marks consisting of four upright strokes with a diagonal line across them. "How long have *you* been here?" asked Dushma, horrified.

"God, I don't know," muttered the girl. "Hours." She scratched several more lines angrily into the wall.

For the next few minutes there was no sound in the cell but the loud rasp of the girl's stone against the breeze blocks. At last, desperate for some sort of conversation, Dushma asked, "So . . . what did you do, then?"

Before she had even finished speaking, the girl began to hum tunelessly, as if trying to drown out the question. Dushma opened her mouth to repeat herself more loudly but then changed her mind. Biting her lip, she looked angrily round for something she could use to write on the wall with as well.

"Nicked a car, didn't I?" said the girl abruptly. "Everybody else got away. But I got my dress caught in the passenger door and they just left me. Bastards!" She threw down her stone in a sudden fit of anger. It bounced off the floor and jumped, spinning, high into the air.

"What are they going to do to us?"

"I don't know. Me, I'll probably have to watch some stupid film. Last time they took me to this place for smashed-up cars. You could still see the blood on the seats in some of them. You were supposed to get really freaked but I was just like 'yeah, yeah, yeah'. They had this machine that squashed them up into blocks of metal *this* big. Wouldn't mind a go on that!"

"Is that all? I mean, that doesn't sound too bad. . ."

"Oh yeah, only my second time, ain't it? Come on, what about you? What've you done? Hope it's something really juicy. That'd take their minds off me."

"I haven't done anything! At least, nothing I could help doing, anyway. I'm not registered you see, and. . ."

She broke off. The girl had started to laugh.

"Oh, ain't it my lucky day?" she cackled maliciously. "They wouldn't have time for me if I was Bonnie and Clyde!"

"What do you mean?" This was what Dushma had been trying not to think about. "What are they going to do to me?"

"How should I know? Anything they bloody well like!"

"But . . . they can't, can they?" Dushma's voice came out high and unsteady. She struggled to stop her face from crumpling. "I must still have some rights, mustn't I?"

"Ahh, don't worry," mocked the girl. "*Course* you have. None of the important ones, but yeah, you've still got a few."

"Have I? Are you sure? What are they?"

"Oh, I don't know." The girl's attention was beginning to wander again. "That thing, you know, that Swiss one . . . the Jennifer Convention."

"The what? What's that?"

"*I* don't know! Some woman that got tortured. But now they're not allowed to do anything that's cruel and unusual. They can be cruel, *or* they can be unusual, but not both at once."

Dushma struggled to take all this in. She sensed a trick. "So which are they, then?" she asked. "Cruel or unusual? And which is worse?"

The girl was chewing on one of her crimson fingernails and looking Dushma up and down intently. "You're a bit weird, aren't you?" she said, stepping closer. Her small eyes were wide and very mobile, flickering restlessly this way and that and never alighting on Dushma's face for more than a second at a time.

"Did they search you?" she demanded. "Have you got any, you know, stuff?"

"No. . . What do you. . .? Get *off*!"

The girl reached out towards Dushma and began to pluck at her clothing. Dushma shrank back, not sure if she dared try and push her away.

The girl's hand reached Dushma's skirt and with a quick movement pulled the pocket inside out. There was nothing in it but a crumpled paper handkerchief, which fell to the floor.

The girl scraped at the lining of the pocket with her fingernails, then peered intently down at her hand.

Seeing her chance, Dushma slid along the wall and out of her reach.

"What was all that. . .?" she began angrily.

"Can you write?" interrupted the girl, brushing fluff disappointedly from her fingers.

"Of course!" snapped Dushma, nettled. She looked at the patterns the girl had been making in the corner of the cell, and added sarcastically, "Why? Want me to scratch your name for you?"

"No. It's just, I thought unregistered people were a bit . . . you know?" The girl pushed her tongue into her cheek and rolled her eyes to indicate simple-mindedness.

"Oh really? Maybe it's just the ones you hang out with!"

The girl licked her lips and made a chewing motion with her jaw. "I was going to give you some advice," she said matter-of-factly. "No idea why, but I was going to. I was going to say: if they give you any bits of paper, don't sign them whatever you do. But now I won't have to bother, 'cos instead I'm going to break your fingers."

She reached out, hands clenching the air. Dushma backed away.

The cell door clanged open. On the threshold stood a thickset woman in uniform, carrying a clipboard. "Duss. . ." she began, reading from the clipboard. "Duss. . . Dush. . ."

"That's her! She's the one!" shouted Dushma's cell mate, leaping into the centre of the room and pointing accusingly. "Get her out of here! She attacked me, she's weird. Kept asking me for, you know, stuff."

"I did not!"

"She did! She's weird. What are you going to do to her?" The girl's tongue flickered eagerly over her wet lips. "Can I see? Are you going to bring her back afterwards?"

"Shut your mouth, you tart," said the woman in uniform. She grabbed hold of Dushma's arm and pulled her out of the cell. "If it was up to me you'd soon find out 'cos we'd do it to you an' all."

Glancing back over her shoulder, Dushma saw the girl gesturing obscenely through the barred opening in the door. As she was marched away down the corridor she could hear her thumping the wall and chanting, "*No* more weirdos in with *me!*"

Dushma was taken back to the doctor's room. This time there was somebody with him.

"It's very kind of you to come at such short notice," the doctor was saying. He sounded grateful, deferential even.

As soon as Dushma appeared in the doorway he began casting quick glances in her direction.

"Not at all." The new arrival was a middle-aged man, perhaps about fifty, immaculately dressed in a suit with a waistcoat. He held a rectangle of celluloid in his hands and was studying it intently. "You were absolutely right to call me. It certainly is most unusual."

"I remembered from your lectures it was an interest of yours," said the doctor.

"Indeed," said the man in the suit. "Well, I'm glad somebody was listening." He switched his thin smile quickly on and off, then turned towards Dushma. First he peered at her through his spectacles, then he tilted his head forward to look at her over the tops of the semicircular lenses.

"Good evening," he said politely.

She was taken aback. It was surprising how quickly she had got out of the habit of being treated civilly. It was difficult to keep herself from replying.

"Come in, sit down." He was indicating the chair where she had sat to have her knee tapped. She shuffled cautiously forward. "Would you mind if we had a few words together alone?"

"Ah, wait a minute," interrupted the doctor. "I don't know if that would be safe. You see. . ."

"Don't worry, she'll be perfectly all right. My bedside manner is impeccable."

"No no, I didn't mean that, of course. . ." The doctor

gave a nervous laugh. "It's just that she. . ." He lowered his voice. Dushma assumed he was relating what had happened to the priest. She felt a guilty twinge of pride.

"Really?" The man in the suit was staring at Dushma again, his eyebrows raised. "You did search her, didn't you? I presume she doesn't have any axes, carving knives or lengths of lead piping about her person? Hmm? It is just her bare hands I have to worry about, isn't it?"

"I don't know. I think so. I mean, I didn't personally. . ."

"Well, I think I'll risk it anyway. I'm sure I'll be all right. Although of course, if you should by any chance hear an explosion, or the sound of gunfire . . . do hurry back, won't you?" He said it very seriously, but as he spoke Dushma saw his gaze flicker momentarily in her direction and his right eyelid tremble in what might have been a wink.

Her lips twitched in spite of herself. She set her face and stared away from him but he had seen it, she was sure.

When the door had closed he sat down opposite her. He was close enough for her to see the individual threads in the finely woven material of his suit jacket. She heard the crisp white cotton of his shirt scrunch like trodden snow as he leaned towards her.

He raised his hand, took her jaw gently between finger and thumb and moved her head slowly from side to side. From his pocket he brought out a small torch no bigger than a pen, switched it on and shone it into her eyes.

Then, still not speaking, he let go of her jaw and tapped

her chin to indicate that she should open her mouth. She did so and he shone the torch inside.

"A piece of advice," he murmured, more to himself than to her. "People tell you very little with their eyes. But the mouth is a different matter. Remember that, when you meet someone. Look at their teeth, watch their tongue, see how their lips move. The mouth is the chimney of the soul."

He snapped off the torch and sat back. "You have no next of kin? As far as you're aware?"

She shook her head.

He held her gaze for some moments, face impassive. Rather than look away she simply let her eyes relax, dissolving him into a pair of blurred, overlapping images. If she had to rejoin the girl in the cell she was going to pretend something awful had happened to her. She would assume this vacant stare, the same expression she had seen in a war film, worn by a soldier who had witnessed unspeakable horrors.

". . .and of course we'll have to get you a new pair of shoes." The man in the suit had been speaking to her. She blinked and looked down at her feet. Her shoes were indeed in a terrible state, soles coming loose at the welts, frayed tongues lolling from the scuffed and laceless uppers.

"But I can't do anything without your cooperation. There'll be formalities. Certain documents you'll need to sign. . . You don't have to. It's entirely up to you. But I believe I can help you more than these people can. What do you say?"

Dushma felt weightless, detached. She should ask him to repeat what he had just said, ask him what he meant, ask for time to think.

She noticed how shabby the room was. The paintwork was chipped and peeling, the furniture old and battered. She looked at the gleaming shoes of the man in the suit, the sharp crease of his trousers, the plump knot of his tie.

She nodded.

"Good." He was on his feet at once, taking a phone from inside his jacket. He turned away from her, walking to the far side of the room as he dialled a number.

"Hello? . . . Can I speak to Mr Ashpool? . . . Yes, I know. Just tell him Marlstroy, will you? . . . What? . . . Oh, he really *is* busy then. Well, listen, I'm afraid it's rather urgent. So, if you could just ask him if he remembers Nicola, Nicola Auquin. . . Yes, that's right."

He waited for a few seconds, his back to Dushma, foot tapping impatiently. When next he spoke it was much more quietly. "Hello old chap. . . Yes, I know, I'm sorry. . . They're from where? Peru? And they've got coal to sell you? Well, obviously, that would be good, if it comes off, and. . . Yes, of course I understand how important it is. Help a lot, I'm sure, so of course I don't want to keep you."

He lowered his voice yet further and moved behind a green fabric screen on wheels that stood in one corner. Dushma heard him talking rapidly but couldn't make out the words.

When he emerged, hardly thirty seconds later, his lips wore a tight smile of private satisfaction. "And a full set of registration documents?" he was saying. "Yes, the sooner the better, really. . . Bike them? Perfect. . . And rest assured, I'll keep you fully informed. Oh, one other thing. . . There's a charge. . . No, a criminal one. Actual bodily harm. . . If you could do something. . . What? . . . No, not me! She. . . All right, later then, and. . . Yes, I'm sure. . . Yes, don't worry, I know what I'm doing."

He switched off the phone and tucked it back inside his jacket. "Friends in high places," he murmured. "We should be able to have you out of here tonight, with luck. But in the meantime –" his face twisted into a sardonic grin – "I think we'd better call your minders back in. Just in case they're starting to get worried about me."

For the first time, Dushma let herself smile cautiously back at him.

PART
II

I

Needle

Dushma never found out how Auntie Megan discovered where she was.

One evening after she had gone up to bed she heard the front door banging and the sound of raised voices in the hallway. She left her room and leaned out over the banisters on the landing, trying to see what was happening.

Footsteps clattered on the tiled floor. Mrs Breckle, Marlstroy's housekeeper, shouted something Dushma couldn't make out. A draught of cold air blew up the stairs.

Her nightdress billowing around her knees, Dushma crept silently down into the hall. Now the commotion was clearly coming from the direction of Marlstroy's study, towards the back of the house. He must have been working late, as was his habit. She hurried along the corridor, the tiles chilly beneath her bare feet.

". . .No need for that, Mrs Breckle," she heard

Marlstroy say. "I'm sure I can manage." Then, to someone else, "Now what did you say your name was?"

As she approached the study she saw the housekeeper backing hurriedly out. Not noticing Dushma, Mrs Breckle scuttled away down the corridor in the direction of the kitchen, leaving the study door half open.

Another voice came from inside the room. Although Dushma didn't catch what it said, the hoarse and wheedling tones were all too familiar.

She almost turned and fled immediately. Auntie Megan's voice brought back vivid and hurtful memories of their many and bitter confrontations. While Dushma no longer feared what her aunt might be able to do to her, she doubted that any new encounter would turn out pleasantly. But after hesitating for a heartbeat or so, she pushed her misgivings aside and continued on down the corridor. It was not until later that she was able to admit to herself that her decision came at least in part from an ignoble wish to see her aunt humiliated.

Auntie Megan stood in front of Marlstroy's desk, her head bobbing and trembling on her narrow shoulders. She wore a short skirt and fishnet tights and carried a tiny PVC handbag. A runnel of sweat gleamed behind one ear.

When Dushma appeared in the doorway she turned and for an instant a spasm of some strong emotion worked its way across her face. Then she fixed a gruesome smile to her lips and flung out her arms in pathetic supplication.

"Oh my darling!" she squawked. "You've no idea how worried I've been! I've been out of my mind! . . .I mean, with worry, you know?"

When Dushma didn't react Auntie Megan turned back to Marlstroy.

"See!" she exclaimed. "She's overcome! She can't say a word."

Dushma had often imagined a moment like this. She had rehearsed in her head the things she might say, the blame she would heap on Auntie Megan for her selfishness and neglect, the sarcastic revenge she could now take for years of being made to feel unwanted and useless. "You always complained what a burden I was to you," she could say. "Well now I'm not and I hope you're happy."

But now that she had the opportunity she found she had no wish to say such things. Despite the memories of all that she had endured from her one-time guardian, the sight of Auntie Megan's sunken face and flinching gaze didn't stir the feelings of resentment she would have expected.

She thought of the solitary days she had spent in the cathedral annexe and wondered what loneliness had driven the obviously terrified Auntie Megan to confront someone such as Marlstroy in his own home. She realized that rather than reviling her aunt, she wanted to tell her the details of her new life. She wanted to talk to her about Marlstroy's library, his garden and all the people she had met. Her encounter with the morbid and drunken Alex would delight her aunt, she felt sure. And it occurred to her that

111

she could ask about the problems she was having at school; the cunning and worldly Auntie Megan might be able to offer some useful advice.

But at the same time as she was thinking this, she knew, she was waiting with a mixture of anticipation and dread for Marlstroy to strike.

"It's been *rarely* kind of you to look after her," Auntie Megan was saying. She was trying her best to sound genteel but so great was her agitation that the effort was sometimes apparent. "We 'ad . . . *had* some difficulties . . . all sorted out now, let me assure you. We'll be on our way just as soon as she gets her things." She ducked her head and smirked ingratiatingly.

"It's most thoughtful of you to come and enquire . . . Ms Crate, I think you said your name was? But as you can see –" Marlstroy gestured towards Dushma – "your former charge has no need of your further assistance."

"How like her not to have complained. Such a stoical child, and so polite. That's how I brung her up, bless her heart. You've been so kind, but we simply couldn't impose on you a moment longer. She can be a handful, I know. And since she isn't *registered*. . ." She was unable to keep a hint of venom out of her voice. She obviously hoped that this would be news to Marlstroy.

"Oh but she is *now*."

"But . . . what do you mean? I mean, how. . .?"

"I don't think you need to worry too much about the details, Ms Crate. I'm sure she'll be most touched by your concern, but we really wouldn't want you to put yourself out more than you have already. So. . ." He began to rise dismissively to his feet.

"But . . . wait a minute, you can't just. . . I've got rights too!" Auntie Megan licked her lips and glanced this way and that, rubbing her hands distractedly together. Then her gaze settled on Dushma and a look of feral cunning stole across her face. "What did she tell you, eh? No next of kin, I suppose? Well I never told her, see . . . so as to, to protect her it was, that's right, to protect her! She don't know, she thinks I was just a family friend, but I'm her mother really, see? Her only living relative! And it's kidnapping, that's what it is, depriving me of my only daughter, the only solace of my declining years, what I've nurtured and cared for as if she was me own . . . which of course she was in fact . . . with no thought to myself, though for all the gratitude I got you'd think she'd of rather been in the workhouse. But I'm sure now she knows the truth she'll see where her responsibilities lie and take this opportunity to repay the loving kindness what I lavished on her through all the years of sacrifice and making do, and I gave you some good times, didn't I, in spite of everything, don't you remember, back in the viaduct?"

Thick with emotion, Auntie Megan's voice trailed away into silence. Her eyes were moist and her bird-like chest heaved.

Marlstroy lifted his chin and looked her up and down through narrowed eyes, his face impassive as he took in her scanty attire and heavy makeup. "You're quite right," he said, his voice silky. "That does indeed put a completely different complexion on things. You will of course need proof of your claim, but fortunately we're in a position to establish that immediately."

He opened a drawer of his desk and drew out a glittering object of metal and glass. It was the size of a rolling pin, and because of this it took Dushma several seconds to recognize it as a hypodermic needle.

"The DNA test is relatively simple." Marlstroy smiled at his pun. "That is to say, it should be simple to determine whether or not the two of you are relatives."

"Just . . . just a second. . ." Auntie Megan's eyes bulged as she stared at the needle gleaming in Marlstroy's grasp.

"It's very sharp," Marlstroy reassured her. "You'll hardly feel a thing." He picked up an apple from the fruit bowl on his desk, tossed it into the air and impaled it on the upraised hypodermic as it fell. The point of the needle slid all the way through. Apple juice dripped on to the carpet.

Stepping out from behind his desk, Marlstroy walked towards Auntie Megan, the hypodermic held out in front of him. She backed away, staggering a little in her high heels.

"Now, just hang on a minute. . ." Auntie Megan flashed Dushma a sickly smile. Her breath came in quick rasps. "Wait, I said! Can't you use nail-clippings these days. . .?"

"I find the neck is the best place for a quick result," said Marlstroy. "Tip your head to one side please, Ms Crate."

Auntie Megan's shoulders bumped the mantelpiece and she began to edge sideways towards the door.

Advancing like a fencer, Marlstroy moved to cut her off. "Tell you what," he offered, "I'll throw in some other tests as well. Just to make sure everything's nice and clean. How about that? Hepatitis, HIV. . . Banned substances, too. Clean living carries a lot of weight in custody suits you know. . . But you seem reluctant. Come come! This kind of thing would cost you a fortune on Harley Street."

"Get away from me! I don't know what you're talking about!" Auntie Megan was flicking her eyes back and forth from the point of Marlstroy's hypodermic to the threshold of the study a few metres from where she stood. "I've got nothing to hide. . . Thicker than water, isn't it? What else d'you need to know? And what about my moral rights? Where were you with your money when she was tiny?"

Marlstroy didn't reply and the two of them glared at each other in silence for several seconds. Auntie Megan was the first to look away.

"God! You're all the same! Why does it always boil down to bodily fluids? Think you know her like I do, do you? Well you don't! So listen to me while I tell you something." She pointed a spindly finger like a witch delivering a curse. "She'll make you regret this, I promise you! You think you've won but it'll do you no good at all. Just you remember that. Just you remember!"

Marlstroy cocked his head and raised one eyebrow in a parody of polite interest. But instead of elaborating, Auntie

Megan lurched away from the mantelpiece, wriggled round the point of the needle and darted towards the door.

Dushma drew back. Breathing raggedly, Auntie Megan slipped past her and out into the corridor. Then she stopped, turned round and for a moment they were looking right into each other's eyes. Dushma could clearly see her aunt's dilated pupils and the broken capillaries in her nose and cheeks.

Auntie Megan's lips worked as if trying to spit out the words that were clogging her mouth. But no sound came. Instead her face squeezed up as if she was stifling a sneeze. Then she turned and stumbled away.

Marlstroy and Dushma stood listening to the sound of high heels retreating over the tiles in the hallway. The front door slammed and there was silence.

An expression of satisfaction on his face, Marlstroy tugged the apple off the hypodermic and threw it into the waste-paper basket. "Better not eat that," he said. "No idea what I last used this thing for."

Dushma looked at the long, gleaming needle. "You weren't. . ." She had to swallow. "You weren't really going to. . .?"

Marlstroy looked at her intently. "If she'd called my bluff? Of course. I doubt it would have done her much harm. But what if it had? She's obviously nothing but a scheming lowlife. A liar, a harlot and a craven sponger. The world would be a better place without her."

"But she did look after me," ventured Dushma.

Marlstroy frowned. "Give yourself some credit. Don't imagine it's just some random act of fate that we're here while she slinks back to whatever benighted hideaway she calls home. Survival of the fittest. Social Darwinism. You looked after yourself."

Dushma had to admit it was easier to think of it like that. It helped to suppress the twinge of guilt she was feeling. Should she have said something to Auntie Megan? But what? She had no idea. Her so-called aunt had been lying, she knew. They weren't related at all, a fact that Auntie Megan had sometimes been cruel enough to express gratitude for, during their more heated arguments. She tried to push the whole encounter out of her mind. She wished she had never ventured downstairs.

Marlstroy returned to his desk and opened the drawer to replace the hypodermic. "The details of your past life are your own affair. As far as I'm concerned when you came to me you started with a clean slate. You're able to help me with my research and in return there are things I can do for you. I don't want to know any more than absolutely necessary about who you were or what you did before we met. And I certainly don't need to know any more about that woman than I've already gathered. I don't think she'll come back but if she does. . ." He slammed the drawer shut. "I won't let her waste my time like that again."

II

Astronomy

During her first few days at Marlstroy's house, Dushma had felt like a visitor who might be asked to leave at any moment. Still in the habit of secrecy, she made herself as unobtrusive as possible, creeping from room to room as quietly as she could. Even when she knew she was alone she kept to the shadows and closed doors silently behind her. Anything she touched she tried to leave exactly as she found it.

Sometimes there were notes from Marlstroy in the hall, telling her of arrangements he had made for her, but apart from these she had little contact with him. If they met on the stairs or passed each other in the corridor he treated her as if they were casual acquaintances, nodding politely and enquiring after her health, or making some remark about the weather. She wanted to talk to him, find out more about him, ask him who he was and what he did, but she never seemed to catch him at an appropriate moment. He always looked too busy or distracted, his heavy brows squeezed together in a frown that did not suggest he would welcome questions. And even if she had dared she wouldn't have known where to start.

It was several weeks before he asked her, as an afterthought, whether she had seen his library. She had, of course, and had already spent a great deal of time there. She said as much, adding that it was often difficult to know where to find things in such a large collection.

He had been on his way across the hall to his study, a briefcase in his hand. But now he hesitated. He looked at his watch, then put his briefcase down and turned towards the stairs, beckoning her to follow.

In the library he paced the length of the shelves, pointing out things he thought might interest her. Here was art, there was reference (two shelves full of dictionaries alone), and here was a catalogue of sorts, begun a long time ago and never anywhere near finished. There was supposed to be some kind of order, he said, but he was no longer sure himself what was where. He didn't have as much time for reading as he would have liked.

Pausing by a shelf of smaller, worn-looking books, he gave an exclamation of recognition and pulled out several slim volumes. "Well I never. Look at these." He blew dust from the covers. "Here. Must've read them when I was about your age."

They were adventure stories, science fiction mostly. And, sure enough, there inside each flyleaf was Marlstroy's name. They wouldn't have been Dushma's first choice, but even so she resolved there and then that she would read them. In effect they were, she felt, the first pieces of personal information he had imparted to her.

When she looked up again Marlstroy had moved on. He was still taking books down from the shelves, but now instead of handing them to her he was leafing through them himself, searching for a favourite passage or smiling at some inscription on the title page.

Apart from the library, Dushma's favourite place in Marlstroy's house was on the roof.

A dormer window led from the crammed and dusty attic out on to a flat terrace floored with mossy bricks. Directly in front of the window was a set of wrought-iron railings and a three-storey drop down to the flagstoned patio. On the other three sides of the terrace rose steeply tilted slopes of grey slate, crowned with twin rows of fat terracotta chimney-pots that glowed a hot orange when the evening sunlight caught them.

Beyond the sharply angled branches of the firetrees and the wall at the bottom of the garden stretched the dense crowd of steeples and towers that made up the city centre. Many of London's famous landmarks were visible, including, of course, the striding arches of the railway viaduct and the proud spire of St Gotha's Cathedral. The view wasn't as good as from her bedroom in the viaduct, but nevertheless, when the haze of traffic fumes wasn't too thick, Dushma could see all the way to the cranes, gasometers and winking tower blocks of Docklands.

She liked to sit on the terrace on these early autumn evenings with her back to the sun-warmed tiles. She would read a book, attempt her homework, or just look at the buildings and try to work out which must be which among the many churches she could see.

Rummaging through the junk in the attic, Dushma discovered several things that may once have been intended for use on the terrace. There were a pair of old canvas deckchairs and a folding card table, but these proved too rickety to be much good. There was an easel, too, which she extricated with some effort before realizing that there were no paints or brushes to go with it.

Much more promising than these was the tarnished brass tube she found standing upright in one corner of the attic with a parasol in it. It was almost big enough for her to have climbed into, and at first she thought it was a shell case from a battleship. Only when she looked more closely and noticed the adjustable stand attached to it did she realize it must be an old reflecting telescope.

She set it up on its tripod on the roof terrace and tried looking through it. But she could see nothing except, at certain angles, her own vastly magnified eye peering back at her out of the darkness inside the tube.

Instead she cleaned it until the sunlight showered in golden needles off its polished curves. She was sure that if only her ears, like a dog's, had been sensitive enough she would have been able to hear it ringing like a cymbal.

121

It wasn't until Marlstroy helped her that she was able to make the telescope work properly. It was Marlstroy who pointed out that the eyepiece was missing, and then found it for her in a leather case among the piles of junk, along with some books about stars.

He was becoming less reluctant to abandon his study in the evenings. He could only stay a few minutes, he said, arriving in the attic still in suit, waistcoat and tie. But soon he had taken off his jacket and folded back his cuffs, his intention to return to work apparently forgotten. The current situation meant that there was less light pollution in the night sky over London than there had been for decades. Since the energy crisis surely couldn't last much longer, he reasoned, they should make the most of this opportunity. He would arrange for a thermos of tea and some cake.

Dushma still found that sometimes he seemed difficult to approach. He could often be distant, even severe. But in his shirtsleeves, helping her align and focus the telescope, he became almost boyish in his enthusiasm. She could tell he enjoyed the challenge of discovering how it worked.

They took turns, one looking through the telescope while the other moved the wheels of the mechanism that changed the field of view. There were no instructions, but between them they soon worked out how to make the right adjustments in order to see what they wanted.

When they had the central London skyline in focus Dushma remained for longer at the eyepiece. It was the cathedral she really wanted to see, rather than stars or planets.

"My God, these must be pretty old," murmured Marlstroy, looking through the books he had discovered. He picked one up and began to turn its yellowing pages. It was called *The Bumper Eagle Book of Astronomical Phenomena*, and on the cover was a picture of a man with a pipe watching two rosy-cheeked schoolboys leaning over a telescope. In the background the sky was filled with constellations, planets and comets.

It had surprised Dushma to discover that the view through the telescope was inverted. The city's steeples and towers pointed downwards, shimmering in the updraughts of warmth from the streets. They looked like reflections on the surface of a lake.

"No, I don't think it's broken," said Marlstroy when she mentioned this to him. "It's a reflecting telescope, isn't it? There's a mirror in it."

"But I'm not upside-down when I look at myself in a mirror."

"True, no. Here. . ." He took a pen and a piece of paper from his pocket. "I think it works like this." Resting the paper on the *The Bumper Eagle Book of Astronomical Phenomena*, he began to draw her a diagram.

Although upside-down and a little unsteady, St Gotha's Cathedral looked remarkably detailed when seen through the telescope. Dushma was able to make out much more than she had ever been able to from ground level. She

123

could see the individual tiles of the spire and the patches of green and orange lichen that grew here and there on the stone. There were clusters of statues and gargoyles that she was sure weren't even visible from the street, yet through the telescope she could discern the expressions on their faces.

She ate sandwiches and cake, remembering another rooftop picnic she had enjoyed not that many months before, behind the low parapet at the base of the cathedral's central spire. She could see the very place quite clearly through the telescope. She knew it was hopeless to expect to see anything there now, but nevertheless she stared until her eye watered, vainly watching for some sign of movement.

When dusk had fallen they angled the telescope more steeply to try and see the stars. More by luck than knowledge they found what they decided must be Jupiter, a silver disc with two rusty stripes across one side.

"What are those lines?" Dushma wanted to know.

"Smoke, I think." Marlstroy thumbed through one of his books. "'Giant clouds of coloured gas hurled up into the atmosphere by volcanic eruptions then spun out into distinctive bands by the rotation of the planet.' Like jam in rice pudding I suppose. You drop in a dollop of jam then swirl it around with your spoon and it makes a coloured ring. And the interesting thing is of course that you can't unstir it again, just by moving your spoon the other way."

It was getting colder on the terrace. They drank their tea

and then, unable to locate any more planets, tried to train the telescope on one of the aeroplanes coming in over the city. But here they had little success. Flights were far less frequent than they had been, and those aircraft they did see slid much too quickly across the field of view, staying in focus for no more than a few seconds.

"Not that long ago we wouldn't've been able to see anything at all," Marlstroy pointed out. "Even when there wasn't any cloud there was this orange haze everywhere from the streetlights."

A few months previously the government had begun rationing domestic electricity. Not long afterwards, local councils started having to cut their streetlighting budgets. No one expected the crisis to last very long. Anyway, said older people, it wasn't nearly as bad as the blackouts during the Blitz.

The shortage of power had dragged on through the summer. Priority was given to hospitals, the elderly and people with young children. There were demonstrations in the streets.

"'The stars like dust. . .'" murmured Marlstroy. "Was that in a poem? Or was it a book?"

He leaned back against the tiles and stared up into space. "Ah, this takes me back. Haven't seen a sky like this in goodness knows how long. I spent a year in Africa, oh . . . a long time ago, just after I'd qualified. It was an overseas aid thing, helping people in developing countries. Amazing experience. There were places out there where there was no electric light for hundreds of miles. The view at night was incredible. Living here, you get used to the idea of the night sky as some big black space with a few dots of light in it. But there you could step out of your front door after dark, with no sound except the lions coughing in the bush, and overhead would be these thousands, no literally *millions* of stars, as if great handfuls, shovelfuls of sugar had been flung into the air and then just stayed hanging there. You could stand there and gaze up at them and almost forget where you were, until it seemed like they were all around you and you were floating up there in the middle of them. . ."

He sat up and frowned at Dushma. "You know, I haven't even thought about that in years. Forgotten all about it. Been too busy, I suppose. I should go back some time." He looked up towards the sky again. "I tell you, if one good thing comes out of this mess it'll be the realization that we use far too much electricity."

"What's going to happen?" In fact, Dushma wasn't really that concerned. She had never been afraid of the dark, and rather liked going to bed by candle-light. She asked mainly because she was enjoying the sound of Marlstroy's voice, and the manner in which he was talking to her.

"Oh, Ashpool's the man to sort it out. I'm just glad it's him involved and not somebody from the other lot. They'd've backed down months ago and the unions and the Greens would've seen their tactics vindicated. Once they've been led to think they can get away with it, they'll be holding us to ransom every couple of years, striking and demonstrating whenever they feel like it."

Dushma nodded. "I see," she said, then added, "I mean, I don't, not really."

"Well, we've got a domestic fuel shortage, together with problems importing from the usual places. Energy's had to be rationed, that much you know. But that can't go on for ever. The government's got to find a different solution. And there are several options: for example, they can look for alternative domestic sources, which was already being done with the new rig on Mythgate Sands; and at the same time they can look at making what we've got go further: relax emission restrictions at the power stations, and maybe un-mothball some of the old nuclear reactors. All of this is anathema to the environmentalists, of course. They want to see the shortfall made up from renewable sources – wind power, solar energy. It's a long-term solution, it won't help us now, but they won't accept that. And the energy workers' unions aren't happy either. They've got safety concerns, some of which I must say I think are pretty legitimate. The trouble is they know they're in a strong position, so they're also insisting on a raft of measures relating to job security, pay and conditions. A tactic like that, though, it's like a red rag to a bull where someone like Ashpool's concerned. He won't even talk to them."

"He was that man at your party, wasn't he? The one in spectacles."

"Yes, that was him. We go back a long way. We were at college together. We've both done each other a lot of favours since. I reckon if he sees this crisis through he'll be in a pretty strong position to make a bid for the leadership."

Although much less bright than it would have normally been, the city was by no means completely dark. There was a faint glow of streetlights from the city's major thoroughfares, and a few of the most important buildings were still illuminated. Eastwards, towards the City and Docklands, lights flashed on top of blacked-out tower blocks. It occurred to Dushma that London probably looked no brighter now than it had done in Victorian times, when the streets had been lit by gas-lamps.

Marlstroy had brought a lantern and it now flickered at his feet, casting an orange glow across the terrace. Nocturnal insects rushed towards it like tiny meteorites. The faint sound of traffic swelled and diminished on the gusting breeze like the distant bellowing of some wild animal.

Dushma tipped back her head so that she could see nothing but the stars. They could be anywhere. Far from civilization; miles even from the nearest human being.

"Do lions really cough?" she asked.

Marlstroy had clambered to his feet and was dusting down his jacket. "Oh yes. I mean, of course they roar too, but more often they just cough."

III

Larchmuir

Though inclined to slip into the vernacular when emotional, Auntie Megan had done her best to ensure that Dushma was well-spoken. "The punters like a bit of posh," she had said once. She often used to tune their old wireless to Radio Three.

If this hadn't been the case then Dushma's experiences at Larchmuir College for Girls would probably have been worse. The school had seemed like an obvious choice. It was nearby and had, according to Marlstroy, an excellent reputation. Normally there was a waiting list, he explained, but he had connections among the governors and they had been willing to do him a favour.

It certainly looked impressive enough. Even before the autumn term began Dushma had already been several times to gaze at the buildings from the outside. Peering through the curled iron gates, she could see a spacious gravel courtyard surrounded on three sides by low facades of worn and patterned brick. This part of the school was so old that the ridge of the roof had sagged over the years and now dipped and rose like a telephone wire from chimney to chimney. The more modern blocks were further back, rising in a glitter of steel and glass from behind the uneven tiles of the older buildings. These would be the science labs, thought Dushma. And the music studio and the concert hall and the darkroom and the pottery kiln and all the other amenities she couldn't wait to begin using.

She was more apprehensive about the traditional subjects. She had taken some tests before the start of term and been told she had a lot of catching up to do. Apart from French and geography, most of what she didn't know had to do with triangles. She would have thought that there wasn't much to know about triangles, apart from the fact that they had three sides. But apparently there was a great deal more to it than that. There was quite a bit about circles, too. To make matters worse, quite a lot of the circles had triangles in them.

For the last few weeks of the summer holidays, Marlstroy arranged for a private tutor to visit Dushma daily. She learned nouns and verbs, chemicals, composers and capital cities, lists of prime ministers and dates, and the names of rivers and mountain ranges. Having never been to school, she didn't know that she wasn't supposed to enjoy this sort of thing.

They stuck a map of the world on a cork board on the wall and threw darts at it. The objective was to go round as many different countries as possible, buying produce to trade with at subsequent destinations. They competed in card games in which historical rulers made up the suits. Then they played pétanque in the back garden and kept the score in French.

In this way Dushma learned a remarkable amount in a short time. But her tutor didn't seem to know any games for making maths more interesting.

"Did *you* have to know about triangles?" she asked Marlstroy, encountering him one evening in the library.

"God, no. Geometry's not much use for medicine. No triangles in the human body. Though once when I was a junior houseman we had a teacher brought into casualty with a set square stuck between his ribs."

He went to the shelves and with difficulty pulled out one of the largest books in his collection. Its leather-bound covers were so big that if it had been laid half-open on the floor, spine upwards like a roof, Dushma was sure she could have crawled beneath it and been completely invisible.

Together they lifted it on to a table and turned its crackling pages. It was full of architectural drawings of churches. There were floor plans with pillars and walls marked in fine cross-hatching. Elevations of the exterior walls showed every brick and pane of glass. There were meticulously inked diagrams of spires with some of the tiles missing to show the supporting struts beneath. Beside each drawing long lines as thin as hairs indicated the dimensions.

"So you see," said Marlstroy, frowning at Dushma's exercise book, "this formula here means that if this terrace is three cubits wide, and this wall is four cubits high, then this buttress must be, let me see, three times three plus four times four . . . five cubits long. Although I shouldn't think anybody still uses cubits these days."

This practical application made the theory more interesting and a little easier to grasp. Dushma even went so far as to go out one sunny afternoon and try to work out the heights of some of her favourite buildings by pacing the length of their shadows. But in most cases this proved impossible, as the shadows fell across busy roads, or were interrupted by other buildings.

Although he was becoming less reclusive than when she had first known him, generally she still saw little of Marlstroy. Occasions when they spent any length of time in each other's company, such as the evening they had set up the telescope on the roof, remained the exception rather than the rule. Their only regular meetings came about through the help Marlstroy required from her with his work. Otherwise he seemed content to leave her to her own devices. She had the run of his library and a key to the front door of his large and elegant house; she could come and go as she wished. It suited her perfectly. It seemed like she had never had so many interesting things to do.

He never asked her about her previous life, and she in her turn hardly mentioned it at all. She rarely thought about it, and when she did she found it easier to pretend that her adventures had happened to somebody else. Her whole existence had changed, she told herself, and the easiest way to think of it was to imagine herself as having become a different person.

One of the few details she let slip of her life in the viaduct was the fact that she had owned a guitar. It had been a battered old instrument left behind at the flat by one of Auntie Megan's lodgers, and she had taught herself to play on it. It was a slow process but eventually she had learnt enough to be able to enjoy picking out simple tunes and sequences of chords.

It had surprised her at first, but Marlstroy seemed to like arranging things like this. Within a day or two he had found her a guitar and organized a series of lessons.

The teacher was a spiky-haired man with an accent that veered from public school to cockney and back again, often in the space of a few words. He had first asked her what football team she supported, and seemed perturbed when she told him none. It was important, he insisted. She would have to find one.

The extreme rustiness of her playing had worried him less. She had a good sense of rhythm, he said, and a sharp ear. They could start on some easy pieces by Dowland, he thought, and she might soon get the hang of that. Then they might be able to move on to Bach before too long. There was just one other thing, he said. She held her guitar the wrong way round. But that was cool. "Hendrix played it like that," he explained. "And he was a cat. Totally monster."

He showed her how to bite the neck so that the imprint of her teeth would identify the instrument as hers.

When at last the time came for Dushma to actually start at Larchmuir, her expectations were so high that it was almost inevitable she was going to be disappointed.

The first lesson involved a man in a bow tie standing at the whiteboard and talking to them solidly for more than an hour. Occasionally he drew a diagram, and the faintly sweet smell of the marker pen floated across the classroom.

After a few minutes Dushma realized that the other girls were taking notes. She hastily opened an exercise book and began to try and jot down what the teacher was saying. She found it difficult to write and listen at the same time and before long she had filled a page with clumsy, half-finished sentences that she doubted she would be able to understand when she came to re-read them.

The lesson seemed to be about how peasants had used their land several hundred years ago. Apparently they had divided it up into strips and planted different crops in rotation. Dushma waited for the teacher to do something more interesting to illustrate his points. Perhaps they would go outside, she thought, and see how they might divide up the lawn to resemble medieval farmland. Or at the very least they could rotate crops of cress on strips of wet blotting paper. Instead the teacher droned on about phosphates and fallow fields almost without a pause until at last the bell rang.

At break no one talked to her. The class was a small one, no more than a dozen pupils, and everyone seemed to have something to do. Some of them huddled into small groups and talked in excited whispers. Others rummaged in their desks or performed useful tasks such as cleaning the board and tidying up the marker pens. Everyone seemed to defer to the tallest girl, a strikingly pretty brunette named Praline Maisefield. She held court over a group of several elegant-looking girls, her frequent laughter echoed dutifully by her audience. Dushma hovered in vain for a sign that she might be welcome to join in.

After break things got worse. An elderly man with a goatee beard arrived and drew circles on the white board. Everything that had made sense to Dushma when it related to diagrams of buildings now seemed completely incomprehensible. Everyone laughed at her when, in response to a question, she guessed that pi was short for Pythagoras.

By lunchtime she was thoroughly miserable. School wasn't turning out to be at all like she had hoped. As soon as the teacher had left she made straight for the classroom door, not bothering to try and catch anyone's eye.

"Excuse me, what did you say your name was?"

She was already a few steps down the corridor. She stopped and turned. Praline Maisefield was standing in the doorway, one arm stretched out to stop anyone else leaving the classroom.

"Dushma," said Dushma. "Hello."

"I say, I did like your joke. Did you see old Thornton's face? He couldn't decide whether you were pulling his leg or not." Praline laughed musically, showing a perfect set of glistening teeth. "Wait *on*, girls. We can't talk with you lot charging past like a herd. Anyway . . . Dushma, is it? How are you fixed for after lunch? Why don't you come down to the locker room and me, Laureth and Natalie'll show you the ropes?"

With an effort, Dushma managed to control her feelings of almost pathetic gratitude. She forced herself to pause and frown for a moment as if considering the offer. "Yes, I think I can make it," she said.

"Good." Praline nodded, clearly not expecting any other answer. "We'll see you there then." She lowered her arm to let the other girls out of the classroom.

The locker room was in the basement in the oldest part of the school. Dushma had been shown it that morning, and given a key to her own locker. It was for storing sports kit, spare clothes, bags, anything that wouldn't go in her desk.

The room itself was large and low. There was an open area near the door with comfortable seating and a low table, a fridge and a kettle. Beyond this communal space the room was divided up into narrow, criss-crossing aisles by ranks and files of lockers. At the ends of some of these aisles, just within the reach of the strip lights running down the centre of the ceiling, were gloomy spaces stacked with boxes and old desks.

"Some people seem to prefer it to the common room," the headmistress had explained. "It can be quite cosy. Though we encourage you to go outside when the weather's nice."

It was at the end of one of the rows of lockers that Praline held court. She perched elegantly on top of an upturned tea chest with Laureth and Natalie on either side of her. Felt-covered office partitions were propped up around them, making a small private enclave.

"So, how do you like it here so far then?"

Dushma thought of her dreary morning and the lukewarm, tasteless lunch she had just eaten. "It's excellent, thank you," she said, trying to sound as cheerful as she could. "I'm really glad I came."

"Hmm," said Praline. "I think that's going a little far. But it can at least be bearable if you agree to adhere to certain simple principles. And I don't mean the rules Mrs Perrets-Cheevy explained to you this morning. We like the cut of your cloth, as they say. We feel you could, with the right sort of encouragement, become an asset to the form. There are, however, certain areas in which you'll be required to improve." She stretched out a hand to Laureth, who handed her a piece of paper.

"One: vocabulary. Nothing is 'excellent'. That's used

exclusively by teachers on end-of-term reports. Though if they write it too many times on yours then I'm afraid we'll have to have words. Anyway, I hope you'll quickly pick up some alternatives. 'Dreamy' would be quite acceptable. Tennis player Brad Backenforth, for example, could quite easily be described as dreamy. . ."

She looked to her cohorts for confirmation. They both nodded enthusiastically.

". . .whereas Ferrari's Jürgen Trummell, I'm sure we'll agree, is a dream on wheels. This may, of course, go out of fashion at any moment. Don't worry, we'll keep you informed.

"Next, appearance is obviously really important. We like to think of ourselves as standard-bearers to a certain extent, something the other girls can aspire to. You've clearly made an effort with your clothing and that's something we like to see."

Dushma glanced surreptitiously down at her uniform. She hadn't, in fact, made much of an effort at all. Marlstroy had arranged for someone to come round and measure her, and a set of blazers, skirts, blouses and shoes had arrived the following week, each with her name and address on a label inside. But this didn't seem the time to admit it, so she said nothing that might call her dress sense into question.

"And just in case you're tempted to let things slide, remember that hand-me-downs, polyester and visible mends are all completely unacceptable."

"Sartorial suicide," said Laureth.

"And posture, that's important too. Straight back, head high, no shuffling. You don't seem to have any problems in that respect. But you really will have to do something about your hair. It's rather too long and, if you don't mind my saying so, somewhat unkempt. We'll be happy to recommend some suitable places. I swear by Valentino's on the Strand. This —" she tilted her head self-consciously — "is his Art Deco look. Obviously you couldn't have the same, but I'm sure he could do something for you."

Dushma raised her hand instinctively to touch the pins and clips that held her dark and lustrous hair in place. She had been feeling an increasing glow of self-satisfaction as Praline praised her clothes and her bearing. This slighting reference to her hair, however, provoked a twinge of annoyance. What business was it of theirs? Covertly, she examined the Art Deco look more closely. From Praline's example, it seemed to involve sleeking the hair away from the left side of the head and gathering it into a knot like a rose behind the right ear. It was certainly a striking style, and although Dushma thought the effect rather too doll-like she didn't dare say so.

"Cosmetics," said Praline, moving on to the next item on her piece of paper. "The school rules are quite firm here so you'll have to be subtle. Strictly no harlots. And I need hardly add that own-brand chain-store products are utterly proscribed. In the event of doubt a receipt will be required.

"Now. . ." Praline ran her finger down the list she held. "Is there anything I've forgotten under appearance?"

Natalie leaned over and, glancing sideways at Dushma, whispered something into Praline's ear.

"Oh yes. And underwear. . ." Praline tipped back her head and pressed her lips together as if Dushma herself had suggested something unseemly ". . .is entirely your own affair. We'd really rather not know, thank you very much." Laureth and Natalie tittered appreciatively.

"Boyfriends!" announced Praline, silencing them with a look. "Must be approved collectively. This is for your own good. I give you the salutary example of Simone Braithwaite whom may I remind you Natalie we are *still* not speaking to. We told her at the time it wouldn't last but she utterly refused to listen to us. And it didn't, of course, but she still won't admit that she was wrong and we were right. Bloody obvious with hindsight really. He was called *Trev*, went to a *comprehensive*, and took her *ferret*-racing. All of which, while amusing. . ."

"We giggled considerably," said Laureth. Dushma smiled uncertainly.

". . .was clearly quite unacceptable. We had to have words. Something like that could reflect badly on us all. Even if, as she claimed, she was only there to watch."

"I suppose that's all you can do, really, when you go ferret-racing," Dushma was unable to resist pointing out. "Unless of course you're a ferret."

This did not go down well.

"She *means*, of course, they didn't actually gamble," explained Laureth. "But it was obviously the thin end of the wedge."

There was an uncomfortable pause. "Being new here," said Praline coolly, "for the first term or so you'll be expected to offer your opinions with a certain diffidence."

"She said, witheringly," added Laureth.

"They have these, like, tube thingies," said Natalie. "They're like, see-through, you know? So you can see through them? You can watch them running down them. It's, you know, quite sweet really, I suppose." She caught Praline's eye. "I mean, that's what I've heard. You know? Of course, I'd never go!" She shook her head firmly.

"So," said Praline, "now you know where you stand you can think it over and let us know. We'll see you down here again same time tomorrow." She jumped down from her perch on top of the tea chest and brushed fussily at her skirt. "Of course, we wouldn't *normally* be seen dead down here. There are *much* better places to go for those with certain privileges, and as soon as we've got these little formalities over with we'll see what we can do for you in that respect, shall we?"

Without waiting for Dushma to reply, she tossed her head and swept out of the locker room, Laureth and Natalie trailing in her wake.

That afternoon and the following morning passed much as the first two lessons had done. By lunchtime on her second day Dushma's wrist was aching from the notes she had taken.

She briefly considered not going down to the locker room at all. But in the end boredom triumphed over rebelliousness. Everyone else seemed to have something to do, somewhere to go. And still no one was talking to her.

She was early and the locker room was deserted. The lights were off, but at the far end of one of the aisles a fan of sunlight had spread itself out across the ceiling, making it bright enough for her to see her way. There was no sound except the occasional distant shout from the playing fields.

Dushma crossed the room towards the light. Looking up, she could see bars of illuminated air swirling with gold flecks of dust. She tipped back her head and exhaled, enjoying the small satisfaction of seeing the motes jink and scatter in the turbulence of her breath.

A locker door banged nearby. She jumped, then moved cautiously round the end of the aisle to look down the next row of lockers.

It wasn't Praline or one of her lieutenants but another girl, her back turned and her head bowed as she struggled with a bunch of keys.

Dushma cleared her throat. "Hello," she said.

The other girl gave no sign of having heard.

"Well, *be* like that then!" A surge of annoyance welling up inside her, Dushma strode along the aisle, intending

142

to flounce from the room in a way that would quite clearly express her day and a half's worth of injured feelings.

As she pushed her way past the girl she caught a glimpse of a pale, startled face and a pair of wide eyes behind thick spectacles. As the face turned towards her she saw, beyond the swinging curtain of lank hair, the beige crescent of plastic tucked behind the girl's ear.

She stopped abruptly. "Oh. I'm sorry. . ."

"You're new, aren't you," said the girl, matter-of-factly. "You have to speak clearly and wait till I'm facing you. If you actually want me to hear you, that is. If you don't, just mutter up your sleeve like everybody else does."

"I . . . of course, yes." Casting round for some way of dispelling her embarrassment, Dushma noticed the writing on the door of the girl's locker. U OWLMIEN, it said. "Sorry, what was your name?"

"Ursula," said Ursula.

"Oh. That's nice."

"No it isn't. It's a horrible name. And don't tell me it means 'little bear', thank you very much. I know that already, strangely enough. My mother's a sadist. Anyway, nobody calls me that."

"What do they call you?" Dushma asked.

"Moth. It's my mother's pet name for me. Don't ask why. I suppose I must have lisped endearingly when I was little or something. She got upset one open evening and called me it, despite strict instructions. 'Oh Moth,' she said. Loudly. I told you she was a sadist. It was all round the classroom by the next morning of course."

"I'll call you something else if you like," suggested Dushma.

"Oh yes? What?" Moth seemed genuinely interested.

"Well . . . I don't know."

"No, it's kind of you to offer but I've got used to it now. What are you doing down here anyway? They like us to be out in the fresh air you know. It's healthier. Haven't you read the rules? 'We strive to instil in all our girls a wholesome regard for outdoor pursuits and a something something for the invigorating qualities of something something.' I had to write it out fifty times once when I skipped games."

"I came down to meet Praline," Dushma admitted. "I'm early though."

"Aren't you lucky? *She* wouldn't normally be seen dead down here."

"I know. She said so. She wants me to get my hair cut at Valentino's. And then she'll talk to me."

"Oh. I see. And are you going to?"

"I don't know. I haven't decided. She's very nice, if she wants to be . . . and maybe it is a bit untidy. . ."

"'Children can be *so* cruel'," said Moth with a sigh, obviously mimicking someone. Her mother perhaps. "Though not half as cruel as their parents sometimes are, believe me."

"What about you? Aren't you supposed to be getting the something benefits of fresh air too?"

"Look at me." Moth gestured helplessly at her pasty complexion. "If I try and absorb any more wholesome qualities I shall burst. No, seriously, they tend not to bother about me. They're worried I'll fall into a daze and be gobbled up unawares by a passing combine-harvester or something. And besides, I like it down here. Listen, can you keep a secret? I'll show you something if you want."

She led Dushma down the narrow gap behind a row of lockers. They squeezed past a table standing up on its end and found themselves in a small space containing a low cupboard and a sagging armchair. Greenish light filtered in from a barred window, most of which was below ground level. All that could be seen through the dusty glass was a crumbling brick alcove and, right at the top, some trailing fronds of creeper and a small patch of sky.

Dushma was just thinking that, though rather snug, this corner of the locker room wasn't all that secret, when Moth pointed triumphantly to a patch of bare wall below the window.

"There," she said. "Look at that. What can you see?"

"Nothing," said Dushma.

"Exactly! Good, isn't it? They left some paint in one of the cupboards the last time they decorated the place. So I wrote on the wall and then painted it over."

"OK. . . Why?"

"So that when it peels off in hundreds of years I'll be famous, of course!"

"Oh, I see." Dushma nodded admiringly. This was long-term planning on a grand scale.

"It's educational as well. I got the idea from this thing we did in history a couple of terms ago. There was this architect — what was he called again? Anyway, he built this lighthouse and carved the king's name in really soft stone so that after a while it wore away and left the architect's name there in granite underneath, so he'd be remembered for ever."

"So what did you put? Was it just your name?"

"Oh no, loads of things. It's, like, my testament. For future generations. I'll go down in school lore. I'll be a legend."

Dushma crouched and peered more closely at the wall. The section Moth had indicated did look slightly cleaner than the surrounding area, but otherwise there was no way to tell what might lie underneath.

"You can have a go too if you like," offered Moth. "But we'll have to find some more paint first. I used up the last of the stuff they left in here."

"No, it's OK thanks." Dushma looked at her watch. "Praline's going to be here any minute. Besides, I don't think I've been here long enough to be able to leave much of a testament for future generations."

They made their way back to the main area of the locker room. There was still no one else there, so Dushma sat down in one of the chairs and began tapping on the arm with her fingers, glancing at her watch every few seconds.

Moth hovered by the door. "Don't worry," she said. "I'll go when she comes. I'm sure it won't do you any good to be seen hanging out with me."

"Why not? What's it got to do with her?"

"You'll see." Moth ran her fingers through her lank hair. "Let's just say, I don't think she can have thought it was worth trying to get *me* to go to some posh salon."

"She told me not to be late." Dushma drummed her heels impatiently on the floor. "Where's she got to?"

"She's toying with you," said Moth knowingly. "To make it easier for her to bend you to her will."

Dushma shook her head firmly. "I'm not going to get bent to anybody's will."

Moth gave her a pitying look. "I'm afraid it happens to most of us. If you're lucky you'll be able to choose whose will you get bent to, that's all. Praline's got no time for me, I'm glad to say."

"But why not?" Dushma tried to introduce a more light-hearted note. "Doesn't she know you're going to be a school legend?"

"God no, don't tell *her*. I'd rather just be ignored. She doesn't think that much of me." She tapped the side of her head. "Poor old Moth. Daft as a hat."

"Oh go on," said Dushma gallantly. "You seem to manage all right." She remembered Moth answering several questions in that morning's lessons.

"It's a miracle if I do, considering all the effort they make to help. I'll tell you something: I happen to know they charge my mother a hefty extra whack for my 'special needs'. They don't actually *do* anything at all, of course, apart from now and then reminding the teachers not to mumble at the whiteboard."

"That doesn't sound very fair."

"*She* doesn't care. She just adds it to the alimony bill. The school gets a grant from the local authority too. I know for a fact they're supposed to have fitted an induction loop in the hall. But I still can't make head nor tail of anything they do in there. Assemblies aren't too bad. Five minutes of watching old Fox-Watson thumping the piano's enough to make me glad I'm deaf. It's these talks they lay on that are really unbearable. I'm hoping if I look pale enough they might send me to lie down and I'll miss it. Do I look pale?"

"Well . . . yes, a bit. What talk is this?"

"Oh dear. She hasn't read the notice-board. Weren't you shown the notice-board? Be careful. You're in danger of making me look positively clued-up. We have them now and then. This one's from some company director. His daughter's in the sixth form. 'The ethical . . . something something, environmental something', I think it was. Pure propaganda."

"That mightn't be too bad," said Dushma, thinking that almost anything would be preferable to the lessons she had experienced so far.

"Don't you believe it. They're *always* deadly. Without exception. They never get anybody interesting. It's just people they want to suck up to so they'll donate some money to mend the roof, or re-upholster the leopard-skin chaise-longue in the staffroom. Not that I can tell anyway. I just sit there for an hour without a clue what's going on. It sounds like they've got their mouths full of cotton wool. 'Omya hum rarnum nyah mahurr nyum nararr,' that's what it sounds like to me." She pressed the back of her hand dramatically to her forehead. "P'raps I'll faint. Or pretend to be sleep-walking. Will you back me up? 'Don't wake her! She's sleep-walking,' you could say."

"Why don't we just do something else? We could go out somewhere."

"Out somewhere?" Seeing that she was serious, Moth stared incredulously at Dushma. She obviously hadn't meant it about the sleep-walking.

"Yes, why not?"

"But . . . where?"

"Just . . . anywhere. Around. There were loads of barricades up on the way in this morning. I think there was something going on. It might be interesting."

"Oh, that. One of those marches, I suppose. They're always having them these days. Mrs Wilson bangs on about them sometimes. Telling us not to get involved. Because there are undesirable elements. I pretend I think she's said elephants. 'What are undesirable elephants?' I say. 'Don't be silly, Ursula,' she says. But it gets her off the subject."

"I think this must be a big one. The bus had to take a different route."

"In that case I'm surprised they haven't locked us all in and put barbed wire round the. . . Wait a minute." Moth blinked at her. "You come to school on the *bus*?"

"Oh yes. I've always been quite independent actually."

"Well, don't tell Praline, that's all. She'd have a fit if she knew. *She* wouldn't let herself be seen dead on one, I bet you."

Dushma looked at her watch yet again. It was now well past the time of her appointment. Perhaps they had just forgotten. Or perhaps she had already been judged and found wanting. Well, she didn't care, she told herself. But it was galling to think of returning to class and having to continue to suffer the *froideur* of Praline and her companions.

The more she thought about it the more she felt the urge to get away from school for a while. She hadn't been there two days yet, but already she disliked the chewy squeak of her soles on the corridor lino, hated the inescapable smells of polish, disinfectant and dust, and resented the way everywhere that looked interesting seemed to be out of bounds. She felt stifled. She hated the stuffiness of the overheated classrooms and the uncomfortable feel of her starched collar rubbing against her neck every time she turned her head.

She stood up decisively. "Come on then. Why don't we just go? We can join this march. No one'll notice us in the crowd. And we can wear our coats so's our badges don't show." She undid the top button of her blouse and tugged at the stiff collar to loosen it a little.

150

"Wait a minute. We can't. We'll get caught." Moth's eyes were wide behind her spectacles.

"Why? Look, it's only this thing, this talk. They probably won't even notice we're not there."

"Well," said Moth slowly, "I suppose we *might* just get away with it. You're new, so you can say you didn't know any better. And they don't expect too much from me anyway. Silly old Moth, they'll say. Probably didn't hear the bell. Probably had a temporary brainstorm and forgot who she was."

A bell rang in the distance.

"Come on then, are you coming?" pressed Dushma. "Hurry up and decide. That was the bell."

A look of blank innocence spread itself slowly across Moth's face. "What bell?" she asked.

IV

An Astounding Feat of Prestidigitation

They agreed that they would have to have placards of some sort. They decided these would be essential if they were to join whatever march was going on, in order that they could blend in with the genuine participants.

Moth opened her locker and took out two sheets of A4 paper, some felt-tip pens, two rulers and some sellotape.

They were hampered in their choice of slogan by the fact that neither of them knew exactly what the march was about.

"It'll be a protest, won't it," reasoned Moth. "They always are. So I reckon I can't go wrong with this." She wrote a large NO on her piece of paper.

"Perhaps they've been wronged," said Dushma. Her felt-tip pen squeaked as she began to write.

Cutting the sellotape with her teeth, Moth stuck her slogan on to one of her rulers. The paper drooped when she flourished the makeshift placard, but she decided it would have to do.

"Come on. Haven't you done yet?"

"Have you got any more paper? I haven't left enough space to finish."

"J-U-S-T-I. . ." Moth read out, peering over Dushma's shoulder. "Just put an S. People'll think you can't spell, but they'll know what you mean and that's the important thing. Sometimes you just have to make these sacrifices for the good of the cause."

"But I don't know what the cause *is* yet," argued Dushma. "So I don't know if it's worth people thinking I can't spell for."

"In that case you could just put an N. Then people would think you were meeting someone. Come to think of it, that way you might actually meet someone. I'm sure Praline would approve of anyone called Justin."

"I think I'll just leave it as it is," said Dushma, after a little thought. "If anyone asks what it means I'll tell them it's Esperanto."

"I can't believe we're doing this," said Moth. She spoke in an excited stage whisper despite the fact that the street was empty.

It had been surprisingly easy to leave without being seen. The main entrance was in the oldest part of the school, and the narrow, barred windows of the ancient buildings made it unlikely that anyone who wasn't looking would notice them as they walked across the courtyard and out on to the pavement.

Although close to one of the busiest parts of town, the area in which the school was situated was a quiet one. The surrounding buildings were mostly warehouse conversions and there were few people about during the day. Since coming out of the school gates into the mild early autumn afternoon they had seen almost no one.

Dushma was so used to going where she liked at whatever time she pleased that what they were doing hardly worried her. She wasn't yet acclimatized enough to the regimented world of bells and timetables to find an impromptu excursion unusual. Yet despite the deserted streets Moth was clearly a little apprehensive. When their path crossed a patch of bright sunlight she stopped, glanced quickly around her and then scuttled to the next corner. She peered cautiously round it, then stepped out and sauntered casually over the road and into the shade on the far side.

"The secret," she said when Dushma had caught up with her, "is not to look too furtive." She clasped her hands behind her back, pursed her lips and tried to whistle, her eyes darting this way and that.

They made their way down cobbled alleys, through narrow arches and up several flights of steps between high walls. Dushma knew this part of London thoroughly and was familiar with all the shortcuts. Before long they were nearing busier streets. There was a faint sound of music and chanting.

"Hey . . . wait for me," panted Moth, breaking into a

trot to keep up with Dushma. "How come you know your way so well? I thought you grew up abroad. Where was it? Somewhere in the East, Mrs Wilson said."

Dushma was prepared for this question, having already thought of an explanation for her local knowledge. "Oh, I was brought up by nomads," she explained airily. "I'm very good at finding my way."

"Nomads?" Moth sounded impressed. "Did you have to live in a tent?"

"Sometimes." Moth's curiosity encouraged Dushma to elaborate. "It was a huge one though, with rugs and cushions and . . . and embroidered silk canopies. But sometimes it was so warm we just slept under the stars. You should see them when there's no light pollution. There's so many of them. They're like . . . like silver dust."

The noise of the demonstration was getting louder. Dushma could hear drums and whistles, the sound of horns and occasional bursts of applause.

"We're nearly there," said Dushma. "Listen. Oh . . . sorry. There's music and singing and people cheering."

"I can hear *something*. . ." Moth had begun to drag her feet. "Does it sound safe?"

"It sounds quite exciting actually. Come on!"

"I don't know . . . maybe we should go back. The assembly's probably nearly over by now. And they might start throwing bottles and setting light to things. On the demo I mean, not in the assembly."

They rounded the last corner. At the end of the road was

a brightly coloured crowd of people moving slowly along. Moth hung back.

"Oh go on," urged Dushma. "It looks fine. Let's give it a few minutes, then if you don't like it I know . . . I mean, I'm sure I can find an escape route."

Arm in arm, they came out on to the main street and weaved their way through the crowd. The good-natured atmosphere of the demonstration was immediately apparent. There was a wide range of people present, none of whom looked like they were going to be throwing bottles or setting light to things. There were young couples holding hands, mothers with babies, several men in suits and even some tourists. Vendors with handcarts were selling food and drink and a man in a multi-coloured kaftan wandered past, sunglasses and jewellery laid out on a tray slung round his neck.

Dushma jumped up to try and see how far the crowd extended. "There's thousands of people," she said. "It goes all the way to the square at the end, I'm sure. There's someone on stilts further on, I think. And there's this silver stuff like someone's throwing tinsel."

The banners and placards they could see had an environmental theme. Most had obviously been professionally printed and handed out by the demonstration's organizers. Many of them urged the government to CUT GREENHOUSE GASES NOW! Others extolled alternative energy sources as the answer to the current fuel crisis.

156

"Do you think we should get our placards out?" asked Moth. They had tucked them under their coats so as to appear less suspicious on their way out of school.

"I don't know. Maybe not. They're going to look a bit feeble, aren't they?"

"Ear-piercing!" shrieked a tiny, tattooed woman with a megaphone. "Ear-piercing! While you wait!"

"What's she saying?" asked Moth.

"Ear-piercing," said Dushma. "While we wait."

"I should hope so too."

The tattooed woman was filling her lungs ready to give another deafening advertisement for her services. Dushma took Moth's elbow, ready to hurry away. But seeing them looking at her, the woman lowered her megaphone and darted forward.

"'Ere," she whispered. "'Avin' trouble buyin' fags? I'll do you a smoker's tattoo. No questions asked, know what I mean?"

Dushma shook her head and walked quickly on, Moth trailing behind her.

They found themselves among a group of people with straggly hair and flowers painted on their faces. Their banner, a long green piece of fabric hung between two poles, was covered with cut-out pieces of material in the shape of birds and plants. One of them, a man in tattered patchwork clothing, skipped along underneath it playing a tin whistle.

"Can I do you?" A woman appeared in front of them, clutching a handful of face-painting crayons. She swayed unsteadily towards Dushma and reached out to touch her cheek. "You'd make a lovely tiger lily."

"Better not," said Dushma. "I'd probably get in trouble when I got back."

"Oh but that's awful," said the woman dreamily. "Why are some people so intolerant?"

They lingered to watch a man clamber on to a nearby pillar box. "We're marching here together 'cos all we've had from this government is promises!" he shouted. "And are we fed up?"

A mixed response of "Yes!" and "No!" came from the people around him. "That's right!" he exclaimed. "And they'd better believe it!" There were loud cheers. "Thank you, thank you," said the man, waving to the crowd as a policeman helped him down from the pillar box.

Up ahead of them, a space had appeared around a group of people in protective clothing. They wore white overalls, gloves, boots and hoods. Their faces were hidden behind cylinder-snouted gas masks. The logo on their banner was a black and red picture of a burning tree.

At first it seemed as if they were dancing, but as Moth and Dushma drew nearer it became clear that they were miming the effects of being overcome by poisonous gas. They were staggering this way and that, and several were clutching their throats. One had fallen to the ground and was writhing on his back in the gutter.

A three-man camera crew was circling them, filming their antics. "That's lovely, more of that," the director of the camera crew was saying, nodding and adjusting his headphones. "Maybe kick your legs in the air? Bit more . . . lovely! Marvellous! That's it, it's a wrap, thank you all, thank you very much!"

The men in white overalls immediately stopped their pantomime of asphyxiation and began congratulating themselves on what was obviously a publicity coup. They clapped each other on the back and punched each other's shoulders playfully.

"They filmed the crowd!" said Dushma excitedly. "D'you think we'll be on the news?"

"I hope not," said Moth. "There's a TV in the staffroom."

One of the white-overalled men remained on the ground. He was still kicking his legs in the air and had now begun slapping the tarmac with one gloved hand. His companions, noticing him, gestured in his direction and shook their heads at one another at such uncontrollable exhibitionism.

"It's all right," said a passer-by helpfully, "the camera crew's gone now."

"Hey look!" exclaimed Moth.

Through a sudden gap in the surrounding crowd they saw, a little way in front of them, a boy dressed in dark clothing, with close-cropped fair hair and intense blue eyes. He was walking slowly backwards, juggling silver batons as he went.

Though they only saw him for a moment, his skill was immediately apparent. His hands moved backwards and forwards and up and down in front of him almost too fast

159

for the eye to follow. So quickly did he catch and throw the batons it was difficult to tell how many there were. They flew in high arcs from his flexing wrists, sparkling like daytime fireworks in the bars of sunlight slanting between the buildings.

"That was amazing," said Moth, when the jostling crowd had closed in again and he was lost to view. "Let's try and get a closer look."

"Yes," Dushma teased her. "He had really bright blue eyes, didn't he? How old do you think he was?"

"No, I mean the juggling!"

Behind them the white-overalled man who had been lying in the gutter had been helped up by two policemen. He now sat on the kerb, his gas mask pushed back on to his forehead to reveal a bright red face shiny with perspiration. "Thank . . . thank you officer," he panted. "If the nerve gas doesn't get you then the lace-up fastenings will. Isn't life a bitch?"

After weaving their way through the crowd for a few minutes the two girls came upon the juggler. They reached the edge of the small area of clear space around him and found themselves no more than a few feet from his circling hands. He noticed them watching him and nodded in a friendly manner, fixing them with his intense blue eyes. One of his front teeth had a corner chipped off and this gave his smile a jagged appearance.

Embarrassed, Moth tried to pull Dushma away. "We'll put him off," she whispered.

But the juggler had already begun to pluck his batons out of the air. With the last one – Dushma counted, there were five – tucked beneath his arm, he turned and fell into step beside Moth.

"What did you think?" he asked. He had noticed her admiring gaze.

"That was amazing," said Moth, blushing.

He gave a little mock bow, one hand on his chest. Then he turned to Dushma, his expression a mixture of challenge and expectancy.

"I . . . well, yes, it was really good," she said hurriedly.

"But not amazing?"

Dushma couldn't tell whether he really was offended or whether he was just pretending to look hurt. "I don't know . . . I mean, it's just practice really, isn't it?" As soon as she'd spoken it struck her how grudging she must have sounded. She realized she was piqued because he was paying more attention to Moth than he was to her.

"Go on, have a try," he was saying, flourishing a silver baton enticingly.

"Oh no, I couldn't, I'd be dreadful," said Moth, turning away and blushing.

"Yes, maybe you should start with something easier," said the juggler, stowing his batons away in a velvet bag that hung over his shoulder. "Like those juggling balls you've got, for instance."

"What do you mean?" asked Moth.

Smiling wickedly, the juggler reached up with his left

161

hand and plucked a small, squashy ball from behind her ear. "Ones like this," he said. He rolled his wrist, making the ball run over his knuckles and under his palm. "And these." His other hand darted into her coat pocket. It emerged holding two more balls, which he began to juggle one-handed.

Then with a snap of his fingers the ball in his left hand disappeared. He held his palm out towards them to show that it was empty. His right hand now kept three balls effortlessly in the air.

Moth was mesmerized. "Does it take long to learn to do that?"

"Oh, ages." He dropped the juggling balls one by one into his velvet bag. "Hours every day. It doesn't hurt to have strong hands as well, of course. Some of the jobs I've done have helped with that. I was a clinker monkey for a while, if you know what one of those is."

Dushma shook her head. "No. What?"

The boy looked away and smiled his jagged smile to himself. "Fancy you well brought up young ladies not knowing what a clinker monkey is," he said. "Let's just say, you don't last long if you've not got pretty strong fingers. Here, feel."

He held out one long, pale hand. Moth shrank back, blushing even more. Before the juggler could withdraw his hand again, Dushma reached around Moth and clasped his fingers.

They walked for several paces holding hands awkwardly.

The juggler's skin was dry and warm, with callouses on the palm. Though he didn't exert much strength, Dushma could feel the powerful sinews in his fingers as he flexed them against her own.

"Did you come to protest, or just for fun?" asked Moth.

"A bit of both. I know one of the organizers. I owe him some favours off when I used to work the chimneys. It's good if there's something to keep the crowds amused. So I hope you are. Amused, that is."

"Oh yes," said Dushma, nodding seriously.

"Because I suppose you must be skipping school to be here. And I must say running such a risk shows true dedication to the cause." He was smiling his jagged smile again.

"No we're not!" lied Moth hastily. "We've got permission. We're doing a project. On . . . on. . ."

"You should have one on a Saturday," said Dushma. "I'm sure loads more people would be able to come."

"They've thought of that. But the council seems to agree with you – that there'd be lots of people, that is. Too many, in fact, because it's turned down every application. There's always some feeble excuse, like there are roadworks that weekend, or the forms weren't filled in right or something. But hey, this is pretty good. There's enough people starting to get concerned for there to be a good crowd even on a weekday. Too many rumours going round: typhoons in the Channel; earthquakes in the home counties – people are starting to want to see something done."

"P'raps I could do juggling instead of games," said Moth. "They won't let me do the team sports, you see. Although I'd be useless at them anyway. I always have to do running. I'm sure juggling would help my hand–eye coordination more. Can you think of any other arguments I could use?"

"It'll help you earn a living, if you fall on hard times," said the juggler. "Nobody pays to watch someone go jogging."

He had turned round and was again walking backwards, facing the two girls. Loosening the drawstring of his velvet bag, he began taking out his silver batons. "I do weddings, birthdays, garden parties," he explained. "I've done theatre. And I've been practising with flaming brands. I'm not quite there yet, though." He showed them an angry red stripe across his knuckles.

"They'd never let me do that," Moth had to admit. "Probably just as well."

They were approaching the square at the end of the street and the crowd had thickened and slowed. "So what are they like, your teachers, then?" the juggler wanted to know.

"Ferocious," said Moth.

"Really?" The juggler was looking around for a space in which he could continue his performance. "Is one of them tall, with straight grey hair and big, red-framed spectacles?"

"Yes, that's Mrs Wilson. But how on earth do you. . .?"

"Well, she's coming this way and she looks like she wants to talk to you. And you know what? Whatever it is your project's on – that one you've got permission to be here for — something tells me she doesn't know anything about it." He smiled his wicked smile. "Good luck!"

Gripping each of them tightly by the arm, Mrs Wilson marched Dushma and Moth to her car. It was parked in a side street a few hundred metres away, two wheels up on the kerb and its hazard warning lights flashing.

"Oh miss, what's happened to your windscreen?" asked Moth as they approached.

There were dozens of leaflets tucked under the wipers. GO BY BIKE ITS GREENER, said one. MY OTHER CAR'S A WASTE OF PRECIOUS NATURAL RESOURCE'S TOO, said another. There was also a penalty notice from a traffic warden and a sticker on the bumper that read, I'M POLLUTING THE PLANET.

Tight-lipped, Mrs Wilson said nothing. She bundled the two girls into the back seat and then slammed the door shut so hard the car shook. Striding to the front of the vehicle, she gathered up an armful of leaflets from the windscreen, scrunched them into a ball and threw them down into the gutter.

"Oh miss," said Moth mournfully, oblivious of the thunderous expression on Mrs Wilson's face as she climbed into the driver's seat.

"That's enough!" snapped Mrs Wilson, stabbing the key into the ignition and starting the car.

They drove in silence for several minutes before she spoke again. "I suppose you're going to claim you didn't hear the bell or something," she said sarcastically, glaring at them in the rear view mirror.

"Pardon?" asked Moth innocently.

The car lurched to a halt, cherry-coloured lights glowing on the dashboard as Mrs Wilson stamped on the brake and stalled the engine. She twisted round in her seat to face her passengers.

"Don't you dare try that with me, Ursula Owlmien! I'm perfectly aware that you know everything I'm saying! Can you have any *idea* how mortified we were when we saw you on the staffroom television? The very thought of *our* girls associating with those dreadful people, reading their leaflets, picking up their bad grammar. . . Thank goodness your uniforms weren't showing! I can't bear to think of the effect *that* might have had on our admissions!"

A small traffic jam was beginning to form behind them. One of the waiting drivers sounded his horn. Mrs Wilson started the car and moved off again, gears scrunching.

"And then there's your own safety, of course." Her head trembled with emotion as she spoke, causing her gold hoop earrings to oscillate. "Haven't I warned you often enough? You know how events like that are rife with undesirable elements. You could've been robbed, or trampled, or kidnapped and inveigled into a sinister underground environmentalist cult!"

"I'm afraid it was my fault," confessed Dushma gallantly. "It was my idea. I persuaded. . ."

Moth nudged her sharply. "I became confused, miss," she

said. "Dushma had to follow me to make sure I didn't. . ."

"Oh for heaven's *sake* Ursula, will you stop pretending to be some kind of half-wit!" Mrs Wilson turned round in her seat again and drove through a red light without noticing. A van coming in the other direction swerved out of the way. "Idiot! . . . You knew perfectly well you were being flagrantly disobedient. Do you think we make rules for fun? Do you think they're there to be flouted with impunity? Well funnily enough they're for your own protection. We've got your best interests at heart, believe it or not." She put the car into the wrong gear and the engine buzzed crossly.

It was already too late in the day for the girls to return to school, so Mrs Wilson drove them home. When they reached Marlstroy's house she left Moth in the car, marched Dushma up the path to the front door, rang the bell and waited with her for someone to answer.

Marlstroy didn't seem surprised to see Mrs Wilson. He stood in the doorway and listened impassively while she recounted Dushma's crime.

"Not a good start, not a good start at all, most disappointing," she concluded at last, shaking her head. She waited for Marlstroy to say something. When he didn't she repeated, "Most disappointing, most disappointing indeed, wouldn't you say?"

"Oh yes, most disappointing," said Marlstroy. He still wore his pinstripe trousers and waistcoat, but he had taken off his jacket and his shirt-sleeves were rolled up to the elbows. He was stroking his jaw with one hand, tugging at the loose flesh of his jowls and making his lean face look even thinner and more deeply lined. All at once Dushma knew from his distant, severe expression that he was concocting some unpleasant punishment for her. For the first time since the two of them had been caught she felt a surge of anxiety squeeze its way up into her chest. She had been hoping he wouldn't be too angry with her.

"A night in the cellar, I think," he said. "In the dark."

"Oh." Mrs Wilson looked as if she hadn't been expecting quite this response. "I don't know if I'd. . ."

"With bread and water. How will that do?"

"Well, perhaps that's a little. . . It's not exactly what I. . . But I'm sure you know best of course." Mrs Wilson glanced over her shoulder at her car, parked at an angle with one wheel up on the kerb. "She'll be having to see Mrs Perrets-Cheevy tomorrow." She began backing her way down the garden path. "The question of her continued attendance will have to be discussed, I'm sure you'll understand. . ."

Dushma tried to wave encouragingly to Moth before the door closed. She was determined she wasn't going to spend the night in the cellar. She would lock herself in her room if she had to, no matter if it meant not getting any food at all, not even bread and water. She sidled into the shadows of the hallway, ready to make a run for the stairs.

Marlstroy shut the door and turned to her. "What was

that thing she said you missed?" he asked. His voice was sympathetic. "That lecture, I mean. Sounded deadly. Can't blame you at all. I'd've legged it too." He strode off in the direction of the kitchen, his footsteps ringing on the flagstones. "Come on, your supper will spoil."

Dushma hurried to catch him up. "So I'm not going to have to spend the night in the cellar, then?"

"God no. Who d'you think I am? Wackford Squeers? I couldn't resist pulling her leg. She looked so righteously indignant. Maybe I shouldn't've done. She did seem rather taken aback. If they ask tomorrow you'd better say I wouldn't let you watch TV or something."

"But I might be going to get expelled," said Dushma. She wasn't sure how much she really cared, but was a little surprised that Marlstroy seemed so unconcerned.

"You won't get expelled. I've told you, I know the chairman of the board of governors. Don't murder anyone, will you, or hijack an aeroplane. But otherwise, do what you like. Next time just don't get caught, all right? They'll probably give you lines or something. It'll all have blown over by the end of the week. Don't let it ruin your appetite."

They walked down the narrow corridor that led to the kitchen at the back of the house. A thick-walled, low-beamed room, it was cosy after the echoing space of the hallway.

Mrs Breckle had left a casserole in the lower oven of the cooking range and a rich smell filled the air, reminding

Dushma that she hadn't eaten a thing since picking at her lunch in the school canteen many hours ago. She helped herself and sat down at the table.

Instead of retreating to his study, as he usually did in the evenings, Marlstroy lingered. He poured himself some wine and swirled it in his glass.

"Don't look so worried," he said.

"I don't know if I am, really. I thought you might be, though. Or cross, anyway."

"Me? God no. I used to do it too. We used to have some dreadful lessons. Greek was the worst. It's much more fun these days. They call it classical studies and tell you all about the sex lives of the gods. But back then it was dreary stuff and I'd get out of it whenever I could. When I was at prep school the grounds backed on to the town library. It had a small museum attached, and a friend and I sometimes used to climb over the wall and spend an hour or two there. There was only one curator, this old chap who thought we had permission to come and help him out. Most of the things on display were fairly dull. Broken pottery, bits of old furniture, that kind of thing. But the storeroom was stacked with dozens of crates that had been donated to the museum by an eccentric Victorian explorer. None of them even catalogued. Must be places like that all over the country, and the things in them are probably nothing but junk, except that there might just be something really sensational waiting to be rediscovered."

He smiled distantly into the dregs of his wine. "But if

there was anything like that there then we'd never have found it. These old crates were full to the brim with bones. Vertebrae, shin bones, ribs and skulls. . . The curator had no idea what to do with them, so he used to let us try and put them together. We hadn't a clue what we were doing." He shook his head. "We came up with some outlandish creatures."

Later, as she was getting ready for bed, Dushma found a rectangle of card in one of the pockets of her coat. *The Astonishing . . . ARBILOW*, it said. *Juggling, Conjuring, Astounding Feats of Prestidigitation*.

That wasn't very astonishing, she told herself. It couldn't have been that difficult to slip something into her pocket while her attention was elsewhere. Why couldn't he just have given it to her? He had been trying to show off, she decided. Well, it hadn't worked because she simply wasn't impressed, let alone astounded. It would serve him right if she just threw it away.

She dangled the card over the waste-paper basket, but before she could let it go something caught her eye. There were a few words scrawled on the back in shaky biro. *Dear Dushma*, she read. *You have beautiful hands. See you again soon I hope, A.*

She read the brief message several times. Then, instead of throwing the card away, she tucked it between two books on the shelf above her bed.

V

The Herb Garden

As Marlstroy had predicted, Dushma's interview with Mrs Perrets-Cheevy did not go as badly as she had feared. She and Moth were told at length about the irresponsible nature of their escapade, and then made to stay in every lunchtime and break until they had copied out the text of the lecture they had missed.

This proved to be more onerous than it sounded. The visiting company director had managed to say a great deal in his allotted hour. It wasn't until two days later that they were able to meet in the privacy of Moth's hidden corner of the locker room.

"Wasn't it dreary?" said Dushma, cradling her aching wrist. "You said it would be."

Moth considered this. "I couldn't really say," she admitted at last. "I can't remember a word of it."

"Listen, I'm sorry, about what happened. . . It was my fault, persuading you to come. You said we'd get caught."

"Oh, that's all right. If I'd had to go to that talk I'd've probably gone mad and run out screaming and got in even worse trouble. Anyway, it was fun. Worth missing a couple of lunchtimes for." She began to giggle. "Those people in those funny suits. . .!"

"Weren't they ridiculous? Hey – we were on TV. D'you think anyone's got a recording of it?"

"And did you see her car? All those leaflets on it!"

"She got a parking ticket!"

"It was for her own good." Moth frowned severely, in imitation of Mrs Wilson.

"What about that juggler?" Dushma asked casually. "He wasn't bad, was he?" She felt too shy to mention the card he had put into her coat pocket, but she wanted to know if he had done the same thing to Moth.

"Oh yes," said Moth knowingly. "You two did rather hit it off, didn't you?"

"Oh go on! He talked much more to you than he did to me."

"Ah, but he kept *looking* at you, didn't you notice?"

"No he didn't! . . . Did he?"

"Anyway, I've decided, I'm going to take up juggling."

"You could call yourself . . . The Astonishing Moth."

"Hmm. I think I've got a long way to go before I'm ready to astonish anybody. I've been practising with rolled-up socks but it's harder than it looks. I broke a glass last night. Perhaps we should try and persuade the school to offer it. As an extra-mural activity."

"A what?"

"It means 'off the wall'. It's all those weird things like abseiling and Eton fives that you can do after hours."

"Really? So you think they'd let us?"

"Well, you never know. They might. You could be my glamorous assistant—"

"Why *thank* you. . ."

"—and I could saw you in half at the Christmas concert. I found this book that tells you how to do it. You just need the right apparatus."

"Like, a saw, for instance?"

"And a special kind of box. It's got a hollow compartment underneath with someone else inside it. So they stick their legs out and the other person curls up with just their head showing."

"So actually you'd need two assistants. Could I wear sequins?"

"If you liked. Nothing too tacky though."

"Escapology. Like Houdini. We could tie ourselves up in chains and padlocks and then wriggle free in the nick of time."

They fell silent. Even with her limited experience of Larchmuir, Dushma could imagine that the chances of the school encouraging such activities were slim.

"Was that your guardian?" asked Moth. "That man with grey hair who answered the door? He looked really fierce. Mrs Wilson said he'd said you were going to be spending the night in the cellar."

"Well I didn't. I think he was just saying that to wind her up."

"Ugh. That would be horrible. Imagine it. All damp and full of scuttling things." Moth was sitting on the floor with her back to an old filing cabinet. She drew up her legs, hugged her knees and allowed herself a shudder of comfortably vicarious distaste. She leaned her head against the smooth metal behind her, then sat upright again with an exclamation of surprise.

"Oh. . . There it is again. Look. Feel that." She laid the palm of one hand lightly on the side of the filing cabinet.

Dushma reached out obligingly. "What? I can't feel anything."

"It's like a humming or a rumbling feeling," Moth explained. "I've felt it before. It's very faint." She looked a little smug, and added, "My other senses compensate, you see."

"It must be a train. Or a lorry in the distance, or something."

"No, I know what *those* feel like. This is different. This is something new. It hasn't been happening for very long. It's hard to describe. It's like the ground's hungry, you know what I mean? Or like when you lie on your hand in the night and get pins and needles and wake up with your fingers tingling."

Dushma looked searchingly at Moth but she seemed perfectly serious. Perhaps she wasn't well. "Have you told anybody else?"

"Well, yes." Moth sighed. "I did foolishly mention it to my dear mother a few weeks ago."

"And what did she say?"

"She said, 'Darling, you'll be changing a lot over the next few years, but whatever happens just remember, it's perfectly natural.' And then she started leaving back issues of *Cosmo* lying around all over the place. Honestly! 'Mother,' I should've said to her, 'mother, hello? Where have you been for the last quarter of my life? And what kind of change did *you* go through that made it seem perfectly natural to feel the ground buzzing underneath your feet?'"

"She doesn't sound very helpful."

"I suppose it's probably just as well. If she'd actually cared about anything I did I'd've probably rebelled in a totally major way. Gone completely wild. Tattoos, body-piercing, hair dye, the lot. As it is, I just know there wouldn't be any point. She simply wouldn't notice." She sighed again. "Isn't it wonderful, the variety of ways in which young people of today can express themselves?"

Dushma remembered her home in the arch of the viaduct, and the way the air in her room beneath the railway line had sizzled with electricity whenever a train passed overhead. She thought of her difficulties with light switches, irons and other electrical appliances. It hadn't really been that long ago, but already the recollections were losing their vividness. She tried to think of some way to share them with Moth without contradicting the alternative history she had constructed for herself.

"You could try mentioning it to someone else," she suggested. "Even if they don't know exactly what it is they still might be able to help." She touched the front of her blouse, feeling the heavy lozenge of Marlstroy's locket through the cotton. It had been one of the first things he had done for her, and she was now so used to it she hardly noticed it was there. It had been a relief to be able to approach a television without seeing the picture dissolve into scrolling zigzags, and to know that she could now switch on a light without the risk of tripping a fuse or shattering the bulb. Even Marlstroy denied knowing exactly why the locket worked, but this did little to diminish Dushma's faith in modern medicine.

"Go on," she urged Moth. "They can do all sorts of things these days. And anyway, it mightn't even be anything to worry about. It could just be that you're tired, d'you think?"

"Don't you start. It isn't 'cos of anything wrong with *me*. Look." She gestured sarcastically at her peaky appearance. "Isn't it obvious I'm positively bursting with energy and vitamins? And I grow things, too. How wholesome is that?"

She scrambled to her feet and reached up to the high window-sill. A handful of straggling plants grew in pots in the greeny-gold sunlight filtering down into the locker room. Taking one down, Moth flourished it proudly under Dushma's nose.

"Go on, smell that. It'll invigorate you."

Dushma inhaled. The plant was little more than a

spindly shoot sprouting from a few square centimetres of crumbly soil, and she could smell nothing but dust and mould. "I'm not sure I can. . ."

"Oh, you must be able to. Go on, rub a leaf. It's all right. I know it looks a bit weedy, but it's guaranteed free of all pesticides, colourings, artificial preservatives and genetic modification."

Dushma pinched a leaf between finger and thumb. As she stroked the ribbed, papery frond the bell rang to mark the end of the lunch break.

"Yes," she said, "you're right, that's nice."

The aroma had brought back a sudden mental image of another subterranean garden she had known, in the ticket hall of an abandoned Underground station she had lived in for a while. Though much more ambitious, it had also been lit by indirect sunlight channelled down through a small opening overhead.

She tried to say something light-hearted in order to dispel the unexpected and painful memory. "But you've got a long way to go before you're self-sufficient, though, haven't you?" And as they turned to make their way back out of the locker room, she added, "Don't know if it's going to keep me awake all afternoon, either."

Trudging up the stairs to their classroom, she could still smell the piercing green chewing-gum-and-toothpaste scent of mint on her fingers.

VI

Nicola

"Who was Nicola Auquin?" asked Dushma.

The question had been preying on her mind since the garden party some weeks previously. The name had been given to her casually, but the more she thought about it the more it seemed that it must belong to an important figure from Marlstroy's past. She'd heard it before, too: Marlstroy had mentioned it himself on the phone to his friend Ashpool the first time she had met him, probably thinking she wouldn't hear, or wouldn't remember. Had Nicola been another ward of his, or perhaps – and the idea felt strange, as if by even entertaining it she was prying – a lover?

Discreetly, she had looked for signs around the house: a photograph on a wall or mantelpiece, or the name inside a book. But there was nothing. This in itself began to strike her as odd, as if these omissions must be deliberate. By the time she had plucked up the courage to ask, the identity of Nicola Auquin was something she half wanted, half feared to know.

"What? Who's been talking to you about her?" demanded Marlstroy, looking up sharply.

"I don't know. Someone at your garden party. I didn't know his name. Naval yarns were his line, he said."

Marlstroy grunted. "That's Fordyke. Just like him to try and stir up trouble. I don't know, I must be just about the only person who hasn't cut him dead since that betting scandal he got involved with. I still invite him to my house, I even still buy his books, and he goes round slandering me behind my back. What did he say?"

"Nothing. Just mentioned her, that's all."

Marlstroy sat back in his chair and thoughtfully pressed his fingertips together. "Well, I suppose you're going to hear about her eventually, so you may as well get the truth from me rather than hear some lurid fiction from someone out to damage my reputation. Nicola Auquin was a patient of mine. This was some time ago now, but I should say before I go on that the details of this are still confidential, do you understand?" He looked at her intently over the top of his half-moon spectacles.

Dushma nodded.

"Well then. She was a patient of mine, as I say. She'd been a doctor herself. A very good one. Outstanding, in fact. Even though she was still young, she could have been making a fortune in consulting. But she'd chosen not to. When her houseman's year in hospital came to an end, she stayed on in casualty. It's thankless work, gruelling hours, inadequate facilities and the worst kinds of injuries to deal with. Many people get out of it as soon as they can, but it was where she felt she could do most good. She even found time to do unpaid community work, helping people who otherwise would have no access to medical care: down-and-outs, the unregistered.

"I don't know what would have happened to her if she'd gone on like that. Perhaps she'd have burned herself out, had a breakdown of some kind. But instead she was involved in a car crash, a bad one. Head injuries. She was in intensive care for weeks. Then there were the months of physiotherapy, having to re-learn simple things virtually from scratch, regaining control of her feet, her hands and her speech. It took time, but she was determined and she made good progress. There was one thing, though, that was impossible to repair, and that was the damage to her memory. Whole areas of her life were now just a blank. She remembered her medical training, how to read and write, the French she'd learned at school. But there were places she'd been to and things she'd done that she couldn't recall, and people she'd known for years who she simply didn't recognize any more.

"Although she never recovered those gaps in her past, she did eventually get better in other respects. Nothing to do with me. It was only afterwards I got involved, when the case began to show certain . . . interesting peculiarities. The brain is an astonishing thing. You lose an arm, then that's it. You'll never grow another one. But if parts of the brain are damaged, then somehow other parts can learn to take over their functionality. What happened, it seems, was that in Nicola's case this recovery mechanism overcompensated. Her memory became phenomenal. She stopped being able to forget.

"Soon her head was full of trivia. Telephone numbers, car number plates, newspaper articles, lists of ingredients from things she bought at the supermarket, the daily barrage of information that just slips out of our minds as soon as we don't need it any more. It happened gradually at first, but by the time I began seeing her, everything she read or saw or heard was being stored away in perfect detail in her new, improved memory.

"I was fascinated. I'd never seen anything like it and nor had anyone else, as far as I could gather. There have been other cases of photographic memory, certainly, but people tend to be born with it, or to develop an innate skill through practice. But there was no one else who had acquired it as the result of an accident. Nicola Auquin was unique to the literature. What had happened? I took scans, ran tests, did everything I could think of to try and work out why what was going on in her head was so different from what happened in everybody else's.

"Although it sounds like an extraordinarily useful ability, she found it wasn't a benefit for long. As her memories accumulated, she stopped being able to control them. She described it to me once as being like having countless television channels playing in her head, but with someone else in charge of the remote control, flicking randomly from one station to another. She had returned to work but began to find she couldn't concentrate. Her memories were becoming so vivid they distracted her. Worse, sometimes her recollections would be so realistic that she'd be unable to distinguish her memories from what was actually going on at the time. She struggled on, but she began to make mistakes. She might prescribe an unsuitable dose of medication because the situation of the patient she was currently treating was driven out of her mind by facts relating to someone she'd seen days previously.

"She had to leave her job. It was a blow to her, it had been her life. But she couldn't forget about it. Worse, her memories of events at the hospital didn't fade with time but stayed as fresh as they'd seemed when she first experienced them. She remembered every patient she'd seen since returning to work. Pensioners blue with hypothermia, car-drivers with their faces mashed by shattered windscreens, battered wives so bruised it looked like someone had thrown ink in their eyes, mugging victims with a knife in their guts or their heads caved in. And all the accidents, domestic and industrial. There was machinery that ran amok, drills that slipped, deep-fat fryers that overturned, appliances that fused, and the parents she had to tell that their little boy who'd impaled himself on railings wasn't coming home.

"She'd seen all those things. So had I, when I did my year in casualty. So does everybody. We all know why you shouldn't run with a knife in your hand, or keep bleach in lemonade bottles. We've had to deal with the consequences. The only way you survive is by blanking it out. You see it, but at the same time you don't. Then as soon as it's over you push it out of your head and move on to the next one. But she couldn't do that any more. Everything she saw stayed as vivid in her mind as if it was still there in front of her.

"I prescribed sedatives, advised her to do as little as possible, to rest, to sleep or just to stare out of the window. I thought this would help stop yet more memories building up. She said she felt ready to burst with colours and words and faces all thrusting themselves into her mind's eye one after another, clamouring for her attention. But doing nothing made it harder for her to distract herself from the scenes inside her head. And every random switch of channels might confront her not with a banal recollection of day-to-day activity, but with an image of some horrific mutilation so real that the only way she could be sure it wasn't there was to force herself to reach out to try and touch it.

"She was tormented. She started begging me to do something. She wanted powerful drugs, or an operation. She knew either course of action would damage her, and possibly destroy her mind. She didn't care.

"I . . . hesitated. I felt that by that stage there was more at stake than her own health and sanity. When might such a chance come again, not to me necessarily, but to anyone, to study such an extreme example of what the human brain is capable of? Do you think I was self-serving and callous? Then think about what she was asking me to do. To wilfully harm another person, for whatever reason, isn't an action to be taken lightly. Well, obviously, but. . . Particularly when that person is someone one has come to . . . to admire, for their fortitude, to feel, well, responsible for, perhaps even close to. . ."

For the first time since he had begun his story, Marlstroy's fluent delivery faltered. He paused, removed his spectacles and pinched the bridge of his nose. "There was another factor too. Ashpool was at the Ministry of Defence at the time, and I'd mentioned the case to him in passing. He'd immediately seen the possibilities. He thought at first of spies with perfect recall of everything they saw. Then he realized the wider implications for the good of society: imagine the benefits to learning, to progress, to quality of life as a whole, of being able to improve the memory of anyone who wanted it. Not of course to a pathological degree, as had happened to Nicola, but in a controlled manner, perhaps through drugs or electrical implants. Imagine, say, being able to save or delete your memories like you do files on a computer. A far-fetched goal, I know, but I felt that if we could understand what was wrong with Nicola we might be at least a little way along the road to achieving it. And Ashpool had the vision to see it too. He arranged for some funding to come my way, discreetly of course, so I could spend more time on the case.

"So as I say, for whatever mix of reasons, good and bad, I hesitated to agree to Nicola's demands for more radical and possibly devastating treatment. I felt I was on the brink of knowing more. I needed just a little time, a few more results. And I believed that the potential for the greater good outweighed the risks to the well-being of just one person.

"She'd been hospitalized by now. Her memories had grown so numerous and insistent that for long periods of time she found it difficult to be sure exactly where she was or what she was doing. But she was strong-willed, and a fighter. I thought she could still cope. She could still be rational, even make jokes sometimes. She wanted me to wear something different every time I visited her, so that she wouldn't get confused with a previous occasion. I bought some horrible ties. . . And smell, you know, is a powerful associative. I had a cupboardful of aftershaves I'd used just the once. She used to like roses, there'd always be some by her bed. . . It's funny, even now, every time I smell them I remember. . ." Marlstroy had risen to his feet and begun pacing the room, lost in his narrative. Now he paused, a faraway look in his eyes, his spectacles still in one hand. Then he shook his head abruptly.

"I was wrong. I spent all that time looking at pictures of her brain but I failed to fathom her state of mind. Nicola Auquin killed herself. She threw herself under a car." He stopped and then forced himself to go on. "My car. She left the ward while I was seeing other patients. She waited on the main road outside the hospital. It was dark and raining, I didn't see her till too late. There was nothing I could do.

"Perhaps it wasn't suicide. Perhaps she'd just become overwhelmed by her memories and lost all notion of what was going on. Or perhaps she did know, but it was just a coincidence she chose the car I happened to be driving.

"Her family took legal action. They blamed me for not giving her the stronger treatment she'd wanted. I told them I was a neurologist, not a psychiatrist. I asked if they'd really have been prepared to see their daughter reduced to a mindless husk just to remove the unquantifiable possibility of her harming herself. But it seemed that wasn't the kind of decision that should be left to experts such as myself. It could have been the end of my career. I've Ashpool to thank that it wasn't. He couldn't intervene directly, but he arranged for certain records relating to my work to be classified under the Official Secrets Act. The case against me collapsed through lack of evidence. I emerged without a stain on my character."

He pushed his spectacles back on and began to take instruments out of cupboards and drawers, ranging them before him on his desk.

"I was guilty of nothing. Anything else you hear is insinuation, slander, gossip and lies. It was a tragedy, of course it was. That doesn't mean there had to be someone to blame. It was an extreme situation, a unique one. I was mistaken, I admit, but the right course of action was only obvious with hindsight. We may never know what it was that was wrong with her and how we might have cured her. My findings were incomplete. I was only able to publish one rather inconclusive paper on the subject, but perhaps later generations will be able to examine my results and reach a diagnosis."

He paused for a moment, then shrugged and spread his hands. "So. There you are." His voice was brisk. "I hope that answers your question."

"But what did she look like?" Dushma asked. "Was she beautiful?"

Marlstroy turned towards her and his face was set like a mask. "I really can't remember," he said in an offhand tone. "She was small, I think. And she fidgeted a lot."

There was a long silence. Dushma wanted to know more but wasn't sure what to ask. It was the first time, she realized, that Marlstroy had told her more than bland anecdotes about himself.

"I'm sorry, about what happened," she said carefully. "I think she sounds nice. I didn't know, when I wasn't registered, that there were people who might be willing to help me if I got ill."

Marlstroy busied himself with preparing his equipment. His story finished, he was clearly unwilling to discuss the subject further.

"There probably weren't," he said. "This was years ago. Are you ready?"

Dushma reached behind her head, lifted her hair from the nape of her neck and unclipped the chain that held her locket. Leaning forward, she dropped it in a heap on the corner of the desk.

Marlstroy had positioned an oscilloscope in front of him and now he turned it on. Green lines wriggled across the screen.

He pulled a pair of surgical gloves from a box and snapped them on to his hands. Then he began to unravel a pair of wires that came out of the back of the oscilloscope. On the end of each was a flat, flexible pad the size of a large coin.

Peeling the shiny paper circles from the sticky faces of the pads, he reached out and pressed them against Dushma's temples.

"Now close your eyes and try and empty your mind," he instructed her.

VII

Clinker Monkey

Dushma twisted and muttered in her sleep. In her dream, sunlight was flooding the streets. It poured between the houses and shops like a glowing river of treacle, rolling slowly over the cars and people in its path, engulfing them in billows of radiance.

Standing in the middle of a road she didn't recognize, Dushma found herself directly in front of the advancing tide of light. She could see, gently tumbling in its bright golden depths, the tiny splayed figures of those already swallowed.

With the strange simultaneity of dreams, she also witnessed the dawn from another vantage point high above the city. She saw the sun perched on the horizon, shuddering with heat like the mouth of a furnace. From it streamed rivers of liquid light, filling the dark grid of streets like molten metal trickling slowly into an elaborate mould.

Down on the road she turned to run but the light was already at her heels. She felt its warmth on her calves and its viscous tug at her ankles, slowing her down. People around her were screaming.

She woke, the duvet tangled round her legs and a ray of early morning sunlight shining in her eyes through a gap in the curtain. For a few disoriented seconds she thrashed her feet to free them from the bedclothes. She had half fallen, half leapt out of bed, ready for flight, before she realized where she was. Clutching at the dressing table to steady herself, she sat back on the edge of her mattress and breathed deeply to calm her racing pulse.

A sound sleeper, she did not normally dream so vividly. She found it difficult to shake off a feeling of being trapped. She stared round her room at the familiar objects it contained – her school uniform slung over a chair, a pile of books on the desk – reassuring herself with their presence.

Once her panic had subsided she walked over to the window, flapping her nightdress around her body to let the cool morning air dry the rivulets of sweat sliding down her back. Pulling the curtains properly apart, she looked out into the garden. The sun was just up, the sky was cloudless and a light mist was dispersing from the garden.

She turned back to her rumpled bed. She was now fully awake and did not think she would be able to go back to sleep again. The morning had looked crisp and inviting. She glanced at her watch; it was some time before she would have to think about getting ready for school. Impulsively, she threw some clothes on over her nightdress, left her bedroom and glided silently down the stairs.

The key was in the lock of the back door. It turned easily and she let herself out on to the patio.

The morning felt as pleasant as the view from her bedroom window had promised. The air, cool and damp with evaporating dew, seemed freshly washed. At the bottom of the garden, moisture glistened on the angular limbs of the firetrees, giving them a velvety texture. From somewhere came the sound of a cooing pigeon like a breathy organ note.

She was about to make her way down one of the winding gravel paths between the flower beds when a noise brought her abruptly to a halt. It was the sound of screaming she had heard in her dream.

Sweat broke out on her scalp like icy fingers touching her head. She spun round, her heel scrunching in the gravel. There it was again. It was coming from round the side of the house. Closer to, it sounded more like a wail than a scream, an undulating whine like a child in pain.

She resisted the urge to hurl herself back inside, lock the door and run upstairs to her room. That would do no good. She would still be able to hear it.

She crept to the iron gate in the side wall of the garden and, before she could change her mind, pulled it open. Ready to dart back again and slam the gate in the face of whatever might be beyond it, she stepped out into the long narrow drive that ran the length of the house and garden, separating it from its neighbour.

Halfway along this drive was the low wooden shed

where the rubbish bins and recycling bags and boxes were kept ready for collection. The front of the shed was normally closed off by a latched gate, but this morning it stood half open. A black plastic bag had spilled out into the driveway and a small group of animals were raking through its contents.

There were three of them, one of them larger than the other two. Sensing Dushma watching them, they swivelled their pointed snouts and sharp triangular ears in her direction. At first she thought they must be dogs. It was only when they turned and fled that she realized they were foxes.

She had never seen one in real life before, and they looked completely different to the pictures she remembered from television and in books. Foxes in pictures were bright orange with gleaming white bibs, but these had dirty, mud-brown fur that clung in matted tufts to their scrawny bodies. Their tails, as they whipped out of sight round the pillar at the end of the drive, were not the full, flowing brushes she would have expected, but looked more like straggling lengths of spiky rope.

They must have been more afraid of her than she had been of them, Dushma told herself. A little ashamed of her temerity, she walked along the drive to the shed, pushed the torn plastic bag back inside with her foot and closed the gate on it. Continuing to the end of the drive, she peered out into the road but saw no sign of the foxes.

She was about to return to the garden when she heard a scraping noise behind her. Turning to look down the driveway of the next-door neighbour's house, she saw that the gate of their dustbin shed had also come open.

Perhaps they had learned how to do it, she thought. Standing on each other's shoulders to lift the latch with their paws. Well *this* time she wasn't going to be frightened. She stepped boldly forward. "Shoo!" she exclaimed, although in an unsteadier, more high-pitched voice than she had intended.

A figure rose up from the other side of the half-open gate. She started backwards, throwing up her hands defensively. Then the figure smiled at her, deep-set blue eyes flashing, and she realized who it was.

"Hello," said the juggler she and Moth had met at the demonstration. "Nice morning, isn't it?"

Unsure if she was angry or pleased, Dushma leaned against the wall and searched her mind for something to say. She remembered the card he had given her. *The Astonishing . . . ARBILOW*, it had said. "OK," she conceded. "You win. *Now* I'm astonished."

He took this as a compliment. "All part of the service," he said, looking flattered.

Dushma saw that at his feet was a box of paper for recycling. He had obviously been leafing through it when she had disturbed him.

"Beaten you to it, have I?" he asked, following the direction of her gaze.

"What? No, of course not. *I* live here. Well, next door anyway."

194

He looked up at the old, ivy-strung brick walls rising up on either side of him. "I see. Very nice."

"And even if I didn't, what would I want to come rummaging through other people's recycling for?" As soon as she had spoken, she realized how haughty she must have sounded.

"It's all right for *you*. You don't know what it's like." He held up what looked like a thick pamphlet, or a floppy paperback book. "You've probably never even been in a public library in your life."

"That's not fair! How do you know that?"

"Well? Have you?"

"Actually, no," Dushma had to admit. "But. . ."

"There you are, see! I bet you've been able to have everything you've ever wanted to read. *If* you're interested in books at all, that is."

"Of course I am!" She resisted the urge to boast about the access she enjoyed to Marlstroy's extensive collection. "What did you find?" she asked instead. "Is it something good?"

"Poetry. Someone's torn the covers off, but it's in good nick apart from that." The pages purred as he drew his thumb rapidly over the closed edge of the book. "What, not your thing?" He smiled at her and she saw his jagged front tooth.

"I don't know much poetry. It's all about flowers and feelings, isn't it? I'm more into stories."

"You can have stories in poetry." He tucked the

mutilated book away inside his coat. "Tell you what. . . Why don't you come for breakfast? There's a place I know just down the road. They do great pastries."

Dushma hesitated.

"Go on, my shout," he offered. "You're not going back to bed, are you?"

"I don't know. I'm not sure if I should come for breakfast. . . I mean, I don't know if it's a good idea. . ." And besides, she remembered, she still had her nightdress on under her clothes.

He pretended to misunderstand her. "Breakfast? Not a good idea? How can you say that? I think it's a very good idea. Especially at this time of day. Tell you what: come and have breakfast with me, and I'll tell you what a clinker monkey is. How about that?"

Still Dushma hesitated. "Well . . . how long will it take? Is it interesting?"

He laughed. "Oh, she's a hard girl to please! She wants breakfast, she wants entertaining. . ."

"Go on, breakfast was your. . ."

"But yes, it's interesting all right. You might find it a little bit shocking. Some of it's maybe not suitable for rich and sheltered young ladies. It's about death, and treasure. It's not poetry, but it's worth hearing if you think things like that are interesting."

"*Un espresso, un cappuccino, e. . .*" he pointed at the pastries on plates inside the curved glass cabinet, "*questo, e questo.*"

"You speak Italian?" asked Dushma.

"Some," he said, shrugging modestly. He basked briefly in her impressed reaction, then admitted, "And you just heard it all."

They sat on stools beside a high marble counter at the front of the café. They could look out through the reversed gold lettering on the window into the sunlit street beyond.

Arbilow held his small, thick-sided cup between finger and thumb and swirled what looked like a few thimblefuls of black sludge around the bottom of it. Then he threw back his head and drained it with one swallow.

Dushma bit into her pastry. Inside the flaky exterior was a sweet, sticky paste of coarsely ground almonds.

"They're not bad, are they?" said Arbilow. "Bet you've had the real thing though. You know, on holiday in Tuscany?"

"Mmm," she said noncommittally. If he wanted to think she was sophisticated, she decided she wasn't going to mind. She raised her own coffee cup, feeling the hot liquid touch her lip through the sweet froth. "Go on then. You said you'd tell me what a clinker monkey is."

"Well. . . Are you sure you want to know?"

"Come on, try me. I'm feeling strong this morning. But be careful –" Dushma clutched her temples – "rich, sheltered young ladies like me are very highly strung. Especially if there's blood or sharp implements involved. Be ready to catch me if I faint, OK?"

"I'll have to come closer then. . ." He shuffled his stool

nearer to hers. "Right. You know those factory chimneys they have? The tall brick ones, round ones mostly. Hundreds of years old, some of them, but they've been modernized a lot inside. They've had to be, for environmental and efficiency reasons. They've got all kinds of filters and electrostatic gadgets to get rid of the particles of pollution before they reach the atmosphere. The trouble is, eventually these things clog up, the chimneys stop working, and someone has to go and clean them out."

"What, you go up the chimneys?" She stared at him. For a moment she thought he must be teasing her.

"Well, down, not up, but basically yes." He was trying to look sombre but she could tell he was pleased with the effect his words were having. "There. I thought you'd be shocked. Bet you thought that kind of thing went out with the Victorians."

"But . . . is that the only way? Can't they make machines to do it?"

"Yes, of course they've got machines. They look like big metal spiders. I've seen one. They've got hooks on their legs, and drills and chisels for loosening the clinker. Trouble is, they're incredibly expensive. To buy, and then to maintain as well. Companies that used them found they couldn't compete. The odd dead clinker monkey's far cheaper than a broken robot. Quite often they can't find any next of kin so they get away without paying a penny in compensation. These firms, you see, they're not fussy who they take. You don't need any training and they don't ask many questions before they sign you up. Which was fine by me. I wasn't old enough for something more legitimate. But I soon found out why they had to cut corners to get their labour.

"You work in teams. The size depends on how big the chimney is, but usually there's about six of you. You've got protective clothing, a face mask and gloves, and a helmet like a miner's with a lamp on the front. If you're lucky it's actually working. Sometimes they give you a power drill, other times it's a hammer and chisel or a canister of solvent. Then they strap you into a harness and lower you down the chimney.

"Inside, the brickwork's all caked with stuff: there's this crust of solidified chemicals that needs to be dissolved or chipped away. Sometimes it's still hot because they didn't shut the factory down long enough ago. Sometimes it's still *glowing*. But every day the chimney's not working costs the factory owner a fortune. So they always want the job to start as soon as possible, and there's a bonus for finishing early. They make you work fast. There's an overseer at the top of the chimney, paying out the rope on your harness as fast as you can chip the clinker. The most important thing is to make sure you don't end up underneath someone else. The stuff comes off in big enough chunks to finish you off if it hits you."

"That sounds horrible. Did people get hurt?"

"Oh yes. One person died in the first chimney I worked on. And in the one after that the guy in the harness next to mine broke his spine."

"My God!" Dushma was wide-eyed. "It sounds suicidal. Why did you keep doing it?"

"I didn't think there was anything else I could do. And I got good at it, after a while. I've got strong fingers, and I'm dextrous. I could change a broken drill-bit with one hand." He gestured as he spoke, sketching the motions in the air. "There's something satisfying about hanging there, hacking away at a sheet of clinker, working at it for hours, feeling it begin to crumble under your chisel, then finally watching it collapse with a roar into the darkness beneath your feet. And there were other reasons too. We were a close-knit group, proud of what we did, in a funny way. I mean, we knew nobody would envy us, but we knew our job was difficult, and not many people could do it. And there were stories, too. Legends, I suppose, about the things that people had found.

"The conditions in those chimneys are pretty extreme. They were bad enough even when they weren't being used. But depending on what processes were going on in the factory, you'd get whole labfuls of stuff pouring up inside them, especially below the level of the filters. Acid mists, clouds of carbon, vaporized metal condensing inside the chimney and streaming down the brickwork . . . it's not impossible that in circumstances like that you might get some unpredictable reactions taking place. Up close the clinker could look like the crust of some alien planet, riddled with craters, charred black like volcanic debris, gleaming with minerals in the light of your lamp. There was one person I worked with who swore that a friend of his had gone home one night with his pockets full of clinker, dissolved it in bleach in his bathtub and been left with two fistfuls of gold. There were others who said that was nothing: the heat in a chimney could cook coal dust into diamonds, they said. People they knew had seen precious stones twinkling in the clinker, chipped them free and become rich beyond imagination.

"It sounds unlikely, I know, sitting here telling it now. Perhaps they were just rumours, spread by the people who ran the company. But in extreme situations things like that can keep you going. And I don't think any of us ever stopped hoping, looking for that sparkle in the lamplight, the sign that something precious beyond measure was embedded there. I know I didn't. And that's what nearly did for me in the end.

"We were working on a chimney in Battersea. It was a funny place, that factory. Set in acres of waste ground, high barbed-wire fences everywhere, no signs outside, soldiers on the gate. And the chimney was a mess. They'd left it far too long, but they wanted it done by some ridiculous deadline. They'd offered a huge bonus, though, so we were working virtually round the clock. It was dangerous, too, and not just because we got so tired. The clinker was solid as concrete, really difficult to shift. And they must have been using a lot of sand for something. When it gets hot enough sand turns to glass, and the inside of the chimney was coated in the stuff. Lots of it had shattered and there were splinters everywhere, ragged edges like those broken bottles you see on top of walls to keep burglars out. You had to be careful they didn't slice your hands and knees, or worse, the rope that was holding you up. We always said we should have metal hawsers, especially on a job like that. But the company was too mean to pay for them, and made us work with the same old nylon climbing ropes we always used.

"In spite of all this we got on pretty well. We'd most of us worked together before, we got a good rhythm going. By the time we were halfway down the chimney we were just ahead of schedule. This was where the clinker was thickest. I was using a crowbar, levering these great chunks of it off the wall, prising them off like giant, filthy scabs, hearing them go crashing down to the bottom of the chimney way below me. And then I saw it. It was smoother than the bits of glass around it, and darker, almost black, but with a multi-coloured sheen like oil when it caught the light. It was just out of reach but I had to get a closer look. I went across towards it. I pulled one glove off, reached out and got my hand on it. It felt extraordinary. Part of it was icy cold, but the rest was warm, hot even. It felt smooth and slippery in my fingers; it almost seemed to be moving, flowing under my touch. It was hard to get a firm grip so I tried to get nearer, pushing myself along the wall with my feet. But I'd forgotten to be careful with the rope. It must've been rubbing over a ridge of glass further up the chimney. It snapped.

"I fell a couple of metres before I hit an outcrop of clinker and managed to hold on. It was embedded with glass, cutting into my hand. I could feel the blood trickling down my arms. I thought the others might just leave me. My helmet had come off so they couldn't see where I was. I was shouting but the echo in the chimney meant it was impossible to tell where the sound was coming from.

"It felt like I was hanging there for hours, just waiting to drop. I think they only came to get me because they were worried they wouldn't finish the job in time otherwise. But when they got me back up to the platform at the top of the chimney I was a wreck. I could hardly bend my arms. One hand was in shreds where I'd taken my glove off. They wanted to bandage it up and send me straight back down but I couldn't do it. Just the thought of climbing into that chimney again had me shivering so much I couldn't hold a rope. The foreman was furious. So were the others when they started thinking they might not get their bonus.

"There was one guy stuck up for me. He could see I wasn't going to be any use even if I did go back down. Said he'd report them if they made me. Well, I didn't want that, for . . . various reasons, but I didn't want to break my neck either. For a while it looked like it was going to get nasty. Then the foreman ran out of patience and just sacked me on the spot.

"It took me twenty minutes to climb down the ladder from the platform to the ground. I had to keep resting, just holding on with my eyes closed until I stopped shaking enough to carry on."

He reached out across the table and unfolded his hand. A fine white mesh of scars criss-crossed his palm. "From the glass," he explained. "Nearly lost a finger. Still can't stand confined spaces. I get flashbacks, thinking I'm still in the chimney."

Dushma grimaced into her cup. The dregs of her coffee were almost cold. "So what did you do after that?"

"That was how I got to know Marcus. You know Marcus Torrelguard? You must've seen him, he's always campaigning for something."

The name was familiar. Dushma recalled a face from news broadcasts: a middle-aged man with a thick moustache and sagging cheeks under tired-looking eyes.

"Yes, I've heard of him."

"Well, at the time he was trying to get better regulation for industry, clean up outfits like the one I used to work for. I was trying to get the money I was still owed. He heard about it, and wanted to know as much as I could tell him. And in return he helped me: found someone who'd patch my hand up properly; got me some work with a couple of organizations he's involved with; lent me some books. . . I was pretty lucky. He's really not the dangerous subversive he's sometimes made out to be, you know."

He shot a quick glance at Dushma, as if to see how she was reacting. She nodded sympathetically. "Is that why you were on that march? He's pretty into the environment, isn't he?" She remembered snatches of an interview with Torrelguard she'd seen recently, but not paid much attention to at the time.

"Yes. He was one of the people behind it. He's always been dead set against any drilling on Mythgate Sands. They've tried to build a rig there before but there's always been too much opposition. It's a crazy idea. It's virtually at the mouth of the Thames. The only reason they think they'll be able to get away with it now is because of this so-called energy crisis."

"But they have, haven't they? Got away with it, I mean. It's almost done, isn't it?" Dushma remembered Marlstroy mentioning the matter several times, most recently over his newspaper at the breakfast table just a few days ago. He had seemed to be in favour, but she couldn't remember why. Probably because his friend Ashpool was involved, she thought.

"Ah, don't bet on it." For a moment Arbilow looked infuriatingly knowing. "Marcus has still got a trick up his sleeve."

"Oh yes? How do you know?"

"Well. . ." He hesitated, toying with his empty coffee cup. "Have you heard of somewhere called the Factory?" He looked proud but at the same time uneasy, as if he was telling her too much.

She shook her head.

"Oh. Are you sure? Well, anyway, I live there. Marcus set it up and helps run it. It's not a factory any more. I suppose it's a sort of community, you could call it. We're just about self-sufficient now. There's a moat, and a garden on the roof. Trees and all sorts. You'd recognize it when you saw it, I'm sure. You know the canal near here? It's not far from there. Don't know if it's your kind of place."

"No? How do you know what my kind of place is?"

"All right then, what *is* your kind of place?"

"Wait a minute." She wasn't going to be so easily distracted. "You were going to say something about the rig, something. . ."

"No, no, it was nothing, honestly. Shouldn't've mentioned it. Come on, your turn to tell me something."

He leaned his elbow on the table, supporting his head on one hand and looking at her intently, pale eyebrows arching above his piercing blue eyes. His sudden interest was unexpectedly flattering. "Well. . ." She found herself thinking of high buildings: the viaduct, the cathedral spire. How much should she tell him?

Hesitating, she glanced down at her watch. It was later than she had thought. She rose hurriedly to her feet. "Look, I'm sorry, I can't. I've got to go."

Walking back with him, she hoped she hadn't seemed rude. He had taken her for breakfast, after all. When they reached the end of her road she lingered at the junction, unwilling to say goodbye.

"Thank you for breakfast," she said.

"That's OK. And I kept my promise, didn't I?"

"Yes. That was an interesting story. Thanks."

"And you didn't faint."

"No. I must be made of sterner stuff than I thought." She cast a quick glance sideways at him. "I'm sorry. I hope you weren't wanting a more spectacular reaction."

She saw the flash of his crooked grin. "Well, I'll just have to think of some other way to get one, won't I?"

"If you like." She remembered something she had been going to ask him. "Oh, that message you wrote – how did you know my name?"

"Ah." He looked mysterious. "I held your hand, remember? That's enough. Just holding someone's hand, perhaps even just touching them, that's all I need to do to know their name."

"Oh, go on. . ." She laughed.

"No, it's true." He seemed quite serious. "I know your size, where you shop. . ."

For a moment she was unnerved by him. Then his intense expression melted into one of amusement. He reached behind her head and flicked at her collar with his forefinger. "Your label's sticking out, Dushma," he said.

VIII
The Girl at the Galen

Despite her growing friendship with Moth, Dushma continued to find attending Larchmuir College for Girls an onerous experience. Every lesson seemed to promise nothing but equal measures of boredom and humiliation.

At the end of a perfectly dreadful day exactly a month after she had started, she felt she now actually knew less than she had done before setting foot inside the school gates. Her form had been given a series of tests and she had come bottom in every one except for chemistry. This was the only subject she was any good at. The other girls seemed to find the equations difficult, but to Dushma it made perfect sense that compounds could separate and recombine to become different things entirely. It was a process she felt she could relate to. Unfortunately, of all the subjects, chemistry was the one which carried least cachet among her peers. Her aptitude for it merely confirmed her lowly status in the eyes of some of her form-mates. Praline

Maisefield, in particular, had gone from ignoring her to tutting and shaking her head when she was in the vicinity.

She knew that at least one letter had already been sent to Marlstroy about her performance, but her guardian had seemed unconcerned. This time she was taken by Mrs Wilson to see the headmistress and have her shortcomings enumerated. She couldn't remember them all, although inattentiveness was one of them, and the list ended with the claim that she was unwilling to accept criticism.

"That's fair enough," she said reasonably, in response to this last accusation.

"*And* she's contrary!" added Mrs Wilson. (Had Dushma been asked to state her form-mistress's failings, lack of a sense of humour would have figured prominently.)

Even her guitar lesson that evening wasn't the usual enjoyable hour she had been looking forward to. Her teacher's favourite football team had suffered a humiliating defeat and he made her listen to *Purple Haze* three times in a row.

The first lesson the next day was supposed to be biology but Mrs Wilson had allowed the class to head her off into a discussion about pets. Praline had told an interminable and self-satisfied story about how her pedigree Siamese had stolen an entire chicken from the fridge and devoured it in the airing cupboard. Everyone giggled appreciatively. Before Mrs Wilson could resume teaching, Natalie launched into a story remarkably similar to Praline's, although told with her own infuriating mixture of archness and incoherence.

"That's nothing. We used to have a pet vulture," interrupted Dushma impulsively. "We did, he was called . . . he was called Hitchcock. And one day we came home and he'd eaten my grandmother. We weren't certain at first, there was nothing left but bones. But then we found some scraps of her dress under Hitchcock's perch."

"But weren't the police concerned?" asked Mrs Wilson sceptically, after a few moments' silence.

"Oh yes," said Dushma. Like a vertigo-sufferer about to step off a tall building, she felt unable to stop herself. "Very concerned. There was a big investigation. They were worried we hadn't been looking after him properly. But eventually they realized he was just greedy."

"*Behavioural* problems?" exclaimed Marlstroy. He was sitting at the breakfast table, a letter from Dushma's school in front of him. "It wasn't a terribly clever thing to say, but I think a therapist is going a little far."

"It was supposed to be biology, but everyone was going on and on about their cats," said Dushma defensively.

"Cats are biology."

"So are vultures. *I* wasn't to know Laureth's grandmother had just died. I said I was sorry. If I'd had *real* behavioural problems I'd probably just've laughed or something."

"Perhaps I could offer to take you into work instead," said Marlstroy thoughtfully. "They're big on that kind of thing, aren't they? Just for a day, or a morning even."

"Really? Can I?"

"On one of my rounds. Don't see why not. I'm sure if I phrased it right. . . 'Appreciation of the suffering of others. . . Social responsibility. . .'"

"Today? Can I wear a white coat?" asked Dushma eagerly. She was sure it would be more interesting than whatever was happening at school, even chemistry.

"No, no, not today. I'll have to speak to Mrs – what's her name? – Mrs Perrets-Cheevy first. Let me see. . ." He reached behind him into the inside pocket of the jacket slung over his chair. "Tomorrow I'm at the Royal Trent," he said, consulting a diary. "Then the Galen on Friday. . ."

"Will it be gory? I don't know if I'd like to see an operation."

"Oh no, just the ward. Nothing terribly exciting. Bound to be better than some shrink though. I don't want anyone else. . ."

"Ink blots," said Dushma. "I knew someone once who said they made her look at ink blots."

Marlstroy had opened another letter. It contained a short note which he scanned quickly and then threw down on to the table with a snort.

"Fordyke," he said. "Asking if Alex could come over again on Saturday. Apparently the lad's been acting strangely and he thinks you'd be a calming influence."

"I . . . I might be busy on Saturday," said Dushma hastily.

"Oh yes?" Marlstroy raised an eyebrow.

Dushma found herself blushing. "It's . . . well, just a friend. We might go out. That's all."

211

"I'll put Fordyke off then." Marlstroy rose to his feet and picked up his jacket. A thought struck him and he laughed briefly. "I know. Perhaps he won't be so keen when he hears you've got behavioural problems of your own."

That Friday Marlstroy drove Dushma across London to the Galen Infirmary. It was an old building of dark brick with heavy iron grilles over the ground-floor windows. At some point a modern ventilation system had been fitted, and silver pipes slanted across patches of crumbling wall like surgical callipers over burned skin.

They parked in a reserved space to one side of the hospital and walked round to the main entrance. Dushma wore a white coat of Marlstroy's which, although a little too long, was a reasonable fit with the sleeves turned up. She had a couple of biros in the top pocket and a badge with her name on it pinned to one lapel.

The Galen had no accident and emergency department and the courtyard outside the main entrance was almost devoid of traffic. Her white coat flapping round her legs, Dushma followed Marlstroy across the pot-holed tarmac, through a pair of creaking wooden doors and into an almost deserted foyer. Feeling rather pleased with how she looked, she began to wish there were more people around.

"Morning Tony," said Marlstroy to a squat old man in a blue shirt and tie standing by an empty trolley near the reception desk.

"Morning sir," said Tony. "What's this? Got yourself a

new recruit? Start 'em young, eh? It's not like on the telly, you know love." He threw himself back on his heels, his face convulsed with silent amusement.

"Oh no. Not yet anyway. She's not old enough. It's just for the day."

"Tell you what then. We'll 'ave 'er. Like a shot. We ain't fussed. Though you'd be an asset wherever you worked, I'm sure." He laid a finger along the side of his nose and cocked one eyebrow at Dushma. "So just let me know if you want some extra pocket money, eh? Just a bit of light lifting – we'd only give you the skinniest patients. And plenty of walking to keep you fit."

They went through more doors and up a wide flight of stairs, following the signs to the neurology department. The corridors they passed through reeked of polish and disinfectant. Beneath this smell, however, Dushma thought she could detect something else, a curious sweetness, as if cheap perfume had been sprayed liberally about in a not-quite successful attempt to mask an unpleasant odour.

They came to a ward. The walls were tiled to shoulder height in cracked cream ceramic. Above that the paint was smudged and peeling. To compensate for the fading decor, a collage of a sailing ship at sea had been hung just inside the door. The waves were made of blue and silver foil that glittered in the light from the tall, narrow windows. Flags of crêpe and tissue paper shivered in the breeze.

Seeing them enter, a nurse came hurrying over. "Oh Doctor, do you have a moment?" she asked as soon as she reached them. "It's Mr Ransome, yes it's bad I'm afraid. . . I don't know what to say to him, I. . ."

"I say! Are you in charge? I want a word with you." A man in pyjamas was walking briskly along the ward towards them.

The nurse smiled weakly at Marlstroy and began backing quickly away in the direction of her desk.

"I think there's been some mistake," announced the man in pyjamas. "There's absolutely nothing wrong with me. I'm fit as a fiddle. Never felt better. I've just done ten press-ups. Straight off like that, no problems. Ask that chap over there. I demand to be discharged immediately."

"Of course you can leave any time you like," said Marlstroy. "But please, may I ask you not to be hasty. There's something you should know."

"Rubbish. I'll discharge myself in that case. Where are my clothes? Who are you anyway?"

"My name's Marlstroy. You don't remember me?"

"Should I? Have we met?" The man in pyjamas looked puzzled as he grasped Marlstroy's outstretched hand.

"I'm afraid so, Mr Ransome. That's why you're here. I've been treating you for some time now. I'm afraid to say you've had an accident. Physically, you've made a complete recovery. But unfortunately, for reasons I don't yet understand – how else can I say this? – your short-term memory has become . . . erratic."

"But that's ridiculous! I can remember who I am, where I live, I can remember. . ." His voice trailed off. He stared around him, frowning. "Oh God. Wait a minute. It's . . . that's right, it's Wednesday. Yes, of course it is, I'm going to visit my parents for Easter. In fact, I have to go at once, they'll be expecting me. What are you looking at me like that for? It *is* Wednesday, isn't it?" He turned to Dushma for confirmation, panic in his face. Unable to meet his eye, she looked away.

"It's Friday, Mr Ransome," said Marlstroy gently. "It's October. I'm sorry."

Shaking his head, the man reached out towards a nearby drip-stand for support. His urge to leave had gone. He stared unseeingly into the distance, his forehead creased with effort. He offered no resistance when Marlstroy took him by the elbow and led him into a small room off to one side of the ward.

They were still in there when the students arrived. There were three of them, carrying clipboards and wearing white coats similar to Dushma's. They were in high spirits, pushing each other as they scuffed their way into the ward, whispering and chuckling amongst themselves.

"He's in there with Mr Ransome," Dushma explained.

The name was clearly familiar to them. Expressions of sympathy crossed their faces and they were quiet for a few moments. But they soon recovered their good humour and gathered round Dushma to tease her.

"I've been telling him for ages we needed someone to take our notes for us," said one of them, offering her his clipboard. "Here, you'll need this."

"How many words per minute can you do?" asked another. "And can you spell 'facio-maxillary'?"

"We're having a sweepstake," said the third. "Small outlay, big prizes. Profits to rag. It's kind of like bingo. You pick an anatomical term; then whoever's got the one that he says first, they're the winner."

"It's going to be me," said the second student. "I've picked 'bollocks' and I'm going to tell him something really stupid and see what he says."

"That's vulgarity, not anatomy. Besides, he'd never say that. He'd just look at you till you shrivelled. And you should watch your language."

"Why? She'll have to get used to a lot worse than that. This is no place for anyone with overdeveloped sensibilities. *Are* your sensibilities overdeveloped, do you think?"

"I. . ." began Dushma. To her relief the door opposite them swung open.

"A sedative," said Marlstroy, a brown bottle of pills in his hand. "He'll feel better after he's rested." He pulled the door quietly closed behind him. "You remember Mr Ransome? We saw him last time, making good progress. A relapse, I'm afraid." He turned to Dushma. "I hope these reprobates haven't been annoying you."

"Of course not," said one of the students. "Just, you know, been going through the details of the initiation ceremony."

They walked through into the main part of the ward.

"You remember I told you about Nicola?" Marlstroy

murmured to Dushma as they went. "Hers was the opposite affliction. Too much short-term memory. Maybe at the time you thought I'd treated her unfairly. But if I could have understood what it was that had happened to her, maybe I'd be better able to help that poor chap."

They moved from bed to bed. Marlstroy chatted with his patients, asking them how they were and swapping pleasantries with those he seemed to know best. Then he would discuss each invalid's condition with his students, pointing out particular aspects of the treatment he had prescribed.

Dushma could make no sense of the medical terms and abbreviations, and soon found her attention wandering. The porter in the foyer had been right. It wasn't like on television, where conversations like these always took place with everyone moving at high speed down a long corridor, accompanied by a beeping machine.

Mostly the students were quiet and attentive. They took notes and asked the occasional question. The only time one of them betrayed any excitement was when Marlstroy mentioned the risk of a pulmonary aneurysm. The student who had mentioned the sweepstake reared up suddenly on to his toes and gave a small yelp of excitement, which he quickly turned into a cough.

At last they came to a room at the far end of the ward. Marlstroy tried the handle but the door was locked. He waited while the nurse fetched the key.

"A new admission," he said, consulting his notes.

"Someone mentioned this. I haven't seen her yet. Can't think why they've sent her here. Oh. . ." He stopped and looked at Dushma. "I don't know if you ought to. . ."

"I'm all right," said Dushma quickly. In truth she had become a little bored and was hoping that the locked room would contain something more interesting than what she had seen so far.

The nurse had opened the door. Marlstroy shrugged and stepped to one side to allow Dushma through.

Here, at least, there was a machine. In the room was a single bed, and on a trolley beside it stood a metal box the size of a suitcase. Needles twitched and trembled beneath the round glass windows of its many dials. Orange lights pulsed and a small screen set into one end displayed a twanging green line. Beside the box, hissing softly, stood a large black cylinder like a bomb.

The occupant of the bed was a woman, apparently deeply asleep. Tubes and wires trailed over her. It was hard to tell how old she was, or even what she looked like, because of the oxygen mask that obscured the lower part of her face.

Her hair had been dyed blonde but the roots were now growing out, leaving two or three centimetres of black close to her scalp. Her skin looked slack and pasty and her closed eyes were puffy. There was a tiny puncture in her earlobe where an earring should have been.

"A suicide attempt, I'm afraid to say," said Marlstroy. "While on remand in a young offenders' institute. That's why they're keeping the door locked, I suppose. They take your shoelaces off you in those kinds of places, and any belts or anything like that you might be wearing. Just to make sure you don't try and kill yourself. But she had a plastic bag in her pocket. She tried to smother herself with it. Fortunately she'd only been unconscious for a little while before someone noticed what she'd done."

He reached out towards the girl and peeled back one of her eyelids with his thumb. Taking a small torch from his pocket, he shone it into her unseeing pupil.

"Doesn't say what she did to get arrested. But apparently she was depressed because her boyfriend had been deported."

Behind him one of the students mimed playing a violin.

"She's been in a coma ever since, although from the scans —" he leafed through some papers — "the permanent damage should be minimal." He spread a set of diagrams out at the foot of the bed. "Prognosis?" he asked.

"Good," said one of the students, leaning forward to examine the graphs.

"Correct."

"Provided no complications arise, that is."

"Of course." Marlstroy shook his head. "As I say, I can't see why they sent her here. It's a perfectly straightforward case. Not my kind of thing at all."

"Maybe she's got rich relatives," said another student. "Maybe they're going to bribe someone to let her escape when she wakes up."

Marlstroy turned on him. "In that case," he snapped, "I shall want my *cut*. Understood?"

Unsure if he was joking, the student sniggered, then blushed and cleared his throat.

Marlstroy was already gathering up his notes in readiness to leave. "I'll have a word," he said. "See if I can't get her moved. There must be more interesting cases. Not to say more deserving ones. . ."

Dushma was standing by the window, taking in little of what was being said. When the breeze billowed the net curtain she could see out into the hospital grounds, over the wall and beyond towards the towers and rooftops of central London. The steel and glass of office blocks glittered in the sunlight, cranes wavered through rising draughts of warm air, and the spire of the cathedral appeared to sail among them beneath the drifting clouds.

It was a beautiful day to be outside. She wondered how long it was since she had been on one of her long, aimless excursions through the city. Weeks, it must be. She found herself wishing she could just walk out and lose herself in the maze of streets.

She heard the jingle of keys. The others were waiting for her outside the door. She shook herself free of her daydream and hurried to join them. Glancing back as she left the room, she felt a twinge of pity for the unconscious girl, who could have no idea what fine weather it was.

She saw the name on the clipboard at the foot of the bed.

Automatically, she kept on walking through the door. She thought about stopping but her feet moved of their own accord. She should be feeling some strong emotion, she knew, but she wasn't sure what. Her heart and lungs seemed to be in freefall inside her. When they landed she would know how she felt.

"A Catfinger", the clipboard had said.

Her step faltered. Then she heard the lock click home. Was it too late to say something, to get them to let her back in?

But no, she didn't want to. *I'm glad*, she forced herself to think. *It's what she deserves!* Yet still she felt hollow. Each breath and each pulse seemed impossibly prolonged.

It serves her right! she told herself fiercely. *After what she did to you and . . . and the others, it serves her right!*

"No, I can't understand it either," the nurse was saying to Marlstroy. "But we didn't get any choice. Express instructions from the director, apparently."

But it didn't seem right at all. Dushma thought of Alison's face, vacant and motionless against the pillow. Then she remembered the girl she had met and come to know in the multi-storey car park they had both frequented.

In Alison's company the car park had seemed a far less gloomy place. They used to sit on the roof and talk and enjoy the view or watch the sunset. On other occasions, in the evenings when the cars had all gone, they would trundle down the ramps on Alison's skateboard or play a complicated game they had invented that involved bouncing tennis balls off pillars and down the central stairwell.

Alison's gusty, abrasive laughter could fill an entire level of the empty car park. When she was there with Dushma it had been not a brutalist sixties stack of concrete slabs but a playground, a dancefloor, a stage, a catwalk, a stronghold against the hordes of frumpy squaws that Alison liked to observe and despise as they scurried to and from the offices and wine bars in the streets below.

"Look at them," she would say with contempt. "Can't you just tell they're going to be doing the same sensible things and wearing the same sensible clothes and even thinking the same oh-so-sensible *thoughts* every day for the next thirty years of their lives? Spare me, Dush love, spare me *now*."

The saying about it being better to live for one day as a tiger than a thousand years as a sheep had seemed to Dushma to describe her friend perfectly. However, when she had put it to her, Alison hadn't been so sure. "I dunno, Dush honey," she had said after some thought. "Given a thousand years, guaranteed, I reckon even a sheep could get up to some pretty wacky things."

When Dushma had first met her, Alison was already a seasoned shoplifter. There was the time she had arrived at the car park with a radio, and Dushma had immediately assumed she must have stolen it. Alison had been outraged at the suggestion. She had found it in a skip, she said. It turned out she had only stolen the batteries.

Its aerial was broken, but they found a length of wire to

replace it with. They wrapped one end round the stub that remained and attached the other to a metal drainpipe that ran down the outside of the car park. The reception was excellent. They could even get foreign stations.

Alison liked to practise new moves to the sound of the latest dance tracks. "How's this, Dush?" she would ask. "How long will they be able to resist me for, d'you think? We curvy girls just have to sway our hips, you know," she added challengingly. "Skinny ones like you need to work lots harder."

But Dushma preferred to sit with her back to the wall, listening to the songs and trying to memorize the chord changes of the ones she liked so that she could play them later.

Alison had often been like that: restless, full of schemes and always eager to enlist Dushma as her co-conspirator. They would start a pirate radio station, form a band and storm the charts, turn the car park into a venue for a team version of their tennis-ball game and start a craze that would sweep the country.

Remembering those times, Dushma found herself blinking miserably. Whatever Alison had done to her, did she deserve this living death that made a mockery of all the ideas and energy she used to have? Better to live one day as anything at all than spend a thousand years in a coma.

Without Dushma noticing they had left the ward and were out in the corridor again. It was much too late to turn back now.

But what if she could have said something, or touched her, done something to try and reach her through the depths of her unconsciousness? But then, why *should* she have done? She remembered one of the last things Alison had said to her. "At the end of the day it's every girl for herself, honey," she had said. And Alison had indeed tried to look after herself and this was where it had got her. It was nothing to do with Dushma. Besides, she was going to get better anyway. They had said the prognosis was good. She thought that was what it meant.

The medical students were scuffling along behind her, joking amongst themselves and trying to trip each other up. She turned to them. "What does prognosis mean?" she asked.

"Prognosis?" said one, nudging his nearest companion. "It's, like, a big nose, isn't it?"

"No," said another. "It was that rock band from the seventies."

"Don't worry," said the third, seeing Dushma's distress and laying a kindly hand on her arm. "She'll be all right. And if the conventional treatment doesn't wake her up, then I personally will volunteer to kiss her. Or –" he smirked at her – "whatever it takes these days, y'know? Always works in stories, doesn't it?"

IX

Barefoot in the Nave

"Aren't you doing anything today?" Arbilow feigned surprise. "No pony club? Ballet class?"

Dushma refused to rise to his teasing. "No," she said, with an indifferent shrug.

They were sitting side by side on the wall of Marlstroy's front garden. It was Saturday morning and another particularly fine day for the time of year. The sun shone warmly and a gentle breeze hardly rustled the few leaves still on the trees.

"You do whatever you want, don't you?" Arbilow drummed his heels against the wall.

"So do you, it looks like." In fact, she thought she had already guessed the reason for his independence, but had decided it was up to him to mention it first. "What *are* you doing this morning, anyway?"

He looked thoughtful. "Well, I thought I might go and organize a one-man demonstration somewhere. I could chain myself to some railings and chant anti-capitalist slogans till they cut me free. Coming?"

"I'd rather not. Besides, maybe I am a capitalist, for all you know. A bloated plutocrat!" She rolled the phrase challengingly off her tongue.

He looked at her thoughtfully, then wrinkled up his nose and shook his head dismissively. "No. . . I wouldn't say so. I had you down as more of a *petite bourgeoise*."

She found herself gasping with indignation and laughing at the same time. All she could think of to say in reply was, "Oh, you . . . you really are infuriating!" It sounded terribly lame. Why did he make her behave like a character out of some costume drama? She was nothing like he thought she was at all, if only he knew.

"So are you coming then?" he persisted. "It's more fun with two. And they probably wouldn't beat me up so badly if you were around as well."

"Oh go on. Nobody gets beaten up for demonstrating. Not nowadays."

"You don't think so? You've got no idea, have you?" His voice took on an edge of bitterness. "You probably think policemen are kind, friendly people who'll tell you the time if you ask them nicely."

"Do I? You've no idea what I know about policemen!"

"I can guess." He looked pointedly past her at the elegant stucco and brick front of Marlstroy's house. "But if you're . . . the wrong sort of person, they can do pretty much what they like to you and nobody cares. Marcus got arrested a while back on some ridiculous charge. They said, because he hadn't promised not to break the law if he felt it was necessary, they were allowed to keep him in prison indefinitely. For public safety. That's completely against his human rights, and habeas corpus and everything. Fortunately the campaign had the funds to get him a decent lawyer. He was out in a couple of days. But even so, he had three broken ribs and a detached retina. They said he'd been 'resisting arrest'."

This, Dushma knew, was the point at which she was supposed to express horror and disbelief at the thought of the forces of law and order behaving in such a way. But she didn't want to give him the opportunity to flaunt what he obviously thought was his superior worldliness. "Well in that case," she said, "I think you should definitely forget chaining yourself to anything and do something law-abiding instead."

"Such as?"

Dushma reviewed her own options for the morning. She had been planning to spend some time in Marlstroy's library, but the weather was beautiful, and she could always read all day Sunday if she wanted. "Actually, I thought I might go for a walk," she said. "Then later I'm meeting Moth – you remember, my friend from the march? – and we might have some coffee and go shopping. Do you want to come?"

"Keep me out of mischief, eh?" He grinned. "Well, I should do some practice, but . . . yeah, OK. Thanks."

He waited while Dushma ran inside to get her bag. When she emerged they set off at a saunter down the tree-lined road in the direction of the centre of town.

The morning was peaceful, and at first they walked in silence. There were hardly any people about, and even fewer cars. There was almost no noise except for birdsong and the occasional distant sound of an aeroplane grinding its way across the sky.

Looking at the elegant houses that rose up on either side, Dushma was struck by the thought that the street where Marlstroy lived must hardly have changed in a hundred years, or even longer. She wondered what she would look like wearing a bonnet and gloves and carrying a parasol. In the library there were bound sets of old magazines containing numerous sketches of women dressed in this fashion. Would it suit her?

Next she tried to imagine Arbilow in a top hat and tail coat. Perhaps he would have her arm in his. But when she glanced at the restless figure by her side she had to admit that the picture that came to mind was an incongruous one. He did not look genteel, with his thin face, cropped hair and deep-set, mobile eyes. His dark jacket and trousers, with their frayed hems and their zippers and buckles and press studs, were far more fitting than anything old-fashioned would have been.

"So, have you got many engagements coming up?" she asked. "You know, juggling and things."

"To tell you the truth, no, not really. Now the nights are drawing in, it's more or less the end of the season for garden parties. They're the best gigs. Tips and a fee, and plenty of odds and ends to eat and drink, if you're lucky."

"Didn't you say you were doing something on the stage as well? In a play?"

"Yeah, that's just finished though. Can't say I'm that bothered. It was mostly just hours of waiting around doing nothing. And the money was pitiful."

"That's a shame. Do you think you'll do another one?"

"Mmm, don't know. Depends what else comes up. This is the first year I've been doing it, so I don't really know what to expect. Things might pick up towards Christmas. Or round bonfire night, maybe. Specially if I can get the knack of that thing with the burning torches. That'll look great in the dark."

"It does sound good," said Dushma. She imagined him at dusk in Marlstroy's garden, juggling flaming batons while in the background the firetrees blazed.

"I don't know, needs more practice. And I'm working on this other routine as well, bit of light relief, really. I call it the junk druggler. I have these cocktail glasses full of coloured water and I drink them one by one and after each one I get more and more unsteady. It's really difficult, pretending to be hopeless without actually dropping anything, but I'm nearly there. I could show you it when it's ready, if you liked. I might need a bit of help, though."

"Oh yes." Dushma tossed her head. "I suppose I'd have to be your glamorous assistant."

"We-ell, I don't know about *that*." Arbilow put his head on one side and considered her through narrowed eyes. "Competition will be fierce, I warn you. You'll have to audition along with all the other hopefuls, I'm afraid. You know, so I can get an idea what you look like in the costume, that kind of thing."

"Oh *I* see! In that case I'm going to have a contract drawn up by a lawyer beforehand specifying exactly how much leg I'm going to show. So you may be disappointed."

He turned to her and looked her up and down with a gaze of frank appraisal. "I doubt it," he said.

"Anyway," she went on quickly, suddenly flustered, "I was going to say, if you're looking for something to do, you know, in the meantime. . ." She hesitated, not wanting to sound patronizing. "I don't know if you'd be interested, but you know the Galen Infirmary in the East End? I think they're looking for people. Porters, I reckon. And I don't think they'd be too bothered about, well, experience, or. . . And they'd probably be flexible if you wanted to . . . rehearse, or. . ." She didn't like to say, *And they won't mind if you're not registered*. "Anyway, just ask for Tony."

"Tony, eh? What's this sudden familiarity with the grey economy? Don't get enough pocket money?"

"No, I was there the other day, that's all. My guardian works there."

"What, as a porter?"

"No! He's a consultant. A neurologist. If you must know, he's a fellow of the Royal College of Physicians, and. . ."

"All right, all right!" Arbilow held up his hands placatingly. "I know, just joking."

Dushma hadn't been intending to walk anywhere in particular, but after about half an hour she found that they had reached the cathedral.

They came upon it suddenly. The streets surrounding it were too narrow and the buildings lining them too tall to afford a view of the spire. They turned out of a cobbled alley into a wide square and it was suddenly there in front of them, reaching dizzyingly up into the clear morning sky.

They crossed the square and, pausing on the steps outside the main entrance, looked up at the teeming facade of the west front. Not yet in the sunlight, it reared above them like a dark cliff, deeply gouged with shadowy clefts and bristling with outcrops of crenellated masonry. There were statues everywhere, standing or crouching in niches and on protruding pedestals, clinging to window ledges and peering out from behind gutters and drainpipes. Some of them were easily distinguishable as saints or clergy: they wore robes and mitres and clutched croziers or crucifixes. Others had a more demonic aspect, snarling out from their alcoves with wide, toothy mouths, or clutching at the air with taloned claws.

By gaslight these gargoyles must have seemed luridly lifelike. The pipes of long-dormant lamps still coiled among them, fan-shaped patches of discolouration darkening the wall behind each nozzle. Overall the effect was slightly sinister. Even the stained-glass windows, so magnificent from inside, did little to relieve the forbidding aspect. Without light streaming through them, they looked like nothing but collages of dull grey glass set into the fretted stonework.

"Creepy, isn't it?" said Arbilow. "Specially when you know some of the stories."

"Oh, I'm not so sure. I think it's . . . it's pretty impressive," said Dushma a little breathlessly.

She had noticed with annoyance that, although they hadn't been walking quickly, she had a stitch and her heart was bumping uncomfortably inside her ribs. In only a few months she had become out of condition. Such a brief journey would never have bothered her so during the days when she lived in the viaduct, when she had often spent almost every waking moment of the day out on the street. Now she passed her time in Marlstroy's library, and went to school on the bus. How long would it be, she wondered, before she began to forget her old haunts?

"Have you been inside?" she asked.

"No."

"It's interesting. Come on, there's something I want to show you."

She led him up the steps to the heavy wooden door, turned the handle and pushed it open.

At first the interior of the cathedral seemed almost

completely dark after the brightness outside. They stood just beyond the threshold for some moments while their vision adjusted to the half-light. Straining her eyes, Dushma peered into the gloom of the cavernous nave. It was the first time she had been here since her arrest. What if she was recognized? Automatically, she dipped one hand into her pocket. Her fingers touched a rectangle of plastic and she gripped it tightly. It was an action she had performed many times since being given her registration card. Now the comforting feel of its rounded corners and raised lettering reassured her that she had the right to be here. No one could drag her away, terrified and humiliated, the way they had done last time she was here.

You do what you like, don't you? Arbilow had said. And it was true; why shouldn't she?

"Take your shoes off," whispered Dushma.

"What? Why? I thought that was mosques, not. . ."

"Just do it. You'll see." She pulled off her sandals. Gripping the straps firmly in one hand, she set out barefoot across the nave. The dangling buckles jingled faintly as she walked.

Arbilow hesitated, then removed his training shoes and stuffed his socks inside them. Knotting the laces together, he slung the shoes around his neck and hurried after her.

The flagstones of the cathedral floor were cold beneath Dushma's feet. Without shoes she could feel that they weren't flat but worn into slight undulations by the tread of congregations over the years. Now and then she noticed a sharper chill as she passed over a brass plaque set into the floor, or a different texture to the stone where an inscription had been carved.

Reaching the middle of the nave she stopped in disappointment. She bent her knees and peered down to check where she was, then moved one foot in an arc around her.

"Do we have to do this?" grumbled Arbilow. "My feet are freezing."

"But it wasn't. . ." She sounded as if she was trying to convince herself. "Last time it was really warm, just here." Had she imagined it? She was sure she remembered lying exactly here and basking in the heat rising up from beneath Selwyn Champion's gravestone. Hadn't it been cosy enough to send her to sleep, curled like a cat on a sun-drenched path?

"Probably some kind of under-floor heating. Hot-air ducts or something. It's certainly not on now though."

"No, there's nothing like that."

"Are you sure? How d'you know?"

"I. . . I've seen under here. There's just a tunnel. It's empty. There's nothing in it. No pipes or anything."

"Well, whatever. Maybe they've just fitted it. And maybe it's broken already. I'm sure it couldn't be very efficient, place the size of this."

Dushma took a pace forward, then another to one side. Everywhere she trod the floor was numbingly cold. She pictured the tunnel beneath her, trying to guess what

234

might have caused the warmth she had felt. Despite the plausibility of Arbilow's reasoning she found a much stranger and more disturbing scenario taking shape in her imagination. In her mind's eye there was something in the tunnel, something hot, something that glowed red as it moved through the dark, paused beneath the gravestone, lingered there a while and then continued on. It would have been no more remarkable an event than others she had witnessed during her time as a fugitive underground.

Arbilow interrupted her train of thought. "You know, this is really fun and everything, but . . . are you sure it's allowed? What if somebody sees us?"

"Oh, they won't. It's too dark."

Arbilow peered down at his feet. "*You* might be all right. But compared to yours, mine might as well've been covered in luminous paint." It was true that his pale feet were noticeable even in the gloom of the cathedral's interior. Clad in black, his legs were almost invisible, so that his ankles seemed to emerge from nowhere.

"It's just, I wouldn't want to frighten anybody," he went on. "You know the story, don't you?"

Dushma tried to think of a story to do with the cathedral that also involved feet, but she couldn't. She shook her head. "No. How does it go?"

Holding on to a pew to steady himself, Arbilow balanced on one leg and moved his right foot slowly towards her, wriggling his toes as he did so.

"It's a funny thought, isn't it?" he murmured. "Parts of your body, having a life of their own. . ."

She giggled nervously and drew back, but he was too quick for her. His foot pressed gently but firmly down on hers and she stiffened into immobility. She stole a quick glance at his face but he was looking away from her into the depths of the cathedral, his expression distant.

The sole of his foot felt cold and dry as he moved it slowly over her toes and then up to her ankle. The callouses on his heel brushed with a not-unpleasant roughness over her own smooth skin.

Out of the corner of her half-closed eyes she saw his knee rise. His toes began to stroke their way up the sharp ridge of her shin.

A shiver ran down her spine and she stepped away from him. "I don't think. . ." Her mouth was dry. She swallowed and began again. "I don't . . . I'm not sure we should. . ." She broke off, still trying to understand her reaction. Was it because of what he had been doing, or where they were? Or because of who he was, or wasn't?

"OK. Sure." Apparently unconcerned, he shrugged, turned his back on her and unslung his shoes from round his neck.

"So what was the story, anyway?" she asked quickly, trying to dispel the sudden awkwardness she felt.

"I don't know if you really want to hear that. It's a bit scary."

"Oh go on, of course I do."

"All right then, if you insist." He turned back to her, his shoes in his hand and a wicked grin on his face. "Although actually I don't think it can have been here, it's not old enough. It was one of those medieval places with tombs of crusaders in it."

"There are some of those here. They're from a much older church that used to be on the site. Most of it got burned down."

"Well, maybe it was here then. Anyway, there was this man who'd murdered someone, a woman. I forget why. I think it was a *crime passionnel*. Perhaps she'd been unfaithful. So he'd smothered her as she slept, or something. And now he had to get rid of the body. But he'd thought of a plan. He waited until the middle of the night, wrapped the corpse in a blanket, slung a bag of tools over his shoulder and crept through the streets to the cathedral. He let himself in through a side door and made his way to the darkest, least-frequented chapel in the building. Right at the back, in an alcove, there was a stone sarcophagus. It had a massive lid with a statue of a knight on top of it, but this murderer was a brute of a man. He stuck his candle on a ledge, took out his chisel and levered the lid right off.

"There was nothing inside but dust and a few old bones, of course. Plenty of room for a new occupant. Except the tomb was too small. People were shorter in medieval times, and his victim wouldn't fit. He tried to bend the limbs, but rigor mortis had already set in. The corpse was stiff as a board. So instead he got a saw from his tool bag and cut off its feet."

"It's like that Greek in the fable," said Dushma. "The one with the bed that fitted everyone. What was his name?"

"So now the body goes in beautifully. He lowers the lid and mixes up a bit of putty for the cracks. He thinks he's thought of everything. He gathers up his tools and gets ready to leave. It's not long till dawn and there's already a faint grey light inside the cathedral. Enough for him not to need his candle, so he blows it out and puts it in his bag.

"He's half way along the nave when he realizes what he's forgotten. They were right by him on the floor; how can he have missed them? He stops and turns round, but before he can start back to the chapel he hears a noise. It's faint at first, but getting louder as he listens. It's the sound of footsteps coming towards him. Slap, slap, slap on the cold stone floor. And just before he turns to flee in terror he sees, dimly visible in the gloom, a pair of naked feet striding towards him over the flagstones. But where each ankle should be, there's nothing but a ring of ragged flesh around a peg of splintered bone."

Arbilow paused for a few seconds to let the image sink in. Then he sat down at the end of the nearest pew and began to put his shoes back on.

"So what happened to him?" Dushma wanted to know.

"In some versions he runs and runs but can't escape the sound of the feet always just behind him. Then eventually he dies of exhaustion or falls into a river or over a cliff. In others he goes mad, confesses his crime, hangs at Tyburn or dies in Bedlam."

He was trying to scare her, thought Dushma. "It's like those stories about the ghosts of Roman soldiers," she said calmly. "Only the other way round. They say you can see them marching sometimes where their old roads used to be. But now the level of the pavement's risen so you can't see the lower half of their legs. It looks like they're wading through the ground."

She stood first on one leg then the other while she buckled on her sandals. "Although I suppose," she added, after a few seconds' thought, "if there was a cellar underneath and you were in it, you'd just see their feet sticking down through the ceiling."

They walked back to the door and out into the square. It was just past midday and the sun now shone on the steps outside the west front of the cathedral. They stood there for a minute, enjoying the warmth.

"Hope I didn't scare you with that story," said Arbilow.

"No, of course not."

"Had you heard it before?"

"No."

"Well then," he said triumphantly, "that's two you owe me now. That one about the Romans doesn't count 'cos I'd heard it already."

They made their way across the square and down one of the cobbled streets that surrounded the cathedral. On either side stood tall old houses that had been turned into the offices of lawyers and accountants or the surgeries of private doctors. Iron railings fenced them off from the pavement and a discreet brass plaque by each door gave the name of the firm that plied its trade within.

They rounded several corners and the road began to widen. Cobbles turned to tarmac and narrow, dark sash windows gave way to the brightly decorated displays of music shops, clothes boutiques and electronics showrooms.

They had reached the outskirts of one of the busiest shopping districts. Weekend crowds pressed around them. By the time Dushma caught sight of Moth outside the café where they had arranged to meet, it was impossible to walk with any gait other than a meandering shuffle, so full had the streets become.

"*There* you are! Where've you *been?*" cried Moth, catching at Dushma's sleeve as if to pluck her from the passing tide of people before she drifted away. "Hurry up or we won't get anywhere to sit."

Without waiting for Dushma to reply, she pushed open the door of the café and made her way over to an empty table in the corner. "I can't go too long without a cup of coffee," she explained loudly over her shoulder. "It's my only vice. I have to have several cups a day or I become sluggish and frankly dull company. In fact, I. . . Oh." Turning round to sit down she caught sight of Arbilow and fell abruptly silent, her cheeks colouring.

"Hello. How are you?" asked Arbilow.

"Fine, thanks."

"And how's the juggling going?"

"Fine, thanks. No, actually, it's a disaster. I'm not allowed to practise in my room any more. I have to go outside, and I've already lost one ball in the shrubbery."

Arbilow nodded in sympathy. "Yeah, it's difficult to start with. I remember, I used to get these dreadful aches in my back and my neck. Do you get those?"

"No. Not really."

"Oh. Well, I was going to say, if you do, I found a hot bath and a massage really helpful."

Moth blushed more deeply and looked down at her entwined fingers. A silence followed.

"I find going for a walk good for stress," said Dushma. "Exercise, fresh air. . ." Her voice trailed off.

"I like to pretend I'm in a balloon, if I can't sleep," said Arbilow. "Floating over the fields, watching the shadows of the clouds. . ." He tipped his chair back on two legs, put his hands behind his head and stared up at the ceiling.

Moth stifled a yawn. "Oh gosh, excuse me!"

"See? It always works."

"I've never flown," said Dushma. "I'd really like to. I don't think it would worry me at all, I've never minded heights."

"Well, I've never actually been in a balloon, so I have to imagine what it's like. But I have flown in . . . well, I have, anyway. How about you?" Arbilow turned to Moth. "Have you been in an aeroplane?"

"Yes," said Moth.

"Really?"

"Yes, lots. I hate it. It makes my ears hurt."

"Oh."

A waitress arrived with their drinks. The coffee came in cups the size of small bowls, and as soon as hers was placed in front of her, Moth seized it and held it up to her face as if trying to hide behind it.

Dushma felt something stroking her calf. She jumped and her knee banged the underside of the table. She glared at Arbilow but he was gazing distractedly off into the distance.

"'Scuse me. Coffee's hot," she mumbled, trying to hide her confusion. She looked at Moth to see if she had noticed anything, but she was still holding her coffee cup under her nose and her spectacles had misted up.

There was another silence.

"I know," said Moth, suddenly inspired. "Look at this." She put down her cup, dug into the pocket of her skirt and drew out a folded square of tissue paper. Unwrapping it, she produced a few fronds of wilted green herbs. The faint smell of mint wafted through the air.

"My latest harvest," she said proudly. "Here, try some. I'm sorry there's not more. It's just, I didn't expect to have to share it three ways." She paused, frowning. "Sorry, that sounds very rude. Try again, Ursula . . . OK: I mean, I wish I could give you lots more, because you're both lovely people. How about that?"

"Is it legal?" asked Arbilow, holding a sprig under his nose and sniffing cautiously.

"Of course it is. I grew it in the locker room at school. Ask Dushma. Well, it's probably against the rules, but. . ."

"Oh in that case, I'm not sure if I ought to."

"Of course you should. It's good for you. A hundred per cent organic. Gives you vitamins, freshens your breath. . . I mean, not that you need to. . . That is, I didn't mean. . . Oh God. Ground, swallow me up now please."

"It's very nice," said Dushma hastily, picking up a stem from the table and dipping it in her coffee.

After that the conversation proceeded fitfully. Still blushing deeply, Moth seemed reluctant to take part. Instead she stared at the table and would speak only in monosyllables. Even when she had finished her coffee she didn't look up, but turned her whole attention to an empty sugar sachet, tearing it with meticulous care into a heap of tiny shreds.

"Listen, I'm afraid I'm going to have to go," said Arbilow eventually. "I've got some things to do. Thanks for the coffee." He stood up and smiled at Dushma. "See you later maybe."

"Oh God!" wailed Moth, as soon as Arbilow had gone. "I'm socially stunted! How will I ever become the witty, urbane hostess my mother wants me to be?"

"I think he was going anyway," Dushma tried to reassure her. "He had to . . . do some practice, I think."

"Why didn't you tell me he was coming? Then I could've prepared some small-talk. To put him at his ease."

243

"Oh, it wasn't anything definite. He just tends to turn up."

"Really? Hey, d'you think he's *stalking* you?"

Dushma had a vision of Arbilow's dismembered feet pursuing her out of the cathedral and through the streets. Out here in the sunlight, surrounded by the bustle of the café, the thought was more ridiculous than frightening. "I . . . well, no, I don't think so," she said. "I think he's just trying to be friendly. I. . . Oh!" For the second time in the space of a few minutes Dushma started in surprise. A cat had sprung up on to the chair where Arbilow had been sitting and was sniffing at the rim of his coffee cup.

The two girls spent the afternoon shopping. It was something which, only a few months ago, Dushma couldn't even have imagined herself doing. Her clothes, often old-fashioned and badly fitting, had always come from Auntie Megan. She had never had enough money to buy her own. As a result clothes shops had never held much interest for her. The only times she had looked in at their windows were when she was out with Alison, in which case she had usually been too busy trying to stop her friend getting them both into trouble to pay much attention to the displays.

"I 'ate to tell you this, love," Alison would say, looking Dushma up and down with a critical eye, "but that kind of neckline went out with Anne Boleyn. With shoulders like yours you should really show 'em off, specially when the weather's nice. How about that strappy number there? Crushed aubergine velour with gold lamé freckling and sheer nylon bodice vents. There's girls that'd kill to be able to get away with wearing that. Go on, I'll get one for you. Look, you don't even have to come in. They're right by the door and the assistant's half asleep."

She could be very difficult to dissuade. Often Dushma would have to feign dissatisfaction with the garment in question. "It's lovely, but I don't think it quite goes with my eyes," she might say. Or, "Beautiful, isn't it, but I've heard gold lamé freckling's going to be so out of fashion next season." This was the only kind of reasoning Alison seemed to understand in what she referred to as "retail situations".

Now that Dushma had money of her own all this had changed. Shops she would never have glanced at twice had become fascinating places now that they contained things she could actually buy. Encouraged by this knowledge, she would stop and peer eagerly into the windows of establishments she had never even known existed before.

The habit of spending money was an easy one to pick up. As the afternoon wore on she even found herself beginning to advise Moth on the things she thought would suit her.

But she was not yet entirely used to her newly elevated consumer status. There were certain instinctive responses she'd still not had time to unlearn. She was browsing in the womenswear section of a large department store, her purchases complete, when she heard a voice behind her.

Something about its tone was enough to bring all her old wariness of authority rushing to the surface of her mind.

"Excuse me miss. . ."

Dushma whirled round to find a policeman standing next to her. She sprang away from him and, almost losing her balance, staggered backwards into a rack of coats. She looked desperately this way and that for a means of escape while her hand felt automatically for the registration card in her pocket.

"Sorry to startle you, miss," said the policeman, "but your bag's open. Now there's people around, I'm afraid to say, who'd take that as an invitation."

Trying to slow her panicky breathing, Dushma pushed herself out from among the coats. She looked down at her bag. It was true that one of the straps had slipped off her shoulder, exposing the contents of the bag to anyone who came close enough.

She hitched the strap back into place. "Thanks," she mumbled, not meeting the policeman's eye. What a quivering bundle of guilt she must look, she thought.

She hurried towards the door, sure that everyone must be looking at her. The blood was still moving too fast through her veins by the time she had left the store and rejoined Moth on the pavement outside.

"I think I've got everything I want," she said, not feeling like going in any more shops for a while.

"So've I," said Moth, peering into her purse. "Oh God. Disaster."

"What?"

"I haven't got enough for a taxi home."

"A taxi?"

"Yes. My mother always insists I get one. She's convinced I can't find my way home on my own. In fact, I'm surprised she hasn't forced me to have my name and address tattooed on my forehead."

"We'll get a bus," said Dushma. "You don't have to tell her."

"A bus? But I've never been on a bus. I wouldn't know what to do, I. . ."

"You've flown in all those aeroplanes but you've never been on a bus? Then you'll have to try it. Come on, I'll show you."

There was a row of bus stops just beyond the next junction. Dushma led the way to the nearest and scanned the list of destinations fixed to one side of the shelter. "Look, there's loads we can get," she said. "You have to hang on tight when it goes round corners, and there's a bell you can push when you want to get off."

They did not have long to wait before a bus appeared. Dushma flagged it down and sprang confidently through the doors as soon as they had folded open.

"Two halves, please," she said.

"I think we should go in polite," said Moth anxiously as Dushma counted out the fares. "Is it more expensive? Have you got enough?"

"No, it's all the same," said Dushma. She turned to the

driver. "She's never been on a bus before," she explained.

The driver pressed buttons on his ticket machine and a ribbon of paper chattered out of the slot. Dushma tore their tickets free and scooped up her change. Picking up her shopping bags with her other hand, she made her way along the aisle, staggering a little as the bus moved away from the stop with a loud sneeze of hydraulics.

They found a pair of seats and had just settled themselves when the bus heeled suddenly over as it turned a sharp bend. Dushma had to grab hold of the handle on top of the seat in front to stop herself being flung against Moth. "So what do you think, then?" she asked.

"Well, I suppose it's better than flying. Just about. I just hope they don't bring us a meal 'cos I don't think I could manage one right now." Moth closed her eyes and swallowed hard. It wasn't until the bus had been moving smoothly for a while that she relaxed a little and risked a few quick glances out of the window.

"Anyway, how come you've never been in an aeroplane?" she asked. "Isn't that what you said? I thought you used to live in the Far East."

For a moment Dushma was nonplussed. She had indeed said something about never having flown, she remembered. That had been careless.

"I, er. . ." She hesitated for a second or two before inspiration struck. "Oh, we travelled by boat. We had so much stuff. Furniture and rugs and things. And books. Thousands of books."

But Moth had already lost interest. She had closed her eyes again and her face looked drawn.

Dushma tightened her grip on the handle in front of her. Whenever they stopped at lights or a junction, the idling motor made the whole bus thrum. If she braced herself she could feel its vibration in her bones. When she held her jaw just so it made her teeth buzz.

She thought of the cat that had brushed against her calf under the table in the café. She wasn't sure whether to be relieved or disappointed that it hadn't been Arbilow.

She smiled to herself. She wondered if she should tell him.

X

A Scar in the Tarmac

That night Arbilow took Dushma to the Bunker on Sproule Street. It was a low concrete structure, out of place among the neighbouring red-brick warehouses, offices and mansion flats. Nothing about its blank exterior gave any clue as to what went on inside. The only indication that something must be happening there on that particular evening was the line of young people stretching from the entrance, around one corner of the building and down an adjacent sidestreet.

"It's tiny," said Dushma. "We're never all going to get in."

Arbilow pointed down at his feet. "Most of it's underground," he said. "It used to be a bomb shelter. Then for a while it was an electricity substation. Now it's about the only place these guys can use their gear without someone complaining. You won't believe it. They've got speakers the size of settees. The size of wardrobes, even. They say you can hear it down on the Underground when they really crank it up."

Dushma unslung her handbag. Crouching down and pretending to look for something inside it, she laid the fingertips of her right hand gently on to the pavement. Immediately she flinched away in surprise. She had touched not a flagstone but the lid of a manhole cover. The metal surface had been hot.

She blew on her fingers and then put them carefully down in a different place. Could she detect the faintest of vibrations like the kind that Moth had claimed to be able to feel? She wasn't sure.

She straightened up.

"That metal cover there," she said. "Feel it. It's hot!" She was reminded of the unexpected warmth of Selwyn Champion's gravestone, but they were a long way from the cathedral.

Arbilow didn't seem impressed. "Probably someone's left a tap running. Cold shower for them in the morning. Serves them right. Haven't you seen those pictures of New York in the winter? There's clouds of steam coming up through the drains, just like those geysers in Iceland. Terrible waste. They should harness it to, to . . . I don't know, fill hot-air balloons."

"They might appreciate one in this weather. A cold shower, I mean."

She had worried that the dress she had bought was too thin and too low-cut. But the evening was unseasonably warm and she didn't feel cold. Nor did she think that, compared to some of the other girls in the queue, she was too indiscreetly dressed. There were plenty of necklines that plunged more deeply than hers. She felt rather pleased with herself at not having got her attire wrong. It wasn't as if she'd had any help. Marlstroy had been no use. He had hardly glanced at her when, ready to leave the house, she had presented herself to him in his study. "Hmph. I hope you don't expect me to tell you to be sensible," he had grunted, before returning to the papers that covered his desk. Did that mean that he was sure she would in fact be sensible? Or that he didn't care if she wasn't? She had no idea.

The queue moved forward a little way. It was being administered by a handful of young men in white shirts, dinner jackets and rigid, flat bow ties that looked as if they'd been cut from black cardboard. They prowled the pavement importantly, their arms held slightly out from their sides like Wild West gunslingers about to make their play.

Now and then couples or small groups of people were beckoned from the queue apparently at random. They were taken to the front, to where a folding table had been set up outside the deeply recessed doors of the Bunker. Every time this happened there were catcalls and shouts of annoyance from those still waiting. During one such outburst there came the sound of a window being slammed shut somewhere high up in one of the surrounding mansion blocks. The young men in dinner jackets immediately began hurrying up and down the queue trying to quell the discontent.

"They're worried they'll get done for breaching the

peace," said Arbilow. "The council only lets them use this place as long as they don't advertise when something's happening. Otherwise they'd get too many people. So it helps to know somebody. Doesn't it?"

A bouncer had appeared beside them. "Hey, thought it was you," he said, thumping Arbilow playfully on the arm. "I suppose we're going to have to let you in."

"You could do."

The bouncer leaned closer and whispered, "If anyone asks, you climbed through the window, OK?"

"There isn't a window."

"Whatever. I haven't seen you, OK?" He turned to Dushma and smirked. "I won't ask how old you are. Just make sure he behaves himself."

On the table at the front of the queue was a metal cashbox. Arbilow reached into his pocket and Dushma heard the rustle of notes. "No, wait a minute, let me. . ." she said, fumbling for her purse.

She was too late. "Hand, please," said a voice. Fingers gripped hers and her arm was pulled across the table. Something sticky was pressed against her wrist.

Beyond the metal doors was another bouncer. He looked in Dushma's handbag and patted Arbilow's pockets. "No alcohol, cigarettes, guns, knives or pets," he said in a bored singsong voice. Then he motioned them towards a dark staircase leading downwards. "This way please."

When her eyes had grown used to the dimness Dushma noticed that the walls of the staircase were covered in black or possibly dark blue velvet. She reached out to stroke it and almost tumbled over Arbilow.

"Sorry," she said. "It's so dark."

"Yeah. They have to keep the lights down," he explained. "'Cos otherwise it looks tacky and sad."

As they descended the booming sound of music grew louder. Dushma could feel it pulsing in the steps beneath her feet. She gripped Arbilow's arm to keep her balance and looked down at her wrist. The square of paper stuck there bore a luminous orange picture of a flower.

At the bottom of the steps was a lounge containing chairs, low tables and several leather sofas. Knots of people stood here and there, nodding and smiling and clutching bottles of water.

In the corner of one of the sofas a couple were wrapped around each other, kissing. Their heads were swaying gently as their faces rolled against each other. Everyone else was ignoring them, so Dushma too tried not to stare as she walked past, despite a sudden urge for a closer look at exactly what it was they were doing.

On the far side of the lounge hung a curtain. Arbilow disappeared behind it and Dushma followed him, pushing aside the heavy material and ducking through to the other side.

At first it seemed as if the room she had entered was on fire. She could see nothing but red and black shapes writhing and leaping in front of her. She blinked, trying to make sense of the scene.

Gradually the twisting shapes separated themselves into legs and torsos and rows of waving arms lit up, she now noticed, by coloured lamps set into the floor. These flickered on and off in time to the music, throwing splashes of fiery light up on to the limbs and bodies of the dancers.

Made dizzy by the heat and noise and movement, Dushma drew back as far as she could from this reeling mass of people. Feeling the touch of something hard and sharp against her bare shoulder blades, she looked sideways and saw that the velvet covering on the walls had been inlaid with broken fragments of mirror. In the strobing light these hotly shining splinters looked like showers of sparks spraying across the room.

She turned back to the crowd of bodies on the dance floor. Their footwork seemed impossibly complex. She could never join in. She had no idea what to do. She wished she had paid more attention to Alison's impromptu demonstrations in the multi-storey car park.

Even as she hesitated Arbilow seized her wrists and dragged her in among the dancers. He guided her into an empty space, his strong hands almost lifting her off the floor. Then he spun her round, swung her arms to one side then the other and let her go.

At first she found herself moving whichever way she could just to keep clear of the people nearest her. She took quick, small steps to left and right, forwards and backwards, simply to avoid being bumped into or trodden on. After a few minutes her confidence grew and she raised her arms and began to bend her knees and swing her hips and shoulders. She risked a glance up at Arbilow and saw him grinning his chip-toothed grin at her, eyes sparkling, the ruddy light casting long shadows upwards over his sharp features.

As she danced she started trying to listen to the music. At first she had only been dimly aware of it as waves of noise breaking around her. But now that she concentrated, she realized that this was something different to anything she could remember from television or Alison's salvaged radio. This was music to be felt rather than heard.

Most noticeable of all was the rhythm, so powerful it made the floor shake. She could feel it in her sternum, as if her chest itself was a drum. The low notes, too, were palpable, wrapping themselves round her body and squeezing her with a gentle, pleasant pressure.

Above the beats and the deep chords were other sounds more like textures than tunes. Cymbal rolls as bright and rustling as foil spread themselves over the music. Pianos pecked, guitars buzzed and stung. Smooth string lines and the spongy notes of saxophones slid and bounced over a sharp scree of bells, xylophones and tumbling percussion. And now and again, through all these sounds, there could be heard an extraordinary rustling, rippling sound that swept round the room like a gust of wind.

Speakers as big as wardrobes, Arbilow had said. Dushma looked up, trying to see over the people around her. As if guessing her thoughts, Arbilow nodded backwards over his shoulder and began to move through the crowd of dancers.

256

They neared the far end of the dance floor and once again, as she had been when she came in through the curtain, Dushma was momentarily sure she could see flames. The cart handlers and their decks were on the other side of what seemed like a wall of fire, rising almost to waist height from a narrow trench that ran the full width of the room. But a closer look revealed this too to be an illusion. What had appeared from a distance to be tongues of flame were just triangles of coloured tissue paper, fluttering in a rising draught of air.

In the light shining up from the bottom of the trench two figures could be fitfully glimpsed, toiling behind their stacks of electronics. Apart from their identical white smocks, only their hands could be clearly seen, flipping records on to turntables and pushing cartridges into the mouths of their machines. Their faces were almost invisible: there was just an occasional gleam of dark cheek or forehead through the web of leads dangling from the amplifiers racked up at eye level in front of them.

As Dushma watched, tissue-paper flames licking at her fingers, one of the cart handlers pulled a microphone towards him. The music quietened.

"The cooks are in the kitchen," announced the cart handler menacingly. "And they're turning up the heat."

A cheer went up from the dancers. The music increased in volume and the rhythm speeded up. The cart handler raised a device like a ray gun up to the microphone. He twirled a handle and the rustling sound Dushma had heard earlier swept around the room again. It was a whisk, she realized. She could see the twin wire beaters meshing with each other as they spun.

When eventually they pushed their way out through the curtain again there were many more people in the lounge. There was nowhere to sit, so while Arbilow went to fetch something to drink Dushma perched herself on the arm of a sofa.

A few locks of her long dark hair had come free of their pins and grips and were coiling down over her damp shoulders. Absently trying to tuck them back into place, she looked around the crowded room.

Over in one corner a boy and a girl were embracing. It was too dark for her to be able to tell if it was the same couple she had seen before. As she watched she realized that the V-shaped patch of white down the boy's front was his chest, visible through his open clothing. The girl's left hand was tucked up to the wrist inside his shirt. The fabric rose and fell over her moving knuckles.

Dushma looked up at their faces again to find they had stopped kissing and were both staring back at her. She blushed and turned quickly away.

"Pretty good, isn't it?" Arbilow had returned, holding two bottles of mineral water. "This is all they had, apart from that horrible energy stuff."

"Oh, that's fine. Thanks." She took the bottle he held out to her. "Listen, this is really kind of you, but you must let me. . ."

"So what d'you think? Did you see the speakers?"

"No." Dushma gulped her water. It was icily cold. She pressed the bottle against her forehead. Her temples felt taut where the salt from her sweat had hardened on her skin.

"No, it was pretty dark, wasn't it. But you must've seen the heat sinks on those amplifiers! They were glowing. Must take some volts to drive that lot."

"Watts," said Dushma. It seemed a long time ago, but she had learned the definitions by heart.

"Is it? Anyway, it's really good here compared to some places. Some of them are terrible. You can't hear yourself think, the music's so loud. They've got these tinny little systems so they crank them up too high. And you can't even dance 'cos the floor's too sticky with beer. Or worse."

"Did you see him do that thing with the whisk? I'd never've thought, when I first heard it."

"They're excellent, aren't they? It must take so much practice." He passed his hands through the air, water sloshing in its plastic bottle. "Maybe I could. . . No, you can't get the equipment, that's the trouble."

Dushma remembered what the bouncer had said to them at the top of the stairs. "Do people really bring their pets?"

"Pets? Oh, that. God, no." Arbilow laughed. "A few months ago these flyers started going round for some of the dodgier clubs. All sorts of different stuff, but they all said 'pets welcome' somewhere in the small print. Some people did actually start to bring dogs and cats and things. One of the upmarket Sundays even did a thing on how pets were the latest disco accessory."

"And weren't they?"

"No. What it meant was, the clubs would turn a blind eye to pimping on the dance floor as long as they got a back-hander."

Dushma shook her head. "Pimping? Is that like a kind of dance?"

"Erm, not really." He looked a little discomfited. "It's prostitutes, isn't it? Advertising them. Anyway, there were a couple of raids and one place got closed down. So now everywhere's still pretty nervous. But honestly, this place is fine, don't worry about it."

They finished their water and pushed their way back through the curtain. The music had slowed and intensified, filling the air with a sense of texture and weight. Cascades of percussion rang faintly through the heavy chords, as if in a distant street medieval armies clashed.

The figures on the dance floor moved more languorously now. Several couples were almost motionless, simply standing and swaying against each other. Stepping among them, Dushma hardly bothered to try and dance. She felt the heat of the lights on her skin and the deep notes of the music resonating in her ribcage. She felt soft, as if her flesh had been tenderized by the beat.

How long had she been here? She had no idea. She looked down at her watch but it was too dark to see the hands properly. She would have to angle it towards one of the lights and that would make it obvious she was trying to see what time it was.

She flicked a glance at a couple nearby. They were pressed together, almost completely still, their eyes closed.

Out of the corner of her eye she could see Arbilow close to her. She did not draw back when he reached out and touched her shoulder.

As he steered her through the other dancers Dushma wondered what she should say to him. That there was somebody else? Except there wasn't, but there had been, and she wasn't sure yet if she was ready. . . It would be far too complicated and difficult to explain, she knew.

They reached the wall at the side of the dance floor. Arbilow felt in his pocket, then held out his hand, fingers folded over his cupped palm. "Close your eyes," he said.

She hesitated. "What is it?"

"Go on. You'll see. Oh, and hold your breath, too."

She pressed herself back against the wall, lips squeezed together and eyes wrinkled shut. A soft breeze blew over her face, and something tickled her cheeks and the bare skin of her neck and shoulders. She flinched and stifled a nervous giggle.

She opened her eyes to see Arbilow rubbing his hands together and smiling at her.

"What?" she demanded, half amused and half annoyed at his teasing expression. She touched her face and peered

261

down at her hand. Something glinted on her fingertips.

She turned to the wall, ducking her head so as to get a glimpse of herself in the fragments of mirror embedded in the velvet. It was difficult to tell what she looked like from the jigsaw of images that confronted her. She twisted this way and that, trying to see her reflection more clearly.

Her face, her throat and her shoulders sparkled with glitter. Bright against her dark complexion, flecks of blue, purple, red, green and gold flashed and winked as she moved her head from side to side.

Arbilow was watching her expectantly. "So, what do you think?" he asked.

She grinned at him, then composed her face into an expression of mock hauteur. "I'm sorry if you thought I was looking a little drab." She tossed her head and turned away from him, trying to hide her delight.

She felt his hand on her shoulder-blade, next to the strap of her dress. Despite the warmth of the air, it was as if a cool breeze had eddied across her back and her upper arms, making her tingle. She held herself quite still. She would step away in a moment, she told herself.

She closed her eyes and tilted up her head, leaning back against Arbilow's touch. She felt his fingers move to her spine, then up to the nape of her neck.

"Excuse me, please. . ." A bouncer stood in front of them, obviously agitated. His face glistened with sweat and his bow tie appeared to be wilting.

Dushma jumped guiltily away from Arbilow, ready to

apologize. Then she noticed that behind the bouncer the dance floor was almost deserted. The last couple were hurrying towards the curtained exit.

"Just a precaution, no need to panic," the bouncer was saying. A bell started to ring.

Her feelings a mixture of relief and disappointment, Dushma made her way with Arbilow off the dance floor and out into the lounge. This room too was now almost empty. A cluster of people had gathered at the foot of the stairs.

Fluorescent tubes in the ceiling shivered alight. As her eyes grew used to their glare, Dushma noticed the stains and tears in the velvet wall-coverings, the cigarette burns on the sofas and the holes worn in the brown linoleum on the floor.

She and Arbilow began to climb the stairs. They were among the last to leave. No one seemed in a great hurry. No one really knew what was going on. A few people were grumbling that they weren't getting their money's worth. Others speculated excitedly that there had been some kind of raid on the premises.

Looking back down into the lounge, Dushma saw the cart handlers come through the curtains. One had his arms full of cartridges. The other was arguing with the bouncer. He clearly wanted to go back and rescue their equipment. Shepherding them firmly towards the stairs, the bouncer began to cough.

The fluorescent lights blinked, then went out. For a

moment the lounge was in darkness. Somebody screamed.

Then the curtains over the entrance to the dance floor burst into flames. These were unmistakably real, not coloured lights or tissue paper. Even from the far side of the room Dushma could feel their heat on her face and taste smoke at the back of her mouth.

Sprinklers in the ceiling sputtered into life. Hissing clouds of steam filled the room.

Frozen on the lower steps of the staircase, Dushma panicked. Feelings of helplessness and confusion overwhelmed her. This had happened to her before and she had done the wrong thing, she knew. What if there was someone still down there? Images of a burning, smoke-filled corridor crowded her memory.

This time she wasn't going to run away. She took a step back down the stairs.

The flames reared up through the mist from the sprinklers. One of the sofas was on fire.

Why on earth is the music still playing? she thought wildly. Then she realized it wasn't. She strained her ears and heard nothing but the spitting sound of the sprinklers, the crackling flames and the clanging of the fire alarm. But the steps still trembled beneath her feet. A rhythm still shuddered in her chest.

She looked up at the ceiling but it was already obscured by roiling clouds of smoke. It was going to collapse on her, she was sure. She sank down on to her haunches and raised her arms to protect her head.

She heard someone whimpering and realized it was her. She must pull herself together. Peering round she tried to get her bearings but her eyes were streaming too much for her to be able to see properly. What had she been trying to do? She couldn't remember. She moved her foot to try and feel the next step up and lost her balance.

Strong fingers gripped her arm and caught her as she fell.

"What are you doing? Come *on*!" It was Arbilow's voice.

"But what if someone's. . ." she tried to say, but the smoke caught in her throat and she choked.

"We're the last. Anyway . . . nothing we can. . ." He began to drag her up the stairs.

They reached the foyer and hurried across it towards the open air. Glancing back over her shoulder Dushma saw that the bottom of the staircase was already on fire. Strips of burning velvet were peeling away from the walls and dropping in charred coils on to the step where she had been crouching moments before.

Outside the Bunker, Sproule Street was crammed with milling, shouting people. A bouncer was pacing agitatedly back and forth just outside the doors.

"Yes, yes, I called them, they're coming," he was saying. He broke off as Dushma and Arbilow stumbled out on to the pavement. "Oh God, there's still people. . . Are you the last?"

"I think so." Arbilow guided Dushma away from the entrance. "Are you all right?"

"I'm sorry, I . . . I don't know what I was. . ." She steadied herself against a lamp-post and began to retch.

Clouds of smoke were now belching from the Bunker's open doors. The flames had reached the foyer and were throwing a fierce red glow out into the road.

"I think we'd better move," said Arbilow. He handed Dushma a tissue for her to wipe her streaming eyes.

They joined the crowd moving slowly away from the Bunker along the narrow street. The air was filled with excited chatter. Only those at the back of the crowd were beginning to glance worriedly over their shoulders at the flames and press forward more urgently.

"Could you move along up at the front, please?" someone called, a hint of panic in his voice. Behind them one of the Bunker's metal doors fell from its hinges with a clang.

Somewhere overhead a window slid open. A voice shouted angrily down.

The fresh air had cleared Dushma's head a little, although her eyes still felt scratchy and her chest hurt. People were pushing her from behind and it was becoming harder to stay upright. Looking round for another means of escape, she saw a gap in the wall beside them, so small as to be invisible from all but the right angle. She tugged at Arbilow's sleeve. "Look, this way."

She darted into the unlit opening, hands held out in front of her so she wouldn't run head-first into anything. She didn't know exactly where she was, but was sure passages like this always led through to another street, or at least to a fire escape they could climb.

It was only after she'd rounded a corner that she realized Arbilow wasn't following her. She stopped and turned, cocking her head to listen for footsteps coming down the passage. There were none. Even the crowd she had left behind was now almost inaudible.

She held her breath to try and hear more clearly. Through the ringing in her ears she became aware of a low grinding sound. She touched the wall beside her head and felt the brickwork shivering beneath her fingertips. A gritty dust like loose mortar trickled over her knuckles.

She let out a long shuddering breath and peered indecisively up and down the passageway. Then she took a step back in the direction of the Bunker.

A gust of air rushed past her face and something hit the ground just in front of her with a loud crack. Splinters of brick sprayed her bare shins. She leapt backwards, hands raised protectively.

Looking up she could see nothing but a narrow strip of sky a long way above her. Only the faintest illumination filtered down between the walls, reflected from a bank of low cloud tinted the colour of dirty sulphur by the weak city lights. There was no way of telling where the brick had fallen from, or if more were likely to follow it.

Dushma gathered herself. She hadn't come far. If she ran as fast as she could it should only take her a few seconds to retrace her steps.

She heard another brick strike the ground, just around the corner in the direction she had come from. She froze, her shoulders hunched. Two more bricks fell in quick succession.

She started backing away. "Don't come this way!" she shouted. "There's bricks. . ." Then she turned and fled.

The passage narrowed as she sprinted along it. At one point she had to turn sideways to squeeze her way through. She could hardly see more than a few metres in front of her in the dim light, and she began to worry she would reach a dead end. She had passed no windows, and seen no ladders she could have climbed or flights of metal stairs that might have offered shelter.

At last, to her relief, she rounded a corner and found herself in a proper street again. Stopping to catch her breath, she looked around for a landmark that might enable her to orient herself. She had turned so many corners in her flight along the passageway that she had no idea how far from the Bunker she had come, nor in which direction it now lay.

There was nothing helpful in sight. She had emerged into an alley which curved away to both left and right, making it impossible to see very far along it. There were a few parked cars, some dustbins clustered on the narrow pavement, and two or three streetlamps, much dimmer than usual, but still spreading wings of faint yellow light up the high brick walls. It was bright enough for Dushma to be fairly sure she was alone.

She brushed droplets of sweat from her neck and temples. The night was very close. Each breath she drew parched her lungs.

She listened, but there was no sound of voices or traffic. She shook her head and swallowed to try and clear her ears, but all she could hear was the same deep grinding noise she had first noticed in the passageway. It was a sensation as much as a sound, a shuddering such as might have been caused by heavy stones scouring against each other somewhere underground. It jarred her bones and made her want to clench her teeth together.

She looked up and down the alley, trying to work out where it was coming from. It was impossible to tell. All she could be certain of was that, though intermittent, it was growing louder. Glancing fearfully upwards, she began to back away from the nearest wall.

The pavement shuddered beneath her feet. Caught off balance, she staggered against the door of a parked car. Its alarm went off, an electronic squall that almost drowned out the sound of cracking concrete.

With no idea of where she was going, Dushma ran. Paving stones tilted up in front of her like trapdoors. She leapt to avoid a few of them, then swerved on to the road.

Here the going was no easier. The tarmac had begun to melt, and it stuck to the soles of her shoes with every step she took. Each laborious stride tugged painfully at her knee joints.

Two loud bangs sounded almost simultaneously from

behind her. She turned in time to see a car slump forward as its front tyres burst.

She jumped back to the pavement and ran on, the flagstones crunching under her feet like crusty bread. Momentarily, she had the absurd yet horrifying thought that she was the one who was causing the chaos around her. She imagined herself as a giantess, shattering the pavement with her footsteps.

A streetlight exploded as she passed underneath, showering her with hot splinters of plastic. The next light was some way on and, unable to see where she was putting her feet, she tripped and fell.

She landed in the gutter, her head striking the softened tarmac. Winded and dizzy, she pulled herself free of the sticky surface, struggling to focus on the blurred square shape of a drain a few centimetres in front of her.

She lurched to her hands and knees and a wave of scalding air beat against her cheek. She twisted away, shielding her face with one hand.

The heat was coming from the drain. The metal bars were turning red. As she watched they began to droop, sagging downwards like thick strands of glowing toffee.

She scrambled back on to the pavement, still on her hands and knees. She tried to rise but the kerb crumbled beneath her and spilled her on to her back.

She sat up in time to see the centre of the road begin to lift and split. A glowing, orange substance like burning jam oozed from the fissured tarmac and wriggled in fiery rivulets towards the gutter. Reddish light filled the alley.

Dushma pushed herself back from the kerb, cutting her elbows on the smashed flagstones as she jerked her feet clear of the road.

Coils of lava wrapped themselves round the wheels of a nearby car. The tyres caught fire first, and then the rest of the vehicle, paintwork blistering and windows cracking as the flames took hold.

Dushma staggered to her feet but her melted shoes were too ruined for her to run. She bent to scrabble at the fastenings, breaking her nails on the tangled straps. Her left shoe came off and she lost her balance again, falling to one knee. Long shadows leapt and ducked around her as the fire advanced. She flinched and raised her head.

A figure reared up beyond the flames of the burning car.

Dushma cried out wordlessly. She stumbled back against the wall, hands held out in front of her, eyes streaming. The figure was trapped in the middle of the erupting tarmac. She waited helplessly for it to stagger and fall as the fire engulfed it.

The figure did not move. Wiping her stinging eyes, Dushma saw that it wore what looked like armour. Its torso was encased in a cuirass of black metal, so smooth and highly polished that it looked like smoked glass. Its curved chest glowed and flickered with a reflection of the burning alley. For a moment, through a gap in the flames, Dushma could see her own distorted image staring back at her, blackened face sparkling with glitter.

The figure began to glide slowly forward through the fire. It seemed to look from side to side as it came, the featureless, pointed wedge of its helmeted head swinging back and forth on the articulated column of its neck.

Unable to take her eyes off it, Dushma limped away over the cracked and scorching pavement. One foot bare, she moved crabwise, her back still pressed to the wall.

She had taken all of three steps when the burning car exploded. The doors burst from their hinges and the windscreen dissolved into a cloud of shining splinters that sprayed down the street like a hot shower of hail.

Dushma threw herself to the ground, arms protecting her face. Debris rattled against the wall above her and something sharp struck her shoulder.

As soon as she dared, she pulled herself upright, shook the remaining shoe from her foot and ran. Her feet burned with every stride she took but she set her teeth and ignored the pain. Within a few seconds the pavement began to feel cooler and its surface became less uneven. A burning wheel overtook her, shedding scraps of smouldering rubber as it rolled along the road.

She glanced back over her shoulder just before rounding a curve in the alley. The figure in armour was gone. There was nothing to be seen but the flaming remnants of the car and, beside it, a long, glistening scar in the tarmac like a furrow ploughed in wet earth.

XI

Wound Dressing

"Are you sure?"

"Of course I'm sure!" said Dushma a little snappishly. "It was just there, no further than that cupboard."

"Hmm. But it must have been pretty dark. . ."

"No it wasn't. The road was on fire! It was bright as. . . Ouch!"

"Sorry. . . Hold still. Nearly finished."

Dushma had no idea what time it had been when she had eventually reached home the night before. After letting herself in and creeping upstairs on bare and blistered feet, she had been too exhausted to do anything other than fall into bed.

She had woken late, despite the sunlight flooding the room through the undrawn curtains. There had been a sharp pain under her collarbone, and blood on the sheets from her scraped elbows and knees.

She was worried she would be in serious trouble. Even after she had done her best to wash the smoke stains from her face it was obvious something had happened to her. There was a cut on her forehead, her eyebrows were singed and a bruise was darkening like a stormy sunset on her cheek. Inspecting herself in the mirror, she knew there was no hope of remaining out of sight for the week or more it would take for these blemishes to fade.

When at last she presented herself in the kitchen, Marlstroy was still lingering over the remains of his breakfast, a pile of newspapers at his side. "Morning," he grunted, not looking up.

"Oh my God!" exclaimed Mrs Breckle, turning to stare from her position by the sink.

"I'm all right," Dushma insisted, possessed by the sudden absurd urge to be stoical. She reached out for a chair and winced as the movement jarred her arm.

Ignoring her protestations, Marlstroy had taken her to his study and treated her injuries. With a pair of tweezers he extracted a small nugget of car windscreen glass from the wound in her shoulder. Then he swabbed the melted tarmac from her grazed limbs with clumps of cotton wool soaked in surgical spirit. The alcohol stung her broken skin and the strong antiseptic smell burned in her nostrils, making her eyes water.

While Marlstroy worked Dushma recounted the events of the previous evening. As she told the story it struck her how far-fetched it must sound. Yet even in the face of her guardian's gently sceptical questioning she was certain that every word of it was true. The images in her mind's eye were still far too vivid for her to be in any doubt about whether she had really seen the things she remembered.

Marlstroy threw the last of his cotton wool into the waste-paper basket and began taping lint to Dushma's elbows. "So, apart from that," he asked, "how was your evening?"

Dushma blinked, a little taken aback by the question. "Oh. I don't know," she said. The events before her flight from the Bunker already seemed very distant, having been almost completely eclipsed by what had happened afterwards. "It was OK, I suppose. The music was really interesting. Really different. And pretty loud."

Reaching into a drawer of his desk, Marlstroy took out a sealed plastic wrapper. He tore it open and removed a disposable hypodermic needle. "I don't suppose you've ever had a tetanus jab?" he asked.

"What's that?" She swallowed as the cold tip of the needle touched her arm.

"It's a disease you can get from untreated cuts. Now just relax. . ."

An icy thread seemed to squeeze its way deep into her bicep. She inhaled sharply, forcing herself not to clench the muscle.

"I've got to tell someone," she said.

"Why?" Marlstroy pressed a sticking plaster over the puncture left by the hypodermic. "It's bound to be all under control by now. And it sounds like there were plenty of other witnesses."

"But nobody else saw what I saw! There could be someone hurt, or, I don't know, something dangerous still around there. I can't just not say anything."

"It was hours ago, Dushma. There's been nothing on the news about it. It can't have been that serious."

"You don't believe me, do you?" she said.

"Now wait a minute, don't sound so cross. I believe you when you say what you think you saw. But it was dark, you were tired, there could be any number of explanations."

"But the road was on fire!" She heard her voice rising and made an effort to sound reasonable. "What explanation could there be for that?"

"Maybe joyriders stole a car, left a cigarette smouldering in the ashtray. Eventually it sets the car alight and the flames make a pillar box or a parking meter seem like something different."

"No! I'm sure it wasn't either of those. It can't have been, I saw it moving!"

"OK, so this *person* you saw. . ."

"I don't know if it was a person or a machine. A person would've been burned alive for certain, you'd've thought, but it was wearing this stuff that looked like armour. . ."

"But whatever it was, it was inside that car that caught fire, do you think?"

"No." She shook her head emphatically. "It was further away, I'm sure. It was on the other side of it."

"Wait a minute. Think about it for a moment. What you're saying is, someone, or some*thing*, came up from *underneath* the road, in a shower of fire and brimstone. . ."

"Yes I *know* it sounds impossible when you just say it like that, but . . . there *are* machines underground, I've seen them. Not like that, but that doesn't mean. . ." She saw Marlstroy's doubtful expression and her voice trailed away. "Anyway, you can't expect me to pretend I didn't see it. I've got to tell somebody, warn them, so they can maybe make sure it doesn't happen again."

"By doing what? Listen, things catch fire. They just do. It's not going to be your fault the next time a car goes up in flames. And suppose they do take you seriously? They'll be round here making enquiries, asking you questions, carrying out medicals on you for all I know. And what if they decide that *you're* suspicious?"

"Me? Why? What have I. . .?"

"You've hurt yourself enough already. You're lucky it wasn't more serious. Now that's enough. Whatever it was you saw, I don't want you getting any further involved!"

Her eyes flashing, Dushma tilted up her chin defiantly. For a few seconds the two of them glared at each other.

Then Marlstroy turned away and threw up his hands. "All right," he said. "You do what you like. But promise me one thing. Please don't tell anyone about what you saw until I've made some enquiries."

"So you do think it might be something dangerous?" Dushma tried not to sound triumphant.

"No! No I don't, not at all. I'm sure there's a perfectly ordinary explanation. I know there've been rumours, recently. Fires that weren't accidental, unexplained tremors underground. People have been talking about terrorist activity, but there's been nothing concrete enough to make the news. Personally I don't believe a word of it, and neither do people whose judgement I value highly."

"Why not?"

"Because there's no point being a terrorist nobody knows anything about. No one's claimed responsibility for anything. When these people blow something up they can't resist letting everyone know how clever they've been."

Marlstroy stood up and began to clear his desk. He put away his tweezers and the unused lint, and returned the bottle of surgical spirit to its place inside a glass-shelved cabinet. "So there you are," he said, turning back to Dushma. "What's there to worry about?"

She hesitated. "I was with someone, you see," she said, "and I . . . we got separated, I don't even know what happened to him. So I was thinking I could ask . . . well, I don't know, whoever. . ."

"No one was hurt, I'm sure. As I said, there's been nothing on the news. But if you like I'll ask about that as well. Just give me a little time. Now is that all right? Do you promise?"

Dushma nodded.

"Good." He handed her a tube of ointment. "Here. Try some witch hazel on that cheek."

Dushma had forgotten about her bruise. She raised a

hand and cautiously touched her face. Her cheekbone felt very tender.

"I look terrible," she said, peering with dismay at her reflection in the polished metal lampshade that angled over Marlstroy's desk. "What am I going to tell them at school tomorrow?"

She had some makeup, bought rather randomly in the first flush of excitement at her new spending power, although she had hardly used any of it. She had so far been too unsure of the unwritten rules obeyed by her classmates to dare to wear any to school. But while it might help to disguise the yellow and purple swelling on her cheek, she doubted there was much she could do about the abrasion on her forehead and the singed remains of her eyebrows.

"You look fine," Marlstroy reassured her. "And you can tell them about most of it. Tell them you were at a night club and it burnt down. Fib about what happened afterwards. Make something up. Have a little fun. They'll be agog, I bet you. It's bound to be more interesting than anything any of the rest of them did last night."

Dushma considered this. It had potential. She could probably make her evening sound quite exciting. "I suppose so." She touched her face again, trying to feel the extent of the bruising. "And will you write me a note?"

"Of course. If it'll help." He stood, and with a sudden, clumsy movement, put his arm round her shoulders and hugged her. "I . . . well, anyway," he said awkwardly. "Glad it's not worse." His smile took his face by surprise. It wasn't the calculated grin Dushma was used to seeing. "I thought you were able to look after yourself," he said. "I don't know if this is evidence for or against."

They returned to the kitchen. After breakfast Dushma went upstairs to her room, but feeling in need of company she soon came down again and sat at the kitchen table with a book.

"There's been all sorts of talk," said Mrs Breckle when Marlstroy had gone back to his study. "My cousin's nephew works at Polegrieve Boys' School and apparently on a class trip out into the country their bus was caught up in a volcanic eruption! They were surrounded by a sea of molten lava! The teacher went for help but all they ever found of him was the melted remains of his wellies in a ditch. It was three days before they got rescued, and by then they'd already organized themselves into a strict social hierarchy. They had laws and basic sanitation and a system of barter based around the buttons on their blazers. I hope you girls would be as sensible."

Dushma looked up from *Lord of the Flies*, which her class were reading that term. "Praline would be in charge," she said. "There'd be complicated rules about dress and vocabulary. I don't think she'd be so hot on sanitation."

XII

Fireglass

By Monday evening the long spell of unseasonably good weather had still not broken. Dushma walked home from school with her heavy winter blazer slung over her shoulder, her skin clammy from the heat. There was not so much as a whisper of a breeze. Now and again brown, shrivelled leaves dropped vertically downwards through the still air like napalmed butterflies.

It was the hottest autumn since records had begun. This was fortunate, the weathermen said, as it meant people could delay turning on their heating and so save energy.

Moth had been unimpressed. They had been in the locker room at lunchtime and she had just discovered that one of her herbs had died. She had forgotten to water it and it had withered, flopping in a tangle of brittle stalks down on to the window-sill among the dust and the husks of trapped insects.

"It's always the somethingest something since sometime," she said grumpily. "What I want to know is, where are the mists and mellow fruitfulness? And how are we supposed to trust these guys when they bang on about what love's like if they can't even get the seasons right?"

"Wasn't that a long time ago? Maybe the weather's changed since then."

"In that case maybe love's changed too. Maybe it's not like a red red rose any more. Maybe it's like a stinging nettle. I think we should be told."

No one had asked about the bruise on Dushma's cheek. She had arrived at school terrified that people would stare at her and whisper, but as the day wore on she began to feel disappointed that no one had even mentioned it. It looked as if she wasn't going to be given the chance to tell her carefully edited version of Saturday night's events.

It began to seem too late to say anything about it herself. She was tempted to tell Moth, who would normally have made a sympathetic audience, but her friend was too preoccupied with the fate of her plant collection.

The only person she was certain had noticed was Praline. They had passed each other in the corridor and Praline had given her a look which had made it quite clear that whatever it was Dushma had been up to, it was sure to be far too sordid for her, Praline, to bear hearing about.

Dushma's feet still hurt and it took her longer than usual to reach home. She had made her blisters worse by going on a long walk the day before. Worried about what might have happened to Arbilow, she had returned to Sproule Street to try and find the Bunker and the site of the destruction she had witnessed on Saturday night. It had been a wasted journey. Eventually she saw a building she thought she recognized, but a little further on she found the street taped off and a policeman standing guard. He told her there had been a gas leak, but would say little more than that. He had claimed he didn't even know whether anyone had been injured or not.

Limping slightly, her blazer swaying uncomfortably across her back, Dushma turned into the road where she lived and saw a long black car with tinted windows parked outside her house. As she approached the front gate she noticed a man in a black suit and dark glasses loitering nearby.

Her first thought was to cross the road and keep on going past the house. She had immediately been certain that the man was waiting for her. She hesitated, her step faltering.

The man was watching her, head tilted slightly back, face impassive. Keeping her nerve, she turned in through the gate and walked up the garden path. She felt his eyes on her all the way to the front door.

Before she could begin climbing the stairs to her room, she heard Marlstroy call out to her from his study. So it was indeed something to do with her.

She put down her bag and crossed the hallway. He hadn't sounded angry or worried, she reassured herself. Nevertheless, she paused outside the study door to put her blazer back on. The thick fabric gave her a feeling of protection.

Inside the study the curtains were closed and the light was low. Marlstroy sat behind his desk. Slumped in the armchair opposite him was a large, grey-haired man in steel-rimmed spectacles holding a cut-glass tumbler of milk.

"Oh yes, you're the one," said Ashpool, waving his drink at her. "I remember. Accountant, wasn't it? Very sensible girl, I thought at the time."

Marlstroy laughed. "Your flattery's wasted, old chap. She sees right through you."

"In that case I shall get straight to the point." He beckoned her forward impatiently. "Come in, come in. Close the door. Yes, let me see. . . Dear me, you have been in the wars, haven't you?"

Dushma blushed, even though she was sure he was exaggerating. Her bruise was already fading and would hardly show up at all in this light, she thought.

"Your guardian tells me you have a story that might interest me," Ashpool continued. "He also tells me, to my great relief, that you have been persuaded, like the sensible girl you are, not to go rushing off telling it to all sorts of the wrong people who might have got the wrong end of the stick and got themselves, and quite possibly you as well, into all sorts of trouble, am I right?"

There was a short silence while Dushma tried to work out what it was Ashpool was asking her. Then she gave up and simply decided that he didn't look like the sort of person who would enjoy being told he was wrong.

"Yes," she said.

At Ashpool's request, Dushma recounted the details of the fire at the Bunker and its aftermath. He listened without interrupting until she reached the appearance of the armoured person or machine from beneath the burning tarmac. At this point he became extremely attentive and began asking a rapid series of questions.

"So this thing you saw, how tall did it seem to be? As tall as me? As tall as that bookcase? Could you draw it for me? What was it made of, would you say?"

Dushma tried as best she could to answer him, even managing a clumsy sketch of the figure she had seen through the flames of the burning car. When she had finished, Ashpool brooded for some time in silence, swirling the dregs of his milk in the bottom of his glass.

"Look, old chap," said Marlstroy at last. "It's terribly good of you to take this so seriously. We're very grateful and all that, but as I've already pointed out to her, it was dark, there was a lot of confusion, the poor girl was very shaken. There must be a perfectly mundane explanation. Joyriders, an abandoned cigarette setting the car alight. . ."

Ashpool stared at Dushma through calculating eyes. "I'm not totally convinced that your version of events can account for exactly what she claims to have seen," he said. "And nor does she appear to be."

"I'm not saying she's made a word of it up, but, frankly. . . She reads a lot of books, she has a vivid imagination. She's not going to interpret what she saw with the same degree of scepticism you or I. . ."

Ashpool raised his hand. "What I'm going to tell you now must remain, it hardly needs to be said, strictly between ourselves." He leaned towards Dushma. "There are people who do not have this country's best interests at heart who would use this information against me. In the current climate of rumour and unease there is a potential for misunderstanding, not to say completely unjustified panic, which I am extremely anxious to avoid. For this reason, young lady, I am very keen that what you have just described to me should not reach the ears of anybody else.

"There are two ways for me to try and achieve this. The first is for me to explain to you the significance of what you have seen and allow you to understand the importance of your absolute discretion. The second way is somewhat cruder. I see no reason to alarm you with the details at this present moment in time, since I have decided to rely on your cooperation. This is because I believe you are a girl of common sense and intelligence who will grasp the legitimacy of my request. It is also due to the high regard in which I hold your guardian, whose help, so invaluable to me in the past, I hope to be able to rely on again in the very near future."

"Oh, you're a smooth-tongued devil," said Marlstroy. "At the risk of sounding like a recalcitrant back-bencher, may I ask just how the right honourable member intends to turn his fine words into deeds?"

Ashpool reached into the inside pocket of his jacket. He

drew forth a cylindrical rod about the size of a pen. He weighed it in the palm of his hand for a few seconds, then leaned forward and rolled it over his fingers and on to the desktop.

Marlstroy picked it up and held it up to his lamp. Then he took a watchmaker's eyeglass from a drawer and fitted it into his eye in order to examine the rod more closely.

"Glass and metal, bonded together?" he asked.

"Aluminium, to be precise."

"Have you any idea," asked Marlstroy, removing his eyeglass, "how much General Motors would pay for this? Or Toyota, or Volkswagen?"

He held out the rod to Dushma. She took it from him cautiously.

The ends were indeed exactly like ordinary pieces of glass and metal, cold and hard against her skin. The middle section of the rod, however, was made of something altogether more unusual. Each end blended seamlessly into a dark, opaque substance, warm to the touch and with an extraordinary texture, neither liquid nor solid. It felt slippery, as if it should be wet, although when Dushma rubbed her fingers together they were perfectly dry. There were hints of movement in its smoky depths, yet when she peered closely all she could see was the distorted reflection of her own face staring back at her.

"There are, no doubt, commercial applications," Ashpool was saying. "But the exigencies of national security come first, of course."

Marlstroy snorted. "So for a few months or even years our aircraft or our tanks or whatever are a bit flashier than everybody else's. Then some American company discovers this stuff too. They patent it and make billions. And then anybody's army who can afford it has got equipment that's just as advanced as ours again. It wouldn't be the first time something like that's happened."

"But what is it?" asked Dushma. Then she gasped and almost dropped the rod. She was sure she had felt it move. Staring down at it in disbelief, she saw that it was indeed now slightly but unmistakably crooked.

"Fireglass," said Ashpool, smiling in superiority at her bafflement. "One of a class of substances known as fluramics to the dozen or so people aware of their existence. It's a ceramic, you see, but one which has certain properties akin to those of a fluid, albeit a highly non-Newtonian one. One of its characteristics is memory. On a molecular level it somehow 'knows' what shape it's supposed to be. If you put it back on the desk you'll see it resume its original form."

Sure enough, when Dushma placed the rod on Marlstroy's blotter it slowly straightened itself of its own accord. She brushed her fingertips against her skirt to try and rid them of the lingering feel of oiliness. She thought of Arbilow's account of his experiences as a clinker monkey. *Moving, flowing under my touch.* . . That had been his description of the substance he had found embedded in the chimney wall a moment before he had fallen.

288

"Paradoxically, it's also harder than porcelain, has twice the tensile strength of steel and is virtually indestructible." Reaching out towards the rod, Ashpool scooped it up and tucked it back inside his jacket.

"So how did you make it?" prompted Marlstroy. "Who discovered how to do it? Why has it been kept so quiet?"

"Who discovered it?" Ashpool paused rhetorically, enjoying the full attention of his audience. "We don't know. We found a description of the process among a collection of old documents. They came to us after the fall of the iron curtain from the archives of a Romanian laboratory. It was attached to a factory making ceramics and glassware since way back, the 1880s at least. Ornaments and trinkets, mostly; angels and gargoyles, that sort of thing. But these writings were more serious stuff altogether. It was like a renegade chemist had tried to sum up his life's work: instructions, diagrams, lists of materials, most of them done in haste. As to their original provenance. . ."

"So someone else had already done it?" interrupted Marlstroy.

"Perhaps. Or tried to, anyway. I said the documents were old. Well, apparently this particular process had been attempted once before, in late nineteenth-century London, although it's not clear how it could have been done without modern apparatus. No record of the outcome appears to have survived, and we assumed that if it took place at all it was a failure. But some of the ideas were intriguing enough for it to be considered worthwhile trying to repeat the experiment. Using, I need hardly add, appropriate alternatives in place of the more *macabre* ingredients."

Ashpool turned and gave Dushma a self-satisfied leer, as if he'd told a joke he didn't expect her to understand. She returned his look with as much composure as she could, yet his words had evoked disturbing memories. Sure that she already knew another side to the story, she thought of Vastruglin the Romanian alchemist, and found herself imagining Ashpool in a fire-lit cellar with a parcel of hair, teeth and bloodied skin in his hands. She willed the thought away. This wasn't the nineteenth century.

"So you succeeded, obviously," said Marlstroy impatiently. "And you've gone and built something with this stuff, is that right?"

"All in good time." Ashpool levered his bulk up out of the armchair. "Now that I've piqued your curiosity, I think we should take a drive."

Outside it was by now almost completely dark. The rationing of electricity meant that only a few dim street lights shone on the quiet road. The man in the suit was scarcely visible against the black bodywork of Ashpool's limousine. Dushma didn't see him until he moved to open the nearside rear door for them to climb inside.

Entering first, she shuffled across creaking, well-sprung leather to the far end of the seat. Close behind her came

Ashpool, already issuing instructions to his driver. The bodyguard climbed in through the front passenger door, slamming it behind him. By the time Marlstroy had pulled the rear door shut the car was on its way.

They had hardly turned out on to the main road when they heard several excited shouts. Figures moved along the pavement, their faces hidden. Some carried banners, the slogans indecipherable in the twilight.

Close by an engine revved. Something struck the side of the limousine with a sharp crack.

Through the windscreen Dushma saw the road ahead become suddenly much less distinct as the driver flicked the headlights off. The car slewed through ninety degrees into a sidestreet, running almost blind.

"I can have a motorcycle escort with us in three minutes, sir," said the bodyguard in the front passenger seat, his hand hovering over a telephone on the dashboard.

"Oh yes," snapped Ashpool. "Why not tell the whole neighbourhood that the Secretary of State for Energy is out for a drive?"

The car turned again. One of its rear wheels clipped the kerb, jolting the occupants.

The driver jumped a set of red lights and went the wrong way round a roundabout. When the road behind seemed clear again, he slowed and turned the headlights back on.

Ashpool removed his spectacles and rubbed a hand

across his eyes. "How am I supposed to do my job," he asked, "when I'm being continually harassed by every extremist anarchist agitator in the entire bloody country? Let me tell you, they'll be a bit keener on my energy policies when it gets colder and they realize they can't put their heating on."

He turned to Dushma. "I suppose you think this is all *terribly* exciting," he said wearily.

In fact she was rather shaken. She had been thrown sideways when the car swerved and had banged one of her scraped elbows. In addition to the pain, she was now beginning to worry that her story was being taken too seriously. It had been infuriating when Marlstroy refused to believe her, but now she was finding Ashpool's intense interest equally unwelcome. Perhaps he had misunderstood her, and would be angry when he realized that she didn't know, or couldn't do, whatever it was he expected.

"This thing moves a bit, doesn't it?" said Marlstroy. He was clinging to a strap above the door with one hand and patting the leather upholstery with the other. His eyes were sparkling. "Though as a taxpayer," he added, "I hope it runs on unleaded."

"I suppose that was Torrelguard's lot," muttered Ashpool to himself. "Though he'll deny it. I'll see if I can't have him picked up for incitement. Should keep him quiet for a day or two while he gets his team of lawyers together."

The car turned on to one of the main roads leading

south of the river. They crossed a bridge, the outline of the city glowing like a night-time mirage of its normal, more brightly lit self.

Soon after leaving the river behind, they turned off the main road again. No one spoke as they drove past high, blank walls and barred gates topped with coils of barbed wire. The only sounds were the faint roar of the engine, the purr of the tyres on the cobbled road, and the occasional barking of a lonely guard dog.

At last they reached a small courtyard in front of a pair of metal doors. A set of floodlights, the brightest lights they had seen that evening, glared down on the car as it pulled to a halt beside a prefabricated booth set against one wall of the courtyard.

Taking his time, a security guard came out of the booth, putting on his uniform jacket as he strolled towards the car. "Got a little lost on the way to the party, have we sir?" he asked. "Might I suggest that wherever you want to go is back the way you came?"

"And might *I* suggest. . ." began the driver.

Leaning out of the rear window, Ashpool cut him off. "You're in danger of getting a little lost on the way up the career ladder, young man," he said mildly. "Please do whatever you need to do to satisfy yourself as to who I am, and hope that, when you've done it, it hasn't taken you more than, oh, about five seconds, shall we say?"

When the metal doors began to swing apart, a short, brick-walled tunnel was revealed beyond them. As soon as the gap was wide enough the car moved forward, rolling a few dozen metres before coming to a halt again.

The soldiers blocking its path were better prepared than the man at the outer entrance. They shone a torch into the back of the car and one of them spoke briefly into a two-way radio. Then the steel shutter that closed off the far end of the tunnel began to rise.

Wherever it was they were, it was obviously intended to be highly secure. Dushma had no idea what there might be behind such heavy fortifications, but guessed that it must be fairly impressive. A scene like in a science fiction film, perhaps, with towers in futuristic shapes and vehicles gliding to and fro to the sound of trumpet fanfares.

In fact the view beyond the shutter was initially disappointing. At first she could see nothing but a small area of rubble and churned-up earth in the headlights of the car. As the shutter rose further she could make out the silhouettes of a few large, unlit buildings. There were no towers, only a pair of tall chimneys. Nothing moved except the distant, winking lights of a solitary aeroplane just above the skyline.

Ashpool leaned forward. "Wait here," he told the men in the front two seats. "You can turn the engine off, but don't leave the car."

He stretched across to throw open a door and the three of them climbed out. "I think we'll have the lights on, if you don't mind," shouted Ashpool to no one in particular. "All of them."

The shutter was still rising as he ducked under it and walked away into the darkness, his long shadow sliding in front of him over the uneven ground.

"I say, wait a moment," Marlstroy called. Then he shrugged and set off after Ashpool.

They seemed to have forgotten about Dushma. She hesitated, one hand on the car door. The group of armed soldiers still stood in front of the shutter, their faces hidden in the shadows cast by their helmets. They didn't move as she sidled among them.

"Mind how you go, love," murmured one of them as she passed him.

The ground was indeed treacherous. Dushma stumbled several times on loose stones and tufts of withered grass as she tried to catch up with the other two.

Ashpool seemed to be having no problem with the difficult terrain. He strode towards the nearest of the unlit buildings, jacket flapping, occasionally kicking stones and pieces of brick out of his path, or shaking wind-blown sheets of newspaper from his feet.

Behind him Marlstroy picked his way more carefully, unwilling to risk scuffing his highly polished shoes. Pausing to regain his balance on an angled slab of concrete, he turned to see Dushma struggling along in his wake and stopped to wait for her.

"Whatever it is, it had better be good after all this," he said, holding out his arm for her to steady herself against.

As they moved further from the car and the glow of its

headlamps it grew more difficult for them to see their way. But then, when they were about halfway across the open stretch of broken ground, the high windows set into the wall in front of them began to light up.

Like a wax drawing becoming visible under the strokes of a paint-brush, the massive structure gradually revealed its full extent as one by one the lights came on along the length of its interior. It was several storeys tall and as long as a street. Inside it looked cavernous and bare. Through the dirty panes of leaded glass, rafters and plain brick walls could be seen.

The only entrance appeared to be a small door set towards one end of the facade. Ashpool reached it first and stood waiting, arms folded. By the time the other two joined him the whole building was ablaze with light, and a wide grid of shadows lay across the illuminated waste ground.

Ashpool slapped the featureless metal surface of the door. "Look at this. No handle, no keyhole, no keypad for entering an access code."

"Very secure, I'm sure," said Marlstroy, a hint of exasperation in his voice. "I hope you're not telling us you've brought us all this way and now you can't get in."

"We used to have fingerprint recognition," continued Ashpool, as if Marlstroy hadn't spoken. "But that didn't work if your hands were dirty, or if you'd cut yourself. Then we had retinal scanners. But they were no good if you'd had a bad night's sleep and your eyes had got too bloodshot. So now. . ." He pointed to a metal plate set into the wall beside the door, then dipped his head towards it as if listening. The door clicked. Ashpool smiled in satisfaction. "So now, it reads my mind."

"Brain waves?" asked Marlstroy. "It picks up your thought patterns?"

"Exactly. Unique as a fingerprint. Impossible to forge, as yet. And with other considerable advantages. The system can be trained not just to recognize an individual, but also to determine their state of mind. Suppose you'd kidnapped me and brought me here against my will. Then it wouldn't open. It would be able to tell I was frightened."

Ashpool slapped the door again and it sprang open under his palm.

Inside the lights were so bright that Dushma instinctively ducked her head, as if this would lessen the glare. She had to shield her eyes with one hand in order to be able to look around.

The building appeared to be nothing more than a shell. No partitions divided its vast interior. It was possible to see all the way from one end to the other, although in the far distance the view was indistinct, perhaps due to the haze of floodlit dust hanging in the air.

The floor on which they stood was made of concrete. Here and there scorch marks and patches of oil discoloured its surface. Wide grooves filled with broken bricks ran across it, marking where rooms must once have been.

Nothing remained to hint at what these rooms might once have contained or been for. The building seemed almost entirely empty. It was only when she screwed up her eyes and peered into the glare of the lights in the direction of the farthest wall that Dushma thought she could make out a low shape, perhaps a vehicle of some kind.

"It was in a workshop near here that we made the first fluramics," said Ashpool. "A year or two ago. The whole site has been virtually sealed off ever since. And not just for the sake of secrecy." He looked at Marlstroy. "You said you thought someone else was bound to discover it too. I have to say I consider that unlikely. The conditions required for its manufacture are, let us say, extreme."

He spun round, indicating their desolate surroundings with a wave of his hand. "This building used to house one of our magnetic induction furnaces. Then one day last summer a power surge caused the fields to spill. Everything within a ten-metre radius simply evaporated."

"But why make the damn stuff here, in the middle of London?" asked Marlstroy. "Wouldn't it have been easier to choose somewhere a little more out of the way?"

"Well – it wasn't quite as simple as that. You see, our discovery of the process for the production of fluramic compounds was . . . fortuitous."

"You mean it was an accident?"

"Let's just say . . . it was *unexpected*, shall we?" Ashpool spoke slowly, choosing his words with care. "By the time it became apparent that we'd discovered something important it was too much of a security risk to recreate the experiment elsewhere. As I've said, we found, or rather *came by*, an old document describing the process. At first it seemed to be the work of a crank. But further study revealed it to be a remarkable mixture of alchemy and science which we didn't – or rather don't – fully understand. To put it bluntly – and I'm sure you'll appreciate that as a politician I find it difficult to say this, even completely off the record. . . To put it bluntly, we didn't really know what we were doing."

"And what *were* you doing?"

Ashpool turned and set off towards the far end of the building. "A few months ago," he began, "we built a machine. We'd made robots before; most of them unsuccessful. This was different. The casing was made entirely of fireglass. We used virtually the whole quantity we'd been able to produce. Highly malleable, almost indestructible, impervious to extremes of pressure and temperature . . . the perfect material for what was to be the first of a new type of exteroceptor. A remote device resistant to the most hostile conditions. A machine able to venture into the depths of the earth and tell us what it found there. Able to distort its shape and flow through narrow openings; driven by a nuclear reactor, giving it the power to roam unattended for years on end, to cut through rock and metal, to go where no man-made creation had ever gone before!"

Carried away by his rhetoric, Ashpool appeared to have forgotten about his companions. He was now striding along at such a pace that they were hard pushed to keep up with him without breaking into a trot.

"And so what was this thing?" prompted Marlstroy. "A bomb? An anti-personnel device?"

"Why do you assume it was bound to be for killing people with? What do you take us for? Warmongers?"

"Well, no, of course not, but. . ."

Ashpool flourished a finger in the air as if addressing a crowd. "This government," he declaimed, "has long anticipated the energy crisis we now face. We have initiated a variety of, er, initiatives to tackle the problem. We have invested in alternative energy projects, we have undertaken a comprehensive survey of potential new sites for oil and gas extraction, soon to bear fruit in the Thames Estuary, and . . . no, please let me make my point –" no one had attempted to interrupt him – "and we have also put considerable effort into developing different, more efficient ways of discovering new deposits of our dwindling natural resources. And *that* was to be the purpose of our new machine. Imagine the untapped reserves of energy it might find, the years of surveying and exploratory drilling that could be saved. The benefits are incalculable. So if we took a risk, it was with the noblest of motives."

"So if it wasn't for defence, why all the secrecy?" asked Marlstroy. "Why not just. . ."

"Because something went wrong." Ashpool had slowed down and was now walking with his arms folded, staring down at the ground in front of him and shaking his head. "Our budget had grown enormously, you see. We had to produce some results. So, against our better judgement, we brought our test date forward. It was too early, we knew. But we thought the worst that could happen was that it wouldn't work. In fact, it worked too well."

There was a dark patch on the floor some distance ahead of them. As they approached, it became obvious that it was an opening in the ground. Not quite circular in shape, it was well over a metre in diameter. The rim was curved inwards, as if something had been forced down through the concrete. Around it was a chaotic scribble of cracks and burn marks.

A little way beyond the hole, the vehicle-like shape which Dushma had first seen on entering the building was now much more clearly visible. It was the size of a large truck. Its body and the turret that surmounted it were made of acutely angled plates of olive-green metal. Caterpillar tracks looped along either side of it and camouflage netting sagged like thick green cobwebs from its downward-pointing barrel.

"Oil," said Ashpool. "Minerals. Gold and diamonds. How do you program a machine to search for those things? We didn't know. So we didn't try. Instead we programmed it to be inquisitive. We programmed it to be interested in loud noises, bright lights and colours. We made it curious about radiation and heat. We made it want to explore. We made it capable of learning. Perhaps we didn't program it well enough; or perhaps we programmed it too well."

They had reached the lip of the hole in the ground. Close to, it was revealed as the mouth of a vertical shaft, the scarred walls of which were lit up to a depth of a metre or so by the floodlights on the nearest wall. Further down than that it was impossible to see.

"We brought it here for the first of our tests," said Ashpool. "To begin with everything went well. The reactor came on line with no problems at all. The motors, drills and lasers all worked perfectly. Then we switched the thing's computer on."

He pointed to the hole at his feet. His face wore a look that was almost proud. "It snapped the restraining cables like chewing gum. It burned its way through fifteen metres of concrete, soil and rock in forty-five seconds. Imagine a film of a volcano erupting, but played backwards in slow motion. That's what it looked like. A fountain of dust and sparks sinking gradually out of sight."

He stretched out one foot and flicked a pebble over the rim of the shaft. It clicked against the sides a few times, the sounds fading as it fell.

"We lost track of it almost immediately. It wouldn't respond to any of the signals we transmitted." He shrugged. "In hindsight, it's obvious really. We'd given it a mind of its own. There was no point trying to give it instructions once it had decided what to do. And it had decided to waste no time in doing what it had been made for. It went exploring.

"For a while afterwards we had no idea what had become of it. Was it lying inert and harmless at the end of some tunnel, its mechanism snarled up and its computer dead? Or was it roaming through the earth beneath us, unreachable and out of control? If it had broken down then our prototype was a failure. If not, then what damage might its unchecked progress cause? Over the last few days and weeks the rumours I've been hearing have left me in less and less doubt as to which of those two scenarios is actually the case."

Marlstroy was rubbing his jaw in consternation. "Excuse me if I'm stating the obvious, but I can't believe you did this. When you think of the dangers. . ."

"But we were so *close*! Think of the good we were trying to do. Compared to that, what's the odd broken water main and a few ploughed-up roads?" Ashpool dismissed them with a wave of his hand. "It would have been a triumph. Articles, documentaries, awards. . . And it's been *mine*. I conceived the project and secured the funding. I've taken a personal interest since the very beginning. You don't know what a strain it's been not to be able to tell anyone all that we achieved, how near we came. . . And now, of course, the whole thing's been shelved."

"But you must be doing something about it. I mean, you can't just leave things as they are, can you?"

"Well, as you see, we've taken precautions in case it comes back here." Ashpool gestured at the tank looming nearby. "Manned with crack troops around the clock."

"And will it come back, do you think?"

"I don't know. But don't worry, it certainly won't come too close while I'm here." He gave a superior smile and tapped the side of his head. "I was the first to recognize the potential of the material we'd discovered, but as the project progressed I saw the dangers too. What if the machine we were building fell into the wrong hands? What if it turned against us and ran amok? So it's been designed to recognize key members of the government, myself included, and avoid them. It knows who I am. It's a safeguard implemented at the most basic level of its programming. If anything's working, that is."

"And what if it does come back here? I thought you said it was indestructible."

Ashpool shrugged. "To be honest, we don't really know. We didn't have sufficient time or material to do the necessary tests. But the one thing that stands a chance of stopping it is a depleted uranium shell."

"This thing," said Dushma. "What's it called?"

Both men turned to her as if surprised to see her still there.

"What's it *called*?" repeated Ashpool.

"Yes," said Dushma. Now that she knew what it was she had seen, it seemed important to her to be able to put a name to it. The two men clearly didn't feel the same way.

"I don't quite see what that's got to do. . ." began Marlstroy.

"Well, it didn't really have a name, as such," said Ashpool. "There was an internal reference code of course, but that wouldn't mean anything to you. No, we were going to wait until we were ready to make an announcement and then leave some PR company to come up with a snappy acronym. Although, come to think of it, someone did coin a word just as the work was beginning. Its purpose was always going to be to drill for natural resources. And in the early stages we were still planning to use electricity – batteries – to power it with, like we'd done in previous projects. So they called the new machine an elidril."

They walked round the tank and on towards the end wall. Here another door led out on to a stretch of wasteland similar to the one they had previously crossed. They stepped out over the rubble-strewn ground, Ashpool in the lead. Marlstroy scrambled closely behind him, still asking questions, wanting to know more about how the elidril worked, how it had been made, what other projects had preceded it. He was obviously concerned by what he had heard, but also clearly unable to suppress a certain boyish awe.

Fragments of their conversation reached Dushma as she made her way unsteadily after them. She found some of what Ashpool was saying unsurprising, such as the fact that before the construction of the elidril there had been other, less successful attempts at building robots from conventional materials. During her time as an underground refugee, Dushma had encountered what she was now sure must have been examples of these earlier efforts: bat-winged, metal-scaled, dragon-like machines too underpowered, much of the time, to work as intended. From what she had seen, the elidril clearly didn't suffer from this drawback. It was easy to understand Ashpool's pride.

They were walking towards a chimney. Its heavily buttressed base, lit by the windows of the building at their backs, was at least the diameter of a large traffic roundabout. Further up, its curved brick sides tapered away into darkness, its top discernible only by the red light that blinked on and off as a warning to aircraft.

At the foot of the chimney, like discarded shoe boxes underneath a tree, was a small collection of temporary offices. Most looked unoccupied, their windows dark, but lights showed from within the nearest. It was towards this one that Ashpool appeared to be heading.

"So . . . you've got no way at all . . . of knowing where this thing is?" asked Marlstroy, his arms outstretched as he tried to keep his balance on a scree of broken slate.

"Obviously we gave it a means of communication." Ashpool spoke over his shoulder, not pausing in his stride. "When at first we heard nothing, we thought maybe the transmitter wasn't working. Then we wondered if it just wasn't able to use it. After all, we'd designed it to actually *know* very little, but to want very much to learn about certain things. In a way it must have been like a child: intensely curious, but with no idea of what it was or what it could do, and needing experience in order to find out the extent of its power. Or perhaps we'd underestimated it completely, and it simply didn't want to tell us where it was."

The nearest prefabricated office was raised off the ground and they had to climb a few steps to reach the entrance. Their footsteps sounded hollow on the flimsy wooden boards.

Ashpool paused with his hand on the door. "And as you'll see," he said, "we're still none the wiser, even now that it has actually begun to send out signals."

He turned and led them into a large, harshly lit room, bare except for a few desks and chairs. At the far end a man sat at a computer with his back to the door. He was reading a newspaper, leaning back in his chair with his feet on the desk. A pair of headphones encased his ears, and he appeared to be unaware that he was no longer alone.

Ashpool rapped the open door sharply with his knuckles.

The man dropped his newspaper, spun his chair round and leapt to his feet. He had forgotten that he was still wearing his headphones and as he rose the jack sprang free of its socket. It flew across the room before being pulled abruptly back as the flex reached its full extent.

"Quiet evening?" asked Ashpool waspishly.

"Yes sir," said the man. He swiped at the swinging headphone flex and managed to catch it in the crook of his elbow.

"Well, don't just stand there. Carry on, don't mind us."

The man sat down again and reached under his desk to plug his headphones back in.

Moving to stand behind him, Ashpool said, "So, nothing at all, then?"

"No sir. It's lying pretty low tonight. Should've heard it Saturday though. Mad, it was. On and on, into the small hours."

"And still always the same thing?"

"Yeah, over and over. Look." He pressed some keys and several rectangular windows appeared on the monitor in front of him. Each showed the same thing: a thin green line undulating wildly between sharp peaks and deep troughs.

Ashpool turned to Marlstroy. "I want you to have a look at this for me." He gestured at the patterns on the screen. "Would you mind?"

Marlstroy opened his mouth as if to protest, but then merely shrugged. "If you like."

Ashpool turned back to the man at the computer. "Could you put a fragment on to a cartridge for me? Just a few minutes'll be enough."

They left the office a few minutes later, Marlstroy tucking a computer cartridge into an inside pocket of his jacket. "I don't know what you expect me to do with this," he grumbled to Ashpool. "You know I don't have the faintest idea about cryptography or cybernetics."

"Just a hunch I have. We gave that thing one of the most complex neural networks ever built. We're still not sure exactly how it might behave. For all I know, it might already have reached the stage of doing what we can only describe as thinking. And that's something you *do* know about."

"But since it's communicating now, can't you just ask it for more information?"

"It's still not responding to our commands. Either they're not reaching it, or, more likely, it's just ignoring them. For weeks we heard nothing from it whatsoever. Now it seems that at last it's discovered something it thinks is interesting. At first I thought it was trying to tell us about it. But I'm beginning to believe it doesn't care about us at all. It's just repeating something, over and over again, like you or I might whistle a favourite tune. I think what you've got there is a neural response – a thought, if you prefer – representing something it's found. Something it likes."

In the car on their way back, Ashpool spoke briefly to Dushma about the things she had seen and heard. "So there you are," he concluded, "now you know as much as I do. I hope you'll see no reason to pursue the matter further. You're far too sensible, I'm sure, but even if you did try and tell someone else about what you've learned this evening, they'd never believe a word you said. But then I hardly need to say that, do I?"

Dushma nodded. She was simply relieved that at the moment nothing more seemed to be required of her. At the moment all she wanted was to get home and go to bed. Her blisters were throbbing uncomfortably and her shins were aching from the effort of floundering after Ashpool across so much rough ground.

When the car drew up outside the house she slid from her seat and limped tiredly up the garden path without waiting for Marlstroy. It was not until she was in the hall that she turned and realized that Ashpool was still with them.

"Goodnight," he said, dismissing her with a nod. Then he touched Marlstroy's elbow and pointed down the corridor towards the study.

Although she was exhausted, Dushma hesitated on the stairs after she had heard the study door close. Her last glimpse of Ashpool had unnerved her. It wasn't the peremptory manner in which he had appeared to be virtually ordering Marlstroy around inside his own house. Rather, it had been his expression that had worried her, although she couldn't think quite why this was.

Often during the last few hours he had seemed eager, even excited, as he had explained how he had overseen the building of the elidril. But as he had stood in the hall, sprinkled with faint light from the low-energy bulbs in the crystal chandelier high above his head, there had no longer been any sign of such emotions on his face. Instead he had looked grimly determined, jaw muscles bunched beneath his ears and lips pinched tightly together.

Dushma reached towards the banister to continue her ascent. Something moved on the steps in front of her and she jumped, momentarily startled by the shadow of her own hand.

That was where she had last seen an expression similar to Ashpool's. It had been on her own face, caught briefly in her bedroom mirror as she had steeled herself to catch a spider in a tumbler and throw it out of the window.

She paused again, hand on the banister. Then she stooped, loosened her laces and slipped her feet out of her shoes. With no sound except a faint click from her tired joints, she glided back down the stairs.

XIII

The Stains of Power

"Something a little stronger this time?" she heard
Marlstroy ask. Glasses clinked.

"Well, I hope you found that worthwhile," said Ashpool.

"Yes, I suppose I should thank you for an intriguing
evening. Although I have to say I don't quite see why you
felt you had to go to so much trouble. And I didn't want
Dushma involved more than she had to be."

"But listen, don't you understand? She's the only one
who's actually seen this thing since it disappeared. I don't
know, maybe I shouldn't have expected anything, but I
thought it might be worth a try, taking her there and seeing
what might happen. . . Now don't look like that, there was
no risk at all. I knew it wouldn't come too close with me
around, but I thought we might feel something, perhaps,
or see some activity from the transmitter."

"But we didn't."

"Well . . . no, but even so, I hope you still found it an
interesting experience. Some of it was right up your

street, after all. That thought-pattern security device, for instance."

"Yes, I suppose it was. First time I've seen a working example, I must say. Not sure if it was worth ruining a perfectly decent pair of shoes for, though. Excuse me while I. . ."

A chair creaked.

"Ah, no, look at these. I'll have to. . . Or maybe Mrs B can do something with them."

Footsteps crossed the room and the door was pulled suddenly open. Dushma sprang backwards, sure she was about to be discovered. But no one came out. Instead, a hand appeared and flung a pair of shoes out into the corridor. They clumped down on to the tiles and the door slammed shut again.

". . .is absolutely state of the art," Ashpool was saying. "It has to get to know you, like those voice recognition programs for word processors. For it to be able to tell when you're frightened, for example, it has to have some data from a situation in which you were genuinely frightened." A note of pride crept into his voice. "Actually, I have to admit I gave them a lot of trouble with that one. In the end they had to mock up a copy of *The Times* with a fake front-page article about how I'd just been embroiled in a scandal and sacked. I was furious when I found out, but it did the trick. Yes . . . incredible technology. Fiendishly complicated stuff."

"I'm sure. In fact, I hold one or two patents on processes

that sound like they might be remarkably similar. I hope you're not treading on my intellectual property rights."

"Oh come on. It's all in a good cause. I wouldn't expect you of all people to be petty where the security of your country was involved. I've never doubted your patriotism."

Marlstroy gave a short bark of laughter at Ashpool's stilted compliment. "You've never even *mentioned* my patriotism. You've got me worried now."

"I mean, I never doubted that you'd do what had to be done, what was necessary for the greater good, even if it involved some sacrifice."

"Yes, you said something earlier this evening about relying on my help in the future. I take it you meant the immediate future?"

"As a matter of fact I did have something specific in mind, yes."

"I see. And is it to do with whatever's on this cartridge?" Something clattered on the desktop.

"Not. . . Well, if you'd have a look at that then yes, I'd be grateful but. . . In fact, there was something a little weightier I wanted to – how shall I phrase this? – to put forward for your consideration, let us say."

"I thought so. Come on then, out with it." He was making an effort to sound light-hearted, Dushma thought. She heard an odd clicking, swishing sound, and then realized it must be Ashpool swirling the ice cubes around in his tumbler.

"So. To business," he said. "You may have recently

noticed a new patient on your ward at the Galen. Her name is Catfinger."

"Oh, *that*. So that was you, was it?"

"I did manage to arrange for her transfer, yes. Although I don't believe the order is traceable to me."

"But why be so cloak and dagger about it, old chap? Why couldn't you have just. . ."

"This is a very delicate situation. The consequences are potentially disastrous."

"In that case let me tell you now, you've very little reason to worry. Her condition is stable and the chances of recovery are good. She really doesn't need any special treatment."

"That's not the point. I need her to be under your personal care."

"I'm afraid I don't. . . Oh. She's not. . ." He cleared his throat. "Do you, by any chance, have a personal interest here? I mean, you're not *related* to her in any way, are you?"

"You seem to be getting the wrong end of the stick. Let me explain from the beginning."

"Please do."

"As you may recall, at the last election we made a pledge to tackle the growing underclass of unregistered people evading their responsibilities to the state. When I was at the Home Office, I was charged with fulfilling that promise."

"I remember, yes. You mentioned it at the time. But I don't see. . ."

"As far as I was concerned we had a mandate from the

electorate and I pursued the policy aggressively. I appointed a task-force and gave them sweeping powers to do whatever was necessary in order to bring the problem under control. In charge of this task-force was an officer from Special Branch called Rapplemann."

"I recognize the name. I saw him mentioned in an article a while ago, I think."

"He got results and that was what I cared about. Arrest rates doubled after his appointment. So I just let them get on with it. By the time I realized what was going on it was too late. Rapplemann was out of control. He was a law unto himself and his methods were extreme. That explosion on the Underground a while ago: it looks like he was to blame. A sting that went wrong. It's impossible to be sure, but what's certain is that no one's seen him since. Officially, he's on indefinite stress-related leave."

"And unofficially?"

"He's probably dead."

"Then what's the problem?"

"He kept few records, thank God, so that should make it more difficult for anyone to prove he did the crazy, brutal things I've heard rumours about. But this Catfinger girl was involved in his last operation. He made some deal with her in exchange for information, and then went back on it. That's all she told anyone before she tried to kill herself. But people are starting to get interested. Her parents have heard there's a chance of compensation. A lawyer wants to ask the girl some questions. And she knows what Rapplemann was up to. If he caused that explosion on the Underground then I'm ultimately responsible and if it gets out then I'm ruined. So I don't want her to have the chance to talk. Do you understand what I'm saying? I don't want her to wake up."

There was a long silence from inside the study. Then Dushma heard Marlstroy's chair creak again as he rose to his feet. At last he spoke but his words were unclear.

"No!" said Ashpool. "If it was just a question of my own position then yes, I'd take my chances. You know me. But there's more at stake than that. Look at the bigger picture. Look at the political situation. This couldn't have come at a worse time. The prime minister's on the verge of caving in. He's watching his ratings plunge as everyone blames him for the strikes, the demonstrations, the soaring price of electricity and the shortages of petrol. If I'm forced out there'll be no one on the cabinet with the spine to stand up to the environmentalists and the trade unions. Who'll replace me? Jackson? Cadogan? The government would capitulate within days. The economy of this country would be put back years, if not decades. Foreign investment would pour out of the City. Manufacturers would abandon us in droves. Just imagine the misery, the thousands of unemployed. Catastrophic! I *will* not stand by and see that happen while I can possibly prevent it, whatever the cost."

There was another long silence. Dushma heard the pad of Marlstroy's stockinged feet on the carpet as he paced back and forth behind his desk.

"You don't know what you're asking me to do," he said eventually. "I'm not a politician, I'm a doctor. There are certain absolutes. . ."

"Don't you quote your Hippocratic oath at me!" Ashpool sounded angry now. "You've always been quick enough to bend the rules when it suited you. Remember Nicola Auquin? They'd have struck you off for that, at the very least, if it hadn't been for me. I saved your career, and at no little risk to my own, let me remind you."

"I never said I was a saint. In the right circumstances, I'm sure I'd abandon my scruples as easily as the next man. But not like this. Not in cold blood. Surely you can see that this seems wrong in a sense that other things we've done never were."

"Don't talk to me about morality," Ashpool sneered. "You mean the cheap certainties of Hollywood westerns where the good cowboy wears a white hat and the bad cowboy wears a black hat and we all know the hero will ride off into the sunset at the end of the film. I'm surprised to have to remind you that real life isn't like that. In the twilight everyone's hat is grey."

If she had been asked to guess Marlstroy's age from his voice at that moment, Dushma would have said he was at least twenty years older than she thought him to be. He sounded tired and hoarse and several times over the last few minutes his laboured breathing had been audible.

"Please. Think again about what you're asking. This isn't about merely avoiding punishment after the event, as it was in the case of Nicola, although God knows I felt I'd been punished enough for that anyway. This is a question of somebody's *life*. . ."

"Listen to me, Arthur." In contrast Ashpool's voice was firm and urgent. "She is *nothing*. Let me tell you a little bit about her. She has no possibility of any qualifications. She's a habitual truant with two convictions for shoplifting. Her father is a violent petty criminal and her mother a borderline alcoholic. Her prospects are nil. She has nothing whatsoever to offer society. Her future holds only poverty, crime and misery. Under current birth legislation she probably wouldn't even qualify for registration."

"You can't be sure of that. She's done nothing to deserve. . ."

"She's no innocent. She was conniving with Rapplemann."

"But that's still no reason to deprive her of a chance to. . ."

"So what are you going to choose? The minuscule possibility that this delinquent can cheat the overwhelming biological and social odds stacked against her? Or the virtual certainty that without me our craven administration will give in to the demands of extremists and reactionaries and drive the country into crisis?"

"You can't force me to make that decision."

"I'm afraid it's already too late for you to leave this room with clean hands. You've come too close to me to avoid the stains of power. Don't torture yourself. This isn't a cosy undergraduate thought-experiment. There *is* no right answer. All you can do is try and make sure the dirt won't show. So ask yourself, what do you *want*? Funds for the Galen? You've always said it's short of resources. If we pull through this I could help you turn it into something world-class. A centre of excellence. Think about it. You know that's not an idle boast."

"I'm sorry. It's no compensation for what you're asking me to do."

Ashpool sighed heavily. There was a loud clunk as he banged his glass down on some wooden surface. "You're living in an ivory tower. If the worst happens, don't think it won't touch you."

"What do you mean?"

"It must be a cosy life. Your experiments, your practice. And what's her name, that girl you've adopted, your latest hobby. . ."

"Wait. You're wrong."

"That's all worked out very nicely, hasn't it? But don't forget how she came to be here. It's not impossible for someone to find out that her registration isn't as legitimate as it appears."

"No! Don't say you'd do that."

"Of course I wouldn't. But if I'm exposed, or even investigated, then all my ministerial actions, every decision I've made, every favour I've granted, everything I've done will be thrown open to scrutiny."

"But I acted in good faith."

"Of course. Unfortunately, where registrations are

320

concerned, the courts, like you, tend not to recognize shades of grey."

"All right!" It was almost a shout. Then, much more quietly, Marlstroy added, "I'll do it."

It was no good telling herself she shouldn't have listened.

Back in her room, lying in bed, Dushma couldn't sleep. Every time she tried to empty her mind some new fragment of what Ashpool had said would seize her attention.

The name of Rapplemann had greatly startled her. She had almost given herself away, only just managing to stifle her gasp of recognition. It had been Detective Inspector Rapplemann who had tracked Dushma and her fellow outlaws to their refuge in the abandoned tunnels of Hitler Street station. *He's probably dead. . .* He was most certainly dead: she had seen him step on an electrified rail, smelled his flesh sear as the current burned through him. It was something she had wished never to be reminded of again.

Most disturbing, however, was the idea that somehow what she had heard had placed some burden of responsibility upon her. She should tell someone, she thought, someone in authority. But there was no one. Her teachers at school? They would never take her seriously. A fantasist. That's what they had called her, to her face. So what would they make of this?

But even if she found someone to tell, even if they believed her, she knew that what Ashpool had said was correct. His ruin would also bring about her own. And that was something Marlstroy clearly didn't want, but for how long could she rely on his protection? How much of his concern for her was on account of his experiment, and how much of it was now personal? Misgivings rose up in her mind, misgivings she had been avoiding ever since she had heard the story of Nicola Auquin. From the way Marlstroy had spoken of her, it seemed possible that he had come to care about Nicola as more than just a subject for his research. But still this hadn't saved her, in the end.

Dushma turned from side to side, unable to get comfortable. When at last she drifted into a shallow, uneasy doze, she dreamed of the elidril. It was directly beneath her, hundreds of metres down through the earth. It flowed through tunnels and caves, dark, gleaming body surging forward on shining silver pistons, featureless head swinging tirelessly from side to side. Indistinctly lit by a fiery glow, it was impossibly strange yet strangely familiar, like the incarnation of some mythical creature.

When it reached an obstacle it didn't stop. It simply carried on in a frenzy of sparks and white-hot splinters of rock.

XIV

The Neon Canal

Throughout the course of her next day at school, Dushma was reprimanded several times for inattentiveness. By the end of the afternoon, she would be able to recall only one incident from any of the lessons she had attended. Even in chemistry, still the one subject she enjoyed, her mind was elsewhere. Oblivious of what she was writing, she copied down notes about the properties of mercury, then stared listlessly out of the window as the teacher held up a vial of the sluggish silver liquid.

Alison had often regaled her with stories of life at school, making her envious of all the excitement she seemed to be missing. Science classes had sounded by far the most interesting. The laboratories became treasure troves to be plundered with abandon: full of futuristic apparatus and lined with glass-doored cabinets packed with jars of coloured substances, they had appeared in Dushma's imagination as a cross between a science fiction film set and the window display of a Victorian sweet shop.

They were places of limitless possibility, where teachers were ineffectual creatures whose only purpose was to offer useful suggestions such as "Remember, *never* add water to acid". In Alison's swaggering descriptions, the enquiring mind always faced an equal chance of enlightenment or hospitalization.

At Larchmuir the reality was rather different. Here, there was no chance that knowledge, or at least the getting of it, might be a dangerous thing. The girls were rarely allowed to do anything by themselves, and even then it was only the most innocuous procedures that were deemed safe enough. The walls were indeed lined with cupboards full of enticing powders and crystals, but mostly the dusty glass doors stayed shut. Anything interesting was always done by the teacher at the desk at the front of the class, well out of anyone else's reach.

Today was no different, and some time after failing to remember any of the properties of mercury, Dushma found herself standing near the front of another lab to witness a demonstration of atmospheric pressure. This particular experiment looked even less promising than most of the others she'd seen, so she hadn't been paying attention to the explanation of what was going to happen. The outcome was to take her utterly by surprise.

The apparatus was simple: an oil can containing a little water, placed above a Bunsen burner. Once the water had begun to boil the can was taken off the heat and the cap screwed down over the steaming opening.

The other girls weren't interested. They'd seen it last term, they grumbled. But as the can collapsed in on itself, sides creasing and dimpling as if squeezed in an invisible fist, Dushma was transfixed. None of the things she had seen in any previous experiment, not the sprays of sparks and fans of rainbow light, not the vividly coloured precipitates, not the sizzling flames and clouds of smoke – none of these could compare in their fascination with such a manifestation of power literally out of thin air. She found it exhilarating to think of being able to harness such a vast and indifferent, amoral force by doing something as apparently harmless as heating a can of water, something that could even be done almost by accident.

Returning home from school, she didn't go straight into the house but lingered outside. She paced up and down the pavement, swishing her feet through the fallen leaves. Dry twigs and seed husks crackled like a bonfire beneath the soles of her shoes. Every now and then she raised her head and looked intently up and down the street.

After five minutes or so she had seen no one and was beginning to get bored. Perhaps she could leave a sign: a pattern of sticks, perhaps? Then a thought occurred to her and she turned into the drive by the side of the house and walked down to the back-garden gate, in case he was already waiting for her.

There was no one there.

She pulled herself up on to the roof of the small wooden shed that housed the bins. She stood with her back to the glare of the setting sun and looked at her shadow stretching away beneath her along the gravel drive and into the road. She was a giantess. She was ten metres tall, at least. She could glide along the pavement, rippling up and over walls, sliding between the wheels of cars and under the bars of gates. She could go anywhere she liked, and when she arrived she could rear up to her full height, dark and terrifying, and. . . But she wasn't sure. Even if she could, she wasn't sure where she would go or what she would do when she got there.

Then she saw him. He was still some way away but walking quickly, thin shoulders swaying in time to his long stride. It was too far for her to make out his expression.

Almost immediately he saw her too, and raised his hand to wave. She jumped down and hurried towards him.

When they met they stood facing each other in awkward silence. Arbilow leaned against a wall and Dushma stirred leaves with her toe. Then they caught each other's eye and found themselves both smiling.

Arbilow pulled a hand from his pocket, hesitated, then reached out and gently touched her forearm. "Hey. Where did you go?" he asked.

"What happened to you?" she said, almost simultaneously.

"I just looked round and you'd disappeared," he said. "I

thought you must've gone on ahead so I pushed my way through but I couldn't see you. Then I thought you might've gone back or something daft like that. But by then there were too many people behind me and I couldn't turn round."

"I'm sorry. I did call out. There was a passageway. I thought it'd be safer. Quicker, you know? But by the time I realized you weren't following it was too late to go back. There were bricks starting to come down – falling, I mean." She had been going to tell him about how she had returned to the vicinity of the Bunker on Sunday morning, trying to find out if anyone had been hurt. But seeing him now, noticing again his wiry figure and air of self-sufficiency, it suddenly seemed absurd to have been concerned. Of course he was all right.

They reached the main road. Walking aimlessly, they followed it for a little way, then turned off it again into a downward-sloping sidestreet. The low sun warmed their backs and their shadows trickled over the cobblestones in front of them.

"I came yesterday," said Arbilow, "but there was someone hanging around outside and giving me suspicious looks so I didn't like to stay. Hey. . ." He had noticed her bruised cheek. "Are you OK?"

"Oh yes. It was dark. I fell over, that's all." Glancing sideways at him, she couldn't resist adding, "Why, were you worried?"

"Well . . . it was me who took you there, wasn't it? So,

327

you know, I'd've felt guilty if anything had happened to you. I mean, it's not like I don't think you can look after yourself or anything, but. . ." His voice trailed away.

"Of course it wouldn't've been your fault," she said quickly. "It was really good, and thanks for taking me." She was no longer sure what she wanted him to have said. To have someone worrying about her suddenly felt like too heavy a responsibility for her to bear. She wasn't sure if she was ready for it. Did Marlstroy worry about her? He seemed too busy to care, most of the time. For the last few years of their relationship, Auntie Megan had never shown the slightest concern for her welfare, yet she came to confront Marlstroy when she found out where Dushma had gone.

Worrying about a person had to mean something different to worrying about losing possessions, say, or money. Who did she really worry about, she wondered. Was it just the people she'd be worse off without? What she had to try and do, she decided, was imagine that she was never going to see someone again, and then ask herself if, despite this, she would care whether they were all right or not.

"Suppose you knew something bad was going to happen to somebody," she began, almost thinking aloud, "and it might actually be better that it happened, in the long run — for everybody, I mean — but you couldn't be sure. If it's not your fault — this thing that's going to happen to her, this person I mean — and you can't do anything about it . . .

then, you shouldn't care, should you? I mean, it's not worth worrying about, is it?"

"I'm sorry, you've lost me," said Arbilow. "Who is this person? Do I know them?"

"No, it's just someone, someone I know, used to know. I was just wondering. . ." She tried to think of a way to explain the chain of reasoning that had led her to hint at Alison's plight, but there seemed no easy way to do so. "Never mind. It doesn't matter."

"No, go on, tell me," said Arbilow. "And anyway, what makes you think you can't do anything?"

Dushma had been taking little notice of where they were going. They had turned several more corners, each new street taking them further downhill. Now they reached the end of another narrow alleyway and came out on to the overgrown towpath of a canal.

She hadn't been here for a long time. She had known this stretch of waterway as a site of neglect and decay; perhaps she'd subconsciously felt that it was no longer a suitable haunt. Now it was the smell she remembered with most immediacy: half enticing and half repellent, an odour of weeds, damp soil and wet, crumbling plaster.

"Look at this place." Arbilow waved his hand to indicate their surroundings, already disappearing as the twilight faded. "It used to be filthy along here. But people got together, made complaints, forced the council to spend some money."

Steep-roofed buildings zigzagged along on either side

of them. They were mostly old warehouses or disused factories, some converted into flats, others boarded up or gutted and left open to the sky. Here and there in the high walls a window glowed, but otherwise the facades were dark. Steel girders protruded from the gable ends, some still equipped with a chain and a hook from the times when wholesalers had hoisted goods up into their storerooms from the barges that plied the canal.

Picking their way carefully, Dushma and Arbilow made their way along the uneven towpath. It was becoming difficult for them to see where they were going, even though the surface of the canal, reflecting the sky, still shone a pale metallic blue as if lit from underneath by neon tubes.

They passed a solitary angler perched motionless on a bollard. A jogger ran by, a torch clipped to a sweatband round his head. Red lights winked on and off in the heels of his training shoes with each stride he took.

They turned a corner to find what looked at first like a crooked portcullis blocking the canal about a hundred metres in front of them. It took Dushma several seconds to see that it was meant to be a giant shopping trolley, as high as a house, dumped on its end in the water, rear wheels in the air.

"I don't remember that. It must be new."

"They put it up about six months ago. It's by that American artist, I forget his name. He does things like that, like giant cutlery and things. It caused lots of arguments at the time. They were worried it might encourage people. In fact since they finished it there've been hardly any trolleys dumped here. I reckon people come trundling along, see that thing and feel a bit upstaged."

They drew level with the sculpture. At water level its slanting bars had become clogged with branches, plastic bags and other flotsam. The canal hissed through this mass of debris, emerging clotted with foam on the other side.

It was now almost completely dark. They had passed several streetlamps but almost all remained unlit. In an attempt to save energy, it must have been decided to minimize the lighting along little-used routes such as this.

Beyond the giant trolley a single light had switched itself on. Warming up, it glowed pale pink like a luminous boiled sweet. They stopped beneath it and leaned against a railing overlooking the canal.

Stretching forward, Dushma could see a little way round the next bend. In the middle distance she at last noticed a building she could remember. In contrast to the sharp angles of the surrounding roofscape, this particular structure had a fuzzy outline, looking in the twilight as if it was surmounted by a crown of motionless black clouds.

"Look." Dushma pointed. "There's that place with the trees on top. Have you seen it?" She narrowed her eyes. Among the silhouettes of branches was a mast supporting what appeared to be a propeller, vanes almost motionless in the still air. "And what's that? I don't think I saw that before. Is it a windmill?"

"It's a generator. Only been up a couple of months. Not much use on a day like this though."

"How come you know that? I could never work out how to get in. It always seemed to be all locked up. Barbed wire around and everything. And I never saw any signs. I've heard that famous people live round here in luxurious conversions. For the privacy, because most other things around are just empty and derelict." Sometimes, when she used to walk along this part of the canal, she had liked to imagine discovering a secret entrance to the tree-crowned warehouse. Once inside, she would befriend the reclusive millionaire film star or musician who lived there, and be shown around their rooftop garden.

"Well, not famous people exactly," said Arbilow. "Not there, anyway."

"Oh? How come you're so sure?" She was reluctant to let the premise of her fantasy be so casually dismissed.

Arbilow hesitated, then shrugged and said, "That's the Factory. You remember. I told you it was near here. That's where I live."

"Really? There?" She tried to picture how the fortress-like building appeared in daylight. She remembered narrow, frosted-glass windows, cargo gantries jutting from the walls, catwalks linking randomly spaced doors high above ground level, and fire escapes twisting like corkscrews up the buttressed facades. "You never said what kind of place it was. How come you live somewhere like that?"

Arbilow shrugged again. "Well, why not?" he asked evasively. "People should live in places like that. It's better than building new houses in the country. It's cheaper for developers to build from scratch, but that's only because no one takes into account the long-term costs of having less fields and trees."

"But what's it *like?* You've hardly said anything about it!"

"I didn't know what you'd think. Some people are terrified of having anything to do with anyone who's not . . . I mean, who's not conventional."

"I don't care."

"But they must teach you all that stuff. You know, 'rights and responsibilities'. Sounds great, doesn't it? But which comes first? You need those rights before you can make a contribution and show that you're entitled to them. If you haven't got them in the first place then you're a bit stuck, aren't you? It's a vicious circle." His thin face wore a bitter expression. His eyes glittered a cold blue in the reflected light from the canal.

"I know . . . I mean, I can imagine." She wanted to say more about understanding how he must feel, but knew he would never believe her to be sincere. Instead she said, "But how can you get away with it? Haven't they tried to arrest you?"

"Nobody knows who owns the building, which helps. Some people did come with search warrants a few months ago, and we got a bit worried. There were rumours they were going to crack down on us. But it's all gone quiet since then. Marcus is quite involved in the place and he could probably whip up some publicity if he had to. He's got quite a bit of clout."

"And how do you survive? What do you do?"

"It's like a cooperative. You'd be surprised, with your sheltered background, but there are places like that around, you know. Where nobody cares whether you've got the right bits of paper or not. Everybody just contributes what they can. I do my juggling, and I've done some work for environmental charities. We're self-sufficient in a lot of things. Most of us are into living in a sustainable way. We quite often go on demonstrations, protests, things like that. It's a way of being able to feel we count for something, I suppose."

A sliver of suspicion darted through Dushma's mind. She thought of the small group of people with banners she had seen the night before. She remembered the stone that had struck the armoured glass of Ashpool's limousine, and the stories she'd heard and read of acts much worse than that.

"You don't do anything violent, do you?" she asked.

"Of course not!" He looked offended. "You must've seen Marcus on TV. He's always condemning that kind of thing. He's all for lying down in front of the bulldozers, not putting spikes in their tracks. If it's that nail thing you're thinking of, I'd never do anything like that. No way."

"Oh, that. . ." It had been a prominent item on the news a few weeks previously. Demonstrators had been trying to prevent an area of woodland being cleared for a new motorway. In spite of their protests the felling had gone ahead, but it had turned out that someone had driven nails into the trunks of several of the trees. A workman had been badly injured when his chainsaw hit one of these nails and jumped from his hands, nearly severing his leg.

Marcus Torrelguard, his name scrolling underneath his picture, had been interviewed not long afterwards. An aggressive journalist had repeatedly tried to get him to admit that he condoned such acts of sabotage. Torrelguard, a weary expression on his face and shadows under his eyes, had patiently explained that he considered trees less important than people.

"We'd never deliberately cause any damage," Arbilow insisted. "It's just about letting people know what's going on. Often that's all you need to do. You think you can't do anything about something, but then you find out you can. You've grown up thinking you're worthless and then you discover you can actually change things. It must be different for you, always knowing you were going to go to college, get some worthwhile job, make important decisions."

"You don't know that!" She could have said more, told Arbilow exactly why he was mistaken, but she didn't, partly because she found it flattering that he thought of her in this way. The idea that she was now a privileged member of society, destined for higher things, was something she wanted to believe in too much herself to feel comfortable explaining the far more complicated truth of her background.

"Oh go on. At least compared to me, anyway. I was never going to change the world working as a clinker monkey, was I? But this spring I went on a protest to a power station that was breaching clean air guidelines. We abseiled down one of the cooling towers and unfurled a banner. It had the name of the company that owned the power station on it, and a skull and crossbones."

"*That* sounds illegal. Not to say pretty dangerous." She didn't want to sound admiring, but she tried not to sound too censorious either. After all, she told herself, it wasn't really any of her business.

Looking rather proud, Arbilow turned his back to the canal and leaned casually against the railings. "Not really. We didn't break anything. And it's much easier going down the outside of a chimney than the inside of one. I couldn't've gone down inside, not after what happened last time. And we had all the gear, so actually it was pretty safe. But, I don't know, even if it hadn't been. . ." He fixed her with his intense and frowning gaze and said, as if quoting something of great significance, "There comes a time when you've got to ask yourself, how far do you go to stop someone doing something wrong?"

The words sounded familiar, and she wondered if she'd heard them before. "Is that something Marcus says?"

"Yes. One of his favourites."

"Is that why they locked him up that time?" Two broken ribs, Arbilow had said: resisting arrest. "Did they think he might go too far?"

"That was probably the excuse. Really they'll just've wanted to shut him up for a bit. Stop him embarrassing shady businessmen who'd donated lots of money to the government."

"So what happened? About the power station?"

"Oh, the banner was on TV all round the world. It was such bad publicity for the company that they had to close the place down while they modernized it. How about that? It's amazing what you can achieve, if you really want to."

Dushma thought of the oil can in the science lab at school, crushed inexorably by the weight of the air around it. She glanced at Arbilow. She supposed he had a right to look a little pleased with himself.

"So, do you often do things like that?"

"Oh, now and again." Then he admitted, "Actually, only the once, so far. But. . ."

"But what?"

"Oh, nothing. I shouldn't really say."

"Oh go on. *I'm* not going to tell anybody." She felt cross at his caginess. She didn't mind if he really didn't want to tell her, but he obviously did want her to know, or at least think he was going to be doing something exciting.

"No, I'm sure you wouldn't, but it isn't even certain it's going to go ahead yet, and I've promised not to say anything."

"Why's it got to be so secret?" she pressed him. "It's illegal, isn't it, or dangerous. Is it?"

But he wouldn't tell her.

"All right then, I don't want to know," she said haughtily. If it didn't have anything to do with her, why should she care whether what he chose to do was dangerous or not?

"I'll tell you a bit more as soon as I can," he offered. "Maybe you could come if you wanted."

"It's getting a bit late. I've got to go," she said. She kicked at the railings and felt them tremble under her fingers. She pushed herself away and looked back along the towpath. It was almost dark. The angler had gone from his bollard and stars were appearing. She hoped she'd still be able to see her way.

"Or come and visit the Factory, if you like. Go on, I'll tell you where to get in. I'll show you round. I'm learning to walk a tightrope, but nobody knows yet. You can watch though, if you like. Be my first audience."

She turned round reluctantly. "I'm sorry, I. . ."

"No, wait. I've been practising. It's all about balance. Look." He sprang up on to the top bar of the railings, swayed there for an instant, then turned and walked a few unsteady steps, his arms outstretched.

"What are you doing? Get down!" said Dushma, horrified.

"No, it's easy, look — throw me some pebbles or something."

She moved towards him and reached out to try and pull

him down. He wobbled and she drew back, afraid she might tip him into the canal instead.

"Don't be *stupid*." She felt furious at his thoughtlessness. What if she had to rescue him? She couldn't swim; *he* didn't know that. What would she do if he fell? She glanced uncertainly down over the edge of the towpath at the smooth, dark blue surface of the canal.

In the light of the single streetlamp she saw a fan of metal prongs sticking upwards out of the wall immediately below the railings. They were rusty and wreathed in slime and weed.

Her anger turned to jittery panic. "Look, just . . . get down, please!" But her consternation seemed to encourage him. He stood with his hands in his pockets, grinning carelessly down at her.

"Like I said, it's all about balance. . ."

"I'm going. I'm not watching. I'm not impressed." She turned her back on him. Willing herself not to look round, she began to walk quickly away.

Almost immediately she heard a thump behind her as Arbilow jumped down on to the towpath.

"All right, all right," he said, catching her up. "Look, I'm sorry, OK?"

"That was really silly," she muttered, not looking at him but striding on, her eyes fixed on the ground in front of her and her hands stuffed deep into her blazer pockets.

"Why, were you worried?" he asked.

"No I wasn't!" she snapped. "But if you'd got hurt I'd've

had to help you and then I'd've been late home and it would've been really irritating. All right?"

"So I'd've got wet, so what? I can swim."

She stopped and turned on him. "Didn't you see them?" She pointed. From where the two of them now stood the spikes below the railing were like a splayed claw reaching up from under the water.

"Oh. . ."

"See?" She spun round and walked away from him, not looking back.

He caught up with her again. "OK, it was stupid," he admitted. "And I'm sorry, I've said."

She didn't reply.

"All right! I was trying to get you to stay for a bit longer. Because I was enjoying your company. There, does that make it any better?"

She had firmly decided not to, but his admission made her stop again. "But I've got to get back. I'm sorry. . ." She caught herself; it wasn't *her* fault. "And what about this other thing you're planning? The one you can't mention but you keep going on about? How do you expect me to believe it's not something just as reckless?"

His contrition was gone already, replaced by his usual self-assurance. "Ah, but that's completely different. It's all organized, it's perfectly safe. And it's not as if I'm going on my own. Come and see if you don't believe me. It'll be worth it."

"Who are you going with? Is it Marcus?"

"I. . . Look, I can't really say just yet. But it's going to be good, honestly. So go on, will you come? Just to see me off?"

"No." But she stole a quick glance at him and, seeing his look of disappointment, she relented. "Oh, I don't know. Maybe. When?"

XV

Oscilloscope

Mrs Breckle had already left for the evening by the time Dushma returned home. She found some cold chicken and salad in the fridge but had little appetite for it.

She knew she was going to have to say something to Marlstroy.

She thought about what Arbilow had said, and how wrong he had been. He had imagined that she must have much more of a feeling of counting for something than he did; that she must feel less marginalized and inconsequential. In fact, she now felt more powerless than she had ever done before she had been registered. She certainly had much less freedom. At school, for example, almost every minute of the day was accounted for. Trying to do anything even slightly different to what was set down for her on the timetable was bound to get her into trouble.

She went up to her room and spent half an hour struggling with her French homework. The class had been told to write a story on a subject of their choice. Pleased at being given such an unusual amount of latitude, Dushma had planned to develop what she thought was a very promising idea about a trapeze artist kidnapped by aliens and forced to perform in a zero-gravity interplanetary circus.

It was only when she actually sat down in front of her open exercise book to begin writing that she realized she knew hardly any of the necessary vocabulary. She was going to have to look up a lot of words. She had a French dictionary, bought for her in the summer. It had been the best available, but was in so many unwieldy volumes that finding anything in it was a laborious procedure. Before long she was forced to admit that the story she wanted to write would take her all evening to complete.

After a brief inward struggle she abandoned her original conception and instead produced a brief narrative about a woman going shopping for clothes in the rain. While terribly dull, it was unlikely to get her told off for letting her imagination run away with her (as had happened before), and its composition had not involved much heavy lifting.

Her story complete, she made a fair copy and then set herself to learning some irregular verbs. She stared unseeingly at the lists on the page for several minutes before finally admitting to herself that she was merely putting off what she knew she had to go and do.

There was a crack of light under the study door but no

answer when she knocked. She tried again, waited a minute or two, then pushed the door open and peered into the room.

Marlstroy stood at the window, an open book in one hand. But instead of reading, he was staring out through the open curtains at the reflections in the glass and the dim shapes of plants in the garden beyond.

"What? Oh yes, sorry, I'd forgotten." He turned away from the window, his expression distracted. There were shadows under his eyes and his face looked craggier than usual.

He shook his head, snapped his book shut and walked over to his chair. "Miles away," he muttered. "Good day at school?"

Before Dushma could reply he began shuffling pens and papers around at random on his desktop, as if he knew he'd lost something but couldn't remember what. "Yes, anyway," he said, "I suppose we'd better get started. Now where's. . .?"

Normally Marlstroy set up his apparatus with quick, precise movements. But tonight he worked slowly, frequently pausing between opening a drawer or a cupboard and taking out from it what he required. Dushma had witnessed this ritual so many times now that she could have assembled the necessary equipment herself but she did nothing, afraid her help might be unwelcome.

At last Marlstroy was ready. Dushma felt the familiar, sticky touch of the electrodes on her temples and saw the green lines on the oscilloscope's screen reflected in Marlstroy's half-moon spectacles. She tried to relax and empty her thoughts but her mouth was dry and she could feel the pulse thumping in her throat.

They hardly ever talked during these regular sessions. Marlstroy might ask her to think of a particular thing, something happy or sad, for example, or he might put on some music intended to suggest a particular mood. But he never spoke about what he was observing.

Despite Marlstroy's hesitancy, this evening seemed set to follow a similar pattern. Dushma sat upright and still, hands folded in her lap. Marlstroy jotted down numbers and brief comments in a notebook he kept in his desk for the purpose, nodding or raising an eyebrow from time to time.

Dushma had never before quite had the courage to question Marlstroy about what he was doing. Partly she was uncertain how she was expected to behave in such a situation. And partly she was afraid that, if she could articulate what it was she wanted to know, she would not like the answers she heard. But tonight these seemed trivial concerns compared to what was really weighing on her mind. It now seemed much easier to ask a question about her health than to bring up the matter of what she had overheard in the study the previous night.

So to postpone the moment further, she waited until Marlstroy appeared to have finished his observations, then asked abruptly, "Can you cure me?"

Marlstroy frowned and thought for a few moments. "I don't think it's a question of *curing*, exactly," he said slowly. "I mean, I never understood that you felt you *needed* curing, am I right? You don't feel ill, do you?"

Dushma shook her head.

"People's minds and nervous systems work in different ways. Some people have better memories than others. . ." Thinking aloud, he doodled in the margin of his notebook. "There's an ambiguous phrase. I may have a good memory, but my memories may not all be good. . . What I'm saying is, I wouldn't presume that what we're dealing with is definitely pathological, as such. I'm a long way from any kind of explanation, I'll admit. But the first step towards the understanding of any phenomenon is an accurate description. There's certainly something strange manifesting itself here. But I don't think it's necessarily anything to get worried about. In fact if anything it's been declining since I've been observing you. Who knows, changes in diet, environment, perhaps even the natural process of ageing, growing up. . . All these may be contributing factors. Difficult to say, but within a year it may have vanished completely, without any need for a cure. In a sense, it may be that there's nothing actually *wrong* at all."

Dushma raised her fingers to the pads at her temples, unsure if she should feel angry or relieved. The entire course of her life had been determined by the assumption that there had indeed been something very wrong. It had been a routine prenatal scan that had first suggested she might be unusual. When, years later, Auntie Megan had shown her the photograph of her unborn self, head wreathed in clouds of inexplicable colour, her only thought had been that someone must have made a mistake. It was somebody else. Or the machine that took the picture had malfunctioned. Whatever the reason, she had been certain that there was nothing wrong with her, certain that a simple error had cost her the right to be registered.

Later she had come to accept the fact that she must indeed have been the baby in the picture, yet she had still felt bitter at how she had been treated. It had seemed unfair to her that she should have been prejudged on the basis of something that the authorities had simply failed to understand, and possibly been afraid of. She had just wanted to be normal, and now it looked as if she was going to get her wish.

Soon she might no longer have to wear the locket that now lay with its chain in a heap on the edge of Marlstroy's desk. She might no longer need it in order to be able to undergo an X-ray without causing the photographic plate to bloom like a stained-glass window; to turn on a light without seeing the bulb flare and shatter; to tune a television or a radio without the signal dissolving into a blur of static. She supposed she should welcome the thought of being rid of whatever it was that had caused things like these to happen. It would mean the loss of one more link with her old life, one less thing to prevent her entering fully into the new role that had so unexpectedly become available to her as Marlstroy's ward. It was as if she was being offered a chance to forget completely about who she had been, the things she had done and the people she had known. It was a tempting thought.

The polished surface of Marlstroy's desk was bright green with reflected light from the screen of the oscilloscope. "You seem a bit agitated. Is everything all right?" he asked, as if reading her mind. Which in a sense he was.

"Yes, fine. Well, actually. . . I know I shouldn't have, but there was something. . ."

"School going badly?" he prompted. "I was thinking about that letter from the headmistress. Discipline isn't everything, these days. Maybe they're a bit old-fashioned. Perhaps you'd be happier at somewhere more progressive. What do you think?"

"I don't know." She twisted her fingers around each other. "You know that girl? The one at the Galen?"

Marlstroy's hand twitched and the pen nearly slipped from his grasp. Recovering himself, he looked up at Dushma and when he spoke his gaze was steady and his voice perfectly neutral.

"I'm sorry. I noticed you were looking a little shaken afterwards. I shouldn't have taken you in there."

Dushma avoided his eye. "I knew . . . I know her," she continued, stumbling over the tenses. "She's . . . she was a friend of mine."

"I'm sorry," said Marlstroy again. "I'm doing what I can

of course but I . . . there's. . . She may be worse than I first thought."

Her lungs seemed to shrivel up inside her. This was awful. He was going to realize that she knew he was lying.

"She . . . she doesn't deserve it," she said breathlessly. "I know she did a lot of things she shouldn't have, but that doesn't mean it's right to. . . Besides, she might not wake up for months. She might not remember anything anyway. She might. . . She. . ."

Marlstroy's face had gone pale and very still. For almost a minute after Dushma's voice had trailed away into silence he did not speak or even blink.

"I see," he said at last. "I suppose I could talk about how you've betrayed my trust, creeping around like a thief in the night, listening at keyholes, intruding into my private affairs. But I think that would be rather to avoid the issue, wouldn't it? So instead let me say that as far as your friend is concerned, I assume you must have heard the arguments Ashpool put forward last night. I'm sorry you don't seem to have been able to grasp them. There are weightier matters at stake here than the welfare of one maladjusted juvenile delinquent."

"But it's not true what he said about her! She could've done something really useful, something important! She could've been. . ." Dushma tried to imagine Alison as a grown-up, doing something useful and important. "She could've been . . . a fashion designer or something," she concluded lamely.

"That's hardly the point," snapped Marlstroy. "I'm not prepared to bandy words with you. This is a situation entirely beyond your experience. Leave difficult decisions to those whose job it is to make them."

"But it isn't *fair!*" It was all she could think of to say and as soon as it passed her lips she knew it sounded pathetic.

"Of course it isn't fair! What about the elderly who aren't going to be able to heat their homes this winter? What about the children who are going to die in the dark on the roads because there isn't enough electricity to light the streetlamps? None of them would think that was terribly fair either, would they? And Ashpool's the only one who's got the nerve to stop that happening."

"You don't know that! How do you know that?" she shot back at him, close to tears.

"Don't be childish. Of course I'm not *certain*. If we only acted when we knew the outcome we'd still be living in caves. And as far as I'm concerned that's the end of the matter. I'm not prepared to discuss it any further."

"Why *not*? What's so difficult about it? Why shouldn't I be allowed to understand why it's the right thing to do?"

Marlstroy pulled off his spectacles and fixed her with his intense, hooded gaze. "You have no idea . . . you have no *conception* of the issues involved here." He jabbed the air to emphasize his words. "This isn't some cosy undergraduate moral philosophy problem. The . . . I don't know, the Jehovah's Witness whose faith forbids him the blood transfusion he needs to save his life. There isn't a *right* answer."

"But there's a better one, there must be," insisted Dushma.

"Is there? And even if you think so, who are you to decide? Has anyone voted for you? Suppose we'd been talking about transport policy. Suppose you'd heard us discussing . . . making cars illegal, say, but then deciding not to. Would you be sitting there telling me it wasn't fair to the thousands of people killed in crashes every year?"

"But that's different!" She was sure it was, but couldn't think of a way to explain how before Marlstroy resumed his remorseless assertion of her naivety.

"Is it really? All the time, people in positions of responsibility are making decisions which they know will leave some people worse off than before. It's a definition of politics, if you like. How to be least unfair to the greatest number of people."

"And how many people like her would there have to be before you'd think it was too many?"

"Listen. You've done what you can for your friend. I appreciate that, even though your intentions are ultimately misguided. I'm sure you'll come to realize, when you grow older, that what we did was for the best. In the meantime all I can say is that I'm sorry you had to get involved, though you've only yourself to blame. I strongly advise you to put the entire episode out of your mind."

Dushma could think of nothing more to say. She was

sure there had been weaknesses in Marlstroy's logic, but could not articulate why she thought he might be wrong. Yet even as they argued she had the feeling that they were both avoiding the real reason why Marlstroy had agreed to cooperate with Ashpool. She hardly dared even to admit it to herself, let alone speak it out loud. She did not want to have to think too hard about what it might mean.

It had been Ashpool's threat to *her*, Dushma, that had finally swayed Marlstroy. What was she prepared to do, what might she have to risk or renounce, in order to counter that? If Ashpool was disgraced, there was the possibility that she might lose her registration. And if she tried to defy him she could be in as much danger as Alison.

"If it's so obvious you're right," she said doggedly, "why not just wait till she wakes up and explain all this to her then?"

"Enough!" shouted Marlstroy, losing his temper at last and bringing the palm of his hand down on the desk with a bang. "You'll do as I say and that's the end of it."

"No I won't! You can't make me! You know she doesn't deserve it! Would you do it to *me* if he told you to?"

"I said *enough!*" Marlstroy sprang to his feet.

It was difficult to tell exactly what happened next. Dushma shrank back in her chair, tightening the wires that ran from the electrodes still attached to her temples. Her face hot with anger and her vision blurred with tears, she plucked at the wires and pulled the electrodes free. Flinging them to the floor, she jumped up to face

Marlstroy, and as she rose her knee hit hard against the back of the desk.

The oscilloscope rocked on its stand and Marlstroy reached out to steady it. But before he could do so the screen shattered, showering the desk with splinters of glass.

For a moment they both stood completely still. There was silence except for the hiss of rapid breathing and the fizz and sputter of a loose connection from within the ruined instrument.

"I'm sorry. I didn't mean. . ." began Dushma, not sure what she hadn't meant. She stared at the wreckage on the desk, her fingers pressed to her forehead. Her knee hurt.

Marlstroy seemed not to hear her. "On too long. . . Must have overheated," he muttered. He brushed glass from his hands. Red smears appeared on his palms and drops of blood spattered the pages of his notebook.

He looked up at Dushma through the cloud of blue smoke drifting between them. "Go," he whispered hoarsely. "Get out. Go to your room."

XVI

The Wide Open Sky

Someone was spitting on her window. She knew it was one of those swollen-cheeked heads that appeared in the corners of old-fashioned maps, a mushroom puff of breath spouting from the round O of their mouths. A single gust could shatter glass, or send a roof-full of tiles cascading down into the street, slicing through the upraised hands of helpless passers-by.

Dushma woke. Her room was completely dark apart from a faint smudge of grey light filtering through the curtain.

The noise came again. She listened, but it didn't seem to be raining. She fumbled for the light beside her bed, the after-image of her nightmare still lingering in her mind. She could picture a huge, cherubic head nestling on a cloud outside her window.

She got out of bed, walked over to the curtain and pulled it open. Outside the night was still and the window-sill dry. A few streetlights glimmered in a ghostly suggestion of their usual bright pattern. The first signs of dawn were just visible on the horizon.

It was chilly and she hugged herself. Had she imagined the noises she had thought she heard? She was about to return to bed when the window rattled again. She glimpsed a swirl of fast-moving grey flecks and flinched away. Someone was throwing handfuls of gravel against the glass.

She undid the catch, lifted the sash and leaned out.

At first she could see nothing in the dark gulf between the houses. Then, as her eyes adjusted, she glimpsed the white blur of an upturned face.

"Hello?" she called. "Who's that?" Although she already had a good idea.

"Come on, we're going!" The voice was Arbilow's. "Come down! You said you would."

She was sure she hadn't.

"What, *now*? Why? Where to?"

"Shh! Just . . . come *down*, I'll explain!"

"All right, but that's as far as I'm going," said Dushma.

She had been appalled by what Arbilow intended to do, but had quickly understood that it was useless to try and dissuade him. She herself had refused point blank to be involved, until she realized it would give her a chance to see the sea. Then she had let herself be talked into joining him for part of the journey. She had never seen the sea.

"And you're sure it isn't illegal?" she added, for the third or fourth time.

"Of course it isn't. We've got a licence and everything. And you'll love it out there. It's really still, really peaceful and atmospheric."

They turned and began walking away from Marlstroy's front gate. Arbilow glanced at his watch. "We'll have to hurry," he said, quickening his stride. "And what did you mean, 'Who's that?', anyway? D'you get many visitors at this time in the morning?"

"No, I suppose not. Most young men come to serenade me in the evening," she teased him.

A van was parked at the end of the road, its engine idling. Arbilow pulled open the nearside door and slid along the wide passenger seat. Dushma hesitated, then ducked down after him and slammed the door shut behind her.

A middle-aged woman sat behind the wheel. She nodded at Dushma as she put the van into gear and drew away from the kerb.

"This is Caroline," said Arbilow. "Caroline – Dushma."

"Hope you're dressed for it," said Caroline shortly. "It's going to get cold, they reckon." She had a narrow face and straight, grey hair pulled back into a clip at the nape of her neck. She kept her eyes on the road in front of her and did not smile.

Dushma had left her room in a hurry. She had given no thought to what she should wear, simply pulling on whatever was to hand before hastily splashing a handful of cold water over her face and creeping down the stairs. She hadn't even bothered to brush or pin her hair, and had instead simply gathered its thick, dark tangles up into a peaked corduroy cap which she had found at the back of her wardrobe and assumed had belonged to Marlstroy.

She glanced down at her unbuttoned jacket, sweater and jeans. She hadn't felt too cold on the short walk from the front gate to the van, but according to Arbilow they were going some distance out of the city. She had no idea what that would be like. She imagined an open, windswept space full of jostling animals and deep, dirty puddles.

This was mad. She was already regretting having agreed to come. Standing at her open window in her nightdress, she had been going to tell Arbilow that she couldn't. It was only the vindictive thought of Marlstroy worrying over her absence that had made her change her mind. This could be a way of showing him that she wasn't as helpless as he might believe. What if he was afraid she had run away, or been kidnapped? Well, good, she told herself. And perhaps she would run away, too, and become a trapeze artist.

The roads were deserted and they drove quickly. Dushma leaned her cheek against the taut seat-belt and stared out of the window at the dark shapes of buildings rushing past. It occurred to her that until recently she had never even been in a car. How easy it would be to get used to being driven around. She wondered where they were. It was too dark to recognize any landmarks, with only the occasional streetlamp lit, and although they hadn't been going for long, she suspected they were already far from anywhere she was familiar with.

Lulled by the noise of the engine and the warm air flowing from the dashboard vents, she fell asleep. When she woke up the van had stopped, and she was alone. The windows had steamed up and she had to rub at the glass with her sleeve to see out.

The van was in a lay-by, parked next to a high hedge. There were no other vehicles in sight apart from a white caravan a little way away. Thinking she must have been forgotten about, she tried to open the passenger door but found herself entangled in her seat-belt. Before she could struggle free the other door swung open and Arbilow appeared, a paper parcel in his hand.

"Breakfast time, sleepy head."

The smell of fried bacon filled the van. It still seemed early, but she realized she was ravenous.

"Thanks," she said, reaching gratefully for the bag Arbilow handed her. "It was supposed to be my turn."

"Don't worry. I'm counting." He grinned at her as he clambered back into his seat.

"How far have we got to go?" she asked, her mouth full of bacon sandwich, ketchup and melted butter trickling down her chin. "Mmf. . . 'Scuse me."

"We've probably passed it three times already. That's the trouble with dead reckoning." He leaned towards the open driver's door. "Isn't it?" he added loudly.

Caroline swung herself into the van and pulled the door shut. Dushma caught the faint reek of cigarette smoke.

"It might help if the co-pilot wasn't navigating with his

358

stomach." Reaching down by her feet, Caroline picked up a thermos flask. "Help yourself," she said, tossing it into Arbilow's lap. "It's black. So if you want it with milk —" and here she allowed herself the ghost of a smile — "tough."

Their destination was a field at the end of a long, rutted lane. Dushma had to scramble out of the van and open the gate.

There were no animals, and no puddles either. Beads of moisture from a fading mist hung from the bars of the gate, but otherwise it had obviously been as dry here as it had been in London over the last few days. The ridges left in the mud by tractor tyres crumbled under Dushma's feet.

The field was bounded on three sides by hedges interspersed with barbed-wire fencing. On the fourth side was a strip of marshy ground dotted with clumps of reeds, and beyond that a restless expanse of white-streaked water stretching away as far as the eye could see. And roughly halfway between the gate and the shore, looking like a long, dark green mound in the dull light, was the reason they were here.

Caroline drove through the gate and a little way onwards over the tussocky grass. Then she stopped the van and cut the engine.

The sudden hush was disconcerting. It felt to Dushma as if all the sound had been sucked from her ears, and she wanted to clap her hands to the sides of her head.

In all the time she had lived in London, she had never experienced silence like this. Even if she had woken in the middle of the night there had always been something: the distant rumble of traffic, perhaps, or the noise of an aeroplane, or the rattle of train wheels. But now she really couldn't hear anything at all. Was this what it felt like to be deaf, she wondered? She quickly took a few steps forward, deliberately swishing her feet through the long grass.

The van doors creaked open. Arbilow stepped out on the passenger side, looking worriedly at his watch. ". . .understand it. He should already be here," he was saying.

Caroline leaned against the wing on the other side of the van, hands thrust casually into her pockets. "We could get ready, I suppose," she said uncertainly. "I'm not going without him."

"He'll be here in a minute, I'm sure."

That was the other really strange thing. For the first time in her life, Dushma realized, she could see no buildings. She turned slowly on her heel, scanning the horizon with one hand raised to the peak of her cap. There was not so much as a chimney pot to be glimpsed in any direction. The only visible shelter of any kind was the canvas marquee, like a camouflaged circus tent in the middle of the field, towards which Caroline and Arbilow were now walking.

The feeling of exposure was even more unnerving than the silence. Although she knew there was no one else here apart from the three of them, Dushma felt much more visible than she had ever done among the hundreds of people in a crowded shopping street.

She could never have been this far from a wall. The sky above her head had never seemed so wide. If the ground should tip, she thought irrationally, there would be very little to stop her sliding all the way to the horizon. Automatically, she stretched out her arms for balance, then stamped her feet to convince herself that the ground was there beneath her, solid and unmoving. She couldn't let on how fazed she was by her first visit to the countryside. After all, she reminded herself, she was supposed to be a seasoned traveller who had lived in a camp in the desert surrounded by nothing but rolling sand dunes.

Eyes fixed firmly on the grass a few paces in front of her, she set off across the field after Arbilow and Caroline.

What she had thought was a tent was in fact, she saw when she reached it, a tarpaulin stretched over some large object. The other two were already pulling pegs out of the ground in order to loosen the covering. Dushma stood and watched them work, thinking she should help but not sure what to do.

Once the material had been slackened it was easier to unhook the remaining fastenings. Caroline and Arbilow worked their way round the covered object in opposite directions, pausing every few paces to fold the loose section of tarpaulin back on itself.

Underneath was a helicopter.

First its snub nose was revealed, followed by a windscreen and a cabin surmounted by drooping, dew-furred blades. Then came a long, tapering fuselage, and finally the stubby fins of the vertically mounted tail rotor.

As soon as it was completely uncovered, Caroline began a systematic inspection of the craft. She opened hatches, tested bolts for tightness, crouched to peer at the wheels that flanked the cabin and stretched up to tug at the mountings that held the rotor assembly. When she was satisfied that everything was as it should be, she opened the cabin door and clambered inside.

Having pulled the tarpaulin well clear of the machine, Arbilow walked over towards Dushma. "Better not stand too close," he advised.

They backed away as Caroline settled herself into the pilot's seat. They saw her make several adjustments to the controls, her movements quick and assured. Then, with a roar and a gust of black smoke, the engine turned over, only to clatter into silence a few moments later.

"Damp, maybe," muttered Arbilow. "Come *on*."

A ragged group of crows had been flushed from their tree by the noise. They flapped away over the hedge off to one side of the field, croaking as they went.

There were several more false starts, but at the fourth or fifth attempt the engine caught and stayed running. Arbilow relaxed visibly, his shoulders slumping forward as the pent-up breath left his lungs.

Dushma wasn't sure whether she had really believed in

his scheme until that moment. Now that it looked like it really might go ahead, she began to think of all sorts of practical questions that hadn't previously occurred to her.

"How am I going to get back, when you've gone?" she wanted to know.

Arbilow didn't seem to have thought of this either. "Oh, I, er. . ." He glanced up from his watch, a distracted frown on his face. "Well, you could wait for us, if you like. We'll only be an hour or two, max. Or there's a station in that village we came through. About a mile back down the road. The trains are terrible, though."

Caroline had engaged the gears and the rotors were beginning to swing. They moved slowly at first, then began to rise towards the horizontal, whistling through the air as they picked up speed. The helicopter moved restlessly on its undercarriage.

Throttling back, Caroline looked up at Arbilow, nodded and raised a thumb. She climbed out of the helicopter and ran towards them over the beaten-down grass, bending low beneath the still-turning blades.

"Sweet as treacle!" She had to raise her voice to make herself heard above the noise of the engine. "Ready to hop." She still looked severe, but Dushma could tell she was pleased with herself.

Arbilow looked at his watch again. "He's late," he muttered.

"I know. We're running out of time," said Caroline.

"We've still got a few more minutes, haven't we?"

"Yes, but. . . We'll have to make a decision pretty soon. And I'm worried about the weather, too."

"This is really unlike him, you know that." Arbilow was shifting with impatience. "We've been planning this for months. He'd never risk wasting all that work. This is just too good an opportunity to miss."

"Maybe there's been some last-minute cancellation. Maybe he just hasn't been able to let you know."

Arbilow shook his head emphatically. "He'd never leave us waiting here like this. He'd at least send someone to tell us, even if he couldn't come himself."

Caroline shrugged and said nothing.

Arbilow turned on his heel and strode back across the field towards the open gate. Climbing up on to it, he stood with his knees braced against the top bar and stared away down the narrow lane.

Caroline took out a phone and began to dial a number. "Tried him in the lay-by," she said, "but. . ."

She put the phone to her ear for a few seconds, then shook her head. "Answering machine again."

Replacing the phone, she reached into another of the many pockets of her sleeveless jacket and produced a small rectangular tin. Prising off the lid, she extracted a cigarette paper and a wiry clump of what looked like dark brown sofa stuffing. Dushma watched curiously as she teased the curly tendrils into shape with yellowish fingertips.

"Look. . . Don't look at me like that." Caroline paused with the finished cigarette halfway to her lips. There was a smoker's tattoo on the inside of her right wrist, partly hidden by the cuff of her shirt. "I can't stop. And it's fair-trade tobacco, OK?"

"Sorry, I didn't. . ."

Caroline nodded towards the gate, where Arbilow still perched. "He thinks I'm not really committed enough."

"Oh, I'm sure he doesn't," said Dushma gallantly. "*I* wouldn't dare do it. I think you're very brave."

Caroline turned her gaze on Dushma, her cheekbones hard and smooth under her steady grey eyes.

"It's my job," she said. "I run a business. Stunts for films and TV. Bit of advertising work here and there. He thinks I only do things like this for the publicity. Fat lot of that I get."

Dushma looked back to where the helicopter stood, its engine growling. She felt a twinge of disappointment at the thought of not being aboard when it flew. Before she could stop herself, she imagined meeting Alison afterwards in the multi-storey car park. "You'll never guess what I did today," she would have announced. And after she'd told her, Alison might have said, "Well you'll just have to get used to it Dush honey, 'cos when we're famous that's the only way we're goin' to travel."

Would she dare, she wondered? She thought she probably would have done, before she was registered, but now she wasn't so sure. She was rather glad that she wasn't going to have the opportunity to find out.

"So why *do* you do it?" she prompted. "If it's not for the publicity?"

Caroline stubbed out her cigarette on the lid of her tobacco tin and dropped the dog end carefully into her pocket. For a while it seemed as if she wasn't going to reply.

Then she said abruptly, "Used to work in the Caribbean. Flying boats. Catalinas. Beautiful things. Old-fashioned. Luxurious, though. Walnut veneer, leather trim, chrome fittings everywhere. We'd fly rich tourists out to some uninhabited atoll, watch the sun go down, have a picnic, champagne, that kind of thing. Idyllic. That was before the first of the big slicks. When they started coming, it got harder and harder to find anywhere that was clean. At first, well, it didn't seem to matter too much. A bit of oil on the surface even made the sunsets more interesting. Sometimes it looked like a rainbow had melted into the water."

Caroline had turned round and was staring past the helicopter and out towards the open sea. "But then it started affecting the wildlife," she continued. She smiled mirthlessly. "It's kind of hard to enjoy your lobster thermidor when there's a flock of seabirds drowning in liquid tar right under your dining table. Sometimes they'd try to climb up on to the plane. No idea what kind they were. All sorts, I suppose. Hard to tell when they get to that stage. Their wings were all splayed and clogged with oil and they looked like slimy hands trying to grip hold of the pontoons. We'd had to ban smoking, it got too dangerous. But the last flight I went on, someone lit up and threw the cigarette overboard. Still don't know if it was deliberate, just for the hell of it. You can guess what happened. Imagine being an insect in a burning frying pan. That's what it felt like. I nearly didn't get us out of there. The pontoons caught fire and I had to bounce the plane to douse them. I wouldn't do it any more after that. Even if there'd still been enough punters up for it. I'd had enough."

When it became clear that Caroline had finished, Dushma said, "I'm sorry. That sounds awful."

Caroline turned away, her face stiff. "Yes, well. At least I've still got a livelihood. Doing something I enjoy." She looked back at the helicopter and her expression softened. "I'm lucky to be doing this, I suppose. I'm qualified, but I'd never pilot a jet unless I had to. Give me something with propellers any day. Completely different experience. You really know you're flying. Might sound silly, but it's like you can really feel them chewing on the air." For a moment she seemed almost proud.

"Does Arbilow know? About what happened to you, I mean. Maybe it's just that he doesn't realize."

"Him? Don't know. Shouldn't think he does. I've never told him. He's never asked. He's only interested in what Torrelguard says. He worships him. And the Pacific slicks are old news now. There's no mileage in protesting about them. Besides, I don't really care what he thinks." She gestured out towards the open water. "This is where I grew up. Don't want to see the same thing happening here, that's all."

"Is this really going to make a difference, do you think?"

"Who knows? He's done things before that have seemed just as impossible. He's got a knack for pricking the public conscience, is how he puts it."

"Is that Marcus, you mean?"

"Who? Oh, Torrelguard. Yes. Have you met him?"

"And he's who we're waiting for now, isn't he?" She remembered Ashpool in the limousine, and his threat to have Torrelguard arrested. "What if he doesn't turn up?"

"Then it's off. It's pretty much too late anyway." She looked at her watch, and then away at the horizon, one hand shielding her eyes, a frown crumpling her forehead.

"Would you not go without him?"

"Don't know. Might've done. But even that might not be an option soon. I think the weather's turning."

As she spoke a sudden gust of wind swept past them. The grass rippled as if a giant brush was being drawn invisibly across it.

Over by the entrance to the field, Arbilow had abandoned his position on the gate and was striding back towards the helicopter. Stopping by the van, he opened the back doors and took out a large bag with something rolled up inside it.

"We're just going to have to go without him," he said when he reached them.

Caroline shook her head. "I'm sorry."

"What's the matter? What do you mean, you're sorry?"

"I mean I don't like the look of *that*." She pointed out to sea. Tendrils of black cloud were crawling up over the horizon like ink seeping through blotting paper. "See how fast that's moving? Can't remember anything like it. Could be here in half an hour. Less."

"But . . . we've got to! When's the next time there'll be a camera crew out there?"

"But you don't even know they're *there*. They might've heard the forecast and postponed it. Or got halfway and turned back rather than risk being trapped on the rig."

Arbilow bit his lip and glanced quickly back over his shoulder at the gate.

"I'm sorry," repeated Caroline gently. "He'd say the same thing. You know he would."

"No. He'd risk it."

"Listen. Maybe he heard something, heard it was off."

"No! I told you, he'd've at least let us know. Something must've gone wrong, but that's all the more reason not to just give up now. Did you try ringing him?"

"No answer. What did you expect?"

"You could try him again. Then maybe try someone else, see if they know anything. If we could at least find out where he was. . ."

"What does it matter where he is? He's not *here*, is he?" But she took the phone out of her pocket again.

Dushma said nothing. They would never believe her if she told them. Or they would be suspicious of how it was she knew.

The phone pressed to one ear and a finger in the other,

Caroline began walking further away from the helicopter. Arbilow watched her for a moment and then set off in the opposite direction, the heavy bag from the van still tucked under one arm, a frown tightening his face.

He reached the helicopter and opened the pilot's door. He threw the bag into the cabin and climbed in after it.

"*What?*" Dushma heard Caroline exclaim. "But, why? What's the charge?"

Arbilow had settled himself into the pilot's seat. He pulled the door shut. Scowling intently, he leaned forward over the dashboard, hands poised over the controls. Dushma recognized his expression. It was the same look of devil-may-care determination he had worn when he had jumped up on to the railings by the canal.

"No!" she shouted, but he didn't hear her. She began to run towards the helicopter, bending low beneath the thrashing rotor blades. The downdraught whipped loose strands of hair across her cheeks.

She tugged at the handle of the pilot's door but couldn't open it. Arbilow shook his head and waved her away. She stepped back, uncertain what to do. Over her shoulder she saw Caroline standing near the van, still with her back to them.

Stumbling in the long grass, Dushma ran round to the other side of the helicopter. When she reached out to steady herself she could feel the whole machine shuddering.

The passenger door was unlocked and she wrenched it open.

"What are you doing?" she yelled above the noise of the engine. "You can't fly this thing!"

"Yes I can! Get back!"

She pulled herself up on to the sill of the door and leaned forward to try and grab his arm. He shook her off and began to open the throttle. The engine roared and the cabin shook. "Last chance!" he shouted. "I. . ."

The suddenness of take-off took them both completely by surprise. The helicopter lurched upwards without warning, tipping slightly sideways as it rose and pitching Dushma forward on to the passenger seat.

Energized by the fear of being trapped, she squirmed round on to her back and levered herself upright. She lunged for the door, intending to throw herself out, but saw to her horror that the ground was already several dozen metres below them and falling rapidly away.

She recoiled, wrapping her arms round the back of the seat as tightly as she could. The helicopter tipped again and the passenger door swung right open, slamming back against the fuselage.

"Get us down! Get us down now!" She became aware that she was shouting, repeating the same phrases over and over again.

"I can't!" Arbilow seemed as astonished as she had been by their rapid ascent. He was gripping the control column with both hands, his forearms shaking with the effort of trying to keep it steady.

Abruptly the helicopter lost height, sideslipping as it

371

dropped. Dushma felt as if two giant hands had seized her torso and were stretching her like plasticine. Through the open door she saw the ruffled surface of the sea rising towards her.

"No, not here!" she shouted, her voice almost a shriek. "Go back!"

The roar of the engine grew louder still. The rotors whipped the air, a dark blur in the sky above the cabin. The noise was like someone running their thumb rapidly over the pages of a book, but amplified a hundred times.

The helicopter began to climb again. It was swaying from side to side and Dushma had to hold on tightly to stop herself being flung from her seat. The flapping passenger door banged shut but she felt very little safer.

"I thought you said you could fly this!" It came out as a panic-stricken wail.

Exhilarated now, Arbilow yelled triumphantly, "We're in the air, aren't we? That's flying, isn't it?"

"All right, all right!" She closed her eyes and drew several shuddering breaths, nausea and terror welling up inside her.

But the helicopter was stabilizing, and in a few seconds she was able to open her eyes again without feeling she was going to be sick. And when she looked around her, so unusual was the sight that she almost forgot to be afraid.

Directly below the helicopter was choppy grey water like a sheet of crumpled foil. Away to the right, already being left behind as they headed at an angle out to sea, stretched a pattern of fields hemmed by straggling hedges and winding roads, and dotted with trees like tufts of fluff on a rug.

She was higher than she had ever been in her life, she decided. Higher than her room in the arch of the viaduct, higher even than when she had climbed to the base of the cathedral spire. She saw a railway line like a pair of silver threads, houses and cars like the scattered tokens from a board game, ponds and lakes like dropped pieces of glass. And, turning almost right round in her seat, she thought for a moment that she could see the tiny figure of Caroline, phone still pressed to her ear, her mouth a dark round O of disbelief in her pale face.

PART
III

I

The Mythgate Rig

The rig stood in the shallow waters over Mythgate Sands a few miles out beyond the mouth of the Thames Estuary. In good weather it would have been an easy flight. In the furious storm which had engulfed them en route, the same storm which had appeared such a remote threat when they had taken off, it had come to seem like an almost insanely foolhardy undertaking.

The clouds were now so dark that there was almost no differentiation between sea and sky. When they did finally glimpse their destination it wasn't its looming silhouette they first saw, but a splash of orange flame smeared out along the horizon by the wind.

"There!"

Dushma's voice cracked with relief. It felt like an age since the lightning strike that had destroyed their compass. She had been growing increasingly worried that she might be mistaken, and they might be going round in circles. Her arm ached from pointing, and her neck was stiff from holding herself still enough to feel the faint tingling on her skin that told her which way was north. She let her hand flop gratefully to her side and leaned forward, staring out into the storm through the rain-spattered windscreen.

Soon the rig itself was visible, rising like a huge metal tree from out of the heaving water. As they drew closer they could make out the three squat columns of its legs and the collection of gantries, towers, pipes and platforms that made up its superstructure.

"That's it, the filthy pile!" shouted Arbilow defiantly. Another plume of fire flourished from the oil rig's vent, flapping like a ragged orange banner.

His original plan had been to fly out to the rig and return without attempting to land. However, the outward journey had been so difficult that this was no longer possible: the needle of the fuel gauge was already trembling a fraction above zero. They would have to try and put down if they were to avoid ending up in the sea.

The helicopter was already showing signs of strain. For a while an irregular knocking had been audible from the back of the cabin, as if a piston had come loose. Now, as they circled the rig looking for the landing platform, the engine began to misfire. Every few seconds a dry coughing noise interrupted its steady roar and the whole helicopter lurched.

"Where is it? Where *is* it?" Arbilow seemed unaware that he was shouting out loud.

378

The engine coughed again and the helicopter dropped several dozen metres.

"We're too low!" They were now almost directly beneath the rig, close enough to one of its enormous legs to make out the flouncing skirts of seaweed clinging to the metal.

"I know, I *know!*" Arbilow pulled the joystick back as hard as he dared. The helicopter began to rise in a series of shallow arcs, its engine stuttering.

The underside of the rig was made from criss-crossed girders like parts from a giant Meccano set. Perforated to save on weight, each strut was secured to the next by bolts with heads as big as lorry wheels. Climbing laboriously past these foundations, they found themselves level with tiers of portholed cabins, storage tanks and covered walkways. But there was still no sign of a platform where they might be able to land.

As they ascended they neared a long run of silver piping protruding at right angles to the superstructure. It jutted out several metres beyond the rest of the rig, ending in a dark hole the size of a dinner plate. A gust of wind pushed them towards it and the helicopter's rotors almost clipped the rim as they passed.

Arbilow had opened up the throttle as far as it would go. The entire machine was shuddering, but it rose only a little further before beginning to drop.

In a few seconds they were once again almost opposite the protruding pipe. Looking down on it Dushma could see streaks of black around its rim. The air above it was shimmering.

She realized what it must be. She opened her mouth to shout a warning but her words were drowned by the roar of the oil rig's vent. A jet of burning vapour streamed from the pipe, enveloping the helicopter.

A window shattered in the heat and the cabin filled with the smell of burning. The helicopter rocked, then steadied and began to rise again, carried upwards on a cushion of hot air.

Gathering speed, they soared above the higher levels of the rig. They passed aerials and the steeply angled booms of cranes, missing them more by luck than any skill on Arbilow's part.

They both saw the platform at the same time, its encircled white H standing out against the grey metal deck. Arbilow pushed the joystick across and the helicopter sloped towards it, shreds of smouldering paint trailing from its rotors.

They came in too fast and too low. The undercarriage clipped the edge of the platform, steel struts crumpling like pipe cleaners. Listing and out of control, the helicopter skidded across the deck, one wheel folded beneath its fuselage. A rotor tip ploughed into the small cabin on the far side of the platform, tearing a deep rent in the thin plywood wall. The rotor twisted and began to buckle. Then, with a sound like the chime of a cracked bell, the whole rotor assembly snapped free and, still burning, spiralled away across the rig.

A moment later the body of the helicopter crashed into the cabin. The front wall caved in but the rest of the structure held firm. The helicopter came to a standstill, its tail hanging over the edge of the platform and its engine still running.

In the tilting cockpit Dushma struggled to her feet and pulled at the door release. It was jammed and she had to twist herself round and kick at it before it would open.

She jumped down on to the deck and staggered as the shrieking wind nearly knocked her over. She steadied herself and turned to help Arbilow as he clambered out after her.

"Get out of the wind!" he shouted. "We'll be swept away!"

Squalls of rain were now blowing almost horizontally across the platform. The two of them had been soaked through within a few seconds of leaving the helicopter. Some of Dushma's thick dark hair had come loose from under the cap she wore and was whipping around her head in sodden rats' tails. Her trousers were drenched and the wet material clung uncomfortably to her legs.

Holding on to one another and bent almost double against the gale, they stumbled towards the covered metal gangplank connecting the platform to the rig's main superstructure. They had just begun to cross when Arbilow stopped and spun round abruptly.

"My banner!" he yelled. "Now I can actually tie it to the rig! That'll be even better."

Dushma was appalled. "For God's sake!" she shouted at him. "Look what we've just done!" She imagined the helicopter's snapped-off rotors shredding their way unstoppably through the rig's interior. "We could've killed someone, and all you can think of is your banner!"

"Listen!" His face was determined. "Because it's been so difficult, that's all the more reason to go through with what we meant to do!"

He turned back towards the helicopter. The wreck was still shuddering. A terrible mangling noise was coming from the engine as it thrashed itself to pieces.

Dushma grabbed Arbilow's jacket to try and restrain him. He shook her loose and stepped back on to the platform.

There was a bang from inside the helicopter. Part of the drive-shaft assembly wrenched itself free of its mountings and burst out through the side of the fuselage. It went flailing across the deck and over the edge like a broken mechanical acrobat.

With less weight to hold it down, the gutted remains of the helicopter tipped tail first off the platform and tumbled into the sea.

At the top of the gangplank was an open hatchway leading through into a stairwell. Glad of some shelter from the wind, they sank down on to the steps for a few minutes' rest.

"Look at that thing," said Arbilow, nodding towards the

landing platform. "It's tiny! They might as well expect you to land on a handkerchief."

"What shall we do now?" Dushma asked.

"I don't know. We could try and hide, I suppose."

"Perhaps nobody's noticed we're here," suggested Dushma hopefully. Apart from the helicopter's rotors, wherever they had gone, the only signs of their arrival were the crushed front of the helideck cabin and the scars on the platform. "I mean, I haven't heard anything, and I'd've thought there might be an alarm, or something." Her only previous experience of what went on at sea had been in films. There was often a scene in which sirens went off, lights flashed and people ran in panic down darkened corridors.

Arbilow was looking at his hands. "They're buzzing," he said. He held them up towards Dushma. There were deep grooves in his palms from the helicopter's joystick.

They were both experiencing the numbing effects of delayed shock at their narrow escape from the wreck of the helicopter. Now that they thought they were safe, neither of them felt terribly concerned about what might happen next.

At last they picked themselves up and began to climb the stairs. They passed a few doors but each one they tried was locked.

After ascending several levels they came out on to a covered balcony. Following it round a corner they found that they were overlooking the central section of the rig. In the middle of a deep well surrounded by cranes and gantries stood the derrick that supported the rig's drilling mechanism. There seemed to have been some work going on: there were metal rods as thick as tree-trunks scattered over the deck, and several spotlights shone through the thick sheets of rain. But there was no sign of any of the oil rig's crew.

In front of them the balcony widened out, leading past a brightly lit room with a commanding view across the rig. From what could be seen through the windows the bridge appeared to be deserted. Holding tightly to the railing in the worsening storm, Arbilow and Dushma hauled themselves along the balcony towards the door.

It was unlocked. They pulled it closed behind them, grateful for the respite from the weather.

For a moment they stood without speaking and looked around them. On the window-sill was a cup, two-thirds full, and Dushma picked it up.

"It's still warm!" she exclaimed, wrapping her hands around it.

They took it in turns to take gulps of the sweet, lukewarm coffee.

A banging noise started up nearby. It sounded as if something had been torn loose by the wind and was swinging against the side of the rig. The whole room began to rattle and creak around them.

"Where did they go? Do you think. . .?" Noticing Arbilow's worried frown, Dushma put the cup down quickly. "It's not safe up here, is it?"

Arbilow was shaking his head. "I don't know. . ." He tried to peer out through the windows of the bridge but it was almost impossible to see anything in the rain-swept darkness beyond the glass.

He moved to the door and opened it. Immediately the wind snatched it from his grasp and slammed it back against the outside wall. He nearly fell and had to clutch at the doorpost for support.

To Dushma, peering over his shoulder, her mouth open in horror, it looked as if the entire surface of the sea was tilting. Disoriented, she felt as if she was overbalancing. She dropped into a crouch, hands on the floor to steady herself. Through her palms she could actually feel the force of the rushing water. The metal deck trembled as the strain on the foundations transmitted itself through the rig.

"Come on!" shouted Arbilow, pulling her back on to her feet.

"Where are we going?"

Arbilow shook his head again. "I don't know. Just . . . down!"

They retraced their steps along the balcony away from the bridge. Below them the rig's central well was a boiling cauldron of water. A crane toppled in a fountain of spray. A gantry followed it a moment later, bringing down lights and power cables as it fell. The rig's extremities were being torn off one by one. The floor shook beneath their feet.

They turned the corner and began to climb back down

the way they had come. Reaching the level at which they had first joined the stairs they paused and looked out through the open hatchway. The helicopter landing platform had disappeared. The only sign of it was the stubby remnant of the gangplank they had used to cross to the main part of the rig.

The sea had subsided a little, but it was still high enough for the wind to blow a stinging cloud of water through the hatchway. They shrank away from the opening, clinging to the handrail in the stairwell.

"Inside," Arbilow was muttering. "We've got to get inside."

"But which way? Which way shall we go?" demanded Dushma, her voice rising.

"Wait! Listen. . ." His head was resting against the wall. "There's something moving. . ."

Dushma put her head to the wall as Arbilow was doing. From somewhere in the depths of the rig she could sense an irregular, grinding vibration.

"Hear that? Another wave like the last one. . ."

Dushma felt her fear beginning to overwhelm her. This was his fault. She wanted to take hold of him and shake him, make him think of some way to save them. "Well, this is what you wanted, isn't it?" she shouted. "The rig to be scrapped!"

"Yes, but not with me on it!" he shouted back at her.

He turned and continued on down the stairs. She hesitated, then hurried after him, face turned away from the windows to try and avoid the awful sight of the sea rearing and swooping beside her.

The stairs took them down below the level of the rig's main platform, ending in a walkway that led towards one of the massive, cylindrical legs. The floor of the walkway wasn't solid, but made of metal slats with narrow spaces in between them. Dushma's stomach heaved. Before she could close her eyes she saw the surging water directly beneath her. She felt as if she was in a plunging lift. Spray splashed up through the gaps in the floor, soaking her feet.

"Look!" Arbilow was pointing to a pair of arching metal rods jutting out like lamp-posts from a raised platform beside the walkway. Several long ropes hung from the end of each rod, thrashing in the wind. "Davits," he said. "For a lifeboat. They've abandoned the rig!"

Dushma's stomach had clenched into a tight knot of panic. She clung to the rail, her eyes squeezed shut and her whole body shivering. Abandoned, she thought irrationally. Left to drown by the crew. How could they do that?

Arbilow was pulling at her arm, then her hands, trying to prise her fingers free of the rail. "Come *on*!" he yelled.

Gripping his jacket, she hurried after him along the walkway, eyes still closed. Pellets of spray stung her face. She blinked.

The sea was wrapping itself round the rig. The swell was already the height of the platform, but the leg they were heading towards broke the flow like a tree trunk in a fast-moving stream, cutting a steep-sided valley into the onrushing waves. Greenish-black walls of water sluiced past the walkway, closing in as the sea rose.

A hatch flapped in the curved metal wall of the leg, swinging open and shut over a dark oval hole in the riveted plates. They struggled towards it, the tilt of the sea making it feel as if they were running uphill.

By the time they reached the hatch they could hardly see. The walls of water had come together behind them, cutting out the light and enclosing them in a narrow, shrinking well of air. Fighting to stay upright, Dushma felt her way after Arbilow through the oval opening. Water boiled in over her knees, threatening to tug her feet away from under her as she turned and tried to close the hatch.

It clanged shut then bounced open. She scrabbled for the handle. Outside she could see nothing but a shifting mass of blackness. She tasted salt and realized her mouth was open. She was screaming but she couldn't hear herself.

She hauled the door shut again and this time the latch caught. Still gripping the handle, she felt water foaming on the other side as the sea encircled the leg. She waited for the waves to claw the hatch from her grasp but it stayed closed.

She turned round. They were in a corridor, faint strip lighting blinking on and off overhead. The walls shuddered as the avalanche of water scoured past outside.

She staggered, throwing out a hand to steady herself. The floor was moving under her feet; the whole corridor was swaying. The air trembled as if the entire leg of the rig was a giant pipe playing an immensely deep and powerful note.

"It's getting worse!" she shouted. "We'll never get out!"

Arbilow was already making his way down the corridor. "Calm *down*. It's all right."

She splashed after him through the puddled seawater. "But how are we going to get out? What if the door caves in? What if. . .?"

"It's all *right*." He was trying to sound reassuring but she could hear the shake in his voice. "Listen. This rig is static. The legs are bedded into the sandbank. If we go down far enough we should be safe even if the upper levels are washed away."

"But then why did they go?" She was thinking of the lifeboat davits.

"I . . . don't know. No, it doesn't make sense, does it? Why leave the rig? They'll be even less safe in a lifeboat on the open sea than they'd've been if they stayed here."

The fluorescent lighting overhead was becoming more haphazard, plunging them into darkness for seconds at a time. Arbilow had taken a small rubber-cased torch from his jacket pocket and was shining it in front of them.

"Maybe there was an accident . . . a fire?" suggested Dushma.

"Maybe. . . But it would've had to be pretty bad, and I haven't seen any sign of one, have you?"

The torch beam had begun to pick out items on the floor. At first there were just a few, looking as if they had been dropped by someone in a hurry. They saw a glove, an aerosol can, a set of screwdrivers. But gradually the items grew more numerous, as if the contents of a tool cupboard had been scattered along the corridor. They stepped over a drill, several saws, a trail of spanners.

"Look." Arbilow stopped and picked up one of the spanners. It was different from the others around it. Instead of a crescent-shaped head at both ends, it had only one. Where the other should have been there was nothing but a melted twist of metal. He touched it with a cautious finger, then snatched his hand away. "Still warm. . ." He let the spanner fall with a clatter.

At the end of the corridor was a round room. It was in almost complete darkness, so that they could only make out the details of its interior bit by bit, as Arbilow swung the torch beam back and forth.

They had come upon a scene of chaos. Broken furniture littered the room: fallen cupboards with their backs caved in; toppled chairs, their fabric coverings scorched to ash; an upside-down table, its legs like candle stubs.

The fluorescent tubes in the ceiling had smashed. The fallen glass, instead of lying in loose, crunching heaps, had fused into spiky, transparent trails that gleamed in the torchlight. Beneath the wreckage the floor itself was uneven. The metal plates had buckled, folding into peaks and hollows like crumpled bedclothes.

In the centre of the room was a hole, wide-mouthed and black. It was here that the floor was most distorted, sagging down towards the rim. This had clearly once been surrounded by a railing, but all that now remained was a circle of bent metal uprights. Inside the hole the top few rungs of a ladder could be seen. Although still intact they had drooped and now looked more like pieces of rope than metal bars.

"A fire, then, it must have been," said Arbilow uncertainly.

"What about that?" Dushma pointed. The torch was shining on a fallen filing cabinet. It was on its side near the middle of the room, as if somebody had tried to use it to block the hole in the floor. It had been chopped in half almost exactly down the middle. The cut edges, streaked with solidified runnels of metal, looked like what might have been left by a red hot knife slicing through grey plastic. Try as she might, she could no longer believe that what they were seeing was simply the aftermath of some accident.

"Or an explosion or something. Gas, maybe. . ."

From somewhere over their heads, up in the body of the rig, came the low, drawn-out groaning sound of tearing metal. Closer to, they could hear the crackle and spit of tumbling water. Debris clattered round their feet. The entire room was swaying slowly back and forth.

The beam of the torch shone on the hole in the centre of the floor. The cone of light was trembling. The shadow of the top of the ladder shivered on the opposite wall.

Dushma looked at Arbilow. His face was sickly in the

torchlight. There were beads of moisture on his forehead that could have been seawater or perspiration. He was shaking his head. She could see his throat moving.

"I can't. You know I can't," he managed to say.

Now that there was no choice Dushma felt surprisingly calm. "There's nowhere else to go," she said.

II

HILR STE

The hollow leg of the oil rig echoed with rushing, slapping noises. The ladder trembled under Dushma's hands. It seemed impossible that there was only water outside the tubular metal and concrete sheath. She heard muffled booms like distant explosions and rasping sounds like chewing teeth. Sometimes the whole leg swayed so much that she had to stop climbing and simply hold on in order to avoid being shaken loose.

She tried not to imagine what might happen if the storm tore the deck of the rig free from its supports. But with every groan of stressed metal she could not help but picture the leg as a mutilated stump swamped by waves, sea water gushing into the exposed opening and cascading down on top of her in an icy, frothing mass.

It was like being inside a huge straw, waiting to be spat out. Pointlessly, she ducked her head.

Eventually the noises merged into one monotonous roaring, punctuated by creaks and clicks as the strength of the surging currents strained the rig's foundations. Dushma decided that this must mean she was now some way below the tumult of the waterline. Other than that, she had no idea how far she had come, nor how much further there was to go. She should have been counting the rungs, she thought, but there didn't seem much sense in starting now.

She rested briefly, then continued her descent, her shoulders still hunched in expectation of a torrent breaching the shaft.

Progress was made more difficult by the unevenness of the ladder. It had been hot enough inside the shaft for the rungs to begin to melt; many of them had sagged in the middle, dripping stalactites of metal down towards the rung underneath. The uprights, too, varied in thickness. In some places they were as thin as a pencil, while in others they bulged as thick as a fist with solidified trickles of molten metal, still warm to the touch.

Once a rung gave way beneath her, snapping like brittle toffee when she put her foot on it. After that she was careful to step as close to the uprights as she could.

As Dushma climbed lower the state of the ladder grew steadily worse. The noise of rushing water was receding, and so she guessed she must have gone below the level of the sea bed. Now that it was quieter it was easier to forget the risk of being swept away by a sudden flood. Instead she began to worry that the ladder hadn't stayed intact all the way to the bottom of the shaft. If the rungs were missing for a large section of the descent she would have to slide down the uprights somehow. She didn't like to think about what might happen if the ladder disappeared entirely. She would have to climb back up to the top again. Or, if she couldn't summon the strength, hang in space until she dropped from exhaustion.

The bottom of the ladder took her by surprise. Her reaching toe stubbed the floor and she nearly lost her grip on the rungs. She swung her foot to left and right to test the ground and then stepped backwards off the ladder. Her aching knees gave way beneath her and she collapsed on to a rough stone floor. Winded, she sat still for several minutes while she recovered her breath.

When she was able to stand she picked herself up and stretched out to take hold of the ladder again. It trembled under her fingers, but she couldn't tell whether this was due to footsteps, or simply a result of the waves still lashing the rig.

Pulling the torch from her jacket pocket, she switched it on and shone it up the shaft. At the limit of the beam she saw a dark shape climbing slowly and mechanically down. She gave a sigh of relief.

The figure stopped moving.

"Nearly there!" she called. Her voice boomed in the enclosed space. Her words were probably incomprehensible by the time they reached him, she thought. She hoped they still sounded encouraging. She switched off the torch in case the light was too dazzling.

It seemed to take an age for Arbilow to descend the last few dozen metres. He paused frequently, and even when his feet were firmly on the ground he wouldn't let go of the rungs. She had to prise his fingers free. There was sweat on his forehead but even so his hands felt icy.

He sank to the floor, keeping his eyes firmly shut. His teeth were chattering and he spoke with difficulty. "S-sorry. . . Thought I was. . . It was like in a chimney. . ." He tried to laugh. "Would've been down in a jiffy in the old days. . ."

"It's OK." Oddly, his evident panic made her feel much calmer.

She shone the torch around the cramped, circular chamber. "We're going to go *that* way," she said, pointing towards the dark opening of a tunnel opposite the ladder. There wasn't any other way to go, but it made her feel better to say it so decisively. The only alternative, waiting until the storm had abated and then climbing back up to the rig, seemed to her to be clearly a bad idea. Any feeling of safety they had from being here at the bottom of the shaft was surely deceptive. They could still drown if the rig collapsed.

Dushma took the lead, picking her way over the rough, rocky floor by the light of the torch. They went slowly, both being still unsteady on their feet after the long climb. Occasionally one of them stumbled on a ridge of stone, or sent a pebble skipping forward into the darkness with the toe of a foot.

The tunnel curved, so it was impossible for them to see

more than a few metres ahead. The walls, floor and ceiling were all of the same solid grey rock, featureless except for the gouge marks of tools. From time to time a warm, gentle breeze stirred the air.

They had been walking for several minutes when Dushma saw a gleam of light ahead of them.

"Look," she said. She stopped and pointed. "Hello! Anybody there?"

"Shh!" hissed Arbilow into her ear. "You don't know who it is."

"What? But . . . what else can we do? We can't hide down here for ever."

"I know! I just think we should be careful, that's all."

Dushma switched off the torch. She listened for a second or two, then reached out towards the wall to feel for any tell-tale trembling in the rock. But the tunnel was silent and still.

Treading even more carefully than before, she moved forward into the darkness. She guided herself by trailing the fingers of her left hand against the wall next to her.

After a few moments she felt a change in the surface under her fingertips. The wall of the tunnel became colder. It was smoother to the touch, and more rippled in texture. The floor, too, seemed different under her feet.

She strained her eyes but could see nothing. She stopped.

"It's gone," she whispered. "It can't have been this far ahead."

She felt Arbilow touch her shoulder. "A flame? A gas leak?" he suggested. "Can't smell burning. . ."

Dushma imagined someone else a little way in front of them, likewise standing listening in the darkness, waiting for a light to show. She turned the torch on.

The walls of the tunnel blazed with light. She stepped back, raising a hand to her dazzled eyes. Above, below and on either side of her, countless reflected fragments of herself swayed in perfect synchronization.

It was as if she was standing in a tube of glass. The undulating surface glittered and sparkled as she swung the torch beam to and fro, throwing back distorted images of herself and Arbilow, images which themselves had been refracted and bounced by internal fissures to create an unending sequence of receding pictures disappearing into the depths of the glass.

She waved her hand, then stepped to one side and back again to watch her reflections move with her. She felt as if she was in the middle of an infinite line of cubist chorus girls.

She turned to Arbilow. "How. . .?"

"Heat," he said. "This part of the tunnel must run through a layer of sandstone."

"So, whatever came through here –" she was talking half to herself – "was hot enough to turn the stone to glass. . ."

"And that would have to've been pretty hot. A fire? Or maybe when they were drilling it. . .?"

Deep within the vitrified walls of the tunnel, Dushma

could see dark, twisted shapes and swirls of colour. There were globules of gold like dollops of treacle, crimson mists, flecks of blue and green and silver like frozen sea spray, and deep blue smudges like boulders or trapped animals. Here and there the glass had clouded as it cooled, leaving it layered with crizzled planes like motionless snowstorms.

"What about the colours?"

"Impurities." He seemed pleased to be telling her something she didn't know. "That's how they make stained-glass windows. In medieval times they used all sorts of things: precious metals; blood; bones. . . Now they use chemicals. It's not all just glass though, I bet you. . ."

He reached out to touch a section of the wall where a cluster of fiery points of light had formed just beneath the surface. "Look at those!" he whispered. "We used to dream of chipping off a bit of clinker and seeing something like that."

Dushma spun slowly, head tipped back and torch raised. She felt as if she was at the centre of a wheel. By a trick of the moving light the shapes in the glass seemed to follow her as she turned. "So are they. . .?"

"Hey! Watch yourself!"

He was pointing at the ground near her feet. She froze and looked down. There was a hole in the floor less than a metre from where she stood. Another two paces down the tunnel and she would have stepped right into it. So confusing was the play of reflections from the walls and ceiling that it was easy to miss.

399

Her mouth dry at the thought of how close she had come to falling, she stared at the curved, scarred lip of the hole. She had seen such an opening once before, in the floor of the disused building to which Ashpool had taken her and Marlstroy. Now it was in glass instead of concrete, but the shape and size were too similar for her to be in any doubt about what had made it.

She crouched and pressed her palm to the ground. It was cool and she could feel no vibration.

"I suppose, if the rig had been drilling, it would've been really loud, wouldn't it?"

Arbilow looked at her. "So? Only down here. And noise pollution wasn't exactly top of our list of environmental concerns."

"I think we should go."

"Well, yeah, of course, but. . ."

"I mean right now. And quickly."

She looked at the hole in the floor, measuring it with her eye. The reflections made distances deceptive, but she didn't think it was too wide.

She drew back several steps, gathered herself and ran. She and the multitude of figures in the surrounding glass sprang simultaneously across the hole.

Her feet slithered over the slippery floor on the other side and she staggered but kept her balance. She turned and shone the torch back up the tunnel for Arbilow to follow her.

He too cleared the opening in the floor without

difficulty but nearly fell as he landed. Dushma caught his elbow to steady him.

"What's the matter?" he wanted to know. "Why the sudden hurry?"

"Shh! Come on." She tugged at his arm. "But tread quietly. Try not to make too much noise."

She led the way on down the tunnel at a trot, running almost on tip-toe. Every squeak and tap of their shoes on the glass floor seemed to echo like a hammer-blow in her ears. Even the rush of breath in her throat sounded to her as loud as a shout.

The tunnel continued to curve, and after a short distance the glass walls began to give way to dull grey rock once more. A few veins of crystal straggled along beside them for a while, growing progressively thinner before vanishing altogether.

They had slowed to a walk by the time they reached the hatch.

A metal architrave encircled the tunnel like the rim of a giant porthole. Its surface was as dull as the surrounding rock and did not reflect the torchlight. Dushma had almost tripped over the sill by the time she saw it.

To one side was a pair of hinges, each the size of a man's thigh. From these hung the hatch itself, a hand-span thick and open just wide enough for them to squeeze through.

"Good job it wasn't shut," said Arbilow, when they stood on the far side. He turned and made as if to continue on down the tunnel, but Dushma did not move.

"I think we should close it," she said.

"Why? The storm's bound to have blown itself out by now. And what if we need to come back in a hurry?"

"I. . . There's. . ." She stopped. She couldn't begin to explain. It would sound too unbelievable. "I'd feel better, that's all."

Arbilow shrugged and did not argue further. Instead he leaned his weight against the hatch and helped her push the ponderous metal disc into place.

It moved slowly, its massive hinges groaning. Dushma winced at the noise, but could see no way of avoiding it.

When at last the hatch had swung shut with a quiet huff of compressed air, she turned her attention to the lock. A spoked metal wheel like the helm of a ship, this too was difficult to move. It took them many laborious turns to wind home the bolt that would secure the tunnel.

"Happy now?" asked Arbilow, when the wheel would go no further.

Dushma stood back and ran the beam of the torch around the sealed rim of the massive hatch. It looked impregnable, and she did indeed feel better now that it was shut. But from what she had seen and heard, she doubted it would impede the elidril for more than a few seconds.

Just beyond the hatch they sat down for a rest with their backs to the wall of the tunnel. Arbilow produced an apple from inside his jacket and Dushma was immediately reminded of how long it was since she had eaten anything.

She couldn't be sure, but the bacon sandwiches in Caroline's van seemed a very long time ago indeed.

Arbilow noticed her hungry look. "Share it?" he offered, holding out the apple.

"Thank you," said Dushma. She sank her teeth into it with a crunch.

They turned off the torch to save the batteries and sat in the dark, passing the apple back and forth between them. They took alternate bites until they had gnawed it right down to the core.

A minute or two after they had finished it, Dushma said, "You know that apple – have you still got the core?"

"No. I ate it."

"Pig." She dug him in the ribs.

"I've still got the stalk though. You can have that if you like."

Dushma considered this. "No," she decided, "better save something for later."

This struck them both as terribly funny. They clung to each other in the dark, laughing uncontrollably. Dushma laughed so much that after several minutes she found that her smile had become a grimace and her cheeks hurt. Tears began to splash her face.

Kneeling on the floor of the tunnel, she wiped her streaming nose and eyes with the back of her hand and tried to pull herself together. Arbilow had stopped laughing too and she tried to sniff as quietly as possible so that he wouldn't hear her.

"What are we going to do?" she asked, when she could trust herself to speak again.

"I don't know. Just . . . keep going, I suppose." Arbilow's voice sounded almost as wobbly as her own had done.

Drying her face with her sleeve, Dushma got to her feet. She switched on the torch, being careful to keep it pointing at the ground.

"But we could be anywhere," she said. "We could be miles underground, heading in completely the wrong direction. . ." She could hear her voice becoming less and less steady as she spoke.

"Listen. I know, I'm sorry. It's a disaster."

A thought struck Dushma and she seized the chance to change the subject. "And what about Caroline? She must be pretty upset."

"I *know*. I didn't mean to wreck the thing, did I? I'd flown it before; I knew it wasn't that difficult. I thought she was being over-cautious about the weather, that's all."

"But she must've told somebody by now. Perhaps they're out looking for us."

"Not down here, I bet you. And don't worry about Caroline. She's insured up to the eyeballs. She only helps us 'cos she feels guilty about all the money she's made."

"Oh, I'm not sure about that. Has she told you. . .?"

"Hey," he interrupted her. "That thing you did in the helicopter, when the compass went haywire. When you figured out where north was. How on earth did you do it? Were you just guessing?"

"That? Oh, it's nothing. . . Just a knack."

"But can you do it again?" he pressed. "Work out where we are now? Which way we ought to go?"

"Not much help if it's *that* way, is it?" She waved the torch towards the wall, noticing as she did so that the light it cast was weakening.

After that, neither of them said anything for some time. They trudged along with their heads down, hardly aware of where they were going in their growing weariness. When a faint glow appeared up ahead, neither of them saw it until they turned a corner and the tunnel opened out in front of them.

They were in an illuminated chamber carved into the rock. The light came from a line of bulbs mounted on walls of the same rough-hewn texture as those in the tunnel, but at least twice the height. To one side was a small platform on perforated struts, with an open cart or truck drawn up on rails in front of it. These rails ran the length of the chamber and disappeared into another tunnel on the far side.

As soon as they had stepped out of the shadows, Arbilow had leapt back out of sight. Only when it became clear that they had the chamber to themselves did he reappear.

"Your carriage awaits," he said unbelievingly, joining Dushma beside the truck. "D'you think it works?"

"If it does, I'm sure you'll think you know how to drive it," said Dushma lightly. Their sudden emergence from the cramped darkness of the tunnel had lifted her spirits considerably.

405

Arbilow swung himself up on to the platform and looked down into the truck. On the dashboard were two large buttons, a green one and a red one. There were no other controls.

He pointed. "You know what? I think I do."

She joined him on the platform. "But why's it here? Where are we?"

"This is an old mine tunnel, I bet you." He too was now visibly more optimistic. "They used to dig miles out to sea. They must've just extended it."

"So where does it go?"

"All the way back? Yeah, must do, or what's the point?"

"All the way back to where? The coast?" She struggled to picture a map in her mind. "Kent? Essex?"

"Further, maybe. Listen, when they were building the rig they took a lot of trouble to prevent people protesting, slowing things down. Sometimes they didn't use the roads at all if they could help it. Eventually we found out they had access tunnels leading down from the Underground. Come on! If we're lucky, this could take us all the way back to London."

The truck did not move quickly; either of them could probably have run faster, but it was a relief to be able to rest their legs. Dushma had felt unsure about negotiating the unknown stretch of tunnel ahead of them aboard such a flimsy vehicle, but once they were moving she soon forgot her misgivings. It was easy to let herself be soothed by the gentle swaying of the truck and the rhythm of the wheels on the joins in the rails. If the bench on which they sat had not been so hard, and if there had been something comfortable to lean back on, she would almost certainly have fallen asleep.

"If we'd had another truck," she said drowsily, "we could've had one for polite and one for impolite, and we could've chosen where to sit."

"What?"

"Like on – oh, excuse me. . ." She swallowed a yawn. "Like on the Underground. But since we've only got one, let's make this one polite, so that's 'pardon', if you please."

There were now lights at intervals along the wall of the tunnel, ensuring that they were never in complete darkness. This was fortunate: their torch had become so faint that it probably wouldn't have picked out any obstacles until they were only a few metres away. Even with the wall lights, for most of the time Dushma could see little save for Arbilow's pale face beside her, and the gleam of the tracks stretching away in front. She felt strangely restful.

Something bumped her cheek and she was jolted upright. It was utterly dark. It took her a few moments to remember where she was.

She fumbled for the torch and switched it on. Next to her she saw Arbilow rubbing his eyes and peering dazedly at her. They must have fallen asleep on each other's shoulders.

She half rose to her feet, shone the feeble torch beam

down over the side of the truck and nearly overbalanced. The floor of the tunnel appeared to be rippling. Disoriented, she clutched at the back of her seat to steady herself. That felt firm enough; just a little vibration from the trundling wheels.

She became aware of a rushing sound close by and realized what was happening. They were moving through water.

She swung the torch in a wide arc all around her. There was nothing there. The walls of the tunnel had gone. There was nothing to be seen beyond the truck except a faintly reflected patch of torchlight stretching and scattering in its wake.

She heard the torch bounce on the floor of the truck although she had not been conscious of letting it go. She pressed both hands to her mouth, biting her palm so hard she drew blood. This was much worse than the temporary unsteadiness she had felt on stepping out into the open field from Caroline's van. Now there were no fixed points to focus on, nothing to interrupt the vertiginous emptiness that surrounded her.

The next thing she knew she was crouching, her eyes tightly shut, with Arbilow gripping her shoulders. He was trying to say something, but all she could hear was her own voice demanding, "But what if we fall? What if we sink?"

"Look!" he shouted. "We *won't*! It isn't getting any deeper!"

She opened her eyes. He had retrieved the torch from

near her feet. It was unbroken, and he was holding it out over the water, angled down towards the surface. They watched in silence for several minutes, and Dushma saw that the level was indeed staying constant, about halfway up the side of the truck.

"And if it does, then we'll have to swim."

"But . . . *I can't*."

He felt her beginning to tremble again and seized her arm.

"Look!" he repeated, shining the torch upwards this time.

His grasp was so tight it was painful and this distraction helped to calm her down. Obediently she tilted back her head. Above her, she made out the merest glimmer of what might have been minerals embedded in the ceiling.

"There!" he said. "We couldn't see anything a minute ago. It must be getting lower. We must be more than half-way across."

It could only have been a guess, but he said it confidently and gradually Dushma's shivering subsided. "S-sorry," she managed to say at last. "I'm OK now."

Arbilow kept the torch on until its light had almost completely faded, then he switched it off. At first the resulting darkness seemed as absolute as when Dushma had woken. But when her eyes had adjusted she noticed a faint illumination coming from overhead. It took her a little while to realize that what she could see were deposits of phosphor, glowing softly like patches of luminous velvet.

Since turning off the torch Arbilow had been talking constantly, an inane patter meant to reassure them both. She listened with half an ear, hardly aware of what he was saying.

"Thank goodness the motor hasn't shorted. They must've designed it with this kind of thing in mind. . . All this water: it can't have been here before, it must be new — so we discovered it. They might call it after us . . . Lake Dushmilow. What a ridiculous name. OK, perhaps they won't. . ."

The faint light from the phosphor in the ceiling was just sufficient for her to make out his silhouette as he moved to the side of the truck and reached out. She heard his hand dip into the water. "Hey, it's fresh!" he exclaimed. "Maybe that's good news. It could mean we're not beneath the sea bed any more."

They drank their fill, leaning over opposite sides so as not to overbalance the truck. After that they were silent, gliding on over the surface of the vast underground lake like passengers aboard a gondola.

It seemed to take a very long time before the ceiling and walls of the tunnel closed in on them again, the lights returned, and the truck rose slowly, dripping, up out of the water.

They abandoned the truck soon after rocks began appearing on the track. They stopped in order to get out and move the first few they encountered, but before long they came upon a boulder that was too large to push aside. It was time to walk again.

Each rock-fall was more substantial than the last. After a while they found themselves having to scramble up treacherous slopes of scree. They pressed on, neither of them able to face the thought of having to turn round and go back.

Eventually, a long ramp of rubble took them up out of the tunnel altogether. They clambered on all fours up into a dark space that could have been another tunnel, a shaft or a cave, it was impossible to tell.

While the bulbs from the tunnel behind them still cast enough light to see by, Dushma made a discovery. Among the splintered stones her hand fell on something much more regular, something far too smooth and square to have come from a roof or a wall made from nothing but living rock. She pulled it free and held it close to her face. It was a half brick.

"Look at this!" She waved it triumphantly, like a shipwrecked sailor with a leafy branch that proves land is close.

Encouraged, they climbed more quickly, their feet sending dislodged pebbles rattling away down the slope behind them. Within a short time a faint light appeared. The ascent grew steeper, but there were plenty of handholds and progress wasn't difficult.

The light became more distinct. Dushma could see a jagged opening above her. Scraping her hands in her eagerness, she hurried towards it, and after a minute or two pulled herself out on to the floor of another tunnel.

The lights here were not bare bulbs but proper lamps with opaque plastic covers. The walls were clad with brick, and along the floor, supported by concrete sleepers, ran a set of metal rails.

Dushma recognized them immediately as proper underground railway rails, not the narrow-gauge tracks their truck had used. It was also clear that this section of tunnel couldn't have been used for some time. Lichen furred the walls, and large sections of brickwork had collapsed. The track too was damaged, and not just above the fissure from which she had emerged. For as far as she could see, one rail was higher than the other, as if the whole tunnel had been twisted.

"Is it safe?" Arbilow had joined her and was looking uneasily around him.

Dushma had at first felt relief at being somewhere she was at least slightly familiar with. It was a welcome change from the unknown environments she had encountered during the rest of the journey. She shivered, remembering the paralysing terror she had experienced while crossing the underground lake. This definitely felt safer than being back there, but at the same time she couldn't help but recall her last experience of a tunnel like this one, and that was not a reassuring thought.

"I don't know," she said. "Keep your ears open, and say if you hear anything at all. These tunnels can be dangerous."

412

"Come here often, do you?" he asked, with a ghost of his ragged grin. "On school trips?"

"Maybe," she replied coolly. "How would you know?"

They set off, moving, as far as they could tell, roughly parallel to the tunnel from which they had climbed. Dushma led the way, alert for steps or a ladder that might enable them to reach a higher level.

The further they went, the more obvious it became that the rock through which the tunnel ran had been subject to some powerful force. They turned several corners that were much too sharp ever to have been negotiated by a train. At each of these the rails were stretched and twisted, or had snapped altogether. Fortunately the cables connecting the lights were more flexible and had stayed intact.

"Do you think this has just happened?" wondered Arbilow. "What if we meet a train?"

"What, *here*? Nothing's ever going to get along. . ."

"No, I mean a trapped train. Full of. . ."

"Don't. It's all right, there's lots of places like this on the Underground. Abandoned tunnels, still lit up. Whole stations, even." She made herself sound confident, despite the fact that she had never seen a tunnel in this mangled condition before.

It was a relief to come upon a set of metal staples in the wall, although she did her best to hide how glad she was. "There, see?" she said, trying to sound as if they were exactly where she had expected them to be.

Arbilow looked uneasily up at the dark hole in the roof, scarcely wider than the staples themselves. "Are you sure?"

"It's the right direction, isn't it?" She tested a few of the rungs. They were still firmly embedded and didn't give when she tugged them. "Come on!" She swung herself up on to the ladder.

But their climb did not lead them to a platform or a warm and brightly lit ticket hall, as she had hoped. Instead they emerged into a small and poorly lit chamber from which radiated a large number of unpromising-looking tunnels.

Arbilow sank to the floor with a groan. Although only a few metres in height, the narrow shaft had affected him badly and he was shaking.

Dushma felt her optimism evaporating. She looked from one dark tunnel mouth to another, searching for something that might differentiate them, a clue that would tell her which one they should choose.

"Climbing's worse," mumbled Arbilow. "Used to have this nightmare. I knew exactly how many rungs I'd come down, but on the way back up there were more and I just kept climbing and counting and climbing and counting and I knew it was never going to end and I had to climb for ever."

"Listen." Dushma crouched beside him and held his shoulder. "I'm going to go a little way down each of these and see if I can see anything, OK?"

She waited until he had managed to nod, then stood up and chose a tunnel at random.

Within a few seconds she was back, stumbling in her hurry to reach him. "There's someone there! Down the first one I tried. I'm sure I heard music, a radio, maybe. And there's a light. Come on! We're nearly there."

Arbilow lifted his head and there was alarm on his face. "Wait a minute. Are you sure it's safe? Who was it?"

"What does it matter who it was? It can't be any less safe than here, can it?"

"No, listen. You don't understand." He hesitated. "The thing is . . . I'm not registered."

It took her a few seconds to remember that he hadn't actually told her this yet.

"So whoever it is," he went on, "they're going to want to see some ID. And when I haven't got any, you know what's going to happen to me then. And I'd rather it didn't."

"Oh." She hadn't thought of this, or rather, she realized, had been deliberately not thinking about it.

He seemed to expect her to say more. "So?" he asked, after a pause. "Is that it? 'Oh'? You're not going to tell me how it's for my own good, and all that back-to-front rights and responsibilities stuff, or whatever it is they force-feed you in schools nowadays?"

"No."

"Well . . . thanks. Saves you some time, I suppose, 'cos whatever anyone says I know I'd rather stay down here than get caught. But I'm not going to try and persuade you to keep me company. I can't expect you to do that. So go on, off you go, get out if you can. I'll . . . I don't know, I might,

415

see if I can . . . I don't know. . ." His voice trailed off and he wouldn't meet her eye.

Dushma remembered the underground lake, and the strong grip of Arbilow's fingers as he had talked her back from the edge of blind panic. "No," she insisted. "I'm not just going to leave you here. Why don't I go and have a look, see who it is? Then I can come back and we can decide what to do. Maybe I can distract them. Or maybe there's nobody there at all. I'll be as quick as I can. OK?"

It was easier to sound decisive about somebody else's problems, she thought. Worrying about Arbilow had temporarily pushed her own fear to the back of her mind. Otherwise she might never have dared suggest making a reconnaissance on her own. But as she picked her way down her chosen tunnel, the danger she herself was still in came back with a suddenness that left her trembling.

By then she was nearly out of range of the dim glow behind her and it was almost completely dark. What if she fell? There could be any number of invisible pitfalls waiting in the darkness at her feet. Or what if she couldn't find her way back? She could see nothing ahead of her. Had she imagined the light she had thought she had seen before?

She was about to give up and turn round when she saw it again. It was very faint, surely too faint to come from a station. Or was it just a long way away?

She wanted to shout out, to run towards it, but she forced herself to keep calm. She trod carefully, making sure the ground in front of her was firm before entrusting her weight to it.

She had not been walking for very much longer before she realized she was in more of a corridor than a tunnel. The further she went, the more the floor began to tilt, until it was at such an angle that she could no longer stand without pressing both palms on the nearer wall to support herself.

A snatch of music caught her ear and she stopped to listen, holding her breath. It was a mouth organ. It was clumsily played, with many wrong notes and long pauses between the phrases, but eventually she recognized the tune. There had been a busker who used to frequent the steps at the front of the cathedral, and he had sung it sometimes, accompanying himself on a hurdy-gurdy. She recalled a fragment of the text. "She was poor but she was honest, ain't it all a bleedin' shame. . ."

Yes it *was* a shame. Tears of pity prickled her eyes, not for this unknown poor but honest person, but for herself.

Her foot scraped through a small pile of debris that had gathered in the V-shaped trough made by the angled floor and the wall. She stooped to see what was there. Her fingers rattled through fragments of china or pottery. She brought one close to her face and saw that it was a broken piece of tile. She let it fall. It dropped with a metallic clink. She searched further and touched something smooth and cold. It was a thin rectangle of brass, a small hole at each end.

417

She continued crabwise along the tilted corridor. The light ahead grew stronger and she saw another piece of metal glinting by her feet. It was brass, like the first one, but this time in the shape of an H. Near it was an L, and a little further on she found an R.

By the time she found an S, a T and an E all together in a little pile, she already knew exactly where she was.

III

The Silver Mask

At the end of the corridor was a room, tilted at an angle of almost forty-five degrees. Dushma paused just before she reached the threshold, her wrists aching from the strain of supporting herself against the slanting wall.

The sound of music still came faintly from somewhere in front of her. Her approach had gone unnoticed. Unsure of how to announce herself, she hesitated, then took another step towards the skewed door-frame and peered through.

Hitler Street, built as an act of appeasement, had become such an embarrassment that it had been abandoned before ever being opened to the public. Expunged from all records, the station had been entirely forgotten. At the time of its destruction, it had been home to the small group of outcasts Dushma had joined after fleeing her home in the viaduct. During her short stay she had not had time to explore much of its vast extent, and she didn't think she had ever seen the room before which she now stood. Yet even if she had been familiar with it once, she would probably not have recognized it in its current wrecked and gloomy state.

She could make out little in the faint light apart from a steep slope of rubble in one corner of the room, and a hammock made of knotted ropes slung between two broken pipes. In the hammock sat a figure, half turned away from her, rocking himself gently to and fro. There was a mouth organ at his lips, but he had given up on the tune he had been playing earlier. He was now simply huffing into the instrument, producing a low metallic buzzing like a distant swarm of robot bees.

"Hello Susskin," she said. "Please stop that awful noise." Her voice wobbled uncomfortably between giggling and tears.

The boy in the hammock lowered his mouth organ and turned to look at her. "Oh. It's *you*." He didn't sound surprised. "I might've known it would only be a matter of time before *you* turned up." He rubbed his eyes and looked at her, head to one side. "Although I was hoping for something a bit more interesting. Perhaps there'll be something better along in a minute." He raised his mouth organ to his lips again.

"What?" Of all the occupants of Hitler Street, Susskin had always been the most difficult. She had forgotten how easily he could nettle her. "All right, so you don't have to be glad about it, but you could at least try and be civil."

"Answered back by a figment of my own imagination.

Perhaps I should get out more." He blew a few grating chords.

"No, it *is* me!" She scrambled into the room. "What's the matter with you? Please don't be like this, because *I'm* glad to see *you*, honestly I am."

Susskin stopped playing in mid-exhalation. He dropped his mouth organ and sprang from the hammock, landing lightly on all fours. Fringes of ragged clothing swinging from his arms and legs, he began to creep towards her, his heavy head still held in profile. She saw the bunched muscle in his tightly clenched jaw and the gleam of one eye.

"She says she's glad to see me," he whispered. "She *thinks* she's glad to see me. But that's because she hasn't. She hasn't seen me properly yet. But she will. She will because we're going to show her. And then we'll see. We'll see if she's still *glad*!"

He swung his head so that his other cheek caught the light.

Dushma flinched backwards, her hand slipped and she fell against the wall. Her elbow cracked against the tiled surface but she didn't notice the pain.

A tangled mesh of polished metal had been pressed into one side of Susskin's face. His flesh was furrowed with criss-crossing channels, each embedded with a glittering filament of wire.

Dushma stared, her eyes wide with horrified fascination, unable to look away. She was torn between pity and fear. The pity was straightforward; she felt sorry for him. But the fear was more complicated. It was fear of him and his unpredictability, and fear of whatever it was that had done *that*.

Susskin grinned cruelly with the good side of his mouth, perversely pleased with the effect he had achieved. "Go on, have a good look. Lovely, isn't it?"

He stretched his neck towards her and the light played on the metal inlay of his scars. Congealed rivulets of silver weaved their way upwards from the collar of his shirt like a branching seam of minerals, or the frozen delta of a river filled with mercury.

Mutely Dushma shook her head. She could think of nothing to say that wouldn't sound hollow and trite.

"Sure you can see properly?" continued Susskin remorselessly. "Perhaps you need a bit more light to get the full, spectacular effect. . ."

Snickering to himself, he turned and began scrambling up the slope of bricks and broken furniture behind the hammock. Half way up he stopped beside a table that had been balanced so that, despite having two missing legs, its top was nearly flat. Reaching underneath it, he drew out two long objects like clubs or paddles and placed them upright on the table-top, jammed between piles of brick.

Stooping again, he picked up a bottle and uncapped it. Dushma heard the trickle of liquid and smelled the oily reek of paraffin. A match bristled into life. A second later the two clubs wedged upright on the table-top caught fire, and Dushma saw that they were cricket bats.

Shadows leapt and dodged across the strangely angled planes of the upended room. Susskin was transformed into a looming silhouette, his features in darkness save for the dancing flames reflected in the metal veins that streaked his face. He looked as if one side of his head had shattered and some fiery substance was oozing out from within.

"Why don't you come closer?" he wheedled. "Make yourself comfortable, and let's talk about the *good* old times, why don't we?"

Dushma stayed where she was, leaning awkwardly against the tilted wall. "What happened?" she asked, shaking her head numbly. "Are you all right?"

"Yes of *course* I'm *perfectly* all right." His voice see-sawed with sarcasm. "Don't you know? There's shops down back streets in Camden where punters pay good money to have this done to them."

"I'm sorry. It must really hurt." She tried to sound as sympathetic as she could, although all she really expected was yet another bitter rebuff.

But Susskin seemed to have lost the will to torment her further. Instead he began to descend from his position beside the burning bats, his head bowed and his shoulders drooping. Reaching the join of the floor and the angled wall, the lowest point of the room, he crouched down beneath the hammock, hugged himself and looked away from Dushma. "Yeah, it hurts," he said. "Sometimes it hurts like hell. Like something with red-hot claws is trying to tear my face off. And sometimes I can hardly feel it. It's like there's only half of me left, and the other half's miles away, just . . . drifting." He waved his arm vaguely.

A cloud of smoke from the burning cricket bats rolled across the room, stinging Dushma's eyes and making her cough.

Susskin fanned the air. "Don't worry about that, it's just the coating. Some sort of protective stuff. It'll burn off in a minute. Then it smells lovely. Best English willow."

"Where did you get them from?" She didn't really want to know, but it seemed like a safe topic of conversation while she thought of how to ask him about finding a way out.

He gave a snort of disgust, as if she'd asked a particularly stupid question. "Never any good at fending for herself, was she? Where d'you think? There's this warehouse I know, in a cellar on Sproule Street. It's easy to get in after hours. I was looking for food but I found these instead. I've just been back for some more. It's not like I've got much else to do on a Saturday night."

"I suppose not." She had hardly heard him. She tried to think of a way to change the subject. "Anyway, if you could. . ."

He ignored her, his gaze fixed on the burning bats. "I like them. They make me feel quite nostalgic. We never used to have ones like that. I mean, with that coating on them. They made us oil them ourselves. It was character-building, they said. Look after your cricket bat and it'll look after you."

He began to rock backwards and forwards, making a breathy sound which Dushma realized was muffled laughter. What had he said? Where had the bats come from? Sproule Street: that was where the Bunker was. And Saturday night – which Saturday night? There was something in what he'd been telling her, a coincidence that might have been worth paying attention to if her immediate need for other information hadn't been so pressing.

"Actually," she began, "I was wondering. . ."

"Remember that autumn Atkinson-Rambler got addicted to linseed?" He didn't seem to be addressing her at all. "They caught him sniffing it behind the bike sheds and put him into detox in the san. The cold turkey was terrible. And then for months afterwards he wasn't even allowed salad dressing in case he had a relapse."

"I remember that story you. . ."

"Come to think of it, I don't think I've done that one yet. Not much to it, more of a vignette . . . no, a bagatelle. . ." He began scrambling up the slope of rubble again, heading this time towards a cupboard balancing on its side up near the ceiling. He seemed to have forgotten about Dushma entirely.

She cleared her throat. "I was wondering. . ." she said again.

He turned and frowned at her. "Still here?"

"Surprisingly enough," she snapped. "Actually, I'm lost, and I was going to ask. . ."

"Look at her!" he mocked. "Can't take the repartee. What a shame. It's what most of my guests like best."

"Oh, so you get lots of visitors then?" She had intended not to rise to his taunts, but his sarcasm prompted her to a similar response despite her best intentions.

"Dozens," he said airily. "Oscar Wilde dropped in the other day, we lit a couple of bats and chewed the fat. He loved the story about Atkinson-Rambler and the meteorites. Laughed like a drain. . . Or was it Noël Coward? Anyway, yeah, dozens, but to tell you the truth there's only one I'm actually sure is really there. One *very* special visitor."

"Oh yes, and who's he?"

"It's not a he. It's an *it*. And it doesn't say anything at all. Just comes and watches. And listens. And if you're *really* unlucky —" he smirked at her unpleasantly — "you just might see it."

He was just trying to scare her, she was sure, but even so Dushma shot a nervous glance back over her shoulder. Of course, there was nothing there.

"Well, I'd love to meet him. . . Or it, I mean," she said, trying to sound as casual as she could. "But. . ."

"All right, all right." He gave a sigh. "So: where is it you've come from?"

"Back there." She gestured behind her. "There's a shaft and a lot of tunnels that all look the same. I couldn't tell which one to take. I just want to get out."

426

"Spider Junction! Oh, now that's a nasty one if you don't know what you're doing."

"Spiders? Why?"

"Because there are *eight* passageways, of course." He shook his head and clicked his tongue exaggeratedly. "You still haven't got a clue, have you? You've still got to have *everything* spelled out for you."

"That's not fair! I. . ." Dushma stopped and bit her lip.

"And what happened to the map we gave you? You had a map, didn't you?"

"Well, yes, but. . ."

"But you lost it. Typical. And now you come down here like a frogging day-tripper wanting the guided tour. Huh."

"Look, I came here by accident. I didn't mean to and now I just want to go."

"Oh yes? That's what you said before, isn't it? But you didn't go, did you? You just hung around and hung around and *then* look what happened!"

"It wasn't my fault! I told you I had no idea what Alison was going to do. I thought she was my friend, how could I have known she was going to give us away?"

Susskin brushed her denials aside, turning away from her as if in disgust. "I was going to do it," he muttered. "I was really going to do it." He sat down on a projecting stone and stared at the burning cricket bats. "I heard them break into the station. I knew you'd had it. I was going to do it. And I *wanted* to! Wanted to turn the whole frogging place into rubble. Didn't care what happened to me. Or

427

you. Didn't care what happened to anybody! Why should I? Nobody ever cared what happened to me! *Did* they?"

He broke off to glare at her, as if daring her to deny it. Half of his face was in shadow, the other half glowed in the flames like red-hot chain mail.

"We did," said Dushma. "I do."

"Sure you do!" he sneered. "Like that's why you're down here now! 'Let's go and see what happened to poor old Susskin,' you said! Well? Is that it?"

"No. It was an accident," she whispered. "But now I'm here, if there's anything I can do to help. . ."

"Anything? Or just enough so you don't feel too bad about yourself?"

Dushma said nothing.

"See? 'Fine words dress no wounds.' That was our motto. Except of course it was in Latin. But I don't suppose you speak Latin."

"No. Actually, I speak French." She folded her arms and forced herself to adopt a bright, matter-of-fact sort of voice. "And if there's really nothing you'd like me to do for you then I suppose I'd better be going. So if you could just tell me. . ."

He continued as if he hadn't heard her. "We had gunpowder," he said. "Tons of it. We'd agreed not to tell you, but you knew about it, didn't you? Beltrowser showed you, didn't he. . ? *Didn't* he?"

"Yes! All right, he did, so what?" Her unsteadily maintained reserve collapsed and she flinched as if from the brutal handling of an unhealed cut. "What did *I* care if you wanted to play soldiers with a load of old. . ."

"'Cos you'd turned his head, hadn't you? He'd gone soft on you, hadn't he?"

Dushma shrugged, lowered her eyes and twisted herself away from him as much as the incline of the room would allow. But he persisted. "Go on, he *had*, hadn't he?" He had risen to his feet again and was pointing at her, jabbing his finger in accusation as he repeated his question over and over again.

"So *what*?" she burst out at last. "What's it got to do with *you*?" She glared at him through unruly strands of hair, her face hot.

"There!" exclaimed Susskin, like a prosecutor who has just wrung a damning statement from the accused. He flung out his arm towards Dushma as if offering her to an imaginary audience. "Now you can't say I'm not being thoughtful, can you?" He winked at her. "'Cos you see, I wouldn't want to hurt your feelings *accidentally*."

He resumed his climb up the slope of rubble towards the cupboard at the top. Dislodged by his scrambling feet, dust and pebbles trickled among the larger pieces of brick and stone.

"Of course I noticed, who wouldn't have?" he murmured, pulling open the cupboard door. "It was rather touching. Showing you his workshop, teaching you to solder. . . Even letting you use his favourite soldering iron, what an *honour*. Bet you've imagined it hundreds of times:

miraculous escapes, tearful reunions, happy-ever-after endings. . ."

Dushma took a step forward, a sudden wild hope jumping up inside her. Susskin's words brought memories rushing back, images and feelings she'd been trying for months to banish from her mind. She thought of Beltrowser as she remembered him most vividly, his thin, serious face tilting towards hers, his strong fingers moving down her spine, his breath stroking her cheek. In that moment she had been more aware than ever before of the surface of her own body, every centimetre of her skin suddenly a place that he might touch. And then she thought of the last she had seen of him, hesitating at the far end of a gloomy tunnel as she hurried to catch him up. He had been turning back to her and raising a hand, a smile just starting to widen on his lips in the instant before the roof caved in and a curtain of fire and dust had blocked her view.

Susskin found what he was searching for. He pulled it from the cupboard and, not bothering to look where he was throwing it, flung it over his shoulder.

It cracked against the tiled wall, slid down and landed in a heap at Dushma's feet. It was a mess of twisted metal and shattered plastic, a little larger than her hand. A length of flex coiled from one side of it, ending in a spray of torn copper filaments where once there might have been a plug.

At first she had no idea what it was. She stirred it with her toe, then stooped, reached out and touched the coil of flex. It was encrusted with crumbled plaster and brick dust that had stuck to the partially melted plastic sheath.

She hesitated, glancing up at Susskin for a sign that he was playing a trick on her. But he seemed to have become distracted again, and was staring into the dying embers of the burning cricket bats.

She picked up the broken object by its flex and lifted it up to examine it more closely. It swung in front of her face, dust and shards of plastic spilling from its innards.

It was a soldering iron, so mangled as to be almost unrecognizable. What remained of its blue moulded handle was crushed and blistered. Torn wires and blackened electronics were visible within the splintered casing. Solidified runnels of melted plastic wreathed the flattened metal barrel.

"It's his, isn't it?" she said dully. She already knew what it meant and now, like the passenger of a speeding car just before the moment of impact, she braced herself to feel it too. But the emotion when it came was not grief but an overwhelming rush of anger. She glared up at Susskin, her eyes dry and flashing.

He didn't even look at her. He continued to stare into the distance, a faraway look on his face. He didn't care, she thought. He didn't care what effect his callousness might have on her. Even his open contempt was better than this.

"Well I hope you're happy now," she spat at him, her voice cracking. "Of all the twisted, nasty, *hurtful* things you could have done, this was the meanest so I hope you're pleased with yourself! Well? *Are* you? And are all your imaginary *friends* going to think it's really *funny* when you tell them all about it?"

Still he ignored her and this incensed her even more. She lunged towards him up the slope of rubble, the soldering iron thrust out in front of her like a dagger. But she must have gripped it too tightly because she had taken only two or three steps when it crumbled in her hand and the barrel dropped into the shadows at her feet.

"Oh. . ." She crouched and scrabbled for the missing part, the bricks shifting beneath her weight.

Susskin had not moved. "How sweet," he murmured. "His dearest possession. I'm sure he'd have wanted you to have it."

It was suddenly very important to Dushma that she should recover the missing piece of the soldering iron. Her hands scraped across the sharp edges of stones. Her eyes began to swim and she could no longer see properly. She heard bits of plastic falling from the disintegrating handle still in her grasp.

She did not notice when Susskin joined her, squatting just above her on the slope. "Here. . ." He spoke with surprising gentleness. "Here it is." He coaxed the remains of the soldering iron from her fingers, slotted the broken barrel back into place and held it out to her.

She took it carefully, cradling it in the palm of one hand while rubbing the back of the other across her wet face. She didn't look up at him.

432

"I didn't mean to upset you," he said. "It could've been worse. At least I cleaned it. The worst of it."

"Don't!" Her voice bubbled in her throat and she had to cough and swallow. "What happened? Where did you get it?"

"Found it, didn't I? After all the dust had settled. After the fires had all gone out. I was going to do it myself. I was going to light the frogging lot myself. I was on my way. I had the matches. I was in the corridor. Once I'd decided, I wasn't scared at all. I was eager. I was *running*! . . . But I was too late.

"I can't remember it that well. An explosion, or some sort of earthquake. I fell, passed out. The next thing I knew. . . There must've been a pipe, or a water tank, maybe. Something metal, melting in the fire. Melting on to me."

A breeze blew through the room. Fed by the draught, the fissured remains of the cricket bats flared briefly and then died back. Almost nothing could be seen of Susskin except the side of his face, a glittering half-mask hanging in the air.

"There was this thing they used to do to new boys. Hold them down, tear off their shirts and splash them with hot candle wax. The ones who did it . . . now I know what it's going to be like for them. When they get to *hell*." He stared at his raised, clenched fists. His breathing was loud and rapid. Still on all fours, Dushma began to back away from him down the rubble slope.

He did not follow her. After a few seconds his breathing began to slow and quieten and he lowered his arms. "I was crawling," he muttered to himself. "Crawling, or dragging myself along. There was glass under my hands, broken medicine bottles, piles of pills spilled everywhere. I ate dozens of them, hundreds. I knew it would be all right if I could just keep crawling. I saw some amazing things. Or imagined them. Once I was sliding down a corridor of glass, reflections everywhere, like those halls of mirrors, you know? But full of these frozen clouds of colour, like . . . I don't know, giant flowers, maybe. You'd love it." Calm again, he turned to Dushma, hand sketching shapes in the air. "I'll show you, if you want. Except I haven't been able to find it for a while. Maybe I did just imagine it. I've still got some stuff from the medicine chest, quite a few bottles of pills. I still need them sometimes, when it gets bad. But most of the time I'm fine. In fact I think in some respects I've even changed for the better, wouldn't you say?"

Dushma didn't dare contradict him. "Yes, definitely." She nodded vigorously.

"D'you think so?" He seemed pleased. "How have I changed, then, in your opinion?"

"Oh. . ." She thought desperately for something convincing she could say. "I think, maybe, you're a bit more serious than you used to be."

"Yes." He nodded. "You're right. I'm sure I'm more thoughtful. I spend lots of time just thinking, now. Better in lots of respects. Everything, even. Except for this. I wonder. . ." He ran his fingertips gently along the silvery mesh etched into the side of his face. "Sometimes I think, how deep does it go? And then I think, if I got a good enough hold, maybe I could just peel it off. But I wonder how much of me would come with it?"

The image of a streaming lattice of ploughed-up flesh sprang unbidden into Dushma's mind. She twitched her head to one side, as if physically trying to dislodge the thought. "Don't talk like that. Look on the bright side! I mean, at least you're still here. It's amazing that you even survived." It was inane babble, she knew, but she couldn't help it. She had to say something, anything, to try and distract herself.

"Yeah, that's it. You're right!" To her surprise, instead of ridiculing her, Susskin rubbed his hands together eagerly. "And now I've not got someone organizing me on stupid missions all the time I can get on with the really important stuff."

He turned and scrambled up the rubble slope, back towards the slanting cupboard. He reached inside and pulled something to the front of one of the shelves. It was a stereo. He pressed a button and waves of static poured from the speakers, crackling and spitting in random peaks and troughs of frothing white noise.

"There," he said. "Listen to that. Recognize it? Beautiful, isn't it?"

Dushma shook her head. "I'm . . . not sure I can quite

make it out," she said carefully. "It sounds just like static to me."

Susskin ignored her. "That was my best cartridge before I lent it to you. Now it's the only one I've got left and I know every second of it."

"Oh." She vaguely remembered borrowing some music from him. "I'm sorry it's ruined. I didn't mean to do anything. I don't know how it happened."

"That doesn't matter. I was annoyed until I realized. 'Cos it's not ordinary static, is it? It's *you*. It's your thoughts, isn't it? A whole cartridge full of them." His one good eye narrowed with predatory concentration. "What *were* you thinking about, I wonder?"

"I don't know. I can't remember!"

He advanced towards her. "It's all right. I couldn't tell at first, but I've worked it out now. You were thinking about me, weren't you?"

"No! I mean, I don't know. Maybe. I told you, I can't remember!" She backed away from him. Should she try calling for help? Would Arbilow hear her?

Susskin stopped. He put his head on one side and stared past her down the tunnel along which she had come. "Sometimes it comes when I play this. I'll hear it moving, or I'll look up and see it gleaming in the distance. It likes the noise. Sometimes it just listens, but sometimes it tries to copy it, hissing and crackling like it's trying to answer back." His voice dropped to an awed whisper. "My special visitor. It goes where it wants. Nothing stops it. Imagine that."

"*What* does?" demanded Dushma, although she was beginning to think she already knew. She pressed her back against the tiled wall, unsure which way to look. She kept turning her head back and forth between Susskin's poised figure and the lopsided black rectangle of the door. She thought of the computer operator in his prefabricated cabin, listening through his headphones to the incomprehensible static of the elidril's transmissions.

"'*What* does?'" Susskin mimicked her. "Just you wait. Just you wait till you see it! It's not like those tatty metal dragons we used to find down here, hauling themselves around with their motors half burned out. This time they got it right. This is the genuine article. The new improved mark two." He rubbed his hands together, almost dancing with glee. "It's like a knight in armour, black and shiny, moving on silver pistons like it's not walking but *flowing*. I thought I must be imagining it, but then I felt the heat in the rock where it had been, the fresh-cut grooves it had made in the walls of the tunnels. Edges sharp enough to slice your fingers. And then I knew it had to be real."

"I know. It is," said Dushma. There was nothing else it could be. "I've seen it too. It's called an elidril."

"So?" Susskin was unimpressed. "So what if you have? I bet it hasn't seen *you*."

"What do you mean?"

"Think about it! This thing, it carves its way through rock like we'd walk through a bank of mist. If it noticed you at all, it wouldn't pay you any more attention than

437

we'd give to a wreath of smoke. But me. . . Me, I'm different." He raised a hand to the metal inlays sunk into his cheek. "It sees *me* all right. It likes me. It follows me around! It thinks I'm *interesting*!"

He backed away from her, turned and reached up into the cupboard. He jabbed at a button on the stereo's cracked fascia and the hiss of static died. The small room was suddenly completely quiet. The silence seemed to swell and recede like the after-echoes of a cymbal clash. Holding her breath, Dushma touched her fingertips to the wall behind her. The tiles were cool and she felt no tremors. She listened but could hear nothing except for the ringing in her ears.

A match scraped and a flare of light danced round the room. Dushma swayed to one side and almost lost her balance, disoriented by the sudden leap of shadows.

Susskin had lit two more cricket bats and now he was clambering down the rubble towards her, a large cardboard box clutched to his chest. Reaching the bottom of the slope, he sat down, settled the box beside him and began rummaging through its contents. He pulled out notebooks and piles of paper, some tied with string, others loose. He riffled through them, searching for something, muttering to himself as he did so.

"Not enough time. . ." Dushma heard him say. "Never be able to finish." He was shaking his head, hands scrabbling through his stack of papers. Some of them billowed from his lap and caught the draught, insinuating themselves

438

towards Dushma's feet. Looking down, she saw sheets of manuscript densely packed with lines of tiny, feverish handwriting. And among them she also saw whole sides filled with nothing but scribble: random marks and swirls gouged so deeply in places as to have torn right through the page.

"Sometimes it seems so important to get it all down." He ceased his frantic search and looked up, an exercise book clenched in his fists. "I'll work for hours, no time for anything else. But then sometimes. . ." He glared past her, a frightful grimace twisting his features. The light from the flames slithered like blood down the wires in his cheek. "Sometimes I just want to set fire to things."

Dushma wondered how much time she had wasted here. Was there any point staying longer?

Susskin was looking at her with a puzzled expression on the good half of his face. "What was it you wanted?" he asked, frowning.

Dushma's mouth was dry. She had to swallow and lick her lips before replying. "I'm lost," she croaked. "I need to know the way out." It was useless. They were going round in circles.

"Oh yes, that's right." He nodded to himself. "Well *I* know the way out. Isn't that lucky?"

"So why don't you come with me?" she suggested in desperation. She could think of something later, anything. Perhaps Marlstroy would help.

"Come *with* you? Why on earth would I want to do that?

It's great down here. Lonely, cold, bad food and no hot water. . . Now what does that remind me of? Oh yeah, it's just like school. Happiest time of my life. And besides, I'm still not certain you're real. Although I have to admit, you're very convincing. But even if you are real I'm not sure if I'm going anywhere with you yet, not after what your friend did to us last time."

"Will you stop going on about that? Please?"

"*I* know *how* to get *out*," he chanted. "But why should I tell you? What did you ever do for me? No, I've got a better idea. Why don't we both just stay down here together?"

Dushma shook her head. She was trembling and she could feel her teeth beginning to chatter.

"Go on!" He leered at her. "Thought you were glad to see me. Thought you said you cared about me. Look — there'll be plenty of entertainment." He waved his exercise book, scattering papers from his lap. "I know how much you like my stories."

It wasn't cold, but Dushma had to hug herself to try and suppress the violent shivers that were running through her whole body. "I'm s-sorry, but I can't. I have to go, I have to get back."

Susskin started to laugh, or perhaps to cough — it was hard to tell which from the painful-sounding gasps he made as he rocked back and forth.

"What for?" he asked, when he had recovered enough to speak. "I bet you whatever it is, you won't have half as much fun as you will if you stay. . . 'Cos, you know my special visitor?" He struck his fist against his knee, half his face alive will malicious delight. "Well, I bet you it'll come more often when we're both here."

She could just leave, thought Dushma. She didn't think he'd try and stop her. But what if she couldn't get out on her own and then couldn't find her way back here either? Or what if she could, but Susskin was gone?

Her trembling knees gave way beneath her. She slid slowly down into a crumpled heap at the bottom of the V-shaped channel made by the wall and the floor of the tipped-up room.

She heard the sound of tearing paper. She looked up to see Susskin ripping pieces from one of the pages of his exercise book. "Tell her," he was muttering, "don't tell her. Tell her, don't tell her. . ."

IV

Joyriding

Arbilow was asleep, curled up in a ball on the floor of Spider Junction. When Dushma tried to wake him, he clutched at her and muttered in fear.

"Don't go, they'll be waiting," she heard him say.

She spoke his name and he woke with a twitch that ran through his thin frame. She saw his eyeballs gleam and dart in the faint light.

"Nobody's waiting!" She gripped his shoulder. "Come on. I know where we are. I know which way to go."

"Sorry. Must've dozed." He pulled himself upright, shaking out his stiffened limbs. "How far did you go? Did you see anybody? Maybe we'd better wait here a bit longer, wait for the fuss to die down."

"But it's not far at all! We're nearly there. And there *isn't* any fuss. Listen!"

They were quiet, not breathing for a couple of heartbeats. It was long enough for Dushma to wish she hadn't made the suggestion. Because, faint but unmistakable, there was indeed a noise.

Arbilow appeared not to have noticed. "All right, I suppose," he said, "but even so. . ."

"No! Come *on!*" It was clear he was frightened of the chimney-like shafts that linked the tunnels, but she was too afraid herself to have any patience with him. She was already unnerved by the hours she had spent underground, and her encounter with Susskin hadn't helped at all. If he had been trying to scare her with his references to a mysterious and powerful visitor then he had succeeded; even more so when she realized what he meant. In her demoralized and susceptible state, what she had just heard was enough to send the thousand tiny feet of terror scuttling across her skin.

She pulled at Arbilow's sleeve. "Stay if you want, but I'm not." He didn't move. She wanted to shake him. Her jaw felt stiff. It was an effort to stop her teeth from chattering. "Do you want to starve to death? Or suffocate? Or worse? Come on, it'll take us hardly any time. We can be home soon. We can get something to eat, get some sleep. Nobody'll be after us, nobody even knows what happened!"

She was talking too much and too loudly, she knew, but she couldn't help herself. She didn't want Arbilow to ask about the noise that was coming from the tunnel she had just left. Nor did she want to hear it herself, and unless she talked or made some other sound to drown it out, it now

443

seemed all too audible. It was the hiss of static, a faint rushing sound like spraying water or a distant, out-of-tune radio.

Arbilow pulled himself upright. His eyes were closed and he leaned on her shoulder. "OK," he whispered. "After you."

He seemed spent. He followed her unquestioningly, one hand still on her arm, as she led him down one of the tunnels. It was a relief not to have to try and explain her sudden fear to him, nor how it was that she had learned the way out.

Susskin had at last grown tired of tormenting her, and had drawn her a map of the way to the surface. With his sketch tucked safely in her pocket, she had made to leave. He had dismissed her with his usual sneering contempt, affecting not to care what she did. But she hadn't wanted to believe that he really meant it. Instead of turning away in silence, or snapping angrily back at him, she had spoken gently.

"I'm sorry, I've really got to go now."

"She's got to go," Susskin had muttered. "Where to? Somewhere nice, is it? *She's* fallen on her feet, I bet you."

It was the first allusion he had made to what might have happened to her since he had seen her last. Even if there had been time, she wouldn't have wanted to talk about it. It would have been impossible not to make it sound as if she had indeed been incredibly lucky.

"Thank you for telling me how to get out," she said.

"That's OK." His voice was unsteady. He had reached out, almost touching her before he snatched back his hand. Lowering his head so that she couldn't see his face, he whispered almost inaudibly, "You said you wanted to help but if you go now you won't have helped one little bit!"

That was when she had given him her address. It was true that she had wanted to help him, and it was the only thing she could think of to do. But even as she took his pen and began to write on a corner of one of his manuscripts, she was aware of a nagging doubt taking shape at the back of her mind. Perhaps there was another reason for her offer, one that she didn't want to think about too carefully in case she found an altogether more complex and disturbing motive lurking in her subconscious.

"There," she said, handing back paper and pen. "Come and see me. Whenever."

"Yeah, I might."

Still she hesitated. She wasn't sure what for. Some indication of gratitude, perhaps? Some sign that he didn't hate her? Or at least that he didn't blame her?

By now the second pair of cricket bats had burned to ashy, smoking stubs. The light from the electric lamp was so faint that when Susskin raised his head, all that could be seen of his face was the gleam of the metal chased into his cheek and the wicked flicker in his narrowed eyes. "Go *on*, are you going or what?" he challenged her. The familiar, abrasive tone had returned. "You want to be careful about staying round here too long. 'Cos of what might turn up, you know?"

She had fled then, her emotions a mixture of anger, pity and fear. What was he going to do? Had that been simply a warning, or a threat? And why had she invited him to visit her? Surely she didn't want to see him again? Had she really just been trying to make herself feel better?

Something he had said was hidden just beneath the surface of her memory like an underwater rock. She steered her thoughts away from the feeling that she had done something far more important than she fully realized, something momentous and irrevocable. Instead, she turned her attention to making her way as quickly as she could along the awkwardly inclined corridor.

Twisting her shoulders, she walked both palms along the tilted wall, forcing her tired arms to bear the weight of her upper body. She had slung Beltrowser's broken soldering iron round her neck by its flex, and it banged against her ribs as she shuffled crabwise in a hurried yet clumsy crawl back towards Spider Junction.

Dushma and Arbilow emerged on to the pavement of a long, deserted street. Tall brick walls topped with barbed wire stretched away for as far as they could see in both directions. It was dark except for a sliver of moon and the irregular, browny-orange glow of a flickering streetlight. There was a high wind, perhaps the vestiges of the storm that had battered the rig. Shreds of cloud raced overhead, luminous in the moonlight.

Dushma had no idea where they might be. The walls on either side of the street were too high for any landmarks to be visible. She listened, but the bluster of the wind was the only sound in her ears, apart from the hollow rattle of a tin can tumbling towards them along the road.

She sank to the ground, hardly able to raise her head. She supposed she should be elated at their escape, but at that moment all she felt was overwhelmingly tired. Nor was it a welcoming kind of tiredness, the kind she could look forward to sliding down into like a warm velvet burrow. Rather it was a heavy, thumping blanket of exhaustion that beat about her head and made her want to cringe away from it.

During the last leg of their journey she had thought of nothing but getting them both safely to ground level. It was the knowledge that Arbilow was relying on her that had kept her going.

The tunnels and shafts had clearly affected him badly. Every time she had glanced back at him she had seen his thin face taut with the effort of forcing himself to continue. Often he had ducked and hunched his shoulders as if in anticipation of some vividly imagined catastrophe. There had been beads of sweat on his forehead, but whenever she had taken his hand to guide him his fingers had been dry and cold.

Yet within minutes of reaching the open air he was

almost his old self. Her chin in her hands, Dushma twisted herself round to look up at him and saw him grinning down at her, his eyes wide and lively once again.

"Hell, what a day!" He stretched, spreading out his arms and flexing his long fingers. "If it still *is* today, that is. How long have we been down there, d'you think?"

Dushma felt a flash of resentment. He had nearly killed them both and now he was talking about it as if it had been a sight-seeing trip.

"Well I'm glad *one* of us is having a good time," she snapped. Despite the encouragement she had given him when he had been reluctant to press on, she knew that they were still a long way from home. She didn't even know which way to go. They were going to have to pick a direction at random and start walking. She wasn't sure if she could muster the energy. It was irritating to see Arbilow so light-hearted.

He crouched down beside her. "Hey, I'm sorry I wasn't much use down there. Good job you figured out which way to go. Your infallible sense of direction again, was it?"

She shook her head. "I wish I knew which way to go *now*."

"Perhaps we could find a phone box," he suggested. "Or knock on someone's door."

"*Here?*" Dushma flapped her hand to indicate their desolate surroundings. "And have you got any money?"

"No. I thought you'd have some."

"*That* would've been convenient, wouldn't it?" As soon as she had spoken she regretted it. She tried to explain why his assumption had annoyed her, but in her tiredness it came out as a self-pitying ramble. "Look, just because I live in a nice house and go to an expensive school, that doesn't mean I've got this carefree life with everything I want and no problems or difficulties. . ."

"So forget I said it! All right?" He rose and turned his back on her, arms folded defensively.

"I'm sorry." She reached out towards him but he was too far away. "I think it's a good idea, I do. Maybe, if we could get someone to come and pick us up, I could go in and get some money when I got home, if they'd wait." If they could find a phone box, she thought, she could always ring Marlstroy, although this would have to be a last resort. When she'd set out she'd enjoyed the thought of him worrying about her absence, but now she was hoping he might not have noticed.

She raised her head and squinted into the wind, looking again for any signs of life. At first the street seemed just as empty as when they had emerged. She was just about to let her head loll back down on to her crossed arms when something caught her attention. Blinking moisture from her eyes, she looked more carefully.

There in the distance was a pair of headlights. A moment later the faint sound of an engine reached her above the roar of the wind.

She staggered to her feet, relief giving her new strength.

"Look, a car. Hey!" She stepped out into the road, her arm raised.

Arbilow pulled her back. "No, wait! It could be anybody."

"Oh *please* don't start that again." She thought he was still worrying about discovery and tiredness made her unsympathetic.

"No, I mean out here, this time of night, you've no idea."

"Oh. . ." Dushma hesitated.

The car sounded its horn. It was approaching fast and showed no signs of slowing. As it drew nearer Dushma glimpsed a long, gleaming bonnet and a shiny radiator grille. She didn't know the make but it looked expensive and this reassured her.

"No, look, it's all right." She raised her arm again.

Just as the car rushed past them it began to brake heavily, tyres scraping on the tarmac and red tail-lights flaring. It came to a halt about twenty metres away and sat there grunting as the driver pumped the accelerator impatiently. The windows were tinted and in the dim light from the moon and the fitful streetlamps nothing could be seen within.

"Come on!"

Dushma was already hurrying unsteadily along the pavement. Her legs were trembling beneath her and it was all she could do to cover the short distance to the car without stumbling. Reaching it, she half fell against the rear wing as she fumbled for the door.

She pulled it open and collapsed on to the back seat. The car smelled of leather and new plastic. She was filled with gratitude at the thought of no longer having to trudge for miles through windswept streets. "Thank you," she mumbled. "There's my friend too, he's just coming."

Then Arbilow was kneeling on the seat beside her, tugging at her arm. "Wait a minute, I think we should. . ."

The door was still open behind him when the car pulled away. The wheels bit and he fell back against the seat, snatching his feet clear of the swinging door as it slammed shut almost on his heels.

The roar of the engine leapt and dipped as the driver moved rapidly up through the gears. The acceleration pressed Dushma back into the soft upholstery. A vague sense of unease penetrated her tiredness. She leaned forward to try and see who it was in the front of the car.

A girl was kneeling on the passenger seat, peering over the headrest. At first Dushma couldn't make out her features, but then the car passed under a series of brighter streetlights and she saw a thin, sharp face framed by straggling blonde ringlets.

"I thought it was you," said the girl. "This is Screely." She nodded at the driver. "He can snag anything. He usually does better ones than this."

"Nuffing wrong wiv it," said Screely.

The girl was looking Dushma up and down with her bright, darting eyes, her gaze never settling on one place for more than a second. "So, how'd you get out then?" she asked.

"I don't know what you're talking about," said Dushma

stiffly. "I think you must have mistaken me for somebody else."

"Yeah, like your twin sister?" She laughed raggedly. "Bet you want to know how *I* got off, don't you?"

"No."

"They said –" she closed her eyes and spoke in a singsong voice as if reciting from memory – "'She has no genetic predisposition to any form of criminal activity.' See? I just hang out with the wrong sort of people, that's all. And is it my fault I've got a trusting nature? I mean, *is* it?"

She glared triumphantly at Dushma, then ducked down and scrabbled on the floor in front of her seat. When she reappeared she had a rectangle of cellophane in one hand. She took a piece of gum from her mouth and used it to stick the cellophane to the top of the windscreen in front of her. There was something stencilled on it in crude felt tip. SHEVETTE, it said, although backwards, so as to be the right way round when seen from outside the car.

"Yeah, tell the world, why not?" said Screely.

"It's not my real name! He won't let me do one for him. *His* real name's Adrian." She slumped down in her seat and pressed a button to wind her window down.

"If you could just drop us at the next corner, that'll be fine, thanks," said Arbilow.

"See?" said Shevette. "He wouldn't be saying that if you'd snagged a Volante."

"Look. There's nuffing wrong wiv these wheels, awright? Don't listen to her, what does she know?"

"But you said you could snag anything!"

"I done Mercs, I done Beemers," said Screely, his hands clenching the steering wheel. "So now she says she wants to snag an Aston or a Scusi. But these days you're lucky to find anyfing wiv petrol in it, never mind a brand new Jag."

"But it's bottom of the range!" cried Shevette, slapping both palms on the dashboard.

"Wosser *matter* wiv you? Check it *out*: 'lectric windows, cruise control, levver uphostelry. . . An' you ain't even *tried* the stereo."

Shevette pushed a button and lush orchestral music filled the car. She shrieked, pulled the cartridge from its slot and hurled it out of the window. "And it hasn't even got a sunroof!" she wailed.

"She wants a sunroof," muttered Screely, shaking his head.

"We could've had that nice new Ford Honcho with roll bars and fog-lamps and chromium flanges, or maybe. . ." She broke off and leaned forward, staring intently out over the long bonnet of the speeding car.

"Look." She pointed. In the distance, directly in front of them, were two glowing red dots.

Screely nodded. He dropped a gear and accelerated, sending the car surging forward. The wind whipped in through the open window. Above the roar of the engine came the reflected whirr of the car's wake riffling over buttressed brick walls.

The red dots were traffic lights marking a junction.

Another road crossed theirs, a busier one: as they neared the intersection Dushma saw several other vehicles flick across their path.

Shevette was rocking backwards and forwards in her seat. "Yes, do it," she shouted. "*Do* it!"

"Anyfing that revs you up, girl," said Screely obligingly.

He let go of the steering wheel. "Look, no hands," he said, waggling his fingers in the air. Then, with a solemn and deliberate gesture, he placed his palms over his eyes.

The Jaguar hurtled through the traffic lights.

From behind them came the sound of a horn and the chirp of skidding tyres. Swinging round, Dushma caught a split-second glimpse of a pair of brake lights swerving away as another car flashed past within arm's length of the Jaguar's rear bumper.

Shevette had stuck the top half of her body out through the front passenger window. Her blonde ringlets were frothing round her head and she was pounding both fists on the outside of the door. Her shouts were just audible inside the car. "Get out of the way!" she crowed. "Get out of the way!"

Screely was roaring with laughter. "Joyridin' years!" he exulted. "The book, the game, the movie deal!" He threw back his head, raised his arms and drummed his knuckles on the roof.

Dushma had hardly had time to be scared. By the time she had realized what was going to happen they had been almost at the lights. No sooner had she braced herself than the danger was past. She felt as if she had just woken from a dream of falling, the panic gone the moment she was aware of it, her trembling limbs slackening with relief, her skin still flushed with the afterburn of fear.

Screely's laughter was infectious. Listening to the rich, unforced merriment bubbling up from within him, Dushma found herself beginning to smile. Slowly the clenched-up muscles of her face began to relax into a stiff grin. Her insides were shaking uncontrollably and each exhalation became a breathy giggle. In a minute she too would be laughing aloud.

Screely dropped his hands and took hold of the wheel again. They were approaching the first of a series of gentle curves, and soon the car was rocking from one side to the other as it rounded each bend. If anything it was now going even faster than it had been before.

Shevette flopped back into the passenger seat. "Again!" she panted. "Do it again!"

Dushma saw Screely's broad shoulders rise and fall. "Why not?" he said, still chuckling, and she felt apprehension and anticipation coiling themselves into a complex knot inside her stomach.

"Hey!" Shevette had turned round and was staring into the back of the car. "I remember." She licked her lips, her eyes slithering over Dushma's dishevelled clothing. "Stuff. That's what they done her for last time. You got any stuff on you?"

Dushma glanced sideways and saw Arbilow's eyes

gleaming in the darkness as he watched her. She tried to compose her face into an expression of incomprehension. "I told you," she said. "You're making a mistake. You must mean somebody else." But she was too tired to make her denial sound at all emphatic.

"'Cos if you've got no stuff then *you're* not much use, are you?" Shevette stretched out a hand and began to pluck at Dushma's jeans, her fingernails pinching through the scuffed material. "Come on," she persisted, "where d'you get it from then? Got contacts have you? Bet you have!" Her voice took on a mocking tone. "Bet you got contacts from the workhouse, haven't you? There's nothing else to do there all day 'cept do *stuff*, is there, when you're not a redgy!"

Dushma drew back, pulling her knees up to her chest defensively and shaking her head. Her hand touched Beltrowser's soldering iron hanging forgotten around her neck and she took hold of it, thinking that she might use it to try and ward off an attack.

"She's not *telling* us!" Shevette punched the headrest of her seat in frustration. "Go on, fling her about a bit, let's see her bounce!"

Obligingly, Screely twitched the wheel. The Jaguar snaked across the road, throwing Dushma heavily against the door.

"See?" said Screely. "Do that in a Honcho an' it'll topple over."

"*Where's* she *go* to get her *stuff*?" chanted Shevette, shaking her headrest as if trying to strangle it.

456

Dushma remembered the name of a pub she passed on the way to school, a few streets away from Marlstroy's house. It was a dingy-looking place with smoke-blackened windows and peeling paint on the door. It seemed plausible enough. "The Snout," she said.

"The *what?*" Shevette looked surprised, as if she hadn't really been expecting an answer, or had perhaps already forgotten the question. "Where's that then?"

Dushma's mind went blank. She couldn't remember the name of the road.

"You've made it up! There's no such place! She's making things *up!*"

Arbilow came to her rescue. "It's on Teardrop Street. D'you know it? Take us there and we'll get you some stuff."

"You shut up," said Shevette. "I'm not talking to you. I don't think I like you anyway." She turned to Screely. "I don't like him. I think we should tip him out."

She lunged over the back of the passenger seat, reaching for the catch on Arbilow's door. She tugged at it, and the door swung open a little way before Arbilow caught hold of her and slammed it shut.

"Ow, let go of me, let *go!*" Limbs thrashing, she tried to pull herself free from Arbilow's grasp. "He's got my arm, he's hurting me, he's *breaking* it!"

Screely jerked the wheel again. The car swerved more wildly this time, hitting the kerb and bouncing up on to the pavement. A low bollard struck the chassis and the car shuddered.

Dushma was hurled to the floor. The car raced on but now a knocking sound came from the drive-shaft almost directly beneath her ear. She could smell new carpet and the reek of spilled petrol.

Screely was shouting. They must be going to crash. She tried frantically to push herself upright, fighting to regain her balance against the swaying of the vehicle.

She was still holding the soldering iron, but instead of dropping it she gripped it more tightly, feeling pieces of broken plastic digging painfully into her palm. She would threaten them with it, she thought desperately. They wouldn't be able to see clearly what it was in the dark. *Stop the car*, she would shout. *Get out with your hands in the air*.

Supporting herself with one hand she tried to lift the soldering iron but the barrel was tangled in the carpet. She wrenched it free and took a deep breath.

A mouthful of smoke caught in her throat. She coughed and choked. Her eyes stung. The floor underneath her was suddenly painfully hot.

The carpet was smouldering. She snatched her hand away, bunching her scorched fingers against her chest as she fell sideways on to her elbow.

Before she could cry out the carpet had caught fire. A line of flames sprang up between the front seats, enveloping the gear lever. In seconds the dashboard was alight, walnut veneer crackling in the heat. Dushma cowered away and as she raised her hands to shield her face she saw the tip of the soldering iron glowing white.

The car was weaving from side to side as Screely struggled to control it. He was coughing and waving his arm as he tried to clear the smoke from the air in front of him. Shevette was screeching wordlessly, though whether in fear or excitement it was impossible to tell.

The car struck the kerb again, leapt into the air and landed with two wheels on the pavement and two on the road. The wall rushed past a hand-span away, lit a lurid orange by the blaze inside the car.

The wing mirror clipped a protruding brick and exploded. A shower of glass splashed the side windows. The distance to the wall shrank to nothing and the car's bodywork began to grind against the bricks in a blizzard of sparks.

They were slowing down. Dushma had pulled herself up on to the back seat as far from the flames as possible; peering out through her window at the blurred tarmac, she was trying to summon up the courage to throw herself out. Already the heat on her face and legs was almost unbearable, and she was afraid that soon her clothes would be set ablaze.

She had steeled herself to jump and was about to fling open her door when the front wing of the car struck a buttress. The bonnet crumpled from the glancing impact and the car spun through a hundred and eighty degrees.

Dushma was hurled against the back of the driver's seat by the collision. She just had time to draw up her knees and tuck her head down beneath her upraised arms before the car slammed into the wall again. A window smashed, scattering her with glass. Going backwards this time, the Jaguar continued its scraping progress along the wall for another few dozen metres before hitting another buttress and coming to a crunching halt.

Thoroughly disoriented by the crash, Dushma's only thought was to escape the flames. She uncurled herself and scrabbled at the handle of her door. She felt it unlatch but though she kicked at it with her feet it would open no more than a crack.

Then she saw the bricks through the broken window. She was on the wrong side of the car. Her door was too close to the wall. She was trapped.

She swivelled in her seat but could see nothing but fire and smoke. Where were the others? Had they left her to burn?

She tried to shout but could only croak. It was getting difficult to breathe. She would have to plunge through the flames before they closed in on her, but she was no longer sure which way was which. She reached out a tentative hand and something hot and sticky looped itself round her wrist.

She gave a choking scream, dropping the soldering iron in her rising terror. As she tried to scrape the clinging substance off her skin, another coil of material sagged down in front of her face. Looking up through the swirling fumes, she saw that the plastic lining of the car roof was melting and peeling away.

As she ducked to avoid the long, dangling strips she felt someone seize her elbow and haul her sideways along the seat. Pain seared down her back for an instant and then she was rolling on tarmac and someone was hitting her, buffeting her head and shoulders and slapping at her legs. She tried feebly to fight back before she realized it was Arbilow. The sleeves of his jacket pulled down over his hands, he was beating her to try and extinguish the flames that had taken hold of her clothes.

She staggered upright, her garments still smoking, a hot mosaic of broken window glass crunching under her feet. She tried to speak, but before she could cough the fumes from her throat Arbilow was pulling her at a stumbling run away from the blazing car.

A few metres from the wreck was a narrow gap in the wall. Just before she followed Arbilow through it, Dushma heard the rich peal of Screely's laughter rising above the spit and roar of the flames. Glancing over her shoulder, she glimpsed Shevette in silhouette, arms flung wide as she danced around the fire like an acolyte at some pagan sacrifice.

Beyond the wall was a steep downward-sloping bank. Dushma slithered on loose soil as she tried to keep her balance. Scrubby bushes caught at her legs, threatening to trip her.

Reaching the bottom she collided with Arbilow and the two of them nearly fell. Recovering, Dushma saw the gleam of reflected moonlight just a step from where she stood. They were on the bank of a river, or perhaps a canal.

They hurried along the rough path as quickly as the dim light allowed, stumbling occasionally on roots and stones. Only when the glow of the burning car had faded from the sky behind them, and the sounds of laughter and flames had died away, did they dare to stop and rest.

By lying flat on the bank of the canal and stretching downwards, they were just able to reach the surface. Dushma immersed her burnt wrist and let the cool water soothe her blistered flesh. Then she splashed her hot and smoke-stained face, pulled off her cap and shook out her tangled hair. A few pieces of glass dropped into the canal.

"Is your back all right?" asked Arbilow.

It wasn't, when she thought about it. It hurt. She crooked an arm behind her and felt a charred hole in her clothes beneath her left shoulder blade. She winced as her fingers touched bare, raw skin.

Arbilow unwound his scarf, dipped one end into the water and pressed it against the burn. "Lucky you were well wrapped up," he said.

Dushma looked at the corduroy cap in her hands. The material was scorched in several places. If she hadn't worn it, or it had been dislodged, her unruly hair would surely have caught fire.

"Anything you want to tell me?" asked Arbilow after a while.

"Thank you," she said with feeling. "My door wouldn't

open. I couldn't see, it was the smoke, I. . . Anyway, thanks."

"Oh, not that." He waved his hand dismissively. "I mean that girl. She seemed to think she knew you from somewhere."

"*Her?*" Even though what he had inferred was true, Dushma was astonished that he should have paid any attention to someone so obviously demented as Shevette. "But she was. . ." She searched her numbed mind for an appropriate comparison. "She was half out of her window."

"Well . . . yes, I suppose she was." He hesitated, and then remembered something else. "But, wait a minute. That thing you had. Where did you get it from? What did it do?"

Dushma put a hand to her chest but the soldering iron was gone. She remembered letting go of it, but its flex had been looped round her neck. The worn plastic must have given way when she was dragged from the car. She had lost it! All at once she felt a terrible sense of misery and failure squeezing down on her. She twisted her head away, refusing to meet Arbilow's gaze.

"What *was* it?" he persisted. "You set light to the car with it, didn't you? How did you do that?"

"I don't know!" she shouted.

"Where did you go, when you left me, down there in the tunnels?"

"Please. . ." She scrambled to her feet, turned her back on him and began to walk on down the canal path, hardly aware of where she was going.

He caught up with her and took her arm. Exhausted, she made no attempt to shake him off.

"So it was true then," he asked more gently, "what she said?"

"All right! Yes, I met her once. We were locked up together — for about five minutes. And yes, I used to be unregistered." There, she had said them, the words which for months she had forbidden herself even to think, so determined had she been to immerse herself as deeply as possible in her new life. "But now I *am* registered," she went on emphatically, "and everything's completely different. Everything that happened before might as well not have done."

"And in the tunnels. . .?"

"Yes, I met someone I used to know. He told me the way out. That's all." But even as she spoke she was nagged once again by the worry that there had been much more to her encounter with Susskin than that, much more even than she was fully aware of. *What had she done?* She pushed the thought away.

"And what about in the car? What happened? What did you do?"

"I told you, I don't *know!*" She was already finding it difficult to remember exactly what had taken place. The order of events was becoming confused in her mind. "And anyway, what does it *matter?*"

"But I told you everything." He sounded hurt. "So why couldn't you tell me you used to be unregistered?"

"Why did you have to know?" She wasn't going to let herself feel guilty. She didn't see why she should, she hadn't done anything wrong. "And you didn't tell me *you* weren't registered," she accused him. "Not till you had to."

"Are you surprised? I was sure I'd never see you again if you knew."

"Oh, I see. Is *that* what you thought about me?" It was Dushma's turn to sound hurt. She pulled away from him and stumbled on along the path, her dragging feet scuffing on the uneven surface.

She had noticed as they bickered that dawn was breaking. The towering shapes of warehouses and chimneys were beginning to appear in outline against a brightening sky. The moon had set and already the first light of day was tingeing the scudding clouds a cold blue-grey and reflecting down on to the steely water of the canal.

"I wonder *what* day it is, though," she said to herself. Realizing she had spoken out loud, she added, "'Cos, you know. . . Feels like weeks."

"'S only tomorrow," said Arbilow. "I mean . . . you know what I mean."

"How d'you know?"

"There was a clock. On the dashboard in the car. It had the date on it. Will you be in trouble?"

Now *he thinks to ask*, she thought. But she refrained from saying so, reminding herself that it was not entirely Arbilow's fault that she was here.

"Might be." She was unconcerned. At the moment it

cost her almost as much effort as she could muster simply to put one foot in front of the other. Retribution seemed far too distant a prospect to be worth worrying about now.

"*I* won't be," said Arbilow, his tone of superiority sounding just a little forced. "I'll just go back to the Factory, sleep for a week if I like. Don't you miss it? The freedom? Doing exactly what you want, whenever you want to?"

"No," she said quickly. "And what about Caroline? Won't she have something to say?"

"Oh. God, yeah, I suppose so. There's probably been people out looking for us. . ." He trailed off into silence. They walked along without speaking for a while, until Dushma stumbled on a tussock of grass and caught Arbilow's arm to steady herself. It was light enough by now for her to see his face and she found herself trying to suppress a smile at the sight of the whorls of soot on his cheeks and forehead and the singed black curves of his eyebrows.

"What?" he demanded.

"You do look funny."

"Oh *thanks*. I do my best. Arbilow the entertainer. Always on the job." He was sagging under her weight as she leaned heavily on his arm. "Sure you don't want carrying?"

"Mm, yes please."

She put her head on his shoulder and looked down at the canal. The water rippled under a rising pall of dawn mist. "Or what we need is a boat," she mumbled. "We could float. On a boat. Ha."

They rounded a curve and in the distance Dushma saw the criss-cross silhouette of the giant shopping trolley sculpture gating the canal. She now recognized the shapes of some of the buildings rearing up on either bank. They didn't have far to go now.

"Here," said Arbilow, when they reached the high walls surrounding the Factory. "Look. Do you want to know how to get in?" He took her arm and drew her a little way off the path.

"That's clever," said Dushma, after he had shown her. "I'd never have guessed."

"Can you find your way home? I'll come with you if you like."

She hesitated, swaying slightly. It seemed so hard just to stay upright. "No, it's all right, thanks. I can manage."

"Are you sure? I don't mind. We could talk. . . Might help stop you falling asleep on your feet. And you owe me a story. Your story."

"Oh." She couldn't tell it now. It would come out all jumbled. And she would have to dredge up deeply buried memories that it might still be too difficult for her to recall with detachment. "Not now, I don't think I can."

"But you will, won't you?"

"Maybe," she said.

V

The Stolen Rose

The house was silent. Dushma saw no one as she let herself in and stumbled across the hall, too tired to try and keep quiet.

The kitchen was deserted. The only sounds were the hum of the fridge and the ticking of the range. She crossed the room and pressed her cold hands to the warm oven door. Then she turned and slid down into a sitting position, hugging her knees. She would rest for a moment before making herself some breakfast.

Her head nodded forward and she slumped sideways, waking with a gasp of pain as the burn on her back touched the hot enamel front of the range. She rolled away from the oven on to all fours. Feeling too weak to stand, she crawled across the flagstone floor towards the fridge. Pulling the door open, she sat cross-legged in the yellow glow and reached ravenously inside.

She ate directly from the fridge, hardly looking at what

she was putting into her mouth. She devoured a chunk of cheese, a yoghurt straight from the carton and half a jar of olives. When she had finished she staggered upright, the effort sending the blood rushing to her head and setting coloured shapes afloat in front of her eyes. She went to the sink and washed her face, and then splashed herself with cold water. Otherwise, she thought, she might fall asleep on the way upstairs.

Drying herself on a warm tea towel, she heard a footstep in the doorway. Looking up, her cheeks still damp, she saw Marlstroy standing there, already dressed and with a briefcase in his hand.

"Up early," he said.

"Yes, I . . . went for a walk." She had to take care to avoid her speech sounding slurred with tiredness.

He seemed satisfied with the half-truth and did not press her further. In the gloom of the kitchen he probably couldn't see her torn and smoke-stained clothing.

He went to the window and peered out into the garden. The glass was old and uneven and put its own flaws and blemishes into the cold grey light falling on his face.

"Where were you last night?" he asked. "I know you can look after yourself, but you really must let me know if you're going out."

"Sorry."

To her surprise Dushma saw that the normally fastidious Marlstroy had a spot of blood on his collar from a razor cut on his jaw.

"We haven't had a chance to talk much recently," he said. "I've been busy, as you know. When things get back to normal I hope I'll have more time. Then we can catch up. Do something, perhaps. We could drive down to the coast, maybe. See the sea before winter sets in." He turned from the window and looked at her, bushy eyebrows rising up his high forehead. Dushma didn't reply.

"Anyway. We'll see." He nodded, spun round and left the kitchen. A few seconds later she heard the front door close behind him.

She trudged up to her room, dragging herself along by the banisters, her leaden feet tripping on the stairs. Sitting down on her bed, she fell back on to her pillow trying to take off her shoes and was asleep before she could push herself back upright.

She woke at midday, one shoe on and one shoe off, her eyes gummy and her mouth dry. She tried to go back to sleep but couldn't. Her head ached and a nervous restlessness possessed her.

She would have to go to school, she decided. It had only been part of her routine for a few weeks but already she had begun to absorb the feeling that the time during the day was not her own. If she went she would have to explain where she had been, but if she didn't go she would be prey to a sense of unease for the rest of the day. And besides, she wanted something to take her mind off the guilt, anxiety and fear that she knew were ready to overwhelm her if she dwelt too long on what she had experienced over the last few days and nights.

She arrived just in time for the first of the afternoon's classes. Everyone looked at her as she hurried to her desk. She had washed and dressed as carefully as she had time for, but worried that she might still look suspiciously dishevelled.

She had been ill, she had decided to say, should anyone ask. She would be as unspecific about the details as possible.

No one spoke to her, but as she passed Praline's desk she heard her remark, "I didn't know we took part-timers."

"She said scatheringly," added Laureth, in case anyone had missed the nuance.

"I think it's about time we had another word with her. Don't let me forget, will you Laureth?"

Actually I went joyriding, Dushma imagined herself telling Praline. *We snagged a Jaguar but it crashed. It caught fire. I'm lucky to be alive.* She liked the sound of that. She practised the insouciant toss of the head with which she would say it. *I'm lucky to be alive. Look.* She would pull the sleeve of her blazer back from her burned wrist and proffer the angry blisters as proof of her exploits.

But even if anyone believed her she doubted they would be impressed. Praline particularly would surely consider joyriding to be the worst kind of slumming. And besides, even as she thought about it, an image of the unconscious

Alison came into her mind, and it seemed cheap to glory in her own survival.

The lessons passed in a blur. Afterwards she wasn't even sure what subjects they had covered. Teachers came and went, wrote on the board or talked to the class, and Dushma opened random textbooks on her desk or doodled in a jotter if it looked like she was supposed to be writing. Fortunately she wasn't asked any questions.

When she was summoned to see the headmistress it was a relief to be able to escape the boredom of the classroom. Tiredness was beginning to overcome her again and she had been afraid she might fall asleep at her desk. Her eyes felt sticky in their sockets and lights stayed in her vision for too long after she'd looked away from them.

The interview was surprisingly easy. Her excuse for her absence was accepted without comment. Was she unhappy, was there anything she wanted to talk about? No, she replied, and after that she wasn't required to say much more at all, just sit and listen and nod while the headmistress told her of all the advantages she had as a pupil at Larchmuir, warned her not to take them for granted, and stressed the importance of everyone doing their best to become part of the school community.

When it was over she made her way down to the locker room and sought out Moth in her sanctuary among the disused filing cabinets and stacked-up chairs and tables.

"You look frazzled," said Moth sympathetically. She

inspected the small collection of wilting herbs lined up on the window-sill. "What you need is camomile. It's supposed to be calming."

"Oh. Have you got any?"

"No. I've got mint and basil and some straggly stuff that doesn't smell of anything. I think it might be a weed. So what did she say? Must've been bad."

"Not really. I was frazzled anyway. Wasn't really listening to most of it." Dushma stifled a yawn. "Oh, I know, something about. . . She wasn't sure if I was making the most of all the opportunities. That the school has to offer."

"Oh dear. That *is* a bad sign, I'm afraid."

"Is it?" Dushma had hardly taken the words in at the time. Thinking about them now, she supposed that they must refer to her poor performance in class. "I know I'm not doing very well, but I haven't been here that long," she defended herself. It was too late now, she knew, but it made her feel better. "And it's not that I don't know things. I do, I know lots of things. It's just that I don't know the things they want me to."

"Something like that happened to me a couple of terms ago," confided Moth. "She usually asks to see people before she writes to their parents. My mother got a letter saying I was cynical! Can you believe it?"

"What did she do?"

"Well, first she looked it up. As she's fond of telling me, she never had the advantages that I'm fortunate enough to enjoy. Then she said she couldn't really see anything wrong with it, and at least where men were concerned it should be positively encouraged."

"My guardian's already had a letter. It said I responded badly to authority."

"And what did he do?"

"He said he supposed he ought to punish me, so I said I'd like to see him try! And he just laughed and tore the letter up."

"That's lucky."

"D'you think so? I suppose it is, but. . . Sometimes I'm not sure how seriously he takes my education."

"Well, I think he sounds great. I wish my mother was like that."

"I don't know. . ." Dushma thought of Marlstroy's planned collusion with Ashpool. "There's other things. . ."

"I do know! Listen. She split up from my father before I was even *born*. You know how it works. She only had me because she knew she could get more money out of him once the tests showed I'd probably go deaf. Mummy's meal ticket, that's what I am."

Dushma nodded understandingly, her mind elsewhere. Should she try and tell Moth? She desperately wanted to tell somebody, even though she didn't see what good it would do apart from providing her with some reassurance. She just wanted to be told that there was nothing she could do, that whatever happened, it wouldn't be her fault.

Moth had plucked a leaf from one of her plants and was slowly shredding it. "That's why she made me sign up for

474

all those extra-mural activities," she continued bitterly. "They were supposed to make me more idealistic but she didn't care, she just wanted to be able to charge my father more maintenance."

But what was the point? If she told someone everything, it would make it all seem more real. And that would make it harder for her to do nothing, whatever Moth or anyone else might say. So it seemed her only option now was to simply forget about it, try and convince herself in time that she had imagined it. There was no alternative. She was powerless.

"I'll tell you what," said Moth impulsively. "If you get expelled, I'll come with you to your next school. Even. . ." The enormity of her promise sank in and she paused, then continued bravely, "Even if it's somewhere cheaper!"

"That's kind of you," said Dushma. Not so long ago she would never have thought such a thing, but now she found herself guiltily wondering how lonely the independent-seeming Moth must actually have been.

In fact the prospect of having to leave Larchmuir didn't worry Dushma that much. Despite the efforts she had made to convince herself that she belonged there, her short career at the school already seemed unreal, as if it had happened to somebody else. It was already beginning to feel strange that she could ever have thought about spending several years in such a place.

The two girls walked back between the rows of filing cabinets and out into the open centre of the locker room.

While they had been talking in their hidden enclave, one of the old sofas that made up the room's sparse furnishing had been moved. Turned through ninety degrees, it now barred the path to the door. On it, in identical attitudes of prim displeasure, sat Praline and her two lieutenants.

"The troglodytes emerge," said Praline disdainfully. "I think you ought to know, we're *very* disappointed."

"Saddened," said Laureth. "Deeply." Next to her, Natalie wrung her hands and was silent. Of the three she was the only one who looked genuinely distressed, although this was her habitual expression when trying to think of something to say.

Praline shook her head slowly from side to side. "A wonderful opportunity, completely wasted."

"She said, regrettably."

"We explained everything perfectly clearly, but it seems you're not prepared to make the slightest bit of effort."

Until recently Dushma had regularly imagined scenes like this, always devising a triumphant ending in which she confounded her tormentors with a devastating riposte. But so much had happened to her over the last few days that it now took her a moment to remember what Praline was talking about. What had she been supposed to do? Something about getting her hair cut. It now seemed so trivial compared to her other preoccupations that she found herself smiling to think that it had ever worried her.

"Dismayed!" exclaimed Natalie. "We're dismayed."

Dushma pushed her way past one arm of the sofa and

walked towards the door. This, it became obvious immediately, was a grave affront.

"Excuse *me*. . ." Praline's voice rose with indignation. Someone – Laureth or Natalie – gave a gasp. Springs groaned as the three girls struggled up from the sagging sofa.

Dushma turned to Moth, who was following behind her. "Did you hear that?"

"No. What?"

"Nothing. It's just, I think the wind's getting up again."

On the way home Dushma took a more round-about route than usual. She left the bus a stop early and then dawdled, playing childish games with herself to prolong the journey. She shuffled through piles of leaves, avoided the cracks in the pavement, held her breath between lamp-posts and walked along the tops of low walls, starting again if she lost her balance.

In one overgrown garden she noticed an unpruned rosebush. Most of its crimson flowers had been stripped away by the wind; a few petals still lay on the surrounding soil like the embers of a dying fire. One of the blooms, more sheltered than the rest, remained intact. It was beginning to wilt and fade but still retained a blowsy beauty. Marlstroy should have roses.

Leaning over the railings to look more closely, Dushma caught hints of its fragrance as the wind gusted. The smell was intoxicating and she inhaled deeply. Everything had seemed more vivid since her return from the rig, she realized. Sight, smell, sounds. . . Even the touch of the iron beneath her palms seemed harder and colder than she would have expected. She raised one hand, her fingers straying unconsciously to the nape of her neck. She felt for the clasp of her locket but of course it was gone. She had torn it from her neck aboard the helicopter.

Why didn't Marlstroy's garden have roses?

She looked up and down the street. It was a quiet side road and there was no one in sight. The bare branches of trees swished overhead like witches' broomsticks. The puddles on the wet road gleamed in the deep orange light of the setting sun so that the gutters seemed to run with gold.

She turned back to the garden. There were no lights on in the house on the far side of the lawn. She glanced about her once more and then pushed a toe into a stirrup of ironmongery and swung herself up and over the railings.

She landed on soft wet grass, slipped and rolled over. She picked herself up. No one shouted out. She ran to the rosebush and, mindful of thorns, bent the stem of the single remaining rose until it snapped.

By the time she got herself back out on to the pavement, she had laddered her tights and scraped the skin from one knee. She limped as quickly as she could away from the scene of her crime, trying to kick the clumps of mud off her shoes as she went.

Once round the corner, she slowed down and removed

the stolen rose from beneath her blazer. She walked the rest of the way home with her nose pressed into the petals and the fingers of both hands delicately holding the spiny stem, like the player of some exotic musical instrument.

The sun had almost vanished by the time she reached Marlstroy's front gate. The last rays caught the remaining leaves of the climbing plants that covered one side of the house. The reddish foliage rippled in the wind like flames licking the wall.

Dushma let herself in, crossed the hall and stood listening outside the door of the study. After a few moments she raised her hand and knocked. When there was no answer she turned the handle and slipped quietly inside.

Nicola Auquin had liked roses. They had filled her sickroom. When Marlstroy had told her the story, it had been obvious that they could still affect him strongly.

Dushma took a vase down from the mantelpiece, placed it in the middle of the desk and stood the rose in it. Would it prick his conscience or merely anger him?

She had not been in the study since they had argued about Alison. The broken oscilloscope was now on a shelf in an alcove, pieces of glass scattered around it. The electrodes still dangled from their sockets at the back of the instrument.

She looked for the cartridge Ashpool had given to Marlstroy but it was nowhere to be seen. Had Marlstroy already examined the contents, trying to guess what the elidril had found that it thought interesting enough to be worth broadcasting? *It's not ordinary static, is it? It's you*, Susskin had said, as the white noise poured from his stereo. Would Marlstroy notice that it resembled the data he had collected from his experiments on her? Should Ashpool learn of it, the similarity would be sure to arouse his suspicions, since the signals had begun before Dushma had ever seen the elidril. And if he discovered her association with Hitler Street and the death of Rapplemann, she would be as much at risk from him as Alison now was.

If she found the cartridge what would she do with it? Perhaps she could take it, record over the tell-tale contents with static from the radio, then replace it before Marlstroy realized it had gone. She tried the desk drawers but they were locked.

By the time she left the study it was almost completely dark. She didn't dare switch on the light to continue her search. She feared that if she did so without her locket the bulb would fuse, or perhaps even literally blow, showering the room with glass.

She hesitated by the door for a moment, looking back across the study. In the faint blue light from the window she could just make out the rose, already beginning to droop in its vase. As she watched, a petal detached itself and fell to the desktop. It landed on a square of fresh white blotting paper and lay there like a splash of dark liquid.

VI

Moonlight and Broken Glass

"People sometimes ask me why," said Ashpool. "Political editors. Idealistic young MPs. They want a stick to beat you with when you fail, or an inspiring quote to rally the faithful. They never actually want to know *why*. Don't suppose you do either."

Marlstroy didn't reply. He stood at the window of his study, staring out through the open curtains. Almost nothing was visible in the garden, and the reflection of his pale, lined face floated in the darkness among the shadows of bushes and trees.

Ashpool stirred in his armchair, leaning forward to pour himself another glass of whisky. "But I'm going to tell you anyway. I was idealistic too, to start with. Really believed I could change the world. Do some good. You remember college, don't you? I must've moaned about it often enough. All those cold church halls. Two old ladies and a dog. If I was lucky. Hundreds of doors slammed in my face. Thousands of leaflets. If you're a rock star they call it paying your dues. When you're a politician they call you power-hungry."

"It never really interested me that much," said Marlstroy. He didn't turn round.

"No, you didn't understand it, did you? All that effort, and for what? To be vilified, caricatured and misunderstood – and that was if you were successful! No, even then you wanted to be revered, didn't you? You wanted to be immortal. But back then I didn't even want gratitude. I just wanted to be someone who had done the right thing. Someone who nurtured the flame and then passed it on. Makes me laugh now to think of it."

Ashpool set his elbows on his knees and stared at the bottom of his glass. His baggy grey suit was rumpled and his heavy face sagged. "Can't remember when I lost my political faith. It happened gradually, I suppose. Eventually I realized that the job wasn't a means to an end any more but an end in itself. I didn't care what I was doing as long as I could keep on doing it. And I was good at it! They predicted everything for me. Environment; then the Home Office, the power behind the throne. I was actor, general and head prefect all rolled into one.

"But now it's all so nearly over I find there's only one thing I'd miss. Not the standing ovations or the cheers from the back bench. I could give up making speeches tomorrow." He raised his hand as if to forestall an imaginary interruption. "No really, I could. The limousine, the bodyguards, the non-executive directorships, all the trappings of power. . . I wouldn't miss them. No, the one thing that would really hurt would be not knowing."

Marlstroy turned from the window and looked at him. "Not knowing? Not knowing what?"

Ashpool sat back in his chair, a superior smile on his lips. "Ah. What indeed. There are things going on now that you've no idea about. There always are. Things I daren't breathe a word of, even to you. This South American business, for example. How many people know the real reasons behind what's going on there? The oil wars, the coal strikes, the things that have had such an effect on our own situation these last months. Speculation, analysis . . . the coverage has been exhaustive. But it's all been wrong. In the whole world there are probably only about a dozen people who'll ever know the truth. And I'm one of them."

"Congratulations." Marlstroy was sarcastic. "So you know which of them's the biggest crook, while the rest of us just have to guess."

"Why does everyone assume that if they're not allowed to know then it must be something bad? Of course there are crimes and compromises. But there's been heroism too, and sacrifice. If I could tell you. . ." Ashpool raised his empty glass and shook it at Marlstroy. "You'd be stirred, you would, even you!"

"You make it sound like a soap opera," sneered Marlstroy. "And you don't want to miss the last episode."

"Laugh if you like. I'm trying to be honest, that's all,

without the risk of having my words twisted round and flung back at me in some fancy editorial. I thought if I could do that with anyone it would be you."

"I'm so flattered."

"Most people, I couldn't say this to them, however obvious it might be. One gets tired of the manipulation, the chicanery involved in getting even the most obviously important things done. When everything else is gone, when the light of idealism has gone out and the thrill of power has turned stale, the one thing that remains is the desire to know what happens. The machine I built. The elidril. It was the culmination of years of work. Do you think I did it to keep myself entertained? It was meant to do immeasurable good. It was going to be my triumph. It still could be! But if my career finishes now then I may never know if I succeeded. Will it simply disappear? Or will they find it and destroy it? Or turn it to their own secret ends? Whatever happens it'll be classified. Suppressed. I'll never find out."

"You seem very pessimistic. You've had setbacks before. I've never heard you talk about the end of your career."

Ashpool pulled off his spectacles, revealing two angry red marks on the bridge of his nose. "You heard the news." He rubbed the back of his hand across his eyes. "You know what happened yesterday. The rig is a wreck! Three mangled stumps in the water. Impossible to hush up a disaster like that. They said it couldn't be done, that we'd find nothing. But it was ready! A new source of oil controlled by non-unionized labour. It was going to be a coup, a sensation. I had camera crews ready to fly out that morning. I had Torrelguard in prison on suspicion of incitement. I was going to outmanoeuvre the strikers and confound the environmentalists. End this whole crisis at a stroke! But now this one piece of bad luck has put us back months, if not ruined us completely."

"So what are you going to do?"

Ashpool hauled himself up out of the armchair and began to pace the study. "We're not quite sure what happened yet – we're still searching for survivors. But as soon as I heard something had gone wrong I put out a rumour of sabotage. Two of the broadsheets have picked up on it already."

"That's hardly constructive."

"Oh, don't be so precious. We'd have to consider it even if we had no evidence. And as a matter of fact I heard this morning that they've found signs of damage to one of the legs of the rig. Fire damage. It's not *constructive* to start looking for scapegoats. The possibility of sabotage at least helps to hold them off from blaming me. Nobody's actually called for my head – yet. But my position is extremely precarious. The merest hint of a scandal now would be enough to finish me."

Ashpool put down his glass, clunking the heavy tumbler loudly on the wooden desktop. He thrust his head forward and glared at Marlstroy's reflection in the study window. "You know why I'm here. But you're making me spell it out, aren't you? There are two lawyers and a journalist wanting to speak to the Catfinger girl. If my involvement with Rapplemann comes out I'm done for. I know we have to be cautious. That's why I came alone tonight. But I can't afford to wait much longer."

Marlstroy turned and faced him. The vase still stood on the desk between them but the rose was gone, as was the petal that had fallen on to the blotter. Nevertheless a faint hint of its scent remained in the air, not quite masked by the smell of whisky.

"I don't think I can do it," said Marlstroy.

"Can't *do* it?" Ashpool looked astonished. "But we've been through all this once. Never mind whatever personal reasons I may have. You know that without me, no scheme bold enough to get us out of this mess will have any chance of succeeding. Now more than ever, after this latest setback. Without me, how long do you think it'll be before the cabinet is crippled by vacillation and compromise? How long before they cave in to the extremists and abandon all drilling on Mythgate Sands for good? How long before the shortages we've seen are a hundred times worse?"

"I'll take the risk," said Marlstroy. "I've told you. I can't do it."

"You know the consequences. For the country, for *you*."

Marlstroy shrugged. "Very well. This time, I'm prepared to face—"

"Wait. Shh. What was that?" Ashpool had spun round

486

towards the study door and now stood poised, feet apart and shoulders hunched, like a wrestler awaiting an attack. "Voices. Outside. Did you hear?"

Marlstroy listened, then shook his head. "No, there's nothing. Your imagination. Wind's getting up again." He turned back to the window. Out in the garden trees and bushes swayed and shook, patches of darker shadow against the night sky.

"No, there it is again," insisted Ashpool. He began to cross the study. "Someone shouting. I. . ."

There was a sound of breaking glass. Ashpool leapt the remaining short distance to the door, seized the handle and flung it open.

Moonlight flooded the hallway, glittering on the pieces of broken glass scattered across the black and white tiled floor. Something had smashed one pane of the wide bay window at the front of the house. A high wind scraped in over the jagged edges remaining in the frame.

Beyond the shattered window a cluster of dark figures could be seen, crowding the pavement outside the front gate. It was impossible to tell how many of them there were. The moon was at their backs and the fitful streetlights illuminated little. Some waved their arms, others clung to the railings. Many were shouting.

Ashpool stood motionless for a moment, listening. Then with a furious hiss of indrawn breath he stepped out across the hall. They were calling his name, chanting it in a ragged, angry chorus. Another window pane broke but he hardly faltered as glass rained down on him. He flapped at the fragments like someone swatting flies.

"Wait!" shouted Marlstroy.

Ashpool ignored him. "I'll give them habeas bloody corpus," he muttered, reaching for the catch on the front door.

"No! Don't let them in." Marlstroy caught up with him and took hold of his arm. "Don't be rash. You don't know what they'll do."

Ashpool shook him off. "They'll do as they're *told*. Don't we have laws? Where do they think they are? The French Revolution?" But he removed his hand from the door and turned his back to it, breathing deeply to try and control his temper. "No, you're right, why take the risk?"

"Come on," Marlstroy urged him. "We can go out through the back. Over the wall." He ducked involuntarily as something struck the outside of the front door.

"You go if you like. But they're probably there as well." Ashpool reached into his jacket and took out a phone. Walking back towards the study, he began to dial a number.

Instead of following him, Marlstroy turned towards the stairs. He grasped the banister and then stopped, one foot on the lowest step, looking upwards into the darkness.

Dushma stood on the landing. She had been asleep, but the shouting and breaking windows had woken her. She was still fully dressed, though her school uniform was crumpled and her hair in disarray.

The noise had subsided, and she wasn't sure if she had imagined it. She stood blinking, her eyes half closed, the moonlight in the hall seeming bright as daylight after the darkness of her room. It was the kind of eerie light, she thought, that should be accompanied by high violins.

Seeing Marlstroy, she began walking down the stairs towards him. She rubbed her eyes and felt grooves on her face where her cheek had rested on folds in her bedclothes.

"What's happening? I thought I. . ." Another window-pane burst inwards in a silvery cascade of glass. A ragged cheer came from outside.

Dushma flinched. As she hesitated, Marlstroy sprang up the stairs towards her.

"Come on!" Out in the street the shouting had resumed and he had to raise his voice to be heard.

"Where? What's happening?"

He took her arm and half dragged her down the remaining stairs. "Just . . . some people. A crowd. A demonstration. Here. . ."

He pulled her along the hallway towards a small door set into the wall beneath the staircase. In his free hand he held a key. It rattled in his trembling fingers as he pushed it into the lock.

The door swung open to reveal a flight of steep stone steps disappearing down into the darkness. A cold draught of air stirred Dushma's skirt against her knees. She shrank away from Marlstroy, tugging her arm free of his grasp.

"Please." He held out the key to her. "You'll be safer here."

She turned back towards the staircase. There were people in the front garden now. She could see their silhouettes moving closer to the house. She imagined them breaking down the door, ransacking the library, bursting into her room and rifling through her belongings. "But. . . I should get some things," she said uncertainly. "What if. . .?"

Several window panes broke at once. Glass skittered over the floor and around her shoes. She leapt backwards, almost falling. Someone began banging on the front door.

Marlstroy steadied her. "Quickly. Lock the door behind you." He guided her towards the cellar, pressing the key into her hand. "Careful on the steps. There's a light switch on the wall inside. Go *on*!"

The cellar door was low enough for Dushma to have to duck her head. She gripped the lintel and placed her foot reluctantly on to the top step.

"I don't . . . *care*!" Ashpool's voice came loudly from the study. "I want it here *now*! Of course I have authorization! . . . What? Of course I am! Look at my voice patterns, idiot! Don't they match? . . . Yes, *immediately*!"

"*Lock* it. Do you understand? Don't open it for anyone except me." Marlstroy raised his hand and squeezed her shoulder. "Don't worry, it won't be for long." He was about to swing the cellar door shut, but seeing her mistrust he paused, then leaned close to her and lowered his voice. "It's all right. I've told him I won't do it. He's not happy, of course, but. . . We'll think of something."

It took her a second or two to realize what he meant. Relief welled up inside her. For a moment she forgot about the breaking glass and the angry shouts coming from outside the house. It was going to be all right. She tried to think of something to say but couldn't. She wanted to show some sign of gratitude, perhaps reach out and touch him, but she was too late.

The last thing she saw before the door closed was the reassuring flicker of a smile warming Marlstroy's hawkish face. Then she was alone in almost total darkness.

At first she didn't dare move in case she fell. The step beneath her feet was invisible, as were the walls around her and even the panels of the door immediately in front of her eyes. All she could see was the light from the keyhole, a silvery blur near her right hand. She fumbled with the key, then slotted it home and twisted it. The lock grated shut.

She listened for a few moments, but could make nothing of the noises coming from the hallway. She heard no more falling glass, but perhaps that simply meant that all the windowpanes were now broken. She heard raised voices, but couldn't tell which direction they came from, or whether any of them belonged to Marlstroy or Ashpool.

Did she dare try the light? She swept the walls on either side of her with the palms of her hands, searching for the light switch. She reached as far as she could without losing her balance, but felt only crumbling plaster and cobwebs. Perhaps it was better to remain in the dark. A light might show through the keyhole and give her away.

She heard more knocking sounds from the hallway. It occurred to her that if someone burst into the cellar she would be flung down the steps. She turned slowly and leaned her back against the door, staring down into the darkness until clouds of coloured mist swam before her eyes.

Then she saw it. She blinked rapidly, rubbed a hand over her face and looked again, but it was still there. Somewhere in the depths of the cellar a light already shone.

Her first thought was that some of the people from outside the house must have found a different way in. She scrabbled for the key in the door, panic driving everything from her mind except the need to escape, to find another hiding place.

Before she could turn it the key slipped from the lock and fell with a jingle on to the steps. She crouched and groped for it but found nothing. Fighting down the urge to scream for help, she looked again at the light.

It hadn't moved. She slapped her hand down on to the cold stone, angry at how easily she had taken fright. It was a bright night. A shaft of moonlight must have found its way into the cellar, that was all. Through a skylight, maybe, or a set of ventilation bricks.

She sat down on the top step and felt around her for the

fallen key. It was nowhere within reach. It didn't matter, she told herself. Marlstroy might have another. And if he didn't he could always force the door. The damage would be minor compared to what had already happened to the front of the house.

Her eyes were beginning to get used to the dark and she could just see the outline of the next few steps. It would be safer to descend than stay up here beside the door, she thought.

Still in a sitting position, she began to work her way down the steps using her feet and hands. At the bottom she stood up cautiously, one arm raised to protect her head from low beams. Grit crunched beneath her shoes as she walked slowly towards the faint patch of light she had glimpsed while standing by the door.

Every few paces she stopped to listen and look around. As she drew nearer to the light she noticed dull smudges of reflection glowing in the dark on either side of her. She reached out and touched a cold, dusty surface. Exploring further, her fingers closed on the neck of a bottle. She was surrounded by wine racks.

From somewhere not far in front of her she heard the clink of glass.

All at once it seemed as if she couldn't draw enough air into her lungs. Her hand flew to her mouth to try and mask the deafening rush of the breath in her throat. She fought the impulse to turn and run, willing herself to stand motionless. She would be sure to trip and fall. Instead she tipped her head and squeezed her eyes shut, straining her ears for a repetition of the sound.

The shouts from above had died down, but as she listened she heard a new noise begin. From somewhere over her head came a hollow, rhythmic booming, as if a heavy object was being pounded against the front door of the house.

The noise, and her subterranean surroundings, made her think of the story she had found in the cathedral annexe. She remembered Vastruglin the alchemist at work in his makeshift laboratory, the walls ringing with the sound of hammer blows.

A current of air wafted over her and she shivered, despite the fact that the draught was warm. Without moving her feet, she twisted round to look back over her shoulder. The slim shaft of light from the keyhole was no longer visible. She couldn't be sure quite which way she should go to get back to the door.

More details of Vastruglin's experiment crowded into her mind: the breaking glassware, the fumes, the flames surging in the grate. She felt an echo of the panic that had possessed her on her last night in the vestry, when the shadowy corners of the room had no longer looked empty, and the candle-light had made the stained glass seem alive.

She forced herself to move further into the cellar, alert for any noise that might be audible above the sound of hammering. Surely if they'd found a way in down here, they wouldn't be trying to break the front door down, would they? The clink of glass she had heard, she reasoned, must have been caused by wine bottles shaking in their racks.

She almost walked into a brick pillar blocking her path. Peering round it she saw that what she had thought to be a moonbeam was far too soft and yellow to be anything of the sort. In front of her, swaying in the draught, a torch hung from the ceiling, shedding a pool of dim light down on to the flagstones.

She pressed her cheek to the pillar, loose cement gritty against her skin. She hoped that the noise from overhead would drown the sound of her breathing.

The torch batteries must be failing. She could see very little by its light. Straining her eyes, she made out the shapes of several more wine racks swathed in fluttering drapes of cobweb. Long shadows stretched away behind them, sliding back and forth over the cellar walls. Much nearer, just a few steps from where she stood, there was a round patch of darkness in the floor like a hole.

A noise caught her ear, a soft rustle or whisper. They were lying in wait for her, planning their attack! She wanted to shout out, leap from her hiding place, anything rather than cower there dreading discovery.

In the dark at the base of one of the wine racks she saw a silvery gleam. Not glass this time but metal. Strands of loose wire perhaps, or discarded shreds of foil.

Among the pools of shadow something moved. A crouching figure dressed in black uncoiled its limbs and stretched itself towards her, spreading like ink across the floor. A pale face turned in her direction, a face half caged in silver mesh.

She cried out at last, a horrified yelp of terror and disgust. But no sooner had the sound passed her lips than she saw who it was. Of course. The manhole she had seen in the floor must lead to a tunnel beneath the house. He must have climbed up through it. The realization dissolved her fear into a mixture of anger and hysterical relief. She clung weakly to the pillar, hiccuping for breath at the same time as she coughed up the dust and cobwebs caught in her throat.

"You. . .!" she exclaimed.

The sound of the blows from the hallway above continued to echo through the cellar like an amplified drumbeat, drowning out her words. She raised her voice to make herself heard and as she did so the awful thought that had been crouching in some hidden corner of her mind came leaping out into her consciousness.

It likes me, he had boasted. *It follows me around!* These were the words she had forgotten, or chosen to ignore, and now they came back to her with all the foreboding of an oracle predicting tragedy.

She staggered away from the pillar, spinning this way and that. The sound of hammering seemed to come from all around her. She was completely disoriented. She had no idea where the door was any more.

She turned back to face the crouching figure on the

floor, already certain of the worst. "What have you done?" she demanded. "What have you *done*?"

Susskin's head lolled and he stared at her blearily. She saw that he held a bottle of wine. He frowned as he tried to focus on her, then turned away, shaking his head.

"Huh!" he grumbled to himself. "Tha's no way to treat a guest."

"Oh, *there* you are," snapped Ashpool. "I can't *believe* you don't have even the most rudimentary security precautions."

Marlstroy shut the study door behind him and turned the key in the lock. "They're in the front garden," he said. "But they don't seem to want to try and come any further at the moment."

"Of course they don't. Their leader's in jail. I put him there. He'd never do anything as stupid as this. Without him they're just a mob."

From outside in the hallway came the sound of something heavy striking the front door.

"Listen to them." Ashpool waved his hand contemptuously. "Like children wanting to smash something. They wouldn't have a clue what to do if they actually got in. They've already gone much too far to hope for any favourable coverage. Those broken windows won't look much good in the papers tomorrow: 'Home of eminent neurosurgeon wrecked by eco-thugs.' I think I've got more than enough justification for a . . . *robust* response." He smiled thinly.

497

"Did you get through?" Marlstroy nodded at the phone still in Ashpool's hand.

"I did. And in a very short time they're going to get the fright of their lives."

"I hope you're not going to take any risks. It's not just us involved, you know."

"No, of course not." Ashpool's eyes were calculating. "That girl of yours. What's her name? She must be terrified. Will she cooperate? Give an interview, I mean. That would be such bad publicity for them. Going round frightening children. Especially if she cried. Would she cry, do you think?"

"No," said Marlstroy. "You'll leave her alone."

They glared at each other. For some seconds neither spoke, and the only sound came from the steady assault on the front door of the house. Then, in the lull between one hollow, booming blow and the next, both men became aware of an altogether different noise.

Something in the room was growling.

At first neither of them could locate the source of the low, steady rumbling. Only when something began to move across the desk did they realize where it came from.

Ashpool's empty whisky glass was travelling slowly over the polished wooden surface, its heavy base vibrating as it went. It reached the edge and toppled over before either of them could move to stop it.

It was unbroken and Marlstroy stooped to pick it up.

When he rose, Ashpool was staring past him, out of the study window.

Something in his expression made Marlstroy pause. "What?"

Ashpool didn't look at him. "This is hardly the time. . ."

Marlstroy turned to follow the direction of his gaze. In the shadows at the bottom of the garden the firetrees were burning.

At first they looked almost festive, with long, soft orange flames wriggling upwards from the tip of each jagged branch. Then these dancing streamers hardened and steadied, turning to sharp blades of blue that quickly thickened and grew to the height of a man and deepened in colour to a vibrant indigo. Crooked shadows shivered on the wall.

Marlstroy shook his head. "Not me," he murmured. "I didn't touch them."

The firetrees roared. Even in the study they could feel the warmth. The branches themselves were beginning to glow. Orange at first, then cherry red. In no time at all the heat had spread to the trunk of each tree and before long the whole row of them was incandescent, pulsing in the dark like growths of luminous coral.

By now the branches were turning white and had become almost too bright to look at. Weakened seams sprang open, venting new leaves of flame. The trees were falling apart. The largest started to sag, its branches twisting away from the trunk as they melted. The broken joints spat showers of sparks and oozed viscous, fiery matter. Soon the other trees were drooping too. Molten metal poured from their splitting limbs and gathered in smoking puddles on the grass.

In the study the cupboards were shuddering. Doors swung open and glassware jangled on the shelves.

Marlstroy was already at the door. The key rattled in the lock of its own accord. "Come on. We've got to get out."

"No!" Ashpool stood his ground.

"Don't be stupid! It's not safe!" Droplets of molten metal smacked against the study window.

"It won't come too close. It'll recognize me. It knows who I am."

"*What* does? What the hell are you talking about? Are you mad?" Marlstroy stepped towards Ashpool and tried to take his arm. Ashpool shook him off.

"The experiment! Don't you remember? It's programmed. A precaution. Like the door to the warehouse. In case someone used it against me." His voice rose to a shout. "It knows who I am!"

Books began to fall to the floor. The mirror above the fireplace shattered and a wave of broken glass poured down over the mantelpiece. Cracks wriggled across the walls. Marlstroy tugged at the door but the frame had warped and it wouldn't open.

"Like the warehouse," Ashpool repeated. His face was running with sweat. His spectacles slipped on the bridge of his nose and he pushed them back into place with a trembling hand. He closed his eyes and breathed in deeply, obviously trying to calm himself.

Susskin sat with his back to the wall, wine bottle cradled in the crook of one elbow. "Nothing to do with me," he muttered. "*I* dunno who they are. Thought you mus' be having a party, tha's all."

The demonstrators at the front of the house were no longer assailing the door. Their voices still carried down into the cellar, but now sounded confused instead of angry.

"Not them. You know what I mean." Hadn't he said he'd broken into a warehouse on Sproule Street the night the Bunker had burned down? "It's here, isn't it. It followed you."

"Goes where it likes," muttered Susskin. "Not *my* fault."

Dushma ran a hand over her forehead. Her palm came away damp. The cellar was already much warmer than it had been when she entered.

She held her breath and listened. A distant rushing noise like pouring water reached her ears. She also heard, nearer at hand, the dry trickling sound of dislodged grit and plaster. She did not need to crouch and touch the floor to feel the ground trembling beneath her feet.

She had to get out. Find the fallen key, or bang on the door of the cellar until someone came to help her. She looked around for some hint of where the door might be but could see nothing.

Susskin's torch still hung from a hook near her head. Its

light was almost gone but it was better than nothing. She reached up and took it. Shaking it to try and strengthen the beam, she swung it in a wide arc in front of her.

She was surrounded by wine racks. They were positioned haphazardly among the pillars, a dozen narrow alleyways opening between them. She had no idea which way she had come. She would have to guess.

She lowered the torch and shone it across the floor. There was little to see except for the round opening near her feet and, to one side, the metal plate that must have covered it. She turned slowly, trying to remember where she'd been standing when she first noticed the manhole.

She saw footprints in the dust on the floor. Hers, they must be. *That* was the way.

"Here. Follow me." She turned and pointed the torch at Susskin. "Come *on!*"

He didn't move. "It likes me," he told her. "More than *you* do. You were just jealous. I could tell."

"Oh, shut *up*. Don't be ridiculous!" She should leave him where he was, she thought. It would serve him right. Instead she stooped and stretched out her free hand towards him but he shrank away, raising his bottle in a feeble attempt to ward her off. Wine splashed his arm.

"And put that down," she scolded him. "You'll make yourself ill."

"Listen to her!" he slurred. "Thinks she's Forence flogging Nightingale. I *am* ill! So I might as well. . ."

A tremor shook the cellar. Dushma staggered and nearly

fell. Behind her a wine rack crashed to the ground. She turned but her path was strewn with broken glass.

Cracking sounds came from all around her. She saw the nearest pillar begin to buckle, bricks splintering and crumbling before her eyes. Rivers of spilled wine poured over the floor and down through the fissures that had opened at her feet. The air was thick with rising dust.

She put a hand to her mouth to try and muffle a whimper of terror. It was too late. She would never reach the door now.

Panicking, she turned to Susskin. He seemed oblivious of the chaos around him, still sitting with his bottle of wine clutched to his chest, swaying to and fro. In her despair, his indifference infuriated Dushma.

"What have you done?" she shouted at him. "Look at it! This is your fault!"

She seized his shoulder but he shrugged her hand away. He raised his head and glared at her. "Don't you dare touch me!" He was shivering. "Don't you *dare!*"

She jumped back but he was already clambering upright. He swung at her with the wine bottle and she flinched, dropping the torch. It broke at her feet but even without its faint light she could still see Susskin's face. A reddish glow bathed his ravaged features, gleaming and flickering in the metal veins of his injured cheek.

Dushma glanced quickly over her shoulder. In the depths of the cellar something was burning. Smoke caught in her throat.

"Now you're going to know," said Susskin. "Now you're going to find out what it feels like."

She stepped backwards away from him and trod on nothing.

She had forgotten about the hole in the cellar floor. She fell a metre or so and landed awkwardly. Her legs crumpled under her, spilling her on to her side. Her right hip and elbow cracked painfully against stone.

It was as if she had been dropped into an oven. A shrivelling heat washed over her. Sweat prickled on her skin. Her clothes stuck to her body like shrink wrap, tugging uncomfortably with every movement she made.

She rolled over on to all fours, blinking and shaking her head. There was an orange glow before her eyes but she couldn't tell if it was real or the result of the jarring impact of her fall. She looked upwards at the opening through which she had tumbled but could see only a confused pattern of moving shadows.

Something splashed on to her upturned face. She choked, her nostrils filled with the dizzying smell of alcohol. Wine from the rackfuls of broken bottles was sluicing across the cellar floor and pouring down on top of her.

She began to crawl blindly towards what felt like cooler air. Rough stone scraped her knees and palms. From behind her came the sound of snapping timber and falling masonry.

Twisting her head to try and look behind her, she saw

nothing but showers of sparks falling through a thick cloud of smoke. It was impossible to tell whether or not Susskin had followed her down into the tunnel.

The smoke caught up with her, stinging her eyes and burning in her lungs. She could crawl no faster. She reached up and waved a hand above her head but couldn't feel the ceiling. She climbed unsteadily to her feet.

The tunnel was still too low for her to stand upright, but at least she no longer had to make her way on all fours. She stumbled on at a crouching run, one hand held out in front of her, the other trailing along the wall at her side.

The floor was uneven and she tripped frequently. At first she had been unable to see her feet at all, but after she had gone a little way she became aware of two faint shadows moving beneath her in time to her tread.

Leaning against the tunnel wall, she stopped to catch her breath and look around. The air was now clear of smoke, but from behind her she could still hear the unmistakable crackle of flames and the occasional, ominous crash. There was no sign of Susskin. Perhaps there were other tunnels that she had missed, opening off from this one.

The ceiling was still a few centimetres lower than her full height and already her bowed back was hurting. She crouched, straightened her neck and peered into the darkness ahead of her.

Although some distance away, what she glimpsed now was undoubtedly moonlight: a pale silver shaft of luminescence cutting at an angle across the tunnel. As soon as she saw it she was sure she could smell fresh air. Straining her ears, she even thought she could hear voices and the rush of wind above the sounds of burning and collapse behind her.

She rose from her crouch, tired joints cracking with the effort. Blood pounded in her ears and coloured wheels of light rolled across her vision. She hurried on.

The heat at her back was growing stronger. When next she risked looking over her shoulder she saw a hot slice of orange light shimmering in the distance. She turned again a few seconds later and it was brighter and closer, obviously now no trick of her eyes but a mass of incandescent material rolling towards her along the tunnel like a wave of fiery treacle. She gagged on scalding, sulphurous air.

Her back ached from stooping. She raised her hand and skinned her knuckles on the tunnel roof. It was still too low.

As she neared the patch of moonlight on the tunnel floor she saw what she had been hoping to find. There was a ladder fixed to the wall, disappearing upwards into the roof. Not daring to waste a second on another glance behind her, she threw herself towards it, gripped the rungs and pulled herself upwards.

As she did so something brushed her dangling left shoe and heat seared the sole of her foot. She gasped in agony and nearly fell from the ladder.

The floor of the tunnel beneath her was awash with

molten rock. The air around her howled with heat. She tried to breathe but some reflex had locked her throat, saving her from sucking the scalding fumes into her lungs.

The blood screamed in her ears. Pain stabbed through her left foot with every step. The heat had melted her shoe so that she had to wrench the sticky sole free of each rung as she climbed. Yet somehow, sweat-drenched palms slipping on the hot metal, she managed to haul herself up the ladder to the grating that capped the shaft.

Moonlight poured down on her through the bars. She beat at them with the palm of her hand but the grating didn't move. She climbed another few rungs so she could press her shoulder against it. It gave a little, then swung open so suddenly that she almost lost her balance.

Nails breaking as she scrabbled at the tarmac, she pulled herself up out of the drain and flopped forward into the gutter. Her whole body shuddered with the effort of forcing enough of the damp night air in and out of her panting lungs.

She lay where she had fallen for what seemed like several minutes, puddled rainwater cooling her scalded hands and feet. She felt sure she was safe, although she was almost too bruised and exhausted to care. How far along the tunnel had she come? It must have been a long way. It felt like she had been down there for hours. And how long would it be before it was safe to go back? She listened but could hear nothing above the roaring in her ears.

She opened her eyes. By her head was the wheel of a

parked car. In the hub-cap she saw a dim reflection of her matted hair and dirt-streaked face. Muffled voices reached her, and the sound of footsteps, oddly distant.

She rolled over and sat up. Her joints throbbed and her clothing, wet from sweat and rainwater, hung heavily on her tired limbs. She looked down at the opening from which she had climbed. The air above it shivered with heat. As she watched, gobbets of molten matter spattered, hissing, on to the wet pavement. She drew her legs hurriedly out of the way. No one else would be coming along the tunnel now.

Her hearing was still muffled. She shook her head and swallowed hard to try and clear her ears. Leaning on the top of the car wheel beside her, she levered herself to her feet.

A wave of heat and light washed over her. She staggered, her hip banging against the car's curved wing.

She was almost directly opposite the blazing ruin of Marlstroy's house.

She stood immobile, hands cupped over her open mouth, as the building began to collapse. Before her eyes the last window that had remained unbroken blew outwards in a spout of glass. Drainpipes bent like liquorice. The stucco crackled like crushed icing on a Christmas cake. Where it had fallen away the crumbling facade spat splinters of brick.

Dark figures still milled in the road before the burning house. Some were backing away and turning to run. Others cheered raggedly at each burst of sparks. They all scattered as, high overhead, chimney pots began to explode, raining hot terracotta down into the garden.

Flames now surged through the shattered windows. Watching in horror, Dushma couldn't help but imagine the passage of the blaze through every room and corridor of the house. She pictured the library, a firestorm of burning books tumbling from the shelves, flaming pages flapping like phoenix wings. In the hall the stairs on which she had stood not long before must now be a ramp of fire, the chandeliers overhead dissolving in showers of molten crystal rain. She thought of her guitar, propped in a corner of her room, the imprints of her incisors on its neck, its strings parting in the heat and whipping away from the blistering fingerboard.

She heard footsteps nearby. Jolted from her stunned and helpless trance, she turned and saw a woman in dark overalls running towards her.

"Stop!" Her voice was a croak. "Listen. . ."

The woman looked into Dushma's eyes but then turned quickly away, veering to the other side of the pavement and running on without a pause.

"Hey. . .!"

Dushma took a few limping steps after her, then gave up. She must look a sight, she thought, her face streaked with wine and crusted with salt from her sweat and tears, her clothing torn and blood on her knees and elbows.

A man rushed past her, almost knocking her over. "Come on!" he shouted back at her.

"Wait! Help! There's people. . . There's people still in there!"

He stopped and turned. He was mouthing something at her. She couldn't hear him; there was too much other noise.

Leaning towards her, he shouted, "Run, you idiot!" He took her arm and tried to pull her along with him but she snatched herself free.

Through the sound of flames and the ringing in her ears she could now hear something else, a rumbling like a heavy lorry climbing a hill. If it was a fire engine, there might still be time. Absurdly, she had the urge to wave her arms, to jump and shout in order to attract the attention of any approaching rescuers. She stepped between the parked cars for a better view down the street but there was no sign of flashing lights.

She turned back to the house in time to see the whole front wall slump down in a cloud of smoke and dust. For a moment the blazing interior stood revealed from ground level to rooftop like a life-size cut-away model. Then blackened joists began to snap like spent matchsticks. One by one the floors collapsed, throwing burning fragments of furniture, plaster and fabric high into the air. The remaining walls trembled and swayed, then folded slowly in on each other.

A hot wind rushed from the ruins. Sparks danced like fiery spray above a rolling surf of flame. Something dark and shining stirred among the burning rubble. Dushma turned to run.

A vehicle blocked the end of the street, the noise of its engine much louder now. It was tall as a lorry and wider. It hardly fitted between the parked cars as it came jangling forward, the links of its tracks tumbling on to the tarmac with a sound like an endless cascade of ironmongery.

Its hatches were closed and clouds of oily diesel smoke blew from its exhausts. Figures darted to and fro in the glare of its searchlights as the last of the demonstrators fled. A stone arced from the shadows and bounced with a clang from one armoured flank but the tank didn't slow.

Dushma stood like an animal caught in car headlights. As the tank drew closer she tried to back away but the melted sole of her shoe had stuck to the road. She knelt to try and undo the lace. The tarmac was hot and soft beneath her hands. The tank rumbled on.

Her fingers slipped on the knot. Hadn't they seen her? Didn't they care? She shouted but the sound was hardly audible even to herself.

In front of her one of the running figures slipped and fell. She heard a shriek.

She wrenched her knee upwards and her foot came free of the tarmac. She threw herself towards the side of the road, staggering round the bumper of the nearest car. Tripping over the kerb, she fell on to the pavement as the tank clamoured past.

Someone was wailing, their voice cracking with pain. It was their leg. Something had happened to their leg.

The tank came to a halt before the burning remnants of

the house. The armoured skirts protecting its tracks rattled with each throb of its idling engine. The shallow, angled planes of its turret stood out in sharp silhouette against the flames.

Dushma crouched in the shadow of a car, scrabbling on the pavement beside her for a stone. The scene before her was like something from television, from news reports of wars and uprisings in distant, foreign cities. In such broadcasts there were often people dodging among the ruins hurling rocks at the enemy's artillery, people who had always seemed to her to be dangerously fanatical or insanely brave. But now she too wanted to throw something, to make her feelings known to whoever was inside the machine that had nearly run her over. She felt neither fanatical nor brave, simply angry and frightened; it was just that there weren't too many other ways of expressing disagreement with a tank.

Finding nothing, she rose to her feet in time to see the tank's turret begin to swing. She was close enough to hear the motors grinding as they drove it round, bringing the barrel of its gun to bear on the flaming wreckage in front of it.

Where Marlstroy's house had stood looked like the launch site of a rocket seconds after lift-off. Clouds of ash and orange smoke still coiled from the ruins. Every few seconds the tangle of burning roof beams flared and shook, sending sparks and trails of vapour spiralling through the air.

As Dushma stood hesitating, torn between an urge to run and a desire to see what was going to happen, a gust of wind swept the heaped-up smoke aside. Now there could be no mistaking what she saw. Bricks and timber spilling like burning confetti from its torso, the elidril reared up like a centaur through the shifting pyre.

Its shield-shaped head shone like black glass, the curved and featureless surface a mask of reflected flame. It swung hypnotically, turning slowly from one side to the other as if searching for something.

Dushma backed away along the pavement, pulling her sticky shoe free of the flagstones with every other step. She should flee, she knew, but the empty visage of the elidril held her as a snake enthrals its prey. Could it sense her? She raised her arms to cover her head, as if she could somehow muffle her thoughts. How close did she have to be? What else might it find interesting?

The elidril began to advance. It moved fluidly through the ruins of the house, flanks glistening like flowing oil. It was coming towards the tank.

Dushma watched in terrified fascination. Odd details caught her eye, such as the shovel and the fire extinguisher clipped incongruously to the tank's near side. Oh good, she thought ridiculously. Whatever was going to happen, someone would be able to clear up afterwards.

An amplified voice rolled down the street. The tank must have a loudspeaker mounted on the turret. The words were incomprehensible. The crackle of static mixed with the sound of flames to drown out whatever was being said.

The voice fell silent and the tank's barrel dropped a few degrees. A split-second pause gave Dushma enough time to stagger backwards a few more paces and clap her hands over her ears.

A long spike of flame jabbed from the muzzle of the gun. The tank rocked on its tracks. The shockwave knocked the breath from Dushma's lungs and shook the ground beneath her. Car windows broke nearby.

The blazing ruins of the house erupted and scattered like a bonfire kicked by an enormous, invisible foot. A swirling cloud of pulverized masonry ballooned from the point of impact, hiding the destruction in a giant red blister of smoking debris.

Dushma turned and ran, her footsteps sounding muffled in her aching ears. Her legs were still unsteady and she nearly fell. Pieces of brick pattered to the ground around her. Shreds of burning paper and cloth swooped through the air.

She stumbled. The pavement beneath her began to crack and rise, threatening to trip her with every step. She found herself no longer running but instead leaping forward from one tilting flagstone to the next. The road looked no safer. No longer appearing solid, the surface gleamed and rippled in the light of the flames.

The heat on her back was intense. She was drenched in sweat. It dripped from her face as she ran. She passed another drain and saw orange light flooding up through the bars. She threw a glance over her shoulder.

The tank was listing. Like a lake of black treacle, the tarmac beneath it was sucking it down. Its engine roared, its tracks churning uselessly through smoking pools of molten asphalt.

The surface of the road began to boil. The tank wallowed and its tracks sank deeper, submerged by the bubbling tar. With a scream of gears the turret swivelled, sending its gun barrel crashing against the bonnet of a car.

The tank tilted further. The liquid seething round its armoured flanks was now no longer black but a deep and angry crimson. Gouts of red-hot fluid surged into the air, spattering and sizzling on the pavement and the sides of nearby cars. The tank's armour plating started to glow. Khaki paint shrivelled and blistered, burning away to reveal bare metal shining dull orange underneath.

A hatch swung open on top of the turret and a figure clambered halfway out, clothes ablaze. The flames streamed in the wind like a ragged red flag. For a moment, even above the noise of the fire, Dushma heard the awful dry rasping sound of choking. Then the figure swayed and dropped limply back into the tank. A plume of smoke poured from the still-open hatch.

A series of muffled detonations came from within the tank and it shuddered with the force of the explosions. A rent appeared in its glowing hull and a flaming jet of gas or oil burst forth.

Dushma staggered backwards along the pavement, hands over her face to try and protect herself from the heat. Scorching air filled her lungs. She was breathing through her mouth but still she couldn't avoid the smell. Burnt tar and petrol vapours scraped across her tongue; the roof of her mouth felt coated with ash and the acrid reek of scorched rubber caught in the back of her throat. Yet the thickness of this chemical miasma couldn't mask another scent, one she had smelled only once before and had hoped never to encounter again. Among the fumes, faint but unmistakable, was the charred, sweet-salty odour of seared human flesh.

Her stomach heaved and she gagged on bile. She wanted to spit but her mouth was too dry. She stumbled on, turning frequently round to look back, one hand still covering her face.

How long had it been since she had started to run? One minute, two? She had come perhaps fifty metres, less even. But already parts of the tank were glowing white hot. The barrel sagged then came loose at the breech, kinking like a bent straw as it fell. As she watched, the molten road splashed up over the armoured skirts that surmounted the tracks, buckling the softened plates.

The tank was imploding. The turret sank down into the hull, its angled surfaces creasing and dimpling like the sides of an oil can crushed by atmospheric pressure. Here and there the armour twisted and tore, leaving long rips in the metal.

Within the tank a storm raged. Through the holes in the

sides could be seen a swirling mass of oily black clouds flecked with silver pins of lightning. Red-gold lava flooded out like rivers of burning syrup.

At last the tremors in the ground began to subside. It became easier to run. The heat lessened and fewer smouldering fragments rained down through the clearing smoke.

At the end of the road Dushma paused and glanced round for a final time. The tank had become almost unrecognizable, just a crumpled mound of misshapen metal. Now less than half its original height, it lay sunk in the tar like some vast splattered fruit dripping glowing juice through a split and burning husk.

She didn't have to feel guilty, Dushma told herself. Nobody could say she'd done anything she shouldn't have. And she hadn't, had she?

Since leaving the burning street behind she had wandered aimlessly, sometimes breaking into a tired trot but mostly just limping along with no clear idea of where she was, let alone where she might be going. At first she had been too shocked to think coherently. She had concentrated on the ground in front of her, and on trying to keep her thoughts free of the images that threatened to surge up from her subconscious in a hideous mix of recent memory and imagination. She was glad of her burnt foot. With every other step the pain drove anything else from her mind.

517

After a time, walking began to hurt less and she was able to form a vague plan. It took her a good while, but eventually she had found herself down on the bank of the canal. The moon was still up, low on the horizon, and by its light she could see enough to pick her way along the narrow towpath.

After she had gone a little way she reached a dip in the bank and stopped, thinking she could bathe her foot. She sat down stiffly and, after some tugging at the tangled laces, managed to loosen her melted shoe. It came off with some difficulty, bringing the toe of her tights with it, as well as what felt like half the skin from her sole. She gasped with the pain, her eyes watering.

She sat for some time with her foot in the water, letting the cold soothe the burn. Her foot began to go numb and before long she could hardly feel it.

The rest of her was still uncomfortably sticky. Her cheeks and forehead throbbed with each beat of her pulse. She raised a hand to touch her face. It was feverishly hot. She imagined her head lit up from within, her skin shining dully like heated metal.

Looking back the way she had come she could still see a faint glow in the sky. For some time she had been listening for the cry of sirens but the night was quiet. Perhaps she just couldn't hear them. Worriedly, she swished her leg back and forth in the canal and was reassured by the sound of churning water.

She didn't have to feel guilty, did she? Could anyone

blame her? Could she have foretold, even caused what had happened? She cast her mind back to her encounter with Susskin in the ruins of Hitler Street, remembering what he had said. *It likes me*, he had told her. Had she thought it was just an idle boast, meant to frighten her? Or was that why, impulsively, she had given him her address? Marlstroy's address. She didn't know, and now several people were dead. Could she have intended that, even subconsciously?

In a late-night science fiction film this would all be a dream, a dream dreamt by somebody else, in which she had no control over or responsibility for her actions. She imagined Alison lying peacefully asleep in her hospital bed, oblivious of the negotiations that had taken place over her life.

She remembered Arbilow quoting Torrelguard. *How far do you go to stop someone doing something wrong?*

Lifting her foot from the canal, she swung it back and forth to shake the water from it. She thought of her classmates at Larchmuir, but found it difficult to recall their faces. She didn't have to feel guilty; she could go back without fear of blame, but that didn't mean she had to, not if she didn't want. No one would think to look for her. They would assume she had died along with Ashpool and Marlstroy in the burning ruins of the house.

She had read that sometimes, after a fire, there was nothing left to identify people by except their teeth. Would they sift the wreckage for teeth? She pictured a scattering of blackened stumps on a mound of white ash. It was images like this she had been trying to suppress. *The mouth is the chimney of the soul*, Marlstroy had said to her.

She picked up her mangled shoe. It would be painful to put on, but less so than walking barefoot. She turned it over. Something had stuck to the underneath, making it even more uncomfortable, but she hadn't had the chance to do anything about it before now.

It was a piece of glass, gleaming in the melted rubber. She made a dry, half-stifled noise part way between a mirthless laugh and a sob. Hadn't there already been enough broken glass tonight?

She prised it free with her thumbnail. It felt strangely smooth and heavy in her hand. She had been going to throw it as far away from her as she could, but now she paused and looked at it more closely.

If it was glass, it was a different sort to any she had seen before. It was more like a transparent stone, a piece of crystal. She held it up to the moonlight. Sparks of white, purple and blue danced inside it. She blinked her tired eyes then looked again but the sparks were still there, showering out from the depths of the stone as she turned it in her hand.

It was captivating. She stared at it, tilting it this way and that to reveal sprays of every conceivable colour. When eventually the moon dropped from sight and the stone no longer shone, she closed her fist tightly round it and tucked it carefully away inside her blazer. If there was one thing she could feel sure about, it was that this was rightfully hers.

With some difficulty she pulled on her shoe and stood up. Without the moon it was much darker and she had to pick her way with care. She stumbled frequently on broken bricks, jarring her burnt foot. The canal was a deep blue pit on her right-hand side.

There was just enough light for her to see the silhouettes of the buildings around her. She turned a corner and, peering ahead of her into the darkness, thought she could make out the faint grid of the shopping trolley sculpture that spanned the canal. Nearby, among the vague outlines of towers and chimneys and warehouse rooftops, she saw the softer shapes of the trees that crowned the Factory.

She quickened her pace, pressing her arm to her chest to feel the stone in her blazer pocket, a small, hard lump against her ribs.

She hoped Arbilow would be there. She had a story to tell him.